The Pendulum War

Pendulum Heroes, Volume 3

James Beamon

Published by Nadi Cat Press, 2021.

Nadi Cat Press

Published by Nadi Cat Press 2021
Leesburg, VA United States
ISBN: 978-1-7323862-4-2
This book is available in print at most online retailers

For Chance,

You are my future made manifest. May yours be as bright as your smile.

Chapter 1
A Block of Wood

MIKE FELT PROGRESSIVELY ill at ease the more he climbed Mount Kutsal. Despite the stairs, fashioned from rough hewn logs and set into the mountain to facilitate the ascent... despite Savvy's explanation that it was a protected, holy site immune to the war, Mike's senses tingled. It was not because of the cold, wintry air.

His companions seemed to take the final leg of their long journey with less apprehension. Underneath his brown hood, Jason's head panned up at overcast skies, a slight smile on his gray aian face. Savvy focused on the trail in front of them, trying to guide them along a path partially obscured by recent snowfall. Runt scanned the sparse mountainside and would gather the occasional dead stick protruding from snow tufts which he'd stuff into his pack, no doubt for a campfire when they finally did settle down.

It was cue enough for Mike to relax a bit. But a deployment in Afghanistan had made navigating mountain passes the least relaxing hike he'd ever take. Instead, he kept his awareness turned up to eleven, his fingers flexing rhythmically in the shimmery-silver lightning gloves. Occasionally, he'd tap his fingers against the diskbow at his waist as he made his way up the mountain.

"So," Jason said, "with this blood whisper thing... any special effects?"

"What?" Savvy asked, her features scrunching up. She was probably trying to understand what the hell a special effect was and how it differed from regular effects.

"No," Mike answered.

"Aw, bogus," Jason replied.

They continued on in silence, only for Jason to break it a moment later.

"How do you know that it worked then?"

"You will know," Savvy answered simply, not bothering to look away from the path as she walked.

Jason nodded. Again, silence rushed to fill the gap left by Savvy's reply. Again, Jason broke it a second later.

"But, I mean, is it a feeling? Does the Blood Whisper Fairy leave a dime under my bedroll? Can I get a better tutorial than that?"

Mike grimaced. "Here's a tutorial... shut up and find out."

"Man, so weak," Jason said. But Mike's reply kept him quiet, and this time longer than a moment. Mike's ears returned to listening for sounds of ambush. A hawk screeched as their boots crunched through snow, but nothing else.

Savvy should've never told Jason about blood whispers and the Jutting Finger that sat atop Mount Kutsal. No, Mike took that back; the real problem was the statement Savvy had made after telling them all where they were going and why. "Even aians go there for guidance, to be spoken to in whisper," she had said, "that is the power of this nasran relic, here before the tribes were tribes." That was all she had to say to get Jason's eyes dancing with excitement. He hadn't left it alone for the first week of their trek here; now he was starting up again.

They climbed the steps through snow and trail for another hour until they finally reached the summit. The mountaintop was flat, a giant, crude circle that hosted in its center a gnarled redwood log which seemed to point straight up at the gray, gloomy sky. Next to the log, ten aians sat in a half circle around a generous campfire.

All of them eyed the newcomers. One, a member of horse house Otam, smiled grimly.

"It's a trying time to travel up here, friends," he said with a shake of his head. "I'm afraid any answers you'll get come with a tax. Eighty percent of what you've got. Come warm yourselves by our fire while you empty out your packs and pockets."

"Seriously?" Jason asked to no one in particular. "Bandits way up here?"

Savvy looked hot enough to melt the snow, her face flush with anger. "The *Kurtsaldah* is a sacred site. You blaspheme my ancestors and taint their works with your presence. Leave."

Horsey boy stood up, and the rest followed as if ordered to. "Don't mistake my hospitality as a true dialogue, nasran hag. You have no say here. Now the tax has been raised to ninety percent. One more utterance and we take it all. Now come here and pay."

"Look, Captain Tariff," Jason said. "Do we seem like your ordinary pilgrims? Since I don't see any of the House of Yol here, let me illuminate you all." Jason took down his hood and revealed his unmarked features, followed by pushing his sleeve up to reveal the arm of bone.

All the aians took a step back as if Jason was made of snakes. The bandit leader raised his hand in surrender. "We've got no desire to tangle with the Chosen One."

Mike had heard enough talk. He grabbed his diskbow and fired. The disk shinged out with blurried speed, burying itself into the horse aian's gut with a spray of red mist. The bandit crumpled wordlessly.

"What the hell Mike?" Jason asked.

The other bandits were quicker to recover than Jason and began to brandish their weapons. But at this point it really was only a matter of arithmetic.

There were nine left. Savvy walked toward them briskly, grabbing two gilded wormwood hexes from her belt. "Gather" she named the first hex as she bent to scoop snow. It seemed the snow rushed to collect into her hand. "Fuel" she named the other hex before slapping it onto her massive snowball. She flung the snow into the bandits' fire, where it exploded as if it was made of gasoline. All nine were caught in the violent blast. Two bandits caught fire from the explosion and didn't get up again.

Seven left. Five landed close together which made it easy when Mike clapped his gloved hands together and released arc lightning at them, frying them instantly.

Two left. Runt rushed over in speed that belied his giant mass. Before they could get up, a couple swipes from the half weagr's z-blade staff kept them down permanently.

Jason still looked to be in shock from all this. "What the hell, guys?" he cried. "They were giving up. You don't do that to folks who surrender!"

"Yes, you damn do," Mike said. "They weren't combatants, they were bandits. At best, they honor their deal and slink off the mountain, only to come back after we leave to exploit, rob, and murder the more helpless kind of traveler. At worst, they come back an hour after we're asleep and cut our throats. Now, I got a real serious problem with the second scenario, but I'll be damned if I tolerate the first if I don't have to. Fuck those thieves."

"Since when are we protecting theoretical people?" Jason asked. Mike began cranking his diskbow taut. Runt wiped his blades clean. Savvy carefully checked the fallen bandits for any hints of life. No one answered Jason.

He scratched his head with bone fingers. "I dunno. I feel kinda crappy about what just went down. It all seems very unheroic."

"I don't know what to tell you," Mike said. "Maybe you'll feel heroic tossing these jackasses off the mountain. Unless you want them staring at you tonight with their dead, vacant eyes."

If there was any more protest left in Jason, he kept it there. He wordlessly pulled a female from the mole house Zemishirus toward the ledge. Mike stopped him before Jason could reach down to pick her up.

"Hey, make sure you give them their just desserts. Check their pockets. Let's rob these fools."

In due time, both the mountaintop was clear and their coffers substantially increased by bandit loot. The four of them were left alone with the Jutting Finger.

It did not impress Mike. Of course, very little outside of a portal going home would've impressed him after all this way and time. Getting to the Jutting Finger was no easy task, but an endeavor of two months. The war had disrupted trade lines, and all but the craziest merchants refused to run caravans which could be seized by aian Armsguard, Hierophane mercenaries or marauding bandits not unlike the ones that just got tossed off the mountain. This meant walking for the most part, a slow going pace as news of marching armies forced extended backpedaling and detours.

After all that, it was hard not to see the Jutting Finger as simply a block of wood. It could've at least looked like a finger. Sure, there were glyphs and symbols like Savvy's hexes carved into the massive redwood log, but it was still a block of wood.

But this was it, Savvy's last and only desperate plan. After Enverpasha ran off with the claims to command virtually all tribes, she had deliberated for days before coming up with this Hail Mary. It involved amplifying her blood whisper and hoping it would shed some light on the location of the Lost Tribe, and with it, the ring of the Buyukata.

Before she led them here, she explained this wouldn't be the first time someone's come to the mountain looking for the same thing. Dreams of bringing home the Lost Tribe, of becoming the Buyuka-ta, had fueled the hearts of aspiring tribal leaders for over a century. She didn't want to be Buyukata, she needed to be Buyukata. This was the only difference between her and all those who came before and failed.

"So..." Jason began, letting the word marinate in the air before adding more to his sentence," we whispering or..."

"*Tabii*, we whisper," Savvy said walking up to the Jutting Finger. She took out her dagger and without ceremony cut across her open palm. She began to smear the blood across the log.

Oh. That wasn't redwood. That was eons of dried blood staining the tree.

Savvy stepped back without saying a word and began applying a bandage to her hand.

"That's it?" Jason asked.

"For me," Savvy said. "If you want your blood to whisper to you, you will have to add it to the Finger."

Jason, warily eyeing the log, raised an eyebrow. "That doesn't look sanitary," he said with a slow shake of his head. "There's gotta be Tetanus or E.coli or something just raging on that stump."

"*Tut*," Savvy shushed Jason. "Then don't whisper."

Mike could almost see the kid's gears turning. Jason looked at his hand and back at the Jutting Finger and back again at his hand. Stuck between wanting to try something new and fear of contracting a flesh-eating bacteria from rubbing the bloody stump, Jason finally decided to risk it when he dug a bone finger into his palm and dragged it across with a grimace. He stepped up to the wood and smeared his blood across it.

"I swear, I better not get visions of me dying from doing this," he said.

As Mike expected, Runt stayed away from the Jutting Finger. The big man wasn't afraid of magic; he just had little use for fortune telling. Any given date in the future Runt would be doing what he was doing right now: exactly what he wanted. Or he'd be dead. Instead of wasting his time and his blood, Runt went about salvaging the bandits' already built fire, now a bit wild and unkempt after Savvy had tossed snow-gasoline on it.

Mike looked at the Jutting Finger, all gleaming and slick now that it sported a coat of its favorite paint. And he thought, "What the hell?" as he pulled a purplish hand out of its glove. A quick cut across the palm later, his blood mingled with Savvy, Jason's and an eon's worth of people seeking answers.

Maybe this thing will give him specifics on a solid return home date.

JASON AWOKE BELIEVING he had somehow died in his sleep and went to heaven. An aian woman floated down to him, gliding gently on silken butterfly wings. Thick blonde curls, the kind he'd only ever seen on women in movies set in Greek and Roman times, framed a fair gray face. Matching her silken wings, a white silk gown draped her body and glowed softly in the moonlight. The gown clung to her, the curve of her breasts and the contours of her flat stomach easily readable across fabric that flowed like water as the breeze rippled it. Her face, her hair, her gown, her descent from heaven, her everything—it was singularly the most beautiful thing Jason had seen in this world or the next.

Too late he noticed the sword.

The tip of her blade at his throat gave him a better sense of gravity. He wasn't floating, having visions of his future Mrs. Cephrin. He was sitting in his bedroll on Mount Kutsal's summit. Around him, his friends stayed asleep. Before him, the sword led the way up to a woman whose dancing blue eyes flashed a cold anger.

"Were it but such a slim chance your death would catch in the waking world, I would drive this blade through your neck with the hopes that it would end this foul war."

Of all the things to know, such as how she got there and why was she angry or if there was any way to not get stabbed tonight, one thing stood out as crucially important in Jason's mind. "Who are you?" he asked.

"Do you not recognize the Temptress, the Kiss of Night, Patroness of Dreamers? Are you really as Yol and Ananna proclaim you to be, some ignorant, bewildered bumpkin bumbling about? How can one such as you cause such chaos?"

Jason should've figured it was Eula, the goddess of the house of moths. She really made an entrance.

"Hey, I didn't cause anything," he told her, a simple plan growing in his head. "It was you guys, your lofty Temple of Houses," he said, his voice progressively rising, "who took an innocent guy, locked him up, tried to kill him, and started a war because he didn't march down to the chopping block with a smile on his face!" he finished in a shout.

Jason cast a questing eye behind Eula to where his friends were. Despite his raised octaves, they remained asleep. So much for help with the beautiful, bloodthirsty goddess.

"I fear the other gods may be right about your bumbling," Eula said, "you just tried to awaken these others when this is strictly a dream." Eula's sword evaporated, as if to prove what Jason saw wasn't quite real. "But what you say befell you has the ring of truth as well."

Jason raised an eyebrow. "Why wouldn't it be true what I'm saying?"

"Simply because the Temple says otherwise. Officially, you rode into the city and proceeded to the High Fane where you declared yourself a god and demanded your place on the Twelfth Throne. That's when you were held for trial but before the High Fane could ascertain the validity of your claims, you abandoned the test of legitimacy and destroyed part of the Temple with the help of your allies in the Hierophane. Now you're roaming the countryside, raising an army to combat the High Fane."

"What?!" Jason cried, jumping to his feet. "I was minding my own business when the Armsguard bumrushed me. They made me go to Nasreddin. And ever since, every time I try to go back to my business, a god comes out of nowhere and drags me back into the temple's mix. Now they're lying on me? Does this look like an army to you? I can't get these guys to do what I want even in my own dreams."

However Eula may have felt about the situation—a growing mystery to Jason—she smiled at his last words, a faint smirk that appeared on her lips as her oscillating eyes looked him over once again.

"This makes a lot more sense now that I've met you, Cephrin," she said. "The official portrait of you being a diabolical rebel mastermind didn't quite mesh with the personal assessment of most gods that you were a strange, likable dunce."

Jason shrugged. "Glad the likable dunce could help you make sense of it all. Me? I'm trying to figure out how you got misinformed about me. You're a goddess. Shouldn't you know what's really going on?"

"That must be the wholly ignorant thinking everyone warned me about," Eula said. "Just because we're gods and goddesses and lead our respective houses doesn't mean we share the same personality or same agendas. Not all of us are in love with the day to day of governing the Holy Aian Empire. The ones who are, Ananna, Menanderus, and Nadi were there in Nasreddin to meet you. Apparently, my three siblings decided between themselves to get rid of you quickly before the other House Masters could weigh in with their opinions. But you got away and they've retold the story of that escape to sell us a war that could've been prevented if they had exercised a bit of patience."

"Maybe you could spread the word," Jason said. "Because when I ran into Yol, he seemed beyond sold on the idea of stopping a criminal Chosen One."

"Yol will support the story version which best leads him into battle. But for Yol, you have Baligoz, who will always let the decision to support the Temple and its wars rest with the individual."

"And what about you? Where do you stand?"

"I stand for life."

"Does this mean we're cool? You're not gonna try to kill me with dream swords, right?"

"Truthfully, killing you to end this war is a tempting thought. But an eternity is a long time to have an innocent life weighing down my heart. Besides, at this point I'm hard pressed to believe your death would cease the fighting. If history has anything to teach us, you're most likely just another false Chosen One, of no use to anyone."

For the first time since he heard about the prophecy, Jason wanted to be the actual Chosen One. Not a fake, not a fluke manufactured by mages and their pendulum, but the aian messiah come to mend the twelve houses. Someone Eula could believe in, a god that sat next to her in Nasreddin.

"You know, I could be the Chosen One," Jason said. "I mean, the jury's still out on that one."

"I admit, I thought it strange that I could not see you in the world of dreams until now that you've used this beacon here. Still, you, the Chosen One? I doubt that."

Jason's brow furrowed in indignation. "Why?"

"The prophecy says the Chosen One is a savior of his people, one who leads the beleaguered masses away from tribulation. Who are you leading on this lonely mountaintop?"

He looked around. "How do you know I wasn't just taking a break?"

"You want to do something worthy of the Chosen One? Help the aians who chose life away from the Empire, caught in the turmoil of being stuck between two sides at war. None are more beleaguered than they."

"Too easy," Jason waved away her words with his bone hand. "That sounds like a standard fetch quest, no subs. If that's all it takes to show you I'm chosen all I need for you is to mark my map. Where exactly are they?"

Eula looked Jason up and down. "In war, nothing's easy. But they believe in you because they've seen you and perhaps something in you. In their dreams, you are their deliverance from pens and cages. They wait for you in Suusteren."

Chapter 2

Siege

RUKI PROVOS GRABBED the peacekeeper by a chrome gauntlet and shook vigorously. Captain Erox, the bastard, had driven a hard bargain, getting two casks of Glandier red wine from Ruki's limited stores. Instead of letting the captain see him grimace, Ruki Provos flashed a winning smile, one that shined like the officer's gleaming metallic uniform as they finally sealed the deal.

Ruki remembered when his clothes shined as equally bright as the peacekeepers in their chrome armor and white cloaks. These days white was impossible to keep up with as a civilian in Suusteren. Ruki instead clothed himself in a clean, simple tan tunic and brown pants.

For what it was worth, Ruki looked a far cry better than the city. She wasn't faring so well under the High Fane's assault. The boulders they hurled from catapults outside the wall had obliterated buildings and littered her streets with rocky debris. The air raids were worse, with winged soldiers from House Demir and Eula dropping fire-bombs. The mages garrisoned within her walls did what they could to nullify the attacks, but some always got through, and the town, she bore those scars.

Where Ruki and Captain Erox had met for this extralegal deal was no different. What used to be the resplendent courtyard of the Res Museum now stood barren, the trees lifeless trunks, the once re-gal building surrounding it a broken, blasted husk.

Captain Erox flashed his own smile to match Ruki's. But Ruki trusted smiles the same way he trusted snakes. He was simply glad the captain had taken off his helmet; all peacekeepers looked alike with them on. Behind Captain Erox was a detail of four peacekeepers and a hand-pulled caravan. Ruki could only see the first cart, but that was the only one he cared about. He allowed his eyes to drift away from the captain while they closed the deal—a tad unprofessional—to look over the cart full of brown burlap sacks he'd just procured. The sacks held grain: oat, wheat, rice, millet—all of which would turn a commanding profit in a place under siege. And all of it was procured not with money, but with the one thing the soldiers weren't allowed.

It was like his uncle had always said. *Business thrives anywhere.*

Captain Erox withdrew his gauntleted hand and snapped his fingers. One of the helmeted peacekeepers came to attention and strode briskly behind Ruki, where the merchant kept his wagon. The cart was laden with various odds, ends, and in-betweens... the bulk of what remained of the Provos Trading Company in Suusteren. The peacekeeper grabbed two of what was likely the only three casks of Glandier wine left in the city, tucked one under each arm, and returned to his caravan.

Each of the four peacekeepers shouldered a sack from their caravan, ran over and tossed it into Ruki's wagon. They did this twice, without care or concern for order, until the sacks of grain rose like a ramshackle shanty from the top of his cart.

Great. Now he'd have to rearrange the cart just to pull it, not to mention the time it would take to get it looking a little less inconspicuous. It was never wise to advertise you had plenty of food in a town starving slow.

"As always, a pleasure Provos," Captain Erox said. He turned and ordered his men out of the courtyard.

Two men on each side grabbed handles on their caravan's lead wagon and began to push. Ruki watched the wagons go by, the first with significantly less food that the well-fed garrison would never miss. The second wagon held various armor and weapons. The third held linen, useful for both beds and bandages. The fourth was a cage sparsely populated with aians.

Despite having seen these cages move throughout the city for almost two months, it was no easier to take the sight of this one. These aians weren't enemy soldiers, but residents of Suusteren. But when the Holy Aian Empire attacked, the mages came and the peacekeepers with them, and declared the aian populace of the free city a threat from within.

That's when the hunt began. These aians were headed to the internment camps built along the city walls. Most of them sat despondent, clutching their knees. They were hard to look at, and Ruki almost turned around to handle his own affairs until he saw one lying motionless on the floor of the cage.

"Captain!" Ruki called. "Stop the cart!"

The cart began to groan to a halt. Ruki took a few steps toward the cage, assessing the unconscious girl with a shrewd eye, disbelief telling him it couldn't be her. But it was, cat ears from the House of Nadi peeking out of chestnut brown hair. He remembered her too well despite the brevity of their encounter.

"Gina?" Ruki asked.

She didn't move. She didn't groan.

The clink of metal against metal told Ruki that Captain Erox had made his way to the cage. Ruki turned to face him. "What happened to her?"

"A feisty one, wouldn't go peacefully. A shield bash to the back of the head brought her down, made her more agreeable."

Ruki looked back at Gina. "Will she live?" he asked.

"She took a hard blow to the head. Your guess is as good as anyone's," he said with a nonchalant shrug. "If she awakens, fine. If she doesn't, fine. Did you need something, Provos?"

"I need her," he said. Ruki didn't know what she was still doing in Suusteren but it didn't matter. This woman had traveled from another world, survived parasitic bokoru in Brambelfen and drove Ruki's caravan away from an ambush, rescuing the lot of them from the unkillable Graverobber. He wasn't about to watch her die in a prison wagon or get carted off to an internment slum.

"Got a thing for kitty cats, do we?" Captain Erox said. "There are better things to invest in, trader. Chances are she'll just get picked up again on the next patrol."

"Let that be my worry," Ruki said. "How about we let your worry be what to do with that third cask of Glandier, eh?"

"Sounds like a better worry to me," the captain said. He snapped his fingers and his four enlisted men got to work. While one pulled the wine from Ruki's cart, another opened the door to the cage wagon for the remaining two. Those two brandished their swords before advancing on the cart keeping alert eyes on the prisoners. The other aians remained docile while the peacekeepers each grabbed Gina by an arm hauled her out of the wagon.

They all but threw her in Ruki's arms and he had to take a couple shuffle steps backward lest he drop her. She hung in his grasp limply.

"Enjoy whatever's left of her, Provos," the captain said before turning his head to the side. "Advance!" he barked and his men took their positions on the sides of the caravan. Their wagons lurched with a groan, moving through the rubble of the broken courtyard to parts unknown.

Ruki kept a firm grasp on Gina. He pulled her gently to his cart and laid her to rest against it while he set about rummaging through his stores. He rustled through a few piles and bins until he emerged with a small glass jar that housed a blue gel.

"Stave's Salvation Salve," Ruki said, reading the label aloud. "Let's hope you really are the 'water cleric in a bottle' you claim to be."

Ruki massaged the gel into Gina's scalp. Her head felt a slight bit warmer and Ruki hoped the wetness he felt through her chestnut hair was only the gel and not any blood.

He stood back and waited for what seemed like an eternity, every moment pulled taut as Ruki hoped the salve would do something, anything. Finally, Gina stirred.

"Nooo," she groaned, "no."

Ruki rushed to her. "Don't try to move too quickly, my dear. You've been injured."

Gina's eyes flitted open. "Ruki?" she asked.

"What happened?" Ruki asked. "Why are you still in Suusteren?"

"Long story. I'll explain later. Right now, I need to get back. Not safe for me out here."

She rose to her feet, thanks in no small part to Ruki's supporting arm.

"I don't know where you're trying to get back to," Ruki said "but you won't make it unless we plan carefully, even if it's only around the corner."

Gina stood still, her oscillating eyes focusing on Ruki. "I'm listening."

Ruki realized he didn't have a plan. He thought for a moment and began rummaging through the wagon until he pulled out a drab gray rain slicker. He threw it over Gina and pulled the hood low over her head.

"Keep your head down. And pull my cart."

"Pull your cart?" she asked incredulously "Dude, do you know how wrecked I feel?"

"I can talk us through that," Ruki said. "What I can't explain is having an assistant who's not assisting. Unwell as you feel, it is our best way to keep you safe. Please, pull the cart."

A stream of obscenities may have rolled from under her breath, but Gina complied, grasping the wagon's handles and leaning into her steps. The cart creaked, the wheels turning slowly to set them on their way out of the secluded courtyard and into the city proper.

The skyline of Suusteren looked like jagged teeth, with many of the brick and stone rooftops crumbling and misshapen. Mercenaries, mages and peacekeepers stood on these ruined rooftops throughout the city; up there to either spot the enemy, nullify their missiles or ensure the aians hadn't somehow infiltrated past the walls. This often meant they kept a keen, watchful eye turned inward to the city streets. Instead of trying to hide an aian under their scrutiny, Ruki decided to shift their focus.

"Citizens! All your wartime needs can be met here at the Provos Trading Company. What you are looking for I just may have. Step up, come, come!" Ruki said to errant passersby.

"You, sir, you look like you could use a set of drinking glasses," Ruki said as he pointed to a thin, scraggly man who looked like he needed a meal more. "And for you, ma'am, I've got a selection of rakes and hoes. I see you looking at the cart. Step up, come, come!"

Thus did Ruki navigate the city, shouting at people to come get products he knew they didn't want or couldn't use. The product wasn't important, it was his earnest salesmanship; it kept anyone passing by or looking down from the roofs from looking too closely at his hooded assistant. People either curiously eyed the cart for hidden gems or rushed away from the salesman trying hard to hawk useless junk.

Every now and again, Ruki would retreat a few steps back to Gina. "Where?" he'd ask under his breath. Gina would whisper back a left, right or straight.

They navigated the city without incident, weaving through main streets and back alleys until they got to Old Town. This section of the city wasn't much to look at before the siege, now it was all shambles. Many of the old brick buildings were charred black, more in number than what Ruki saw with the aian fire bomb raids, as if the residents themselves had set fire to them. Debris and detritus covered the streets, making it virtually impossible to see a bit of the cobbled stones underneath. Gina stepped away from the cart and nodded to a tavern with a hanging sign that named the place "Second Chances."

Why did that name sound familiar?

Gina led the way inside. The place was packed from window to wall, all seats and tables taken, standing room only as if the remaining residents of Suusteren planned to party their way through the siege. Only none of their faces seemed festive. If anything they all looked at Ruki as if he was general of the High Fane's Armsguard. And he wasn't even the aian here.

"Uh, are you sure this is the right place, Gina?" Ruki asked. He realized at this point it was probably not the wisest decision to be led by the person who had just recently suffered violent head trauma. Gina stopped, took down her hood, and turned to face Ruki.

She had a human face with creamy yellowish skin as opposed to aian gray, no cat ears. "We're definitely in the right place," she said.

Ruki's face contorted with unspoken questions as he looked at Gina. Instead of saying a word, she pointed at the bar. Ruki's memory of the place came rushing back as soon as he saw the bartender, the girl with the frizzy black hair and ebony skin. Calais the witch.

Calais put down the glass she was drying and charged over to Ruki.

"What are you doing here?" she growled.

"Me? What are you doing? What is this?"

"This is none of your concern. And I have enough of a time keeping this place inconspicuous without a huge wagon full trade goods parked out front."

"Be cool, Calais," Gina said. "I got captured by the patrollers. Ruki here saved my ass. No need to worry."

Gina's new human look brought a smile of understanding to Ruki's face. He looked around the room at the somewhat uncomfortable looking people packing the place.

"They're all aian," he said appreciatively. He looked back at Calais.

"You did this?" Ruki asked.

"Who else?" she asked in return before storming back to the bar.

"Gina!" a male voice called. Ruki turned and saw a megrym wearing a leather apron bolt towards them. It was Vincent, the other pendulum hero that they had pulled out of Bramblefen. Vexation reigned on his face. "What the hell was that, leaving like that? Staying gone til wednes-forever? Are you serious?"

"Vinny, chill," Gina said. "I got captured."

His features softened, "Are you ok?"

She nodded.

Ruki wasn't ok. His confusion had steadily grown since walking into Second Chances. He needed some holes filled in. "Why didn't you guys leave Suusteren?"

"It's complicated," Vincent said. "I mean, this," he indicated the bar packed full of fake humans, "wasn't our intention. While we didn't want the extreme danger of going to the Hierophane with you and your friends, we didn't want to go trekking there by ourselves through a wholly foreign world. So we stayed here to learn more about the world and more about these bodies we inhabit."

"Specifically, our character triggers," Gina said.

"So, eventually I learned mine," Vincent said. "Annoyance. And I found that as a tinkerer I can enterprise all sorts of interesting gadgets when I'm annoyed."

Ruki looked at Gina. "So what's yours?"

She shook her head. "I still don't know."

Vincent nodded. "That's roughly the answer to your question of why we're still in Suusteren. While Gina was busy trying to find her trigger, I went about trying to either build or procure a fast means of travel. Before she could find her trigger or I could find us a ride, the siege came down. Internment followed. We've been hiding out ever since."

"How'd you guys find Calais?" Ruki asked.

"We didn't," Vincent said. "She found us."

Ruki looked at the bar, where Calais worked silently. He found it strange that a witch would use magic to hide these people in plain sight. After all, the penalty for practicing witchcraft was a hot brand driven through your heart. He strode over to her.

"Don't tell me you're going to order another happy ending," she said as she wiped the counter.

"No, I'm curious. You're a witch, and a business woman. Neither one of those are fond of unnecessary costs. So why take on this risk?"

"Most of my clients before the war were aians. It made sense, seeing as how they have little access to magic. I got to know a good many of them while I helped them through one problem or another. I knew firsthand they didn't deserve getting locked up in slums built into the city walls, where death from disease and starvation waited."

Ruki nodded. So much for his former notion of the completely self-serving, selfish, soul-sucking witch. "So what happens now?" he asked.

"It's nice to have allies in this town. So stay for a drink," Calais said with a smile. "Then you've got to take that wagon and move it the hell away from here."

Chapter 3
The Coup

MEL LOVED TO PRACTICE her forms. It was dancing to her as her footfalls glided and darted about the clearing, transitioning from one form to another. Her breathing was music as she would rush the attack or steady the defense, the *shing-shing* of the bastard sword as it sliced through air at would-be targets. There was harmony to be found in all of it. These days it felt as if it was the only harmony to be found anywhere, the only way she could unwind and not think about anything. There was nothing complex about the forms, no special circumstances to consider. She simply stabbed out.

She ended her latest form with her arm fully extended and slightly bent, the sword level with her eye and the blade reaching to point like an accusing finger at wherever she looked. It just so happened to be Rich.

The brown robed mage leaned against a nearby barren oak, the only one in the clearing. The rest of the leafless trees huddled close together in a distant circle that fringed the clearing. It was as if this lone tree was brave enough to venture out from the surrounding forest, to grow in the space occupied by nothing save Vylar's flat-roofed house. Rich's spellbook was open but who knows how long he had been looking at her. A sloppy smile creased his lips.

"Looking good," he said.

"Are you talking about my forms or my ass in this catsuit?" Mel asked. She preferred her previous catsuit, the all black one with one arm exposed, but it had been rendered into dishrags after her fight with Brigitte. Her current leather outfit was more espresso colored, with thick brown stitch work. She perpetually had to fight the urge to tear a sleeve off of like the last one. That said, it did seem to mesh well with the blue cloak billowing behind her.

"The forms," Rich answered. "And probably the catsuit too."

Without another word, Rich delved back into his spellbook. Mel wiped sweat from her brow. She sighed. Vylar's hideaway sat in the southern countryside of the Free States, making for a mild winter that turned rather hot when she started practicing. But the sigh wasn't because of the heat she felt at her collar. A feeling she couldn't quite place lurked under the surface.

She walked over and sat down beside him.

"How's the studying coming along?" she asked.

His attention stayed on the pages as his finger glided along intricately written symbols. "You would think an enterprising mage somewhere would've thought of a spell to make studying magic easier," he said.

"Maybe it's done on purpose, to keep people like me from cracking open those books," Mel said.

"The language isn't too hard to see after awhile," Rich said. "It's the tone and intent that are hard to place. Still messes me up if I'm not careful."

Mel was thankful for the discussion, the distraction of it if nothing else. She leaned her head to rest against his shoulder. His words trailed off, then he shut the spellbook with a crisp snap and rose to his feet suddenly. "I've got to practice these new techniques," he said.

Normally, Mel would just nod and smile. Not this time. She had played this game oh so delicately for two months. She was tired.

"Rich?" she asked.

"Yeah?"

"Do you regret sleeping with me?"

She was done with subtleties, of trying to glean insight from bits and pieces of his speech and mannerisms. All she wanted was simple answers from Rich to help her in trying to understand him, where they stood now, and why.

"What?" Rich asked, confusion on his face. "Definitely not. In fact, I'm really glad we did. I saw your point... we were weirdly situated to have a unique experience while we're here. Plus, since danger just sort of swirls and looms around us all the time, we've gotta carpe diem that kind of thing."

Mel smiled. "Do you even know what carpe diem means?"

He smiled back. "I thought it was 'grab the dimes!' or something like that."

He sat back down next to her. "Speaking of, that's another reason why I can never regret it. You're a total ten. Confession time," he said raising his hand in the air.

"You remember when we first met Runt and were walking away from his house? And your brother accused me of staring at your ass? I was. So help me, I couldn't stop myself."

"Really?" Mel said, "Well, I'm glad you didn't tell me back then when I was mortified of being a girl, it would've weirded me out."

"It wasn't really my fault," Rich said, "you were wearing a steel bikini. Everyone knows those are the worst kind."

"What? How so?"

"There are only naughty bits on a bikini, and all your bits were shiny! It's guaranteed to destroy a man's attention, which is why the steel bikini isn't authorized attire for proms or state dinners. Look it up."

Mel laughed. "I'll be sure to do that," she said. "I remember the awkward kid who used to play this game with me and Jason. You've grown a lot since then."

"I think everyone has. Well, maybe not Jason."

They were quiet for a moment. Mel rubbed her hand across cool, dry grass. She felt a measure of relief, but something still gnawed at her.

"If you don't regret what we did, how come we've never..." she let the question trail off.

"What? You mean again?"

"That's what I'd like to know," a gruff voice said from behind them. Mel turned to face Vylar. Rich's mentor had a stern look on his features, made even more stark by milky white eyes that stared in Rich's direction.

"What do you mean again when I haven't seen you do any spells the first time?" Vylar asked. "I thought you wanted to get out of brown."

"C'mon-"

"C'mon?" Vylar asked. "It looks like you're about to teach me something new, Bendy Sleeves. I've never heard a spell start with that. Makes me wish I had eyesight, so I can see what wonders you unleash with this 'c'mon' spell."

"OK, I get it," Rich said. "Back to work." Rich rose to his feet and walked away thumbing through his spellbook. The opportunity for Mel to understand their relationship better walked away with him. Mel looked at Vylar, who sat down in Rich's recently vacated spot.

"Block much?" she asked.

"I don't understand your phrase but I hear your tone fine and clear, lady," Vylar said, shifting his head in her direction slightly. "If anything, I should sound like that. You're a distraction. Bendy Sleeves there is Brown of the 32nd Kind, one degree from graduating into a master color. And he's gotten here faster than anyone I've ever seen. Let him work."

"I let him work as much as he wants to work," Mel spat. She didn't like being called a distraction, especially when she spent most of her time minding her own damn business. "If he gets distracted, that's on him."

"You're right," Vylar said. "I'm asking you to help him along. He's a fugitive from both the Hierophane and the Temple of Houses, which is a hard spot to be in when you're a lowly brown robe. The faster he gets access to specialized magic, the better equipped he'll be to fend for himself."

Mel didn't respond. Vylar's request to let Rich work felt like some sort of inane gaming sub-quest, an obstacle stacked on top of other obstacles that kept stacking as high as a skyscraper. She wanted to take the Rift Pendulum home. Before she could, they had to depose Druze as Hierophant and reinstate Majora. Before they changed mage tower management, they had to garner enough support to make the coup as bloodless as possible, since a violent civil war between mages would leave the tower helpless against the ongoing aian invasion. Before they could help Rew Majora garner support or stage the coup, they'd have to be strong enough to handle themselves in a fight, which meant Rich out of brown robes. Before he could get out of brown, Mel would have to leave him alone and let him work.

"You can stop gritting your teeth, lady," Vylar said. Only then did Mel realize she was chewing on her frustration, like indigestible gristle.

"I just want to go home," she said.

Now it was Vylar's turn to not respond. A peaceful silence settled between the two. They both, in their own way, watched Rich practice his spellcraft.

RICH ABSOLUTELY HATED this spell, the graduation spell that would take him into the 33rd degree. He believed Vylar when he said it took years for some to get past it.

It involved all four principles of spellcraft. It started simple enough, with the creation of a ball of light in the palm of your hand. Then you had to focus on the fraction-worth of heat the light spell generated and augment it until the spell generated more heat than light. Then you had to bend the light, somehow pulling the light away from the heat you held in the one hand into your empty hand. Finally, you had to destroy the light you just siphoned off, leaving nothing but dark, flameless heat raging in one hand.

Rich's spell kept breaking whenever he tried to siphon off the light. He understood the words, and he was sure he had the right tone and intent. It's not like Vylar hadn't told him again and again what those were. Despite knowing this spell, when it came down to implement he was all fizzle.

He held up his hands to try again, either for the nth or the umpteenth time, when the blue and white shimmering light of a portal swirled into existence near Vylar's house. Rew Majora stepped through the portal.

Like Rich, Rew wore a brown robe. Unlike his, her color was strictly to maintain as much anonymity as possible. While much of her raven hair fell loosely down her back and shoulders, she kept a good many locks braided as they had been the day he helped her escape the Underthral dungeon. She walked toward Rich, Mel and Vylar with an air and confidence that was impossible to hide in dirt colored robes.

"You smell like news," Vylar said sniffing the air.

"Easy enough to smell," Rew said. "It is the one thing I always come back with."

She looked at Rich.

"How goes your training?"

"Still of the 32nd Kind," Rich said.

Rew nodded and didn't ask anything more of him. Her manner had been this way ever since he'd rescued her from the Underthral.

As much as he'd like to chalk it up to her being angry and focused on recovering her rightful place as Hierophant, doubt plagued him. A small voice told him she was still angry and heartbroken because of his lies to her and no amount of rescuing was going to fix that. The voice got louder every time she'd return from her covert fact-finding missions with very little to say to Rich outside of questions about spell progression.

"It will not be easy to remove Druze from power," Rew said gravely. "He cannot be ambushed; he has no predictable schedule outside of regular meetings with his inner circle of mages."

"Who are they?" Mel asked.

"One master from each color school. Once or twice a week they sit in the grand council room and strategize on the war."

"Can we turn one of his inner circle?"

"It is doubtful. They have all sworn loyalty to him, praising him as the Second Hierophant Reborn. To ensure this loyalty is truly spoken, their minds are routinely inspected by Druze's newest advisor, the blue robe Delv Vereyn."

"Delv!" Rich exclaimed. He remembered all too well when the blue mage had played in his mind while he was helplessly caged. "I thought that bastard was dead."

"Can you tell us anything we can work with?" Mel asked.

"The aians are a tenacious foe," Rew said, "especially when all the houses are involved as they are now. The only thing keeping the Hierophane in the fight are the mercenaries procured from the Southern Kingdoms and the intense skirmishes being fought between the aians and nasrans up north. But I have seen bits and pieces of a plan that may take him away from the high security of the Hierophane or battlefield camps. I'm still trying to discover details, but from what I've seen it definitely affects you here."

Mel's features grew more concerned. "What's he planning?"

Rew shook her head. "I do not know how but I do know what. He seeks to amplify the pendulum."

Chapter 4
Another Front

DRUZE LOOKED OUT OVER the Erga Salt Flats, stretching as far as the eye could see, a level plain in all directions. Normally the salt pans were white, but this was winter, which didn't mean cold so much as the little bit of rain to fall in this region had made a dramatic appearance. Half-inch thick water lay as a sheet over the ground, reflecting a totally clear, perfect image of the daytime sky. To look down in all directions was to see giant, fluffy clouds listing across the ground. It was as if the earth had disappeared and Druze was at the meeting point for a heaven above and a heaven below.

It was beautiful. This is why the aians considered the Erga Salt Flats a jewel of their empire. They called it the Mirror of Heaven.

Druze couldn't wait to rip the jewel from their grasp.

With his right hand, he shielded his eyes from the sun to look at the shimmering smudge in the far distance. The Crystal City stood as a beacon on the horizon. Built of shining white brick and encrusted with the salt, it sparkled in the sun like a mirage. It served as both a trading post for the Southern Kingdoms and a gateway into the Holy Aian Empire.

Druze smoothed out the regal purple and white robes of the Hierophant and ran his fingers through his now blonde hair. These robes once belonged to his daughter. The body once belonged to the pendulum reject La Croix. The only thing that didn't feel borrowed, out of place, was the sense of power in being the head of Seat Esotera. That fit like a glove, especially in times such as these.

Behind Druze gathered an army filled with mages of all colors, mercenaries, and soldiers from different distant lands of the Southern Kingdoms. The blue and white glow of open portals shimmered all along the lines of the army, bringing more troops and more mages to open more portals. In less than a minute the army had doubled and still the portals kept firing off.

A ram's horn could be heard over the sound of shuffling soldiers, distant and muted yet loud like the giant bellow of an anguished beast. Druze had held no illusions about keeping this force a secret from those eagle-eyed aians, but he was surprised it had grown to almost its full complement before the ash skins had raised the alarm.

Claiming the Crystal City was key to the Hierophane's strategic goals. It would cut off trade between the Holy Aian Empire and the handful of human kingdoms in the Southern Kingdoms who had refused to openly ally with the Hierophane. This would force a self-reliance upon the aian armies that was ultimately unsustainable. It would also choke out the greedy human kingdoms, perhaps even forcing one or two of them to join the human cause against these ash skins. The second goal was to tear open a whole new war front. A harsh stalemate had developed along the border of the Free States and the Holy Aian Empire.

"Are we all gathered?" Druze asked Vereyn.

"Your armies are fully assembled, liege," the blue robe answered. Scars stretched up Vereyn's face, a road map of pain made even more noticeable by the wild shock of blue hair erupting from his head. Druze pointed to their distant target.

"I want a cadre of Pendulum Heroes, aians from House Yol and Zemishirus, digging tunnels to get under the city. Twenty pendulum heroes working four tunnels should suffice. I want them continually replaced once they expire."

Digging under a city was a costly endeavor. Firetraps were all too common, where the city builders had prepared its defense by digging under the city and placing hexes, wards or even nonmagical incendiary snares. Anyone attempting underground access would set them off, filling their tunnels with certain, purging fire. It was suicide. It just so happened Druze had suicide troops.

"Any other call for pendulum heroes?" Vereyn asked.

"No." The Rift Pendulum had grown increasingly unreliable. The more heroes summoned meant a stronger possibility of unintended consequences, such as the warriors becoming insubstantial as ghosts or disappearing completely. No reason to jeopardize the underground assault by padding their numbers.

Vereyn made a curt bow. "Then I shall see to it, liege."

The Crystal City shimmered with more than just sunlight. Activity along its walls and gates let Druze know this would be no strict siege. An aian force was coming to meet them, some on marching feet, others on the backs of fierce destrier warhorses. The total lack of eagle and moth-winged flying troops was an unexpected boon.

Druze invoked his voice augmentation spell through a smirk as he looked at the distant army. He spoke and his voice boomed over the salt flats like thunder, silencing the growing din of his restless army.

"Creation mages! Destruction mages! Craft your towers."

The white robed creation mages chanted as a team. The air seemed to fold and waver, like heat rising, above the army as the mages remade nothing into something substantial. Thick wooden logs drifted out of these folding waves of air. This is where the destruction mages took over, cutting and blasting the logs until four giant siege towers stood. These would serve to get the standard soldiers over the walls.

"Forward!" Druze called. The red robes, the mages who excelled chiefly at the altering, bending, and manipulation of matter, began to push the siege towers. The giant wooden towers dragged across the landscape with a harsh grate akin to rough sandpaper. The army fell into step behind them.

The enemy destriers had chewed through more than a mile in this time. Druze counted the destriers at fifty abreast, at least three ranks deep. Powerful hooves sent up clumps of sand and violent sprays of water as they charged with reckless speed at their enemy. While the number seemed small, there was no denying their fear-inspiring display, a display made even more menacing with the Mirror of Heaven casting an equal, upside-down advancing horde. Two more minutes and the aian cavalry would be on top of them.

Suddenly, the cavalry broke their formation, splitting the fifty abreast down the middle, with one half turning right and the other half turning left. The bastards were attempting to flank them.

That wasn't all. As the horses turned to the side, each revealed a second rider. These riders unfurled their eagle and moth wings and took to the air. As the horses ran to either end of the human formation, the aian air corps, all archers, rose straight as a stalk into the sky. Exposed by the cavalry parting like a curtain, the aian foot soldiers marched relentlessly to close the distance, to fill the empty space left by the destrier cavalry.

The air corps was the biggest immediate threat. "Mages!" Druze called, pointing up at the ever rising flyers. "Fire volleys at your will!" For emphasis, searing blue netherfire leaped into existence into the hand he pointed with. He brought his other hand up with jarring force into the blue fireball, sending it careening upwards. The missile sped into the rising air corps, where it crashed into a moth aian and dissolved the flyer instantly.

The skies in front of Druze's army turned crimson and hazy as mages sent smoking, fiery red missiles hurtling through the air. Two dozen found their mark, sending flyers writhing in flames to the ground with a satisfying crash. So many more missed as the flyers expertly dodged the relentless stream of fireballs. The flyers kept rising into the sky.

Within moments, the fireballs rose towards the flyers only to have gravity pull them back down to land harmlessly on the ground. The air corps were now effectively out of range. At this safe distance, the remaining flyers pulled arrows for their bows. It was their turn. They loosed.

The arrows rushed like a black tide. Mages tried to bat them away with bent sleeves, armored men hoisted their shields. But there were too many arrows. The piercing screams of the wounded and dying erupted through the ranks as the arrows found homes in the arms, legs, heads and hearts of mage and soldier alike. One volley. Then another. And another.

The flying archers were one of the Aian Empire's most powerful assets. Druze had to stop their rain of destruction. Now.

"Yellow robes!" Druze's voice boomed for the weather manipulation specialists. "Tornado assault!"

The skies darkened as the yellow robes called harsh winds into existence. The cadre of yellow robes made motions in the air as if they were pulling down a ladder. That's when slender funnel clouds began to descend in the midst of the flying units, causing them to scatter. The summoned winds were small as far as tornadoes went, but they were enough to disrupt the flight patterns of the enemy and tossed mercilessly any flyer foolish enough to get caught in the funnels. The enemy archers stayed on the move, unable to aim precisely. Druze's army advanced free of their hail of arrows.

Time to turn the tables. "Razers!" Druze bellowed over the howl of wind. "All report!" In moments, eight mages wearing either purple or orange robes made their way to stand before Druze. Razers were a tactical unit Druze had invented during the War of Six Houses. Composed of two man teams of one orange robe and one purple robe, this unlikely pairing displayed a remarkable tenacity for causing all manners of chaos once the two opposing colors learned how to play nice. Well trained Razers were named such because they could raze any obstacle. Druze had trained these eight mages personally.

"Cavalry Redirect coupled with Catapult Smash Offensive," Druze instructed. "Time your portals for the height of your catapult arc. Move."

The teams of orange robed augmenters and purple robed terrormancers snapped to attention and gave a curt bow before turning their attention to the advancing army.

As if synchronized to the task, all eight mages made a portal root, collective fingers flying in the air as they sealed the root with hovering ink that quickly disappeared.

Next, a purple aura surrounded the terrormancers. Black chains erupted from their sleeves. The chains shot around the orange robes. Unceremoniously, the terrormancers vaulted their teammates into the skies toward the marching aian foot soldiers. The purple robes didn't wait to check their throws. Instead they split up, two each bolting towards the either end of the army's column using the great chains erupting from their sleeves as legs.

High in the air, the orange robes bent and altered their robes, expanding the orange fabric to easily four times its natural size, until they looked like four flat suns hovering over the marching aian force. Next the augmenters made another portal root, the ink barely visible to Druze against the artificially darkened skies.

Meanwhile, the aian cavalrymen had run beyond the length of the human army's column and were turning their destriers again, this time on a curving, scythe-like path directly into the human army. In a few scant minutes they would charge into the army's exposed flanks.

The purple robes, chains tearing into ground between the marching footsteps of human soldiers, were rushing to the flanks.

Even from this distance, Druze could see the inspiring awe of the destriers as they bore down on his unprotected flank. Time seemed to slow as the horses' rippling muscles charged across the plain. He saw breath snort from their flaring nostrils, hot even in a climate such as this, one made humid from the press of bodies and the steaming rise of freshly shed blood.

The purple robes reached the flank. The raze began.

First the orange robes did what they were known for. They augmented their bodies, including the robes, changing the texture to something much more massive. Lead. The four gray disks abruptly dropped from the sky.

The augmenters landed with a sickening crunch on top of the marching aian army with enough force to cause the earth to quake. The soldiers immediately beside the giant lead disks lost their footing and their weapons as they were tossed one way or another. The soldiers who had only gotten an arm or their legs flattened under the massive lead disks howled in unbearable agony.

Meanwhile the purple robes called their portals into existence. The blue and white glowing tunnels flared to life which led back to the middle of the formation where Druze originally gave them their orders. The terrormancers did not take their own portals.

The orange robes reverted back into flesh and blood, their shrunken orange robes now merely fabric as they picked themselves off the ground. They also called their portals into existence. The portals opened up right next to the ones set by the purple robes in the middle of the formation.

The orange robes stepped into their portals, emerging back at the center of the human army. Next to the orange robes were the unused portals freshly opened by their terrormancer partners. They each stepped into these waiting portals. The orange robes emerged on the other side at the flanks of the human army, beside the waiting purple robes.

Finally, the orange robes ran out to meet the galloping destrier cavalry. They called their second portal into existence in front of the rushing horses. These portals, built when the orange robes had expanded to four times their size, opened four times the size of a typical portal, giant maws to swallow the rushing horses.

On either side of the human army, the destrier cavalry was vanishing in the glowing blue and white portals. The destination end of the portals were high in the air above the marching aian soldiers, where the orange robes had placed the portal root. Horses and their riders began to spill out of the hovering portal, falling from dizzying heights onto their own marching comrades below. Horse after horse, rider after rider, flailed screaming as they plummeted to an inescapable death.

The remaining cavalrymen veered to avoid the portals. They plunged into the ranks of the advancing humans, cutting into Druze's men with swords as the horses stomped men underfoot.

The aian foot soldiers cheered at the sight. Bolstered by their cavalry, the foot soldiers raised their weapons and charged.

Suddenly, the walls of the Crystal City shook at the very foundations. A giant plume of fire shot out of the ground. Druze realized a group of Pendulum Heroes must have set off a fire ward.

His were not the only underground units active. The ground opened up in front of the red mages pushing wooden siege towers. Spears shot out from the opening, impaling mages too slow to react. Hands attached to insect exoskeleton armored forearms reached out from the ground, pulling soldiers down by their ankles.

The mercenaries and soldiers began to halt without orders, searching the ground frantically for signs of further betrayal.

Instead of getting more hands and spears coming from holes in the ground, a vast chasm opened up in front of them. Aians from the antennae-headed ant House of Yol and talon-clawed mole House of Zemishirus began to pour out of the opening.

"Stand your ground. Push through them!" Druze called, his amplified voice filled with anger. The men of the Southern Kingdoms were used to standard warfare with other men. A fight with an organized aian force was a wholly different matter. Still, the bulk of them continued the advance toward the city, pushing the siege towers forward and the aian forces backward.

"Razers!" Druze bellowed to his trained specialists. "Worry not about this useless melee. Take the walls as we push through!"

The Razers split off from the fighting on the ground, forming into their own siege team. As they ran at the walls, the orange robes turned themselves into gleaming steel. Chains erupted from the robes of the terrormancers following along the orange robes. Their chains grabbed the steel men and hurled them into the walls. The walls shook and dust rose in a noxious cloud as the steel men impacted. The steel men began to climb.

From the tops of the walls, aians poured boiling oil onto the steel men. One Razer who wasn't fast enough fell screaming from the walls as the oil covered him. The other ones kept climbing.

The purple robes closed the distance to their counterparts on the walls. They shot their chains at the steel men. The chains wrapped around the climbers which allowed the purple robes to pull themselves onto the wall. Once on the wall, the terrormancers opened their robes to unleash nightmare creatures, slathering demon dogs the size of wild boars or toothed serpents with legs as long as ostriches, that ran up the side of the walls and into the crowd of defenders at the top, creating a panic.

By this time the red robes had finished pushing the siege towers into the side of the Crystal Castle. Men rushed the stairs, yelling fiercely as they strove towards the top.

Just like that, the human soldiers and mages were over the walls and into the Crystal City. Briefed on the layout and given specific battle plans for once they breached the walls, the schools of magic went to work.

The terrormancers sowed chaos everywhere the aians clustered for defense, releasing their nightmare creatures which would dissipate after crashing into a group of aians and infusing them with a sense of mortal terror that made them cry for their mothers and their gods. The chaos only increased once the destruction mages were over the wall, raining fire and ice upon the fear-stricken aians.

Within minutes the aian army was broken, routed and in full on flight. Soldiers and mages cheered. Druze held his hands up to quiet them.

"Tonight we shall celebrate. But now we make haste to secure the city. Let us not lose what we worked so hard to gain. Mages! You know your roles. Fill them."

The mages would go through the city, repairing the damage done during the assault, strengthening the defenses. The Crystal City would need to be stronger structurally than it had ever been to withstand an aian assault against it.

And they would assault it. It was too precious a target to lose without response. Now the armies of men were free to tear through the southern reaches of the empire. Meanwhile, the mages and peacekeepers still held the center strongly in the Free States while nasrans were sweeping south in an arc that headed towards Nasreddin.

Instead of two, now the Holy Aian Empire had a war on three fronts.

This is what the world would see. But Druze moved in shadows and the occupation of Crystal City was the beginning of a grander plan, the whole of which was known only to him.

"Bring me the aian garrison commander," he told Vereyn.

Within moments peacekeepers brought forth a male in an overly decorated Armsguard uniform, a wide-eyed and shaking member of the chameleon house of Sen.

"Did the terrormancers get you or were you always this craven?" Druze asked.

The aian commander's response was to gulp and shake his head.

"Not exactly the accomplished conversationalist," Druze said. "That's fine. Vereyn here has unique ways to get people to open up. And you and I have much to discuss."

Chapter 5
Catching Up

SAVASHBAHAR HAD NO words for her anguished, dead son. She could only look upon Dushunmek, tasting shame like acrid ashes upon her tongue. Such was the price of silence. She should have wailed him to the halls of the ancestors.

When a warrior dies, the loved ones must wail. The sound is bitter, unbearable; it forces the fallen spirit to flee from the mortal coil. It also lets the warrior know with absolute finality how loved they were.

Her son, looking at her now, did not mask the hurt on his face. The same silence, the unrepentant voicelessness she had shown when he fell to hollowers at Maltep now kept him lost in the afterlife, unable to find the hall of the ancestors. His look said it all. *Why do you keep me bound here? Why don't you mourn for me?*

Savashbahar shook her head. "I will not mourn. The wail that would lead you home also extinguishes my fire for revenge. It heals me. And I would rather have you glare at me with your brightest hatred than to wail my spirit empty. My poor son, I do not want healing. I want to bathe in mage blood."

Dushunmek clawed his face, as if the thought of being between worlds was too much to bear. He disintegrated, collapsing into so much dust. The dust began to stack and fall into a pattern. Once it had settled, it revealed an ancient city ruined, blasted beyond salvage.

Yasak toprak. Forbidden land.

A moment later the image faded as she bolted upright. Dawn's light crested over the rise of the valley below Mount Kutsal. Morning mist shrouded the valley floor, creating the illusion of a frozen, ghostly sea. The rising sun provided enough light for her to clearly see her breath as she panted in ragged exhaustion. On the summit a short distance away, Mike and Runt sat before the cooking fire. Runt minded the eggs on the cooktop. Mike looked at her, an eyebrow raised in question over blue tinted goggles.

"You okay?"

Savashbahar shook off the image of her son's pained, accusing eyes. "I am better now, little one. I know where my destiny lies. The Sprawl."

Mike grimaced. "I figured," he said holding his bandaged hand up. "Not worth the cut if you ask me. All that for some reruns."

"Blood whispers own!" a yell behind Savashbahar proclaimed, loud enough to create an echo. Apparently Jason's vision went well.

Mike fixed his gaze at the boy. "I don't know why we take you anywhere."

"Comic relief. Badass sniping skills," Jason said walking toward the campfire and counting off fingers as he named reasons. "Lively conversation. Keen dungeon crawling acumen." He sat down beside Mike and Runt and reached into his tunic with his bone hand. The pendant emerged on his fingers, five maggots writhing their way into a heart. "And my running subscription to *God Mode Quarterly*," Jason finished with a smile.

Savashbahar stretched her limbs as she rose from her bedroll. She joined her compatriots around the fire, where the scent of robust woodland herbs mixed with eggs. Even with limited rations, Runt always managed to make the food delectable.

"You know this puts us in a bit of a bind, right Savvy?" Mike said as he handed her a plate with two eggs on it.

"How so?" she asked.

"It took us forever to get here because we couldn't hop a caravan and shortcut it. And this is a place people really try to go to. Remember trying to make the Sprawl? It took days and days on a caravan, through the most inhospitable desert I've ever seen. It ain't made to be walked across."

"Indeed," Savashbahar admitted. They'd have to take a store's worth of supplies to traverse that desert. In this time of war and strife, procuring the necessary supplies would take an age. Then they'd have to defend the supplies from marauders. They needed a faster way. She mulled her meager options as she chewed on egg, coming up with naught but dead ends. Then she noticed Jason's death hand raised in the air.

"I think I can help," he said, the grin on his face smug enough to feel abrasive. He said nothing else and the moment stretched.

"*Eyvah*! Speak it then, child."

"I can get us flown there, courtesy of the House of Eula."

Jason explained his blood whisper, his meeting with the Mistress of Moths. They had made plans to meet in the nearest city, an aian heavy trade town called Nev Tefar.

"Lemme get this straight," Mike said. "The aians wanna kill you, they fighting with the mages over the rights to who gets to lop your head off first, and you decide to go meet these fools for drinks at your neighborhood bar and grill. Word?"

"You left out the part where I ask Eula nicely to fly us all to the Sprawl, but yes."

"Wow," Mike said with an appreciative smile growing on his lips as he nodded. "You are really stupid."

"Hey man, unless great plans look like egg yolk, I don't see any ideas stuck between your teeth. You need to get there. You've got no options. Sounds like it's worth the risk to me."

Mike shook his head. "Do you know how much mouth I'm gonna hear from Melvin if I let his friend get killed being as stupid as you sound right now?"

"I may not be a grown man back in our world, but here I'm a grown aian. It's my call," Jason said. He looked at everybody, a mischievous gleam in his dancing eyes. "Let's do it."

Mike looked at Runt, who nodded slowly. Then Mike turned to Savashbahar. No other alternatives came to her mind, so she nodded as well. Mike faced Jason.

"Bet," Mike said. "But I gotta know one thing, the thing you trying real hard to leave out."

"Whassat?" Jason asked between bites of egg.

"Just how smoking hot is this moth chick?"

BY THE TIME JASON COULD make out the squat buildings of Nev Tefar in the distance, it was well into the afternoon. He ran rightmost with Runt to his left, then Mike, then Savvy. All of them stayed abreast at a moderate jogging pace that had eaten away at some fifteen miles in getting here.

Jason remembered his first day in this world. Specifically, he remembered how long it had taken them to get to Fort Law and how much their feet hurt from that slow walk. Unbidden, he envisioned the scene from Conan the Barbarian—still one of his favorite movies—when Conan had freed Subotai from his "dinner-for-wolves" cage and together than ran, like literally ran, to the next town. Like it was nothing. Now, he knew what that felt like.

If this was a movie, right now the camera would be panned out to a fairly distant shot, so you could get all four of them in the frame, juxtaposed against the sparse winter landscape of barren shrubs and occasional islands of unmelted snow amongst the rocky turf and brown grasses. The shot would be in slow motion, with raw drumbeats rising as they surged toward the town. They could use this scene for the movie trailer because anyone looking would know instantly they were a collective set of badasses, each and every one of them capable of extreme badassery.

But of course, the movie would really be about Jason, so the camera would return for his close up. He was distinctly aware of his well defined pecs rising and falling as he breathed, his taut shoulders moving in rhythm and his abs tight but not clenched. This was definitely not his body back on Earth, where his pudgy original shell had a love-hate relationship with trans fat and high fructose corn syrup.

Here he felt powerful, like when he inhaled air he exhaled better air.

"Feels good, doesn't it?" said a hauntingly familiar voice to his right. The problem was none of his running companions were on his right.

He turned his head as if snapping a whip. Onus the Corruptor was beside Jason. The God of Power did not run so much as glide, his blood red robe listing just above the lifeless ground. The months since Jason had last seen Onus had not been kind to the god's physical host; the lesions and sores on his forehead and arms had completely eaten away all signs of the host's old house of Yol. Onus smiled warmly at Jason, regarding him with cold, still eyes.

Jason looked back to the left. Focusing solely on the town, all his companions moved as if Onus had been there all along, telling jokes and offering to clean their breakfast dishes.

"Feel free to reply, Cephrin," Onus told Jason. "Your allies can hear neither me nor you, at least not when you address me. It's a completely private channel, something that encourages an active dialogue rather than forcing you to sound rather undone to onlookers as if you're talking to yourself."

"How?" Jason asked.

"It's magic, the timeless, ethereal stuff. The very stuff all aians had access to during the Maddening Times. This is the gift which my brothers and sisters sought solace from instead of mastery over."

"No," Jason said, "I mean, how did you know... how I felt just now?"

"I am the God of Power. That feeling, Cephrin, the heady rush of competency, of knowing without doubt you possess mastery over your environment, your employ, yourself, your competition—anything, everything—it calls to me, like a lover with her arms outstretched. I go from place to place embracing that feeling and telling what passes as aiankind to embrace it as well."

Between Eula finding him in a dream and Onus finding him from a feeling, Jason wondered if anything he did was wholly his anymore. Maybe scratching his ass summoned the Horse God Otam.

"Again, I'll ask," Onus said, his smile growing. "Feels good, doesn't it?"

"Sure," Jason said. "But you already knew that. Did you want something else?"

"Although I can sense your thirst for power, I can't read your mind, Cephrin. It's been a couple months since we last spoke. I reasoned it was high time to catch up."

Jason felt the heart pendant bouncing up and down on his chest as he ran, tapping at his skin again and again like a knock on the door.

"I'm afraid there's not much you've missed," Jason said. "A war, me in the midst of this and that, nothing really."

"Idle chatter?" Onus asked, a hint of disgust in his voice. "Spare me the banality. Time is precious to the powerful." He pointed toward the city they were striving to reach. "New adventures await, no?"

Nev Tefar had indeed gotten closer, perhaps two hundred yards out, and it was a rather strange sight. The buildings were all cylindrical. The two-story buildings looked like giant bean cans while the one-story buildings looked like giant tuna cans. Many of the buildings hosted fairly large windows, which made Jason contemplate how the glassmakers curved the glass just so to make it fit. Roofs were either flat or they rose to a point like circus tents. Here and there a place would be made entirely of wood but most of them were constructed of red, brown, or even purple brick. The staggered effect of the varying buildings made the town look like a demented set of pipe organs. It looked like the kind of place that would prompt the words "adventures await".

"I guess so," Jason said, turning back to Onus. Onus, however, was no longer there.

"You guess what?" Mike asked. He slowed his jog down to a walk the remaining distance. Everyone followed suit.

"Nothing," Jason said, "I was just talking to Onus, the God of Power, who apparently thinks it's great to appear only to me and disappear after he asks me questions. Just as a note, guys, if it seems like I'm talking to myself from here on out, it's probably him trying to take me out on a bromantic date, before he permanently wears my body as his meatsuit. OK?"

Jason had seen enough shows where the devil/demon/spirit friend appears to the protagonist who tries to pretend this specter isn't there and comedy hijinx ensue. Not this time, might as well nip this in the bud right now. He didn't have the energy or inclination to keep trying to convince people he wasn't crazy.

The rest of the team stopped. They looked at Jason, all of them remaining silent. The silence stretched. Finally, Mike adjusted his goggles.

"Yo, whatever," he said with a shrug.

Jason reasoned he spoke for the rest of the gang. Back to business.

Nev Tefar was tradelands, a watering hole nestled along the Holy Aian Empire's western and ill-defined northern borders. In these reaches, a town could fall into the Free States or the Aian Empire or that amorphous region where the nasran tribes roamed and dwelled, all dependent upon the predominant race of inhabitants. Here, aians mostly lived, which made it Holy Aian Empire.

This time, Jason remembered to put his hood up. He even remembered to address the hand of his severed arm, which protruded out of a quiver on his back as if it was waving to passers-by. He put a small black cotton bag around the hand and pulled the strings tight to ensure no part of the severed arm was distinctly visible. Finally, he put his bone hand in his pocket. Now he was fully incognito.

Small crowds of shoppers lined cramped streets, browsing as traders of all races hawked gold trinkets, wooden bowls, spears with tassels, wool and silk rugs. A megrym trader showcased steam powered washing machines. The air hung thick with the charcoal tang of grill fires and the savory aroma of spiced meat from local aian vendors cooking meals to order right on the street. Humans and aians browsed alongside nasran elders. Children of all races wove around and between the legs of adults as they ran and played. Leave it to the principles of free trade to not get the memo that all these folks should be fighting. Consequently, no one batted an eye at Jason and his eclectic ensemble of companions as they passed.

The two-story inn held the same nonchalant, accepting diversity found on the streets. The vibe of the town almost encouraged Jason to throw back the hood and relax. Almost. He wasn't going to play his hand like some wet nub. Instead, he kept his head down, passing by the tables and bar to lead the way upstairs.

The second floor didn't have the same open floor plan as downstairs. The stairs led up to a corridor. At the end of the corridor, two moth women stood in gleaming silver armor holding spears and shields. They raised their shields and spears as Jason and his companions approached.

Jason took down his hood, revealing his markless face. "I'm expected," he said.

The guards nodded and lowered their stance. One opened the door and held it open, revealing a balcony area. Eula sat at a table hosting a feast. She smiled at Jason, a smile that made Jason feel warm to gaze at, a smile that made her look even better than he remembered from his dreams. Behind her, three more moth guards stood in silent watch. Below, the streets and their noises seemed muted even though they were only two stories up.

"I see you're a man of your word," Eula said. "I prepared a meal, just in case your honor held."

"Cool." Jason said with a clumsy smile. Immediately he winced because, dammit, now that he thought about it, there were a hundred better lines he could've said. Like 'I'm not a man of my word, just a man who can't say no to a free meal.' Well, maybe not that exactly, she might think he was a hungry ass glutton. But it was better than 'cool'. Anything beat that.

While his friends took a seat, Jason ignored the feeling of being back in high school to make the introductions. As he held his hand out toward Mike and Runt and Savvy, he tried to focus on his calm, hoping perhaps his Cephrin mode could get him through potentially awkward moments with the opposite sex.

"I assume your disciples will accompany us to Suusteren," Eula said.

"Disciple?" Mike asked incredulously. "The fuck?"

Jason held a placating hand up. "Actually, I have a better idea. Rather than go straight to Suusteren we need to head south and rendezvous with Mike's brother."

"Our people suffer needlessly in prison camps and you want to facilitate family reunions?" Eula asked.

"Hear me out, goddess. Our wartime intelligence is a bit sparse, but we've heard the city of Suusteren is under siege, yes?"

Eula nodded.

"So mages and soldiers are entrenched in Suusteren, which is probably why you haven't just flown into the city and freed the people yourself. Also explains why you're looking to see if I have an inkling of Chosen-Oneliness in me despite my bad rap because if I do then maybe I can help. And I can, but I don't fare flying directly into the city any better for you. In fact I make it worse because I'll get detained at the aian siege line. Wanted criminal, enemy of the Fane and all that."

Eula looked at Mike. "And his brother can remedy this problem?"

Jason smiled. "Where his brother is, so are competent human magic users at odds with the Hierophane," he said, thinking of Vylar and Rew. Hell, even Rich counted... maybe. "Where there are human magic users there's the potential for portals directly into Suusteren. Instead of boldly flying in we sneak in and..." he snapped his fingers, "what do they call it when you extract all the people you wanna extract?"

"Exfiltrate," Mike offered.

"Yeah, exfiltrate the aian populace behind enemy lines. And that, my goddess, is the best plan you've heard all breakfast."

Eula considered a moment. She turned her head to one of her guards. "Gather a detail. Enough to carry the big one as well."

The guard rose on fluttery wings and flew off into the town. Runt's jaw tightened at the sight of the departing flyer as if he had just bitten down on leather and nails.

"Man, don't start tensing up," Mike said to Runt. "I bet it won't be that bad this time. They prolly won't even drop you."

Runt growled, a low, dangerous sound. Mike answered Runt with a hearty clap on the back.

"I ask you all to remain here as our escort prepares," Eula said. "This is Temple controlled land; it is not safe to advertise your presence in this town. Please. Eat and rest yourselves." Eula looked at Jason with an expression he couldn't place. Curiosity? Intrigue? It was a look few women ever had for him in his previous life, one that spoke of interest.

"Besides, I'm eager to get to know this Chosen One while we wait," she said.

Jason flashed his cheesiest big smile. Suddenly, the earth shook, evaporating the smile as he clutched his chair in alarm. It shook more. The street below erupted. The packed dirt of the road blossomed into a miniature volcano two stories high. Jason had seen that tell tale volcano before. It was an anthill made into a mountain. His stomach warbled at the sight.

A moment later an aian in gleaming bronze armor jumped onto the rim of the giant anthill.

Yol, the God of Strength, pointed a meaty finger at Jason. His nostrils flared and his chest heaved with wild, ragged breaths. The god's eyes practically glowed with rage.

"Fool Cephrin! Did you think you could always cower from me, the mightiest of the gods? Did you think your treachery at Suusteren came without price? Your death is here, false god, and its name is Yol!"

Chapter 6
A Little Less God Mode

THE SIGHT OF YOL GAVE Jason a wave of dread that ran along his spine and made his stomach roil like an angry sea. The closest feeling he had to match it was when the neighborhood bully Otis Warring had set a time to mangle Jason after school and Jason had to ride that fear for hours. Only now, the livid face of a powerful god glared at him with more anger than Otis Warring could ever command.

"Yol, buddy!" Jason said, managing a wan smile as he waved at the god standing atop his mountainous anthill. The god was only a stone's throw away from the inn's balcony where Jason waved. Jason hoped Yol hadn't brought any stones with him. Jason cast a furtive glance at the table near the end of the balcony, where Mike, Runt, Savvy and Eula sat. Yol had captured all their attention.

Before Yol could utter a reply. Eula stood up and unfurled her wings. They were smoky gray and sported vivid red lines framed in contrasting white, with splashes of purple throughout and two giant orbs of blue on each wing that looked like eyes. They were beautiful, not only arresting Jason's attention, but Yol's as well.

"Brother, Cephrin and his friends are my guests here by invite, afforded the full protection of me and my house. I ask you kindly to cease all aggression."

Yol's face seemed to swim in anger as it swiveled from Jason to Eula. Now incredulity crept into Yol's expression, making the ant god resemble Bruce Lee after he stomps on a nameless adversary, twists his foot and shakes his head in a slow "no"—that look of I 'can't believe this idiot tried to fight me so now I have to grind his soul out of his body by twisting my foot'. Yol's entire everything stayed over the top.

"Sister, would you have me call off the entire war? Is that what you mean by 'cease all aggression' while you have afternoon tea with the number one threat to our beloved Empire?"

"I would gladly have us call a ceasefire," Eula shot back, "to give us time to reexamine the cause of this war in the first place."

"The desecration of the Temple of Houses is cause enough for any right-minded aian. Now, have some spine! You are a goddess." He spread his hands out to show the town, full of aians who were busy trying to get more distance between themselves and Yol as if he was the epicenter of a tornado. "Their goddess!"

Out of nowhere, Onus was standing beside Jason. The Corrupter shook his head as he looked at Eula and Yol.

"These two. Never could get along. Hopefully, Yol's easily ignitable anger explodes soon, otherwise they could argue their points for months on end."

Meanwhile, Mike Savvy and Runt were backing away from the table slowly towards Jason. "Yo," Mike said. "We need to bounce."

"On foot?" Jason asked. "We don't stand a chance." Yol had obviously dug his way here in the minutes it took for one of the hive mind to relay a basic description of Jason to the god. Yol was fast underground. The only way they were getting out of here was in the hands of moths.

Speaking of moth hands, Eula had hers clenched into fists, her arms akimbo as she argued with the ant god.

"It is for every right-minded aian to question what they weren't present to see, in this case the cleaving of the Temple of Houses and the Chosen One's involvement. Until my questions are satisfied, Cephrin dwells under the very roof of my house."

"Will you also pretend that you don't hear what they say of me?" Yol asked. "That this charlatan bested me? Me! I am the mighty Yol, to be bested by no one, least of all this fake sack of lies and tricks. Stand aside, sister. I will have satisfaction."

Eula shook her head. "I care nothing for your ego. Bruised as it is now, it's still bigger than the mountain you climbed out of. My sponsorship of Cephrin doesn't change simply because you want to showboat, to redeem yourself for perceived slights. That only changes when he falls out of my favor. I may not respect our reasons for war but I do respect the covenant between gods. Do the same, brother."

Yol ground his teeth together, as if he could chew through Eula's stance. The ant god turned his sights upon Jason. The anger seemed to bake off Yol in waves.

"This is how you demonstrate your presumption to godliness? This is your testament as Chosen One, to hide behind my sister's pretty wings?"

Jason shrugged. "Works for me."

Yol glared, saying nothing for long, tense moments. Finally, he pointed a meaty finger at Jason. "I will be closer than you can imagine when you fall out of Eula's favor." With that, the god backed slowly down into his anthill, staring at Jason the whole time.

Standing beside Jason, Onus groaned loudly as they watched Yol's slow retreat. "Always so dramatic!" He looked over to Jason with his disconcerting, unmoving eyes and smiled with chapped lips. "You should be glad I gave you the power to talk to me without eavesdroppers."

"Why?"

"Because when you ask me for help, which you will, you won't be seen as a reprehensible monster in league with The Corrupter." Onus winked. "Which you are."

Jason didn't know quite how to take Onus. Why would he ask the god for help? It looked like the crisis had been averted. There was nothing left to do but have a drink and fly on out of here. He was about to ask Onus when the building shook with earthquake force.

"He didn't," was all Eula could say. The next moment the entire inn fell, collapsing in a shower of wooden planks as if the very ground underneath it was suddenly gone. Eula and her moth entourage took to their wings while Jason and his friends fell. Jason reached towards the airborne Eula, but she quickly disappeared as he fell deeper into a sea of broken wood.

He looked down to see meaty, armored hands reaching for him.

"Onus!" Jason called as the god of strength snatched him down by his legs. Without a word, Yol swung Jason by the legs, driving Jason's head into the ground as if his whole body was nothing more than a carnival hammer. Yol hauled Jason up by the legs once more and drove him back down again. Then the god spun and threw Jason like a discus. Jason went flying through packed dirt until he emerged on the surface, landing on his back in the streets of Nev Tefar.

In front of Jason, the broken bones of the inn protruded from a giant sinkhole. Screaming, groaning, grinding—all the sounds of chaos—issued forth from the hole. Yol walked casually out of the sinkhole, his red cape flapping behind him as if even it was scared to be too close to the god.

"I see you are built of stronger stuff than you let on, Chosen One. Perhaps you will make this battle worthy of my bards after all."

"Where are my friends?" Jason asked, dusting himself off as he rose.

"Saving themselves," Yol answered. "Too busy to help you slink away this time. You have no more tricks left with me, false god."

Jason felt the stinging rawness of being pummeled headfirst into the ground. Underneath that pain, the sure sense of Onus' power filled him. One of these feelings, maybe both of them, left Jason decidedly hateful.

He lunged at Yol, quicker than the god probably expected. Instead of punching, Jason grabbed the ant god by an antenna. Jason tried with everything in him to rip that damned stalk off Yol's head. He jerked down and the god's face went with it as Yol yelled in pain. Jason slammed Yol's face into the ground, muffling the god's yells, and dragged Yol's head across the street, pulling solely by the antenna. Then Jason yanked upwards, tossing the god in the air by the feeler.

"I hope the whole hive felt that!" Jason shouted as Yol landed with a crash into a building down the street.

Without a second thought, Jason ran over to the sinkhole. It looked like the hole ran down another twenty feet. Down in the hole, he saw his friends were alive if not OK for the moment. Over a dozen ant-headed aians surrounded them.

Four other aians were already down. Mike was cranking his diskbow taut. Runt had his Z-blades disassembled into twin axes. Saavy held a hex in one hand and her combat knife in the other.

Jason was in a perfect vantage point to assist through archery. He could easily drop two, maybe three of them before they even realized death came from above. It was every archer's wet dream. He reached behind his back to grab his bow. He felt his quiver of arrows, his arm club—the hand still covered with a bag, but no bow.

He looked back where he had come. His bow was on the ground. The string hung limp, coiled on the ground, useless. The wood of the bow was broken in three places.

See? This is why archers ran from melee combat. The bow had taken the brunt of the force when Yol had decided to turn Jason into a drill bit and drive him through six feet of dirt. One day he swore he was going to find an awesome unbreakable bow, his ultimate weapon. He felt robbed. An archer without a bow was like the Pillsbury Doughboy without a cookie sheet.

Jason looked up from his broken bow to see Yol barreling down on him from down the street. The anger on Yol's face was apparent as he charged like a raging bull. Yol thought he was angry... what the hell good was an archer without a bow? Jason yelled his fury and charged down the street to meet Yol halfway.

Imbued with Onus' power, Jason grabbed Yol by the shoulders, determined to shake the god apart. But Yol didn't move when Jason tried to push. Yol flexed and it seemed as if his muscles grew to twice their already swollen size. Jason's hold withered as Yol's strength erupted.

Now it was Jason's turn to get manhandled. Yol caught him in an unrelenting bear hug. Yol's arms felt like a mechanized car crusher. No matter the power Onus had given him, Jason couldn't push back as the steel-like vice slowly, inexorably squeezed Jason insides out.

Jason heard Eula through the blood beating fiercely in his own ears. "Enough, Yol," she said. Jason opened his eyes to see she had flown down behind Yol. She had her sword, the same sword she had wanted to impale Jason with in his dream, trained on her brother. "The fall you engineered for Cephrin and the inn may fit your criteria for 'out of my favor' but I assure you it doesn't pass muster with me. Don't make an enemy of me or my house. Let him go."

"Has it come to this, dear sister?" Yol asked. Jason could feel those vice-like arms loosen a bit, just enough to breathe pained, shallow breaths.

Jason wondered the same question. Every action hero since John fricking Wayne has said "let her go." And here Eula was saying it for him. That almost officially made Eula the leading man. It also made Jason the damsel in distress. Had it come to this?

Onus stood next to Jason as he wheezed itty bitty breaths. The god looked at him with a sly grin.

"I know what you're thinking. How is it you're so utterly helpless before the mighty Yol even after invoking my name? You see, Cephrin, I'm the God of Power. You're fighting the God of Strength in his domain, on his terms. But fear not. Power feeds into strength as surely as strength feeds into power. All you need do is call on me again."

Anything. Anything to be the hero and not the damsel. "Onus," Jason squeaked.

Immediately, he felt the Corrupter's power course through his veins. He broke through Yol's formerly iron grip while the god was in mid sentence with Eula. When Yol turned around to face Jason, the look of shock on the god's face lasted only a second before Jason's fist hit it with all the newfound power Onus had given him.

The punch was so hard it sent Yol careening off his feet. Eula had to take off in flight to avoid the missile that was her brother. Yol landed against a building's brown brick wall with a thud and a clap of dust.

Jason wasn't finished. He charged at the ant god. When he got to Yol, he pushed the god with his forearms, driving him through the brick, into the building. A mountain of mortar dust kicked up, bathing the world in a thick white fog. Jason kept pushing, driving Yol through another brick wall and more mortar dust clouds. They emerged in an alleyway. Jason hit the ant god with another hard hay-maker. Then he threw another punch.

This time Yol caught the fist in his meaty hand. Yol squeezed and Jason could feel the integrity of his own fist disintegrate. The pain al-most made Jason take a knee. Yol looked at Jason with wild, berserker eyes and spoke with a bloodied mouth.

"Think you can ever be mightier than I? Listen to your fathers, grandfathers, forefathers. They have seen me through the ages and they know none stronger. Learn as they have the name of true might. I am Yol!"

Suddenly, blow after blow assaulted Jason's face, a brutal rain of meaty fists. Those few seconds felt like an overwhelming eternity. When the blows stopped Yol had one hand grasping Jason's face like a basketball. Yol reached back and threw. Jason felt like he was floating while the whole world sped past him.

Then the crash came. Jason closed his eyes to the jarring impact and rush of dust. With his eyes closed, Jason had no choice but to focus on the pain he felt all over.

After a moment, Jason forced his eyes open with a groan. The dust from the rubble left the room a hazy outline of shapes. Daylight streamed into the room courtesy of the hole his body had created, illuminating the procession of fine particles marching to the heavens. From without, the mocking laughter of the God of Strength seemed to shake the broken building.

The hazy outline began to clear. A broken table came into view. This looked like a kitchen, with shattered shelves of foodstuffs scattered every which way. In one corner, a mother from the House of Demir held a toddler tightly. In another corner, a teenage daughter, the marks of House Otam starting to show, sat huddled, clutching her knees. Their look of fear and anguish were uniform.

Jason went to rise and felt something awkward underneath him. He looked down and realized he had landed on top of a man. Of House Demir like the mother, the man lay prone on his back, his eyes closed and face contorted in pain.

No. This isn't how this was supposed to be. Heroes don't hurt civilians. Quickly Jason scrambled off the guy, to help him up and make sure nothing was broken. He tried to ask if he was all right but the voice of an angry god shook the building.

"Come out and face me, coward!" Yol bellowed. "Let the whole town witness the glory of Yol as he bests you!"

Jason sat in utter disbelief. These people were nothing more than witnesses to the god's exploits. Yol didn't care if he destroyed this entire town and these people's way of life along with it as long as someone was left alive to tell others the epic tale. Was Yol really this shallow? Had Jason also been like this?

Dammit, this destruction was real. The hapless aian Jason had landed on and the home his family had lived in were real. These people had a way of life before today and Jason was just as guilty of treading on it as Yol was.

He had to stop this. Now.

"You can have the power to stop this," Onus said, once again appearing out of nowhere in the corner of Jason's eye. "Just call on me once more."

"Fuck off, devil," Jason said with a shake of his head as he took his arm club out of its sheath. He should've known better than to listen to Onus. Because of Onus' prodding, Jason had called upon the God of Power twice, just for Yol to match him in strength. Jason realized now it was a never ending cycle; no matter how powerful Onus could make Jason, Yol would grow just as strong. He could not beat the god of strength that way. So Jason went back to what he did best. He bent the rules.

Jason ripped the black bag off his arm club, revealing the fingers. Unceremoniously, Jason placed his teeth around the pinky finger, at the first joint before the tip. He bit down, chomping it off the hand. He spat the dismembered digit into his bone hand. Feeling more himself than ever in his confidence, he swaggered out of the debris, into the street where Yol waited with a broad, toothy smile.

"You're Yol, the Pillar, the strongest of the gods? Well I'm Cephrin, the Archer, the world's most crack shot! So, fuck you, Yol... what's all your strength mean when I can drop you if you say one more word?"

Yol's next word wasn't a word so much as a yell, a roar glazed with anger. But it was all Jason needed, with the quick precision of an experienced barfly playing darts, he flicked his severed fingertip into Yol's gaping maw.

Yol's rage turned instantly into surprise. Perhaps more surprising was Jason's speed. He plowed through the distance to reach Yol. Jason took a hand and clapped it over Yol's mouth. The other hand pinched Yol's nose with an iron grip.

They began to wrestle, God of Strength and Chosen One, as Yol tried to pry Jason's fingers from his nose and mouth. But the God of Strength was slowly losing that strength, leeched away by Jason's spell imbued fingertip. Sleep was setting in, coupled with a lack of air.

Then the inevitable happened. Yol swallowed.

Jason released his grip on Yol, who stumbled after him. The ant god swung, a blow Jason easily side-stepped as he continued to back away from the defeated god.

"You can get mad if you want to," Jason said. "But at the end of the day, not only are you going to be waiting on your entire digestive tract before you see daylight again, but you're also a motherfucking cannibal. Good night, you complete asshole."

Yol fell to his knees. Still, he scrambled after Jason. "No!" he cried, kicking up dust as he struggled to crawl after his quarry. "Not like this. Not by—"

The god swallowed whatever else he was going to say as he collapsed into the dust of the street.

The quiet afterwards made Jason feel like his ears were blown out, the silence deafening in its completeness. He looked up from the sleeping body of Yol. The townspeople kept a respectable distance of about fifty yards away from Jason, surrounding him from all sides as they looked at him from the street and from rooftops.

He saw his friends in the throng, all of them alive and well. Eula stood with them, a look of utter disbelief on her face.

Jason wasn't quite sure what was supposed to happen now. Does the crowd cheer? Do they mob him for beating one of their pantheon gods? They did neither. They all just stared.

"I'm sorry folks. For breaking your town. For everything."

Onus was in the crowd, unseen amongst the townies. He had an appreciative, sly smile on his face. Without a word, he brought his hands up into a slow, silent golf clap.

Chapter 7
War Costs

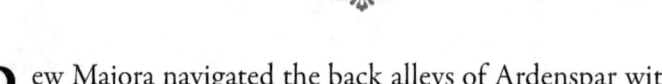

Rew Majora navigated the back alleys of Ardenspar with all the deft surety of a veteran pickpocket. Nights like this she certainly felt more akin to thief than Hierophant, like a vagabond desperate for a home.

The alley she hurried down seemed more of an afterthought than a street. Buildings fed into the alleyway haphazardly, creating strange angles that jutted forward awkwardly or retreated back into a darkness made heavy with the shadows cast by sparse, flickering gaslights. Her boots knocked dully against slick cobblestones.

Hundreds of feet overhead, the iron grid of the suspended monorail crisscrossed, feeding into tower stations which rose like giant pillars throughout the city. They reminded her to keep her head down and hood up. Peacekeepers and mages perpetually scanned the city from the elevated trains, looking for aians, looking for her. The city felt like the maw of a monster ready to snap its jaws closed at any moment.

She fought a cold chill and pushed away dire thoughts as she arrived at her destination. A whitewashed door stood stark against the black of the brick. She knocked rapidly twice then paused for five seconds before giving the door one more knock.

The door opened to the kind face of Breunan. The former head of the Nasreddin Mage Delegation Tower now served as her principle source of intelligence inside the Hierophane. He looked out into the darkness of the alleyway briefly before ushering Rew inside.

This time they met in the kitchen of an abandoned inn. Breunan had a fire glowing in the hearth. Rew could tell it was illusionary, magefire as fitting a brown robe of Breunan's kind, a crude spell that provided all the light and crackle of fire but none of the warmth. The glow cast long shadows throughout the quiet kitchen.

"Did you have any problem finding this place?" Bruenan asked.

"No, your directions were excellent," Rew answered. "Let's hope this location does not become compromised."

"It's anyone's guess," Breunan answered, "the more our network grows the riskier it gets."

"Has it grown?" Rew asked.

"Since we've last talked, four more mages have expressed their desire to see you return as Hierophant, bringing our numbers up to fifty-three."

Rew nodded. It was a small contingent, to be sure. However, fifty-three mages within the walls of the Hierophane, strategically placed, could be enough to ensure Rew access to her father. It would just take careful planning.

Breunan leaned closer, as if the barren wood walls were eavesdropping. "What's more, my lady, I have discovered Druze's plan."

"You mean with the Rift Pendulum?"

Breunan nodded. "My sources tell me he acts quite strangely toward the Pendulum. It is known to all the higher mages that the Rift Pendulum is able to call upon one hundred heroes and still operate its underlying engines without difficulty. However, even in times of dire need during the course of this war, Druze is calling only a fraction of those numbers, ten usually, no more than twenty pendulum heroes. It's one of the reasons why the war along the Western Front has all but ground into a stalemate in the trenches. Would you venture to guess why he's doing this?"

Immediately, Rew recalled Rich's eyewitness account of a pendulum breaking, and of course Rich himself was an indicator.

"The Rift Pendulum is becoming more unstable," she answered.

Yet the answer didn't make sense. Why wouldn't Druze just factor this unpredictability in as an acceptable risk? After all, wasn't it better to risk destabilization bringing a force of one hundred to bear down on the aians during battle than to lose the battle because you played conservatively?

Breunan seemed to anticipate Rew's response. "You will also be interested to know, Lady Majora, that your father's new body once belonged to a pendulum reject."

Rew looked at Breunan with new appreciation, her smile growing as the implication dawned on her. "He's scared," she said. "Magical artifacts aren't exactly beholden to anyone's laws, even natural ones. Who knows what further destabilization would do? Druze's body could altogether disappear. Or the pendulum could recycle the body, thrusting a hero's consciousness into it while Druze still occupied it. That's why he's afraid to draw too much from it."

Breunan returned Rew's smile. "Although Druze won't admit it, most mages believe this to be true. And it isn't something easily stomached for these mages, seeing friends die and having retreats sounded because the aian army has quickly dispatched the ten or so pendulum heroes summoned."

"Who's to say if a faltering pendulum would have any effect on him at all?" Rew asked. "This doesn't sound like my father has a plan, just a weakness, and not a big one at that."

Breunan shook his head and began to rummage within his brown robe. "It's a plan when you take steps to eliminate the threat." He produced a rolled up scroll from his library pocket. Bruenan walked over to the butcher block countertop, where a legion of nicks and scratches were left to tell the story of a time where this inn's kitchen was used to prepare meals and cater to the citizens of the city instead of sitting in darkness to host fugitive mages.

He unfurled the scroll and almost as if that action was the catalyst, there came a knock on the door. Immediately, instinctively, Breunan rolled the scroll back up. He looked first at the door then to Rew. She shook her head. Apparently, neither one of them had invited a third party. The knock came again, louder and more insistent this time.

Breunan hurried over to Rew and thrust the scroll into her hands. Wordlessly, Rew put it into her library pocket. She watched as Breunan went over to the door and cautiously cracked it.

His eyes found hers through the crack. Her father's eyes, his exact stern expression, staring at her from a body that wasn't his.

"I could've easily chosen netherfire over a knock to put to this door," Druze said, still looking at Rew as if the brown robe didn't exist. "Are you going to open it or should I?"

Rew nodded to Breunan to open the door. Silently, she watched as Druze walked into the room with an unconcerned air of indifference, the purple and white robes of the Hierophant swirling about him. She cycled through attack spells, searching for the most efficient and deadly combinations to use with the materials around her.

"I know you, daughter," Druze said as he looked around the abandoned inn. "Perhaps too well. And there's really no point to a duel. We're immortal. The only outcome of our fight would be new bodies and I for one have no interest in trading in this skin. Besides, I already have what I want." He smoothed out the purple and white robes of her former office.

The memory of her father's coup burned fresh and hot. "You put me under my own witchlock, allowed a blue robe to violate my mind to find proof of your one-sided story, then tossed me in the Underthral and for what? You could've had your old robes back any time you wanted them!"

"Oh, I'm not so sure of that," Druze countered. He walked around the room looking about the place as if he was inspecting the furniture or checking the dust. "Your judgment has soured, softened. I had no confidence in the mush of it."

"There's nothing wrong with my judgment."

"Really?" he asked as if stifling a laugh. "I'm here talking to you now because your judgment led you to believe you could get away with making an unauthorized portal into Ardenspar. I'm cleaning up a war with twelve aian houses because you lacked the sense to turn over that fake robe you love so dear."

"If anyone's lacking in this room, it's you *father*," Rew said, spitting the last word out like snake venom. "You are without scruples. Rich and his friends were never ours to turn over to the aians."

"Whose are they then? We created these things out of pure magic."

"We have a moral obligation to see them home."

Druze spun to face her, his expression contorted in rage. "We have a moral obligation to the Free States!" he shouted. "What is your fake robe to the real ones felled in battle? What are his friends to the growing threat of the gray temple's hordes?"

Rew's anger wasn't hot and loud like her father's, but cold and quiet. "Yes, we have a moral obligation to the Free States, and here you are putting its aian citizens in concentration camps in every major city," she stated. "They are blameless, just like my fake robe as you call him. From what I can gather, it was you who massacred nine hundred and ninety-nine Armsguard cavalrymen at Dreft Esker instead of simply holding the pass. If you want a scapegoat for dead mages and a war with the Temple of Houses, look to yourself, Hierophant."

Druze smiled. "Spoken like the leader of Seat Esotera. Where was she when the tower needed her to do what was right?"

"That is all I have ever done."

He shook his head. "No. All you have ever done was what was noble. And the things I've done have allowed that to happen. I've operating in the shadows for the good of the Hierophane while you stood blameless and untarnished in the light. After centuries of being able to do that, I can see how you would confuse the right thing with the noble thing. But what is right isn't necessarily what's noble."

Druze held his hand out toward the dusty chairs turned upside down on the tables. "*Iskemleye bana gel*," he said. One of the chairs flew off the table toward his outstretched hand in a small eruption of dust. He turned the chair right side up and sat down to address Rew.

"Sometimes the right thing will have you feeling as dirty as this inn, despite your intentions. Sometimes what's right will tarnish your soul."

"Is this the lesson you would have had me learn in the belly of the Underthral?" Rew asked coolly. "Or do you tell yourself such things to feel better about being so despicable?"

Druze's jaw clenched tight. The air seemed to crackle in the space of the strained silence. "I'm still your father," he said, "and if I have to kill you a couple times for you to remember that then so it'll go. You find me despicable. Seeing farmers get their crops seized by High Fane Armsguards is what I find despicable. Or the Free States under siege, the populace slowly terrified as these ash skins roam and marauder across the region. All these civilian lives, sacrifices for a war to your sense of nobility. That, my dear daughter, is despicable."

"I stopped listening around the time you said you'd kill me a couple of times," Rew told him. "Would you like to try? I stand ready for you to try. And you'll need to if you think I'm going to go peacefully with you back to a dungeon cell."

Druze held his hands up. "I'm not here to fight you and I don't want to see you caged. I'm here to tell you I forgive you, daughter. I wanted to give you this invitation in person. Come home to the tower. We could surely use a mage of your caliber. Let's end this war to-gether."

The nerve! Rew scoffed. "You forgive me? Does your forgiveness include relinquishing my robes and slinking away to some dark, for-gotten corner of the world for a hundred years?"

"Your robes? Didn't you say these were my robes?"

"Not when you strip them from me by force. And not when you wear them to intern Free States citizenry."

Druze looked at his daughter for a long, silent moment. He held neither anger nor sadness in his eyes.

"Rew, you are entitled to your anger. It will mute over time. Even if you never agree with me you'll eventually see why I took these robes back and these measures. There are costs to war. This was one of them. We couldn't afford your noble sensibilities with so much at stake."

He stood up. Casually, he picked up the chair he had sat in and walked it back to where it came from, placing it back upside down on top of its dusty table.

"As if I was never here," he said with a half smile. He turned to face Rew and his mouth straightened. "Let's cut through any illu-sions we may have. You don't want to kill me because I am your fa-ther. You know I'm not a saint but I'm definitely not some penulti-mate evil either. The fact of the matter is I am the former and current Hierophant, leading the mages through a war in much the same way you would. You are angry with me just as I've been angry with you. And as angry as you made me when you betrayed me and the Free States for some otherworldly strangers, I never wanted you to die. Even if we wanted to kill each other, we can't. Not really. You want these robes back and I'll only give them to you once this war is over. So, will you help me see that happen?"

Her father made sense, which made Rew even madder. They were truths as he saw them. They burned but not more than the thought of joining him as anything less than Hierophant. The hell if she'd join him, not after all he did to her, not after his amoral and callous treatment of innocent people who he was tasked to protect as the wearer of those robes.

"I thought you wanted to cut through the illusions," Rew countered. "Let's not ignore the fact that you tried to trick Rich into being an unwitting sacrifice for your immortality. You were willing to kill his friends for it. Only he got the better of you, this raw kid versus a five hundred year old mage, and you've been fueled by vengeance ever since. Clearly that fuel burns through your ability to reason, which is why you refuse to see that not only is all of this your fault, but untold innocents continue to suffer under your reign."

"I'm talking solutions and you're talking faults?"

"I'm giving you the solution of who to blame when I refuse your offer momentarily."

Rew gave him a moment of perfect silence.

"Go the hell, father."

Druze smiled. "So it goes. You should leave now. This was the only pass you'll get. The next time you portal into Ardenspar or mage held lands, you'll be bound with a witchlock and dragged into the Underthral for the duration of this war. For the time being you are free to go."

He pointed a finger at Breunan, who Rew all but forgot as she focused her seething anger on her father. "This man is not, however."

Rew shook her head. "It looks like you're going to get that duel after all, because he's coming with me."

Druze laughed as if the idea of fighting his daughter was sheer nonsense. "Please. The first thing I would do in a fight with you is kill the brown robe for the spare body... which would be interesting just to see which one of us would be forced to inhabit him first. No, I don't think you want that tonight. You want to stop me. You want these robes back. You want to end this war on your terms and send your boy love back home. I don't see how any of that happens once we start fighting, which will definitely kill this brown robe and send the black robes I have surrounding this place charging in and pitching witchlocks like horseshoes. Let's see how stubbornly you pursue nobility. The first move is yours because you know my speed with netherfire."

He could summon the stuff at a moment's notice, a secret only he knew. Rew cast quick, furtive glances around the room, trying to find a way to nullify Druze for the time necessary to get Breunan out of harm's way. As if Druze knew what she was thinking, he stepped back a few paces, where he could easily see magic coming at him and appropriately react. Maybe if she bent the wooden stools next to him to act as handcuffs. No, she would also have to harden the wood or it would stretch too thin and Druze could just snap the cuffs. Perhaps open a portal and push Druze inside? He was too far away and she doubted he'd let her get closer. Perhaps use the stone of the fireplace as shrapnel? No, that put Breunan in the line of fire.

"I surrender," Breunan said, stepping in between Rew and Druze.

"What?" Rew shook her head as if she hadn't heard Breunan. "No."

"Yes." Breunan replied. "Who am I when the fate of the Free States hangs in the air? Go."

"You are my follower and my friend and you are coming with me, that's who you are, Breunan," Rew answered. "And I'm not going to run away and let Druze kill you."

"Kill him?" Druze asked incredulously. "For showing you loyalty? For displaying bravery? Perish the thought."

Druze walked over to Breunan. "But he is only a brown robe and at his age that's a crime in itself. Magic is a gift all humankind should use to the full of its limitless potential. Not like the stork-legged nasrans scratching rudimentary tricks into wood chips and not the aians who are spell mutes. The complete bounty of magic is humanity's to manipulate. I find it a shame you've yet to reach that potential... Breunan, was it? Personally, I believe it's just a matter of motivation. You've probably never been sufficiently motivated to rise out of brown."

Druze smiled at the increasingly nervous looking Breunan. "War is where men find themselves, Breunan. That's where we're going to find a color for you, once I've stationed you at the most dangerous garrisons this war's seen. The places where the aian assault is deadly and ceaseless, where you will see mages better than you die in their brighter colors. I have every confidence that if you survive there, you will be a real mage for it. How's that sound?"

Breunan gave Rew the briefest of glances, then he set his jaw and looked at Druze. "Sounds like the vacation I've always dreamed of. Lead the way."

"No!" Rew said. "This is madness, Breunan. It's suicide. And I absolutely refuse to sit back and watch this happen. You're coming with me."

Breunan shook his head. "Like your father said. There are costs to war. This is one of them. You keep fighting in ways that make sense, ways that restore the Free States. I'll keep fighting in the ways I know. That's all we can do, Hierophant."

Rew was speechless. What could she say to a man so committed to seeing her triumph that he would condemn himself to such a fate?

"Take your portal," Druze said. "It's not noble, but it's clearly the right thing to do."

Breunan nodded. The part of her that wanted to fight Druze right now knew no good would come of it, not with Breunan in the way, a team of destruction mages waiting outside. She hadn't even gotten a chance to see what Druze's plans were. Breunan had risked everything to deliver the scroll that now sat in her library pocket. She couldn't let his sacrifice be in vain.

"I will fix this Breunan," she told him.

"Nothing to fix, Hierophant," he replied with a smile. "I was never broken."

Rew opened her portal in a shimmering blossom of blue and white air. She walked backward into it, watching Druze and Breunan fade out of existence. Now she was in the remote, snowy wilds amidst a forest of barren trees. Here she would wait for the portal to close without any followers before opening a new one to her real destination.

She had nothing but time to wait. She wished every other moment for the damned portal to close already. In between those moments she wished she could look at the plan Breunan paid so dearly for, but she refused to be distracted until she was somewhere safe.

Through it all, she desperately longed to feel clean again.

Chapter 8
Seeing Red

RICH FAILED. AGAIN. Graduating out of brown was stupid and impossible. This was bullshit. How in the hell did the mages come up with this test as something necessary to graduate?

Vylar had already given up on him for the night and retreated to the modest house over an hour ago. No light came from the house—it's not like Vylar needed it—so it seemed to emanate a feeling of utter emptiness and forlornness. No help from within. No help from anywhere, really. He had to graduate on his own.

"Maybe take a break?" Mel suggested. She sat by the fire. It was a real one that she had made. At least one of them was learning some new skills instead of wasting their time.

Rich sat down next to her and huffed out a sigh. The warmth of the fire was a comforting surprise. He hadn't realized how cold it had gotten while he worked over and over on the graduation spell. He stuck his hands out to the fire so it could heat his digits.

"It's funny," Mel said with a half smile as she looked at the fire. "The aians see Jason as the new messiah and/or antichrist. The mages look at you like you're the former King of Magic hoping you start your comeback tour. Apparently me and Mike got off easy but I'm starting to suspect if I ever travel to Khermer the people there will worship me as some kind of warrior-priestess-queen. Hell, maybe Mike's the long lost prince of the Megrym Hegemony."

Rich shook his head. "The Megrym Hegemony is a loose confederation of city-states ruled by a rich merchant class, like a corporatocracy. I think the ruling city-state changes based on which city has the most economic power. I don't know whether they have princes or CEOs, but if Mike was a ruler there, he'd be filthy rich."

Melvin grimaced. "Apparently back when this was just a game, I was the only one of us not looking up lore and additional content. Now I feel like I'm in the dark on even basic facts about the world."

"Meh," Rich responded with a bat of his hand. "Knowing that stuff hasn't helped me."

"It's nice to know though," Mel said, returning her gaze to the fire. "I hate being in the dark about things."

"If there's anything you wanna know that you think I may have some insight on, feel free to ask. I'm no Wikipedia, but I'll do my best to illuminate you."

"Well, I did have a question you never answered. How come you didn't want to fool around with me again?"

He shrugged. "I don't really have an answer. The thing that keeps me from doing anything is a question more than an answer. What if I fall for you? What if we fall in love with each other?"

Rich didn't have that much experience with love, but it didn't seem to be something you could just turn off when it became inconvenient. What place would they find themselves when they finally got back into their original skins?

Mel nudged a pebble with her boot. "Here's the thing, Rich," she said. "I—"

The rest of her words were cut short as the blue and white light of a portal burst open in the clearing.

"Man, C'mon!" Mel cried at the open portal.

Rew Majora emerged from the portal. Initially happy to see her, Rich quickly became perturbed by the stoic look on her face. Things didn't look like they were going well. She strode over to them, an intimidating tower of presence as she stood over them while they sat.

"Hi Rew," Rich greeted.

"Shouldn't you be practicing?" she asked.

"I was..." he hesitated and glanced over at Melvin, "just taking a break."

Rew looked at Melvin. "Can you excuse yourself? I need a word with Rich."

Melvin's eyebrows furrowed. "Why am I the one that has to get up and leave?" she asked.

"Asking Rich to get up and come with me would clearly interrupt his break," Rew replied. "Since he's still in brown it's quite visible he needs this break. So, please."

Mel's eyes held a certain shrewdness to them as she looked at Rew, and her jaw tightened as if she literally chewed on Rew's request. A moment later, Mel rose to her feet and walked off into the darkness of the surrounding countryside. Rew looked back at Rich.

"What's wrong with you?" she asked.

"What do you mean?" Rich asked.

"At first, you set records climbing through the first half of brown. Now, nothing. You've stagnated. I want to know why."

Rich shrugged. "I don't know."

Rew scoffed. "Of course you do. The easy way is to feign ignorance. Stop taking the easy way. You know what your own troubles are." Rew pointed behind herself. "Is it the warrior girl?"

"No," Rich said, shaking his head. "Maybe. No, no."

"It's not that complicated, Rich," Rew said. "She's a woman. Whether that's forever or not is of no concern right now. There's no need to overthink it, or to let it affect your spellcraft."

"Wait," Rich said, "What's my spellcraft matter to you? It was my spellcraft that blew up the Temple of Houses, turned your father into a body snatching monster and started a war. If anything, I'm no longer a threat."

"You're also not of much use," Rew retorted. "If you haven't noticed, I'm rather short of allies right now. While I can tell you to keep practicing, I haven't the time for subtleties. You need access to color magic, some color other than brown. Because if I learned anything seeing you charge into the Hierophane's dungeons in a harebrained rescue, you're not the type to sit idly by while I go off alone to end the dual menace of my father as Hierophant and the war with the Holy Aian Empire."

Rich stood up. "What do you mean harebrained? I no shit rescued you."

"Don't mistake my assessment for ungratefulness. Still, my gratitude doesn't change my assessment. Your probability of success was extremely low. Not because of any lack of bravery or cleverness but because you simply lacked *access*. How much easier would that rescue have gone if you still wore gray, Rich?"

Rich looked away. The simple truth stung like a cut. Rew kept going in the space of his silence.

"I need you as an asset, Rich, not a liability. Whatever's distracting you from rising out of brown you need to confront it. Now," Rew said. "If it's the warrior girl, you need to—"

"It's you," Rich said.

"—tell her... What?" The confusion on Rew's face couldn't be any plainer.

"I can't tell how you feel about me," Rich explained. "I mean, I used to know. I kissed you, you kissed me and you liked me then. Once you found out I turned your father to stone you hated me. Then I rescued you and it felt good for that moment, you know that moment when I broke the witchlock and held you in my arms and now here we are and I just don't know where I stand. I keep thinking we're simply allies, not even friends any more and a part of you hates me." He looked up at her, trying to find some meaning, some clue in the eyes looking back at him.

"Rich, do you realize I'm a woman three-hundred fifty years old who is seeing a lot of firsts despite these years? My father recently betrayed me and stripped me of the very seat he gave me. He has turned the Hierophane and Ardenspar into a police state ruled by fear. All this while the Free States are at war with every house in the Holy Aian Empire. And your chief concern is how I feel towards you?"

Rich was unapologetic as he shrugged. "I can't help it. The war, Druze, that's all stuff I can fight, you know? I know how to fight it. Throw some spells, then throw some more spells and throw more after that until things are the way they're supposed to be. And they'll get there because that's the way they're supposed to be. But with you, I don't know how to fight it, or if I should fight it, or if this is the way things are supposed to be."

A barely perceptible smile formed on Rew's lips. "What I called you when we first met still stands as true. You are sweet, Rich. And to return your honesty in kind, I wouldn't be able to begin telling you how I feel. My world is upside down now, Rich. Right now I'm confused, trying to wrap my mind around the crazy world you come from where this sort of thing would matter this much. I do know I don't hate you. And I very much would love for you to rise into the mage I know you can be and stop stalling already."

Rich nodded, a lopsided grin fixed on his face. "OK."

From behind Rew, Melvin echoed Rich's "OK" with her own.

"You guys look like you're done," she said walking into view. "Unlike the two of you, I can't just break out the magic fire light when I get tired of stumbling over roots and whatever else is out there in the inky dark."

"You're right, Melvin," Rew said. "I'm done. But Rich here is not."

"I'm not?" he asked.

"You've spoken your problem. Your problem's resolved as much as it can be. And your break's over. Time to graduate into Brown of the 33rd Kind, and with it, entrance into a master color."

"Surprised you didn't finish that up with a 'no pressure,'" Rich said with a raised eyebrow.

"No pressure," Rew said.

At least Rich was going into this attempt with a smile. He took a deep breath while Rew and Melvin watched him under the firelight.

A ball of white light sprang to life in his palm. Rich's brow furrowed in concentration. He began to feel heat emanating from the ball of light.

His breathing deepened. Beads of sweat appeared on his forehead. The heat grew inside the ball until it rolled out in sweltering waves.

Rich was pouring sweat now. It came more from the deep focus than the heat from the ball. He opened up his left hand and began to pull the light away from the ball emanating its intense heat. A couple of times the stream of light faltered, flickering under the torchlight, but Rich kept pulling at the light, tugging it from the ball of heat.

Drenching in sweat, Rich now held an orb in each hand, one of pure light and the other of pitch black heat. Illuminated by the ball of light, the fingers of the left hand began to twitch. The twitching became more earnest. Finally, the fingers began to constrict, pushing the ball of light down smaller and smaller and smaller until...

His hand closed into a fist, squelching out the light. Rich was left with only one orb, the magic that was officially known as the Black Calefaction, but bemoaned by all who had to cast it as dark heat.

"Congratulations, Rich of the 33rd Kind," she welcomed him with a smile.

"Haha! Yes!" he cried with joy. He threw the dark heat into the air where it dissipated into nothing.

"Thank you," he panted.

"It had nothing to do with me and everything to do with you," Rew said with a wry grin.

Rich turned to face Mel. "Did you see? After working all day at it, it was almost too easy."

"Yeah, I saw. Grats," she said. Her smile seemed pained, forced.

"Now you're ready to study higher levels of magic," Rew said. "But first, you've got to choose a color. You'll likely need a day or two to decide which one."

"Oh, no," Rich said. "I've had plenty of time to think about which school I wanted to belong to while I was failing miserably at the graduation. Do you wanna see?"

"Of course," Rew answered.

Rich had already discarded the idea of being a blue or purple robe. He wasn't the type to delve into the heads of others or exploit their fears. Neither did he lean towards the biological based magics of the green robes either. But most of the other schools had made for a harder decision. Rich could easily fit in as a yellow robe and manipulate weather, or a body altering orange robe... he recalled both how he had created a tornado and destroyed the Triptoe Robot. Speaking of destroy, Rich had thought about being a destruction mage, but in the end decided against it simply because he had had it up to his eyeballs with the black robes.

Rich cast the spell to invoke ascension into a master color. Not only did it allow him access to the magic, it also turned his robe the proper color.

Rew took a look and smiled. "I should've known."

It was the school that played with and bent the laws of nature and physics. They were the ones who most augmented their spells with mean, distance and density. It harkened back to the spell Rich used to defend himself from Ananna at the High Fane, the spell that had cut into the Temple of Houses and cast it aside with such aplomb.

The spell that had started this war could only come from them. Rich wore a red robe.

Rew brushed his shoulders. "It suits you well."

Chapter 9
The Tightening Noose

RUKI PROVOS NEVER MET a bargain he didn't like. That is until Calais the Witch wanted to barter in witchcraft.

"Honestly, it's a first rate deal," she said. She sat at the opposite end of a round table, her hand tousling her frizzy hair as she tried to convince Ruki of the supreme advantage he was taking of her. "You know firsthand how much I normally charge for my services."

She may have been errantly playing in her curly locks. Or she could have been some casting some sneaky witchcraft that would leave Ruki drooling and dumb if she so much as touched him. He removed his fingers from his beer mug and took his hands off the table just in case. 'You can't trust a witch. They cheat at magic.' Words Tavis Provos had lived by.

"Do you know what I had to trade to get that food?" Ruki asked. "My uncle would rise from the grave if I just gave it to you."

Calais sighed. "You're not giving it away. We're talking magic here. Can you do magic?"

On either side of Ruki and Calais sat the pendulum rejects Gina and Vincent. Both of them stayed silent for the debate. "I don't need any cosmetic treatments," Ruki said, indicating Gina. She had striking features now that Calais' witchcraft had glamored her into a human woman. Most of those features were now turned into a disapproving scowl. Vincent merely shrugged and took a sip of beer.

"Witchcraft is an intangible," Ruki continued. "And it's a danger-ous intangible. Naturally, I can't resell this to anyone without invit-ing a mob to push a hot brand through my heart. Too much of my profits are tied to the foodstuffs. So giving them away without some sort of goods or money will leave me unable to trade. What you're asking me to do is kill what little business I have left and starve as the city withers."

Calais eyes took on a pleading sadness. "I'm asking for com-passion, Ruki Provos. Look around you. These people are the ones who'll starve, not you. And unlike you, when they leave this inn they leave their human guise as well. They can't forage."

"I take it your abilities don't include making portals, otherwise you'd just move these people out of here instead of trying to sell me vouchers for the cursed kind of magic?"

Calais shook her head. "Even if I could make portals, that kind of spell signature is being fiercely watched. No unauthorized portals in and out. You know that."

Ruki did indeed know the mages were defending against another Dramor Massacre. During the War of Five Houses, the aians cap-tured a mage and forced him to open a portal to the once prosperous city of Dramor. Once the portal was open, they marched an army through. The town was still a blackened ruin hundreds of years later, the tale of its fall told to scare children and to remind mages that some fates are worse than torture and death.

"Do you know what business is?" Ruki asked. "It's an enterprise that doesn't concern itself with who's eating as much as who's pay-ing."

"There are women and children here, Provos."

"What? Men don't have working stomachs now?"

Calais stared at Ruki with deadpan eyes. "You don't want witch-craft as payment. I get it. But this witch refuses to see these people waste away when I'm sitting directly across from the man who can save their lives. That means you're going to get witchcraft as payment. All we're really deciding is if what you get is beneficial because of your generosity or a pox upon your wretched, selfish soul because you didn't want to part with a few bags of grain."

Ruki smiled. "So, am I supposed to shiver a bit and give in to your strong arm tactics? Or do I suddenly change my mind because since you put it that way, it sounds like a bargain? I'm not entirely sure since I'm not a coward. You should know I've dealt with scarier stuff than you for the sake of the Provos Trading Company, everything from robbers to Hollowers to a tribe of angry nasrans to techromancers out in the Sprawl. So maybe this is where you kiss the bottom of my boots as I walk out of here."

Ruki stood to leave. Calais reached for him, causing him to snatch his arm away in a flinch. Calais held her hand up, signifying she wasn't up to anything. "Please," she said, indicating the chair. "Sit." Calais grimaced when Ruki didn't move. "I can't afford to buy all your stock," she said.

"Then don't," Ruki replied, returning to his seat. "If you're done being an evil witch extortionist, then perhaps you should do what I was going to suggest and buy one or two bags of grain to tide these people over until I can get them a portal out of here."

Calais raised an eyebrow. "How are you going to get a portal? There's only one entry portal and one exit portal daily. And the list of people allowed to portal out is beyond stringent."

She was right. Making portals was a low level brown spell, so only those people who had documented proof of minimal magical ability were allowed to take the portal. The last thing the Hierophane wanted was for some random citizen who knew how to make portal roots to try to sell portal access to the aians.

Ruki shrugged. "I know people, people who know how to look the other way. Palms thirst for grease, especially in dry times like these. Our ultimate aim should be to get as many of these folks as possible through that exit portal."

"How?"

Detailed explanations would have to wait. A fevered hush came over the crowd of masquerading aians. A single word filtered its way through their lips until it arrived at Ruki's table.

Mage.

Soon enough Ruki had line of sight on the mage. The crowd parted for him as if he was diseased. Wearing a blue robe, the mage strolled nonchalantly through the bar flanked by two peacekeepers. The mage looked around, nodding appreciatively as he made his way to Ruki's table.

"My! Could business get any better for you?" he pointed his finger at Calais as if the words he wanted were at the tip of his tongue. Then he snapped his fingers as if the recollection hit him. "Calais Fervorush, right?"

Cautiously, Calais nodded.

The mage smiled warmly. He shifted his attention to Ruki. "Speaking of business, I couldn't help but notice that wagon outside, one with the unmistakable markings of the Provos Trading Company. That would make you Ruki Provos, yes?"

Ruki turned on his own warm smile despite his creeping sense of dread. "Indeed it does! For my wares to have caught your eye tells me you are indeed a connoisseur of great caliber. For one such as you, I am ever open for business. But I'm afraid you have me at a slight disadvantage in that you know me—no doubt by customer loyalty and word of mouth—but I don't have the pleasure of your name. You are?"

"Oh, how rude of me," the mage said through a healthy grin. "My name is Leto. Please, don't let the blue robes fool you into thinking I wish to procure materials from your caravan. Behind the battered walls of Suusteren I'm more of an inspector. What I seek from you is information, Mr. Provos."

"By all means, I am happy to serve a robed leader of the Free States," Ruki said. He attempted to rise from his seat when Leto's firm hand on his shoulder kept him down.

"Stay in your seat, Provos." Leto stood over Ruki and leaned in uncomfortably close beside him. "I don't want you to trouble yourself on my account. I shall be brief. It's simply a matter of identity I wish to ask you about."

"You already know who I am, Mage Leto," Ruki said, trying to keep his smile diplomatic.

"Indeed," Leto said with a smile. Immediately his smile became an exaggerated frown. "I wish the same could be said for all of Suusteren's citizenry. Do you realize not everyone in this city is quite as documented as you and the Lady Fervorush here?"

"It hadn't occurred to me," Ruki answered.

"Yes. There are apparently humans who live here without any trace of residency. It's quite anomalous. And it's not the only strange thing. Do you realize that nearly a fifth of the entire aian populace is unaccounted for?"

Ruki raised an eyebrow. "That's quite a number. Are you sure your math is right?"

Leto chuckled. "Well, I wasn't here for the last census, but these numbers seem strange enough to warrant investigation. What kind of inspector would I be to not be curious?"

"I'm not sure how I can help you verify your numbers, Mage Leto."

"I get strange reports of strange numbers from all over the city. For instance, I got a report that eight bags of grain never made it to the peacekeeper stores. There was another report of six fugitive aians recently being captured yet only five were processed into the internment camp." Leto shrugged. "I am simply trying to make sense of all these numbers. Perhaps you can help, Provos."

Ruki's gaze flickered over to one of the peacekeepers. That one stood behind Calais looking imperious in the chrome armor and shiny helmet. The other peacekeeper stood directly behind Ruki's chair where it was impossible to get eyes on. Had one of them been on the trade run and snitched it out to the mages? Ruki looked back at Leto, cracking a smile even though he felt the noose tightening. He breathed through it.

"Why, if nothing else, I'm a businessman, Mage Leto. And information is something that never loses value, depending on what the information is. I'm sure I know things of interest. So why don't we—"

Ruki cut himself off as he panned his head to look at a place almost directly behind Leto.

"You!" Ruki shouted to a human disguised aian, a person who was busy leaning on the bar and trying way too hard to look like he was minding his own business.

"Yes, you!" Ruki pointed. "Can't you see I'm in the company of a mage? How the hell am I supposed to be able to offer this rarest of companions a beverage if your barrel body is blocking the bar?" Ruki waved his hand to the right. "Move!"

The aian turned human looked both confused and scared. Nevertheless, he complied, scurrying over to the right and exposing a few choice bottles of whiskies and gins.

Suddenly, a high pitch *twing* sounded. Leto's stomach exploded into a red mist. A disk from Ruki's diskbow shot out from the mage's back, sped past where the glamored aian had been and kept going to break a bottle of twenty year Ambrose whiskey as the disk embedded itself deeply into the wall.

Leto crumpled, setting off an explosion of action. Calais sprung from her seat, twirled and reached for the peacekeeper. One hand moved in a blur smearing purple chalk lines over his armor. The other hand smacked the peacekeeper's chest, the fingers splaying out to touch the lines the other hand had just drawn. The lines glowed and the peacekeeper went down in a fit of convulsions.

Ruki held no illusions he would be able to move that fast. He visualized the peacekeeper behind him drawing a weapon and running him through while he was stuck dumb watching Calais' foul magic at work. Vincent caught his attention. The megrym leapt from his seat towards Ruki, his hammer raised. Ruki hit the floor. Vincent flew past where Ruki had sat only a moment before. Ruki looked up to see Vincent's hammer come across the peacekeeper's helmet with a jarring clang. The peacekeeper stumbled three steps backwards before hitting the floor with a din like dropped pots.

Calais wasn't done. She hurried over to Leto, who was barely alive, crawling on his stomach. She took out white chalk, kicked him onto his back, then knelt and began to trace lines and symbols on his face and the floor around his head. Leto tried to talk, to perhaps cast a spell in defense, but he couldn't gather the necessary focus to speak above a slurred mumble. Calais put the chalk between the mumbling mage's lips. The mage started to shake from some unseen power. The lines and symbols on Leto's face and on the floor began to glow a fierce cobalt blue. The stick of chalk Calais held in Leto's mouth also turned blue and blue dust the same intense cobalt hue started to well out of the symbols and lines of his face, from his nose, from his ears. After several agonizing seconds, the blue light subsided and the mage stopped shaking altogether.

Ruki grimaced. He wasn't a fan of blue mages, mind pokers all of them, but that was an unkind way to die. Truth of the matter was Ruki wasn't quite sure what Calais had done to Leto. All he knew is that he didn't want to end up like that, with a witch hunched over his dead body, scooping blue powder into a small leather bag and smiling at a new, pretty blue chalk that had once been white.

"You can never have too much of the blue stuff," Calais said as she stowed the chalk in her pocket.

"I know you can have too much conversation," Vincent said as he kneeled down to check the peacekeeper he had beat in the head. "Crap, how annoying were the two of you? 'Good sir, I'd like to ask an exhaustive battery of questions about things I already seem to know the answer to, just to see you squirm.' 'Why? That sounds heavenly! And would you pass the Grey Poupon?' Sheezus! Get a room."

Gina frowned. "Why are you complaining? Didn't you need that annoyance to tap into your character trigger?"

Vincent looked down at the incapacitated peacekeeper, looked back up at Gina and shrugged. "Still annoying though."

Ruki rose from the floor. "It was obvious Leto wasn't going to stop until he pulled our masks off, no doubt subject us to blue magic mind probes. But now we've got to come up with a plan. This turn of events completely wrecks any ideas I had about escape via portal."

"Can't we just dump the bodies and pretend they were never here?" Calais asked.

"We can't be sure no one knew where Leto was heading," he answered. "Leto or the peacekeepers likely told someone. Even if Leto decided to keep a close rein on his investigation and no one comes here in an hour to find him, what happens when a blue robe and two peacekeepers are discovered dead?" Ruki asked. He pointed at Leto's face. The symbols and lines that Calais had drawn into the mage's skin looked burned in. "The mage displays obvious signs of death by witchcraft. How many stones do you think they're willing to turn over to find who did it?"

Ruki looked over the bar, full of people without refuge or recourse. "This ship is sinking," he said.

Chapter 10

Portents and Dark Tidings, Reasoned Out

A BITTER TOUCH OF SORROW clouded Rew's resolve as she stared at the scroll Breunan had sacrificed so much to give her. It was a regional map, an unconventional and stylized physical map she had seen innumerable times in her extended lifetime. There were no country borders or cities, mostly geographical features such as mountains, lakes, rivers and seas. Superimposed over this typical terrain, oblong and irregularly shaped circles were drawn seemingly indiscriminately, over both land and sea. It formed a strange pattern familiar to any advanced student of the tower. The map showed the ley current.

Why, Breunan, why was this so important that you'd risk your life to bring it to me?

"Looks like ocean currents," Rich said tracing a finger along the lines that started from a small irregular circle and emanated out in waves. "Except, you know, that they're all closed circular splotches and some are on land and all."

"This is telluric current," Mel said, nodding at the map. "You don't remember seeing these, in Earth science?"

The look on Rich's face answered a clear and resounding no.

"You know how the Earth is like a giant magnet... poles, how compasses work, all that? Well, it's actually more of an electromagnet. The telluric current is a low frequency electric current that moves underground and through the sea."

"That's what I get for not paying attention in science class," Rich said with a smile. "I was probably too busy paying attention to character stats and reading up on useless lore like what the Megrym Hegemony is."

The two of them smiled at each other for a brief moment before Rich turned to face Rew, the smile still on his face. "Is that what this is... telluric current?"

"Who can be sure," she said. "We're comparing different worlds. The ley currents radiate outward from specific points." She pointed at the middle of a few of the circles for emphasis. "These points are believed to be where the Onesource enters our world. Magic in turn emanates outward from there."

"You don't sound sure," Rich said.

"Cause she's not, Bendy Sleeves," Vylar said. He was seated at the other end of the table, having little need or desire to stand huddled over the map scroll with the other three. "You know what the tower is, don't you? A place to study a subject that defies explanation every chance it gets. Sure, you got practical applications of established procedures, what you would call mage magic, but that's not all there is to the Onesource. Is it living? A part of something living, like its blood or breath? Or its waste product? A force? Does it change? If so, how? If it doesn't will it ever? Why'd it drive the aians mad? Why is there a cost to its use? What determines that?"

"Vylar is right," Rew said, mostly to herself as she studied the map. "I'm not sure what really is behind ley current. No one is."

More to the point, what was Breunan trying to say? He had given her the map but didn't get a chance to explain before Druze interrupted them.

Poor Breunan. Even more of a reason to return as Hierophant and end this senseless war.

"This was important to Breunan," Rew said. "Important enough to sacrifice his safety to make me aware of it. But it's no different than any of the maps we study in magic theory. What Druze would hope to achieve using ley current isn't exactly jumping off the map at me."

"I'm not a mage or anything," Mel said looking at the map with an intensity and curiosity, "but I figure we can reason this out. This feels like troubleshooting with a little bit of deductive reasoning and a dash of scientific method. Unlike magic, all things I like."

She looked at Rew. "Ok, so your dad is in the body of a pendulum reject, right? By your description, the one formerly known as Baron La Croix."

"Indeed."

"Unlike the other times we came across him, Druze isn't swapping bodies out like everyone else changes drawers, so we can reasonably assume holding onto this one body's particularly important to him. The body's special to him and the body's tied to the Pendulum. So is it safe to assume the ley current has something to do with the Rift Pendulum?"

Rew nodded as she mulled it over. "Quite possibly. The Rift Pendulum is one of the few things original to the Hierophane, built well before I was alive. How the underlying engine of the pendulum works was something my father said was lost to time, but I've always suspected he knew more than he let on."

"Okaaaay," Rich sighed, a sound that was dramatically steeped in exasperation. "Before we go any further, is there anything else you suspect Druze knows more than he lets on about? I mean, last time you suspected something like that he jumped out of a portal ring to make me cast a suicide spell while he tortured my friends. Let's not mention the infinite lifespan thing."

"When you've lived for centuries, some things begin to become inconsequential to you," Rew replied coolly. "Like your attitude."

"Now, children," Mel interjected.

"You should let them keep going," Vylar said. "Most entertainment I've seen after watching Bendy Sleeves fail at graduation for a month straight. Least he could've done was graduate during normal waking hours. No... idiot waits until I'm dead sleep."

"Let's focus," Mel said. "So let's say the ley lines have a lot to do with the way the Rift Pendulum works. With that assumption in mind, why would Breunan give you this map? I can only reason that the pendulum's physical location is pertinent to these currents."

"Very astute," Rew said, "the Hierophane sits in the epicenter of this current here." She tapped her finger at one the bigger splotches."

"So," Mel began, "in assuming the Rift Pendulum is powered by ley current, then it's likely powered by the same current the tower is standing on." She pondered the map in silence for a moment. "But the Hierophane's ley node can't be all there is to it, otherwise there'd be no reason for Breunan to smuggle the map to you. It's something you already know and don't need a map for."

Rew nodded her agreement. "So, it wasn't the tower's ley current he was trying to show me."

Mel's eyes widened, her features changing as if she was struck with lightning. "Have you guys ever heard of an Earth battery? Rich?"

Rich shook his head in answer. Mel filled him in.

"An Earth battery is a pair of electrodes made of two dissimilar metals, such as iron and copper, which are buried in the soil or immersed in the sea. The thing is, if the plates are sufficiently far apart, they can tap telluric currents. Earth batteries are also called telluric generators. So if the telluric current and this ley current are one in the same..."

"Then the Rift Pendulum could be a telluric generator," Rich said, venturing to fill in the blanks. "Well, in this case, a ley generator."

Mel nodded. "What's more, the Rift Pendulum seems to be a standalone, self contained system," she said, putting her finger on the Hierophane's solitary ley current splotch. She added another finger onto the ley node directly east of the Hierophane and closest to it. "What would happen if it suddenly went from a self-contained system to a networked system?"

Understanding dawned on Rich's face as he looked at Mel's two fingers on the map.

"Druze is going to double the power of the pendulum."

Rew shook her head as she looked at the map. She reached for the chair closest to her with shaky hands, pulled it closer and collapsed in it with all the grace of getting pulled by magnets. "My father will be beyond stopping," she said in a near whisper.

Rich screwed his face up at the map. "I don't see it being that big of a deal, a little more juice for a toy is all, nothing we can't handle."

She shook her head. "You don't understand. The Hierophane is half a millennium old, with towers and devices built over the ley line to intentionally tap into the source of magic, including the Rift Pendulum. If Druze gets his hands on another, totally untapped source, the power he could feed the Pendulum would be exponentially greater than what's available to him now."

Rich shrugged off her analysis and shot her a charming, lopsided grin. "He can only do so much magic. Even immortal as he seems to be, he's still only human."

Rew shook her head again. "But that's just it. He's not. Not anymore. His body is like yours, one of pure magic. Powered by a weakened pendulum. In a more humanizing analogy, think of that pendulum as a brown robed mage. Brown magic can do some amazing things but it's severely limited in the amount of power it can wield. Now, think of the options available to the pendulum if it went straight from brown caliber power to gray."

Rich's jaw went slack and his eyes danced. No doubt he could visibly see some of the ramifications... they were too clear not to see.

"He could build a character with iron skin. Or a being made of fire. He could build an army of shells, just waiting for his soul to inhabit."

"Exactly. And don't forget, you're a product of the pendulum. You need it to return to your home. What do you think happens to you if Druze gains the power to correct the pendulum's problems without any of your involvement?"

Mel leaned in closer. "You're saying he'll have the power to just delete us?"

"I can't be sure. The way the ley currents work, how the pendulum truly operates, those have always been mysteries to me along with every other mage of the current era except Druze. The possibility that Druze can simply wipe you from this world is there. You are ultimately children of the pendulum, even if your creation was in error."

Silence became thick, weighted in the house. The map of ley currents, a standard map for school mages, felt ominous.

"Where do you think he's going?" Rich asked looking at the map. "Are any of the splotches on the map probable, or just those close to the Hierophane?"

"Distance plays an important role in telluric generators," Mel said. "So it's best to assume the same holds true for the ley kind." She pointed at the ley current emanating roughly east of the Hierophane's.

"Where is this one?"

"You've been there," Rew answered nodding at the map. "That's Nasreddin."

"Hmmm... pretty sure Druze isn't going to the aian capital to set up a magic antenna," Mel said. She moved her finger to the ley node west of the Hierophane. This one sat in the sea.

"And this one?"

"That one is definitely a better target," Rew said. "It's within the boundaries of the Free States, a mile or so off the coast of Suusteren. They say that ley current is why the Opal Horn is so abundant with marine life, which in turn made Suusteren such a prosperous seaport. I would have said this was the best bet before the war. But now the city's under siege, surrounded by aians. No doubt they'll have naval forces deeply entrenched in the waters of the Horn."

Mel nodded. "Can't say that's it for sure, can't rule it out completely like Nasreddin. Moving on." Mel's finger traced a path from the Suusteren node to the one directly north of the Hierophane.

"This one?"

Rew shook her head. "Possible, but even more doubtful than Suusteren. That's in the heart of the Sprawl. The gangs there aren't very friendly towards mages, or any outsiders for that matter. What we know about how those gangs operate indicates they are experts in guerrilla warfare. Druze would need an army of mages and probably years of fighting to clear it out enough to operate. Too much time and magepower to spare right now."

"Oh, I wouldn't rule it out completely, lady," Vylar said. He turned to face Rew and it seemed as if he was looking directly at her through his closed eyelids. "I've been going there for years now. Lot of shadows in the rubble. You'll be surprised how much one person can do when they know how to move in them."

Mel nodded thoughtfully. "A point I can't argue with. And then there's the last one." She took her finger and placed it on the node due south of the Hierophane.

"I'm not familiar with that node," Rew admitted. It's not within the border of the Free States. It appears to be within the kingdom of Colkhis."

At the mention of Colkhis, Vylar nodded. "I know the place. It's a site the Colkhisians call the Blue Grotto. We know it here as Lapis Deep."

Rew grimaced and inhaled sharply at his words. Lapis Deep was a strange cave system, carved out of the blue stone lapis lazuli. Rew had been there a megrym-sized handful of times in the course of her three hundred and fifty years, and never lightly. It was not a place one goes without reason.

Rich and Mel looked at each other curiously, and when both of them shook their heads, they turned to Rew. "What is it?" Mel asked. "What's up with Lapis Deep?"

Rew sighed. "It is home to... unpleasantries," she said. "Creatures. Anomalies warped, maybe by the ley current."

Rich raised an eyebrow. "What sorts of things? And how bad?"

"Of chief concern are the Beautiful Ones," Rew answered.

Rich's eyes widened at the mention of the Beautiful Ones. "Now I remember Lapis Deep! The Beautiful Ones, you mean those things from the Crystal Dark expansion?"

Rew raised a questioning eyebrow. So did Mel for that matter. Rich continued, filling in the blanks.

"I remember the lore from that. Back before the Hierophane, when people pretty much magicked about at their own risk, a bunch of magically inclined artists, sculptors mainly, went to Lapis Deep to work the stone to make their creations so lifelike they could literally breathe. And they succeeded, making these blue lapis statues that moved on their own accord. Inadvertently the creators, so deeply driven by their need to take their art beyond the life it imitated, infused in their statues a driving need to make life as well. First they turned on their creators, tore them apart to see how they worked.

Then they began to build their own fleshy style Beautiful Ones from parts ripped off the sculptors and from the bodies of anyone foolish enough to go there."

"Aw man," Mel said, "You're talking about those stone dungeon bosses with the small army of herky-jerky dudes?"

Rich nodded. "Badass, right?"

Vylar grumped. "I should hardly think so. The creators were foolhardy. Sure, the Beautiful Ones were perfect on the outside but they lacked on the inside. No lungs to breathe or open throat to speak, no stomach to know hunger, and most importantly, no nerves to know pain. The ability to feel pain helps people know empathy. They'll just as soon pull your arm off to see what's in it as stare into your mouth in utter amazement. You don't know what you're getting because it's not like they can speak to you. No one even knows if you can reason with them; it's not like the sculptors built eardrums for their stone ear holes."

"So," Mel said, "There's a siege to the west, a hostile empire to the east, bloodthirsty gangs to the north and unfeeling and potentially murderous museum artwork to the south. All we have to do is pick the right one."

Looking at the map, the southern node made the most sense to Rew. "The Beautiful Ones are not a joy to tangle with, but a competent cadre of mages should be able to navigate Lapis Deep without too much peril. If I was trying to tap one of the nearest ley currents, I'd try there first."

Vylar grumped. "I still say the Sprawl's the easiest bet. The place is a ruin as big as an empire, not to mention what lies underneath. Easy enough to hide, move and operate without too much interference if you halfway know what you're doing."

Rich shrugged. "Same could be said for Suusteren. Sure, you may have some House Baligoz and Menanderus aians out there in the water, but the mages still control the city. Easy enough to portal in and work at breaking the naval siege from that position, or attacking the land forces in a way to distract the aian navy enough to get the job done."

"We better choose carefully," Mel said. "And right the first time. We may have the numbers to cover each point at the same time, but it's not exactly the smartest move. If any one of us run across Druze, we're gonna want the others here at our backs. I know I do. The last time I took on a destruction mage with just a sword and moxy it took two weeks to recover."

Vylar held a hand up. "You hear that?" His neck craned a bit as he listened for things no one else could hear. A tense moment later, he turned to Rew.

"Maybe your daddy isn't going to Lapis Deep, Suusteren or anywhere else with a ley pulse on it right now," the blind man said. "Maybe he's coming here."

Chapter 11
Reunion

MIKE HAD NEVER THOUGHT about it before, but now he realized why moths don't travel in packs. They don't like looking ridiculous. He knew this was how moths would look firsthand because that's how the gang looked airborne thanks to aian moth power.

Apparently the moth wings of House Eula weren't as strong as the eagle wings of Demir. While Mike and Savvy only needed one moth flyer to carry them, Jason needed two and poor Runt was a damn mess. He had four flyers, each manning a limb, holding him up like he was performing the world's longest slow motion freefall, complete with limbs that seemed to flail as each moth went back and forth on their own wing beat.

That was really the worst part of it. More than the lack of strength, it was the complete lack of team coordination that really irked Mike. When they flew with the boys from House Demir, those eagle wings all synced up. Moth wings don't sync, they flutter to their own individual tune. Collectively they looked like the world's worst dance troupe.

It beat walking though, stupid looking or not.

As the countryside drifted past them a mile below, Mike couldn't help but reflect on how good this felt. Not the wind, that shit was cold as hell, but the fact that they had a solid direction, a game plan.

Jason's idea to meet back up with Mel and the mages was actually decent for a change. Once they connected with them, they were bound to have portals to all sorts of spots. Jason planned to hop a portal into Suusteren with his moth friends and the girl he had no hopes of getting with, the rest of them were gonna get an express ticket to the Sprawl. Too easy.

Mike cast his gaze over to Savvy. A while back, before winter had set in, Savvy had placed a hex onto Mel's pack for tracking purposes. Now Savvy was guiding the flying dance troupe thanks to her connection via the hex. She pointed to a speck on the distant landscape and gestured for them all to land.

The speck turned into a small house and the smaller dots gathered near the house turned into people.

"Are they your friends?" Eula asked Jason, who she flew beside. Mike guessed goddesses don't deign to carry common folk.

"That's them," Jason said with a sly smile. "Don't worry about the battle stances. They've all got human eyesight and we haven't gotten close enough for them to really see us."

The moths fluttered onward. Soon enough, everyone's face became readable regardless of race. Rich, Rew, Vylar and Melvin stood in the brown grass. Mel waived at his brother vigorously after sheathing his sword.

Mike had barely touched the ground when Mel bum rushed him, sweeping him up into a fierce hug. He returned the hug with the same gusto. Man, it felt like forever since he had seen his baby brother.

"Heh! What it do?!" Mike exclaimed. "I mean, what's really good?"

"It's all good, now that you're here!" Mel said. "Well, not all good, but mostly good... screw the rest! Ha ha!"

Eventually Mel put Mike down to hug it out with Jason. Mike shook hands with Rich. "New color?" Mike asked, looking at Rich's robe.

"Yeah," Rich smiled and smoothed the front of his robe down. "You like?"

"Seen one Snuggie, you seen 'em all, right? But it is nice to see you moving off fries to the register."

"I'll second that," Jason chimed in behind Mike. "But I figured you'd go for destruction, you know for that sweet bonus to damage, or possibly even white robes for the added stat increases."

"Same old Jason," Rich said smiling. "Still got a gamer's eye for all this."

"Can't unlock the bonus stage without it," Jason said returning the smile.

Mike left them to hug and bro it up. He turned and found Melvin wrapped around Runt's thick neck, one foot on tiptoe, the other bent in the air as Mel tried to hug the half-weagr and keep balance. Mel let go and embraced Savvy and once they were done Savvy held onto Mel's hand as if Mike's brother was Savvy's long lost daughter.

The whole thing looked so strange to Mike. Mel seemed... different. And not just 'same dude in another body' different either.

Meanwhile, Rich and Jason's hushed dialogue made Mike's ears twitch.

"Is that Eula? Jason, you brought an aian goddess to the rightful Hierophant while their nations are at war?"

"Seemed like a good idea at the time."

Mike could almost see Jason shrug as he said it. Instead of looking at the two of them, Mike's eyes found Rew Majora and Eula standing arm's length apart looking at each other.

"Any chance you can get the Temple of Houses to stop this war?" Rew asked.

"About as much chance as you getting the Hierophane to desist," Eula replied.

Rew held her right hand up, letting her robe sleeve fall down around her forearm. It looked as if she was showing Eula nothing was up her sleeve, which made sense when Mike thought about the kind of talents mages had. Then Rew extended the hand to Eula.

"Welcome, Queen of Moths."

Eula took the hand and shook. "Well met, Hierophant in waiting."

"Whew!" Jason said, letting out a big sigh. "Glad they didn't start fighting. That wouldn't have been an easy one to break up."

WHEN MEL HEARD JASON and Mike explain why they were there, the short hairs on the back of her neck stood up.

"There's magic in this," she said.

Everyone—the mages, the dozen moths, her brother, the guy with the bone hand—everyone looked at her with confusion. Except Runt and Savvy.

"Don't you guys see?" she asked everyone in the field. "We were just talking about how there were these three places we needed to be at basically the same time and couldn't, well not be there and really be worth a damn at any case. Then you guys literally drop from the sky and need to be at two of the three. It's gotta be magic."

Rich shook his head. "If there was a color that could do something like that, I would've chosen it."

"No," Mel said. "You've been a mage too long. Not magic as a tool you can use like a hammer. No, it's more like magic the way we know it back on Earth. That thing that dwells with fate and destiny and luck and strange encounters and coincidence and happenstance. We're supposed to be here, all of us, right now, so we can get to these places because we're supposed to be in these places. Why is that? Magic."

Eula bowed her head deferentially. "Life is how the Onesource calls upon us all," she said, "and we are ever in its service."

The words sounded like a mantra or a prayer to Mel, and it occurred to her that Eula and the other aian deities weren't like gods in the usual Earthly sense. The gods and goddesses in this pantheon weren't the end-all and be-all of supernatural power—one god didn't rule the seas and another wasn't the living embodiment of the sun and a third didn't invent music all by him or herself—these aian gods and goddesses prayed to a power higher than themselves. Mel entertained an image of Apollo or Ra or Jupiter on their knees praying, thought about who they'd be praying to and what they'd be asking for and all of it decidedly tripped her out.

"Speaking of magic," Rew Majora said, "I believe with the addition of our newly minted red robe and an accomplished Hexenarii, we have at our disposal the necessary elements to create a magical means to solve any future communication problem."

Vylar, his eyes closed, raised an eyebrow. "Mirror links?"

Rew smiled. "Indeed. It is well past time to coordinate our efforts, no matter where our paths take us."

The magic users talked about the process between themselves, with Rew describing the overall procedure while Vylar chimed in here and there with additional details. Rich nodded earnestly like school was in session. Savvy looked between the three human casters with a stoic poker face. After a couple of minutes of planning, they got started.

As if Vylar knew Mel was the most curious bystander among the crowd, he made his way over to her and talked her through the process as it was happening. Maybe he knew she was going to barrage him with a million questions and was trying to head her off at the pass.

Rich made the foundation, first by holding his right hand out like he was Force choking someone. With his left hand he tossed the powdery contents of three bowls into the air. The different colored dusts stayed suspended in air under his pseudo-Force choke. First, fine yellow grains, then a white powder that looked like baking soda and finally a fine gray powder that was reminiscent of ashes.

"Sand, soda ash, limestone," Vylar told Mel. "The method to convert these can be magical, but the ingredients have to be natural and unaltered. Luckily, I keep odds and ends like this on hand in small quantities."

Rich brought the sand, soda ash and limestone together to mingle magically in the air. He brought his other hand up to get it involved with the Force choking. Spellcraft flowed from his lips and the air where the ingredients hovered began to glow red. Mel felt the heat of this suspended fire grow as the redness of the air swelled and throbbed to lava levels.

Rich snapped off the spell, and the fire died in an instant, leaving a glowing red pane to hover before them all.

"The glass," Vylar said.

Savvy was up next. "After I speak, you must kiss," she said. She pulled a hex from her belt and went over to Mike. "Attune," she said, bringing the hex up to Mike's lips where he gave it a smooch.

"Well, that's all the action Mike's gonna see this year," Jason cracked.

Wordlessly, Savvy took the now green glowing hex over to the super hot glass pane and dropped it. The hex caught fire and melted in an instant into the glass.

"*Sus!*" she spat the word short and sharp, hushing Jason as she went over to him. "Your fool words linger in the air in ceremony as much as the glass. Eat them next time."

"I don't know if that's true," Vylar whispered to Mel, "but I keenly appreciate the sentiment."

Savvy plucked another hex. "Attune," she named it and brought it to Jason's lips for his kiss. This one glowed red after the kiss. Once dissolved, Savvy made her way to Mel. Mel's hex glowed blue after her kiss. And after this third hex was soaked into the hot glass did Savvy turn to Rich. She ducked and weaved between his outstretched arms to present him his hex. Rich's kiss made it glow gray. Savvy dropped the hex into the glass and backed away, her part complete.

"My turn," Vylar said. He stepped towards the glass and held both his hands up towards his mouth as if he was going to yell at someone from far away. "*Donma yeri ellerim arasinda*," he spoke. Next, he exhaled deeply and where he blew frosty air poured forth from his cupped hands over the red hot glass. In a moment it was cooled, a seemingly normal pane of glass if not for the fact that it floated five feet off the ground.

He held a hand up. "*Nereye dokunduu um guumuush olsun*," he intoned. He then placed that hand over the now cooled glass and wiped. Every where his hand passed turned into shiny silver.

His part seemed done but instead of coming back to stand beside Mel he took a place beside Rich, who still had his hands held up to keep the glass suspended.

"Turn it over," Rew asked Rich.

Rich nodded and raised his left palm up while keeping the right static. The left side of the glass pane raised itself into the air before turning over. Mel could see the pane was basically a highly reflective polished silver behind the glass.

Rew stepped up to the mirror perpendicular to where Rich and Vylar stood. She placed both hands on the mirror.

"*Chaa realdaa inda, tanikdiklarena gor ve duy*," she said.

The mirror shimmered, like sunlight sparking across a still lake. Then the shimmer went quiet. She looked up at Vylar.

"If you please, Vylar. On three."

Vylar stepped back up to the mirror where both he and Rew placed a single finger on the dead center of their respective edge perpendicular to one another.

"One, two, three..." Rew counted off.

"*Kopart*!" both Vylar and Rew spat on three. The mirror snapped loudly and cleanly from a line drawn out from their fingers. Now Mel was looking at four floating squares of mirror. Rich flitted his fingers and the mirrors starting coming toward him and stacking into a neat pile for him to grab.

Rich handed a mirror to Mel, Jason and Mike.

"Just hold the mirror up and say one of our names."

Mel held her mirror up. "Mike," she said.

Mike appeared in place of her reflection, him smiling those pointy sharp teeth.

"Whattup bruh," sounded out in stereo as Mel picked up the words from both the mirror and the megrym standing not more than six feet away.

Jason called Rich and Rich called Mel and the three of them tried to three-way call each other until Mike waved a couple of hands in the air to cool them down.

"Magic Facetime's all well and good," Mike said, "but how about we conjure up some grub and a game plan?" He turned to Eula. "Your brother wrecked the best buffet spread I'd seen in months. I'm still weeping bitter tears about them things that looked like deviled eggs."

Vylar's humble abode went from hosting four people to over four times that. Even if everyone could manage to squeeze themselves into the house, they'd be five people past standing room only. Needless to say, Vylar's simple pantry didn't have strong enough shelves to see seventeen people well fed.

But that's where magic came in, the kind that was common in this world and readily accessible to mages. Vylar recruited five of

Eula's guard moths, opened a portal and led them all through it. A minute after the portal closed, another opened and the six of them reappeared, only this time the guard moths were carrying a huge game animal. It looked like an antelope, supersized to five hundred pounds, with a brown coat that sported six vertical white lines. It had some long, seriously wicked horns that spiraled two and a half times.

"What is that?" Mel asked.

"Kudu," Runt answered with an appreciative nod. "Good meat."

That seemed to be his cue to get the fire going. He made it near the solitary tree in the clearing, assisted by Savvy, Mike, and some of the guard moths who set about cleaning and butchering the meat. Meanwhile, Vylar portaled to another place he didn't name, this time with Rich in tow, so he could make a portal root. They came back with a barrel keg.

"See?" Jason said to Eula, an awkward smile on his face. "I told you my people are the top notchiest."

Eula returned his smile. It was nowhere near as awkward looking. "Indeed."

In short order it may not have necessarily looked like a backyard barbecue in the suburbs—with the odd menagerie of aian, nasran, megrym, half-weagr and humans in robes—but it certainly felt like it. It felt good. It was a feeling Mel hadn't had since Suusteren, and even back then any happiness had been muted by the constant search for a means to get Rich out of stone.

Here was a rare moment where nothing was wrong. Soon enough they'd be in different parts of the world, away from one another, all of them no doubt facing some kind of danger. Mel allowed herself to breathe deep, savoring the respite along with the sizzling aroma of game meat. She stretched the brief flash of now for as long as any one moment could stretch. And exhaled.

"Yo," Mike said to Vylar between mouthfuls of savory kudu. "Just so I'm clear, you definitely got a portal to the Sprawl?"

Vylar, his eyes closed as his custom, didn't turn his head towards Mike, but rather took a swig of ale from his mug.

"Got portals everywhere, young man. I can put you into the heart of any of the major Sprawlcrawler territories: Clockwound Warders, Sons of Kaftar, Exhaust. Just name your favorite threat."

"Word," Mike grinned, adjusting his goggles.

"More challenging is the Suusteren dilemma," Vylar said after another drink of ale. "When I open a portal there, it's going to be a whole world of alert and angry mages descending on the scene. You sure you want to go there? And who's all going?"

Jason looked around. "Just us aians," he said, "unless someone else wants in on the adventure of a lifetime."

"Apparently, I do," Vylar said with a grump. "More important than the adventure of it, I'd like to see you get those aians out of the prison camps. Those are people they should be protecting... damned mages prove too much thinking leads to overthinking."

He took another swill of ale before continuing. "Seems to me that just opening a portal and leaving you to your own devices is a recipe for disaster, if not outright suicide. Sure, I imagine the goddess would fare well enough, cause a lot of confusion and bedlam in the city, potentially rally the aians surrounding Suusteren into an assault, but how many more innocent people die that route? No."

He shook his head. "Best way is to go in fast. Use subterfuge, redirection, and the darkness that I live in to cut a path to the camp. Take out the guards as quick and clean as possible, open up some portals out of there and disappear before the cavalry comes. You're going to need me for those portals at the end. As much as I would've found it an easier time in Lapis Deep, it looks like I'll have to leave that with Bendy Sleeves, the Hierophant and the warrior girl."

Mel shook her head. "You're gonna have to leave the warrior girl out of it." She looked at Jason. "I'm going with you."

Jason nodded and smiled appreciatively. "Now we're talking that easy XP."

"Wait, not easy XP," Rich said. He leaned toward Mel. "I thought you were coming with us. How come you're not coming with us?"

"Look, you don't need me here," Mel said. She sighed. "Plus I'm getting in the way. I figure it's time for me to move on, put my talents to use and actually help some people that really do need it."

"You're wrong, Mel," Rich said, his eyes full of care and concern. "I do need you."

I need you. The words felt like barbs to Mel, ones Rich placed on her just to drag them across her heart.

"Need me for what?!" Mel cried, so exasperated she could barely contain herself. "It's like you've been spending all your time on a spell of avoidance. You hardly talk to me. Any time I try to talk to you about us you find a way to avoid it. Maybe you're right in that you don't want to fall for me, but where's that put me? Maybe I'm just murky about shit now but it seems like we were better friends before we slept together. Either way, I need some space, man."

If this backyard barbecue had some music playing, this is when it would've skipped the track. The quiet was surreal. Mel could feel Mike's eyes burrowing at him behind those goggles.

"You two," he said, bringing his greenish-purple megrym hands together and apart like he was playing an air accordion. "Banged?"

"Mike," Mel began. But that was all the answer to the question her brother needed.

"You on some straight bullshit, bruh," Mike said as he got up and walked off, into the barren trees of the surrounding forest.

Mel got up to go after her brother. First, she looked at her best friend.

Jason shrugged.

"It's weird, dude, but what the hell. Some shit you gotta yolo."

Chapter 12
Suusteren, The Raid of

JASON EXPECTED BETTER goodbyes than this. Of course, nothing really felt real or right at this time of morning. It was two hours before dawn, that no-man's-land of time when night owls were all out of hoot and the early risers had yet to rise. This was the best time to infiltrate Suusteren according to Vylar, when the mage watch would be at its lowest and doubtful of an aian strike because of the race's horrible night vision. Looking around at all the assembled players and the dark smudge of shadows beyond, Jason had to agree.

Still, even without sunshine, the thought of them all parting had played out better in his mind.

It wasn't just Mel and Mike. Yeah, the tension was still there, thick like cold meatloaf gravy. Mike still wasn't really airing out what his issue was with Mel, and when Mel tried to talk, Mike wasn't listening.

"Miss me with all that," Mike had said. "I ain't trying to know what you trying to tell me. Keep it."

It wasn't just Mel and Rich either. Mel adjusted the straps on his pack and double checked the contents, completely ignoring the old kid. Meanwhile, Rich was looking at Mel with the world's most adoptable puppy eyes. Maybe not that bad, especially since Jason couldn't really rely on vision in this light, but still, it looked bad, where at least twice he saw Rich rubbing the back of his head, mouth partway open and awkwardly looking as if he was going to walk over and say something but then changing his mind about it.

Jason could understand Rich's predicament. Look at Mel. Remove any context, take away the origin story and really look at Mel. There was no denying he was a beautiful woman even if it was strange for Jason to think about in those terms. Plus, Mel was cool to hang with. A rejection from someone like that has to mess with the very fabric of a dude's soul, much less his psyche.

Finally, there was Jason himself. He tried not to think about his condition as he checked the bow that the Hierophant Majora had created for him, something bent and shaped from the fallen branches around Vylar's house. It wasn't ornately detailed, by no means an ultimate weapon, but it was definitely sturdy, strong and functional.

The bow wasn't his problem, the numbers were his problem. He had three maggots left on the pendant Onus had given him. At this point, there wasn't necessarily an urge to use it, but existence in a normal, unaltered state felt bland and cringeworthy. Honestly, he felt powerless during the whole of his waking hours and was only comforted from the helplessness of it by feeling for the necklace under his brown robe.

That was the other reason this goodbye felt especially sucky. He felt his number was coming up, literally. The next time he saw any of the guys, he could very well be sharing skin and headspace with the aian god of power. And Jason didn't think anyone whose moniker was "The Corrupter" would be a good roommate.

"Everyone ready?" Vylar asked.

Solemn nods all around. This wouldn't do. Jason brought out one of his old gaming sayings.

"Put X's in their eyes and pee on their tactics..."

Silence.

"C'mon!" Jason cajoled. "Story worthy stuff's coming to us, this can't be the start! So let's kick it off right, square in the junk of the opposition. Let's put X's in their eyes and pee on their tactics..."

"Cause it's all about that XP," both Rich and Mel said with a smile. Wan smiles but smiles nonetheless.

Vylar opened the portal to the Sprawl. Mike stepped through without a look back at his brother, followed by Runt and Savvy.

Hierophant Majora opened her portal to Lapis Deep next. Rich hesitated, spared a look back and gave a shaky wave goodbye before following the hierophant into the portal.

Once the portals to the Sprawl and Lapis Deep had closed, Vylar took a deep breath and exhaled. "Steel yourselves. Things will move fast once this thing is opened. Remember the basic plan—everything else will be fluid."

With that, he opened the portal to Suusteren and led the way in. Mel grimaced, shaking his head because portals were never an enjoyable thing for him before leaping through. Eula and Jason followed with the moth guards close behind.

The city that Jason had spent so much time in trying to get a healing spell for Rich had dramatically changed. Rubble and detritus covered the streets. The buildings were all but crumbling to their foundations. Some were little more than a wall or two with a hollow window or doorway.

Jason followed close behind Eula and Vylar. The blind man was moving with purpose through the street. By the time the entire moth guard had come through the portal, Vylar had opened three more portals to who knows where. He figured it was useless to try to sneak a portal past watchful mages, so instead why not inundate them with as many portals as he can spare until they could muster their forces? They'd be stuck investigating them all until the portals closed or until they got more forces out of the barracks to comb the city. Hence,

Portalpalooza was well underway as Vylar opened his fourth, this one above his head as he stepped briskly to the next intersection.

"Which way?" he asked Eula.

Eula closed her eyes. "The majority of my people are dreaming in the east, at the walls."

Vylar took a step in that direction.

"Wait," Eula said. "Another contingent of aiankind dream elsewhere, closer. Smaller, but still sizeable. Their dreams are more troubled than the ones in the prison camps. They have nightmares of getting caught, killed and imprisoned."

"We don't have time," Vylar said.

"They are close," Eula said, "two or three blocks north. We must rescue them."

"Halt!" a voice shouted behind them. Jason spun towards the voice.

Two mages were running, closing the distance towards them. Thanks to shitty aian night sight and the fact that the only illumination here belonged to the blue and white swirl of portals, the mages were either red or brown robes. Jason trusted Vylar's assessment that the tower would have their crappiest mages on watch at this time, which would make these guys brown robes.

Vylar moved at them with speed that defied age and physics, as if had cast some kind of crazy agility spell without uttering a word. He weaved around the portals he had made, left then right then left again, as if he was a speed skater. One brown robe bent his robe and sent the sleeve careening towards Vylar. Vylar held up his staff, "*Santrifuj ol*," he spoke quickly yet calmly. The staff spun on its own axis, blindingly fast. It caught the brown robe's sleeve, which began to wrap around the spinning staff. The action yanked the mage off his feet. Vylar turned, swinging the mage already off his feet into one of the portals, where the mage disappeared with a squelched cry.

There were no new magic words for the next mage. Vylar threw the staff, which was still spinning, at his chest. The mage coughed and spluttered at whatever spell he was in the process of saying as the spinning staff started bunching up his robe. The mage looked like he was being chewed up. Vylar rushed to the mage and grabbed the staff. He turned around, forcing the mage to turn in awkward steps with him. Then Vylar ran at another portal, stopping short and delivered a powerful open hand blow to the staff. The blow launched the mage off his feet, who blasted out of his own robe with a giant ripping noise to go hurtling buck naked through the portal behind him. Vylar's staff was still spinning with damn near a bedsheet's worth of robe material spun around it.

"*Dur*," he commanded the staff, which stopped spinning and allowed the rent robe fall to the ground. He turned to Eula.

"We don't have time," he said.

"We must," she repeated.

Vylar grumped at that but he went north instead of east, rushing through a tight alleyway. The sound of pursuit was growing behind them. All around them, sirens began to wail.

A pack of five peacekeepers met them in the alley. Mel rushed them, sliced into one, spun the sword into another, kicked a third at the end of the spin and kept moving, practically dancing them down as his body and sword moved through them with ballet grace, so fast the rest of the group scarcely had time to register what had happened. Mel finally ended the dance with both knees in the back of a peacekeeper who groaned into unconsciousness at the end of the alley.

"Next street over," Eula yelled over the din of the sirens.

They emerged into the next alleyway to find a lot worse than Jason had hoped for. Directly in front of them, two mages led two dozen peacekeepers. The mages were either blue or black robes. The mages and peacekeepers backs were turned, apparently more concerned with their own business than the city waking up on high alert. They formed a semicircle around a building that had a sign illuminated by a lone gaslight. *Second Chances.*

The mages and peacekeepers turned at the sound of the commotion behind them. One glance at the small horde of aians behind them and they all spun in an instant to face the new threat.

This wasn't going to be a quick and easy fight like the last time. Meanwhile, behind the moth guard, four mages appeared at the end of the alleyway, too far and too dark for Jason to see what color. Even if it was an all brown affair, this wasn't going to be fun.

The twenty-four peacekeepers ran at them, swords out.

Eula stepped in front to meet them. She didn't draw her sword. Instead, she seemed to bring the surrounding darkness to her and amplify it, as if the gaslight grew dimmer or the night became darker. Then she exploded, no, more like fragmented, into a swarm of black moths.

There were dozens of them, moths as big as a man's open palm. Their wings fluttered as fast as hummingbirds, an angry ticking sound. The moths swarmed over the faces of the peacekeepers and mages.

Immediately, Eula's guardsmen drew their axes and rushed the peacekeepers and mages, who were batting erratically at the moth swarm. Jason assumed the moths of Eula—or perhaps it was better to say Eula as moths—weren't poisonous or had sharp fangs or anything that could bring down armed warriors alone. Still, having huge moths the size of beefy hands beating their wings in your face at the rate of a hundred reps per second had to be beyond distracting. Her guardsmen knew and were rushing to capitalize on it. It took Mel a little more time to recover from seeing a woman burst into moths, but a few moments later he ran in to help Eula's guard. Jason took out his bow to put some shots down range.

Vylar nudged him with his staff.

"Behind us, eagle eye," he said.

Jason turned. The four mages had closed the distance in the alleyway rapidly. Their robes were two distinct shades of the same shitty dark color—dammit, why couldn't the sun rise already? Ok, they were probably two brown robes and two black, maybe thirty yards out, not quite in robe bending distance, but getting closer all the time.

"Start shooting," Vylar said.

Jason took a half breath and held it. After months of practice, this was the best way he'd found to quickly channel the inner calm he needed to get immersed into Cephrin mode. In a rapid, fluid motion pulled an arrow from his quiver, nocked it and aimed.

"*Squishy mobs, aim for the head,*" he thought.

He loosed his arrow. Immediately he went for another one, nocked it, fired. And again. Again.

The first arrow got deflected by bent sleeves. And the second. And the third. And the fourth.

These were mages, not practice targets. No mage worth a damn was going to go for catching an arrow with their brain pan, not even a brown robe. All Jason had managed to do was slow them down.

"Keep firing," Vylar instructed. Meanwhile, he reached and pulled an arrow of his own out of Jason's quiver.

"I'm just wasting ammo," Jason said. He, however, did not stop firing. Just because he couldn't see what Vylar was up to didn't mean the old man wasn't up to something.

The four mages had slowed to a walk. Most anyone, mages included, weren't inclined to go running full steam at the business end of a drawn bow. Especially since with Jason's accuracy, these mages had to deflect the arrows unless they wanted their brains skewered. Tired of either the slowed pace or the incessant parade of headshot arrows, the two mages in the front spoke spells. Fire bloomed into their palms, revealing their robes to be the black of destruction mages. They opened their arms wide and the flames stretched, until a wall of fire stood between Jason's bow and the mages.

Their heads, even their feet, were protected by the fire. Under this protection, their pace quickened.

"Now fire this one," Vylar said, handing the arrow he had pulled earlier back to Jason. "Then get ready to clear out the left side."

Jason grabbed the arrow. Instead of the gray steel tip all his arrows had, the metal was now silver-white. He didn't question... he especially didn't question in the middle of a battle. He nocked and shot.

As soon as the arrow touched the wall of fire, it exploded. The explosion itself wasn't lethal or particularly powerful but the light! That arrow transformed into a miniature sun, blinding the mages with a light so uncomfortable, even Jason's aian eyes had to squint at it. He had seen that reaction in chemistry class and it was unmistakable, even a world away. Lithium.

It was as if a pocketful of instant noonday had been made in the alley. Now Jason had no trouble seeing and he saw everything from their fine wrinkles, to their color hair, to their frustrated grimaces as they squinted, to the fact that one of the brown robes was a woman.

Vylar charged down the alley at the blinded mages, clearly more prepared for a condition of sightlessness than these people.

Jason followed his orders to clear the left side. He ran at them, drawing his arm club from its sheath on his back. Two meaty whaps later, the mages on the left side were crumpled on top of one another, sound asleep.

Jason didn't see what Vylar did to the two on the right side, just that they dropped noiselessly. Vylar shook his head at Jason.

"Arrows would've been quicker," he said. "It's only going to get thicker from here. Chivalry doesn't extend to anyone with the skill and desire to actually end you. No pulled punches. Now let's help them."

Jason spun to face the initial threat, the two dozen peacekeepers and two mages. Thirteen of the peacekeepers were down, but so were three of Eula's guardsmen. Both mages still stood. Mel was fighting three guards at once and doing well but one of the mages kept deflecting his blows with strategically timed bent sleeves. Several moths littered the ground.

All the moths that were still hovering fluttered back, towards Jason and Vylar. They flew into the same spot, glowing, until they coalesced into Eula. The goddess dropped to a knee. Her face and arms hosted several cuts and burn marks. Apparently, she bore the wounds of all the dead moths.

Jason rushed to her. "Are you OK?"

She shook her head. "I'll heal soon enough," she panted. "My men need your aid."

Jason looked up. She was right. Mel was tied up in his own fight against three peacekeepers and one mage. The five remaining guards of Eula stood against the other mage and ten peacekeepers. The enemy was regrouping, pulling closer together and retreating in measured steps with their backs to the building called Second Chances.

Just like the lithium experiment, the name of the place seemed to gnaw at Jason. Where had he seen that name before?

As if to answer him, the door to Second Chances suddenly blew apart, sending an explosion of wood fragments, smoke, fire and dust out over the mages and peacekeepers. Holding much more power than Jason's arrow, it forced everyone to the ground, including Mel, Eula's armguard and Jason.

Jason looked up to see shadowy silhouettes darting back and forth through the cloud of dust. One walked towards him and emerged from the fog. Jason couldn't believe his eyes. He said the name as a question.

Chapter 13
Suusteren, The Battle of

"Ruki Provos?"

Ruki hadn't expected any of the aians who had descended upon Second Chances to know his name. His deals were good, but not that good. Definitely not worth fighting it out with mages and peacekeepers. But the fight had set off a hellish commotion, one which alerted them to the danger at their back door and provided enough time for Calais to set up a wicked spell.

Ruki blinked the dust and smoke from his eyes as he staggered out of Second Chances. Soon a familiar face appeared. Even without the face, the bone arm was unmistakable.

"Jason?"

Ruki hurried over to help Jason to his feet. "What are you doing here?"

The question was about more than Jason's presence in Suusteren. He assumed by now Jason would have gotten his ticket home along with Mike, Rich and Mel. Ah, Mel... Ruki missed her. She was by far the prettiest megrym brother he had ever laid eyes on.

Ruki reached a hand out to help Jason up but found his arms intercepted by a woman stepping into them and hugging him fiercely. Mel! This was the first time Ruki put faith in his uncle's belief in positive thinking. He hugged her back.

"Oh, I've missed you," he told her.

"Same," she said.

"Yep, don't worry about me, no need for an assist," Jason said dryly as he picked himself up off the ground.

"Why are you here?" Ruki asked Mel.

"Didn't you just ask me that?" Jason asked.

"We're here to free the aians trapped here." Mel said. "And I guess you too!"

"Capital," Ruki said.

"Plus there's probably a quest reward at the end of this," Jason said, brushing himself off.

Mel and Ruki were disengaging from their embrace, nodding at each other, sharing a moment that didn't include Jason.

"Maybe that quest reward is the ability to get noticed," Jason muttered.

More of the dust cleared, allowing Jason to get better eyes on the others who had emerged from Second Chances. He pointed a bone finger at Gina and Vincent.

"You guys?" Jason asked. "It's been months. What are you two still doing here?"

Before either of them could answer, the blind man interrupted. "Save the reunion," he said. "You think these battle mages gave up and went home to curl up with a good book? Where are all the aians?"

As if in reply, the aian refugees started filtering out of the bar. They looked on with appreciative awe at the bruised and bloody female moth warrior that stood next to Jason. They took long looks at Jason for that matter as well. The aian crowd forming started chattering amongst themselves.

"Our goddess..."

"Lady of the Tenth House..."

"Together with the Chosen One..."

"Here to save us..."

Ruki was shocked. This was Eula. He had been to Nasreddin many times to barter and trade, and whenever he had gotten a glimpse of a god they had been so well attended and thronged by crowds all he could ever catch was a raised hand waving hello. He'd never imagined he would see one here in his home city, with both his city and the god looking worse for wear than they should.

"Vylar is right," Eula said. "We must be brief."

Eula stood tall, with such dignity and poise that the cuts, bruises and burns seemed like jewelry. She held her hands out toward the aians.

"My people, we have come to rescue you along with our family and friends held in the walls of this city. Please, take this man's portal to safety while the Chosen One and I liberate the rest of our kind."

She nodded to Vylar, who in turn brought a portal swirling into existence. Without hesitation aians started running through.

Jason looked at Gina and Vincent, neither of whom were exactly getting in line to go. "Now's your chance to get away from this madness," he said.

Gina and Vincent looked at each other and shook their heads in unison. Gina addressed Jason. "Last time we tried to strike out on our own, it didn't quite work out so well. We're better off sticking with somebody who has a better idea on how to get home than we do. That means you, O' Chosen One."

"And most certainly does not mean me," Ruki said, craning his neck to see where the line to escape ended. "Excuse me, while I take this portal." The end of the line was somewhere behind Calais' frizzy hair.

Why was she shaking her head at him?

"You should ask him where it leads," Calais said.

Did it matter? A legion of angry mages with fireballs and terror dogs and the really nasty stuff was going to descend on them at any moment. Anywhere was better than here. Still, Ruki may as well as ask; he had long enough time to wait while the aians fled. He looked at the old man who had created the portal. "Where's it go?"

"Numbra Keep," Vylar answered.

"What?! Why there?"

"Only place within aian imperial lands not protected by portal dampeners. There is a war going on, you know."

Great. The Aian Empire's most notorious prison. No way was he going to show up on the tail end of this portal, the only human, and convince the Temple of Houses that he wasn't the mage who made it. They'd keep him locked up in the lowest level of Numbra Keep. Even if every aian who took the portal vouched for him, they'd be convinced he set it all up just so he could get into aian territory where he could craft a whole slew of nasty mage spells behind their backs.

Funny thing is, looking at what the mages had done to the aian citizens in Suusteren, Ruki really couldn't blame them if they did lock him away. Not that he was going to give them the opportunity.

"Do you have anywhere a bit more human hospitable?" Ruki asked.

"The Megrym Hegemony," Vylar answered.

Ruki frowned. He had gotten the better end of a few lopsided trades. Not that he had advertised them as lopsided. Needless to say, he wasn't exactly welcome in many parts of the Hegemony.

Before Ruki could ask if there was anywhere else, Vincent pointed with his hammer toward the distant end of the alley.

"Mages!" he announced.

Ruki turned to a sight that caused a rush of mortal terror. He couldn't count the mages. They had filled up the alley, rows upon rows.

The refugees were barely over half evacuated. Running now would condemn the rest of the civilians stuck on this side of the portal. And looking at the downed peacekeepers and mages, Ruki doubted that the horde of robes would be in a charitable spirit of mercy.

"Slow them down!" Calais cried. She pulled out red and black chalks, held one in either hand, and began scrawling like a mad-woman on the brick face of a nearby building on one side of the alley.

Jason grimaced. "Quivers aren't clips," he said as he nocked an arrow. "You better be quick cause ammo's short."

He loosed the arrow at the mages crowding down the alley and it met with the expected result of getting deflected by a sleeve. It did little to stop them.

Ruki joined in, aiming his diskbow at a brown robe in the middle of the pack. The disk shot out with a jarring twang. Ruki heard a yelp and saw the ranks buckle as the brown robe went down. That slowed a handful of them down in the rear, but most of the mages kept moving.

Vylar picked up some discarded paper flyers littering the ground and started shredding them, speaking spellcraft the whole while. He finished speaking, opened his hands and an unending torrent of paper bits erupted from his palms. The paper gusted down the alley with a savage howl, a manufactured blizzard.

Initially, the mages didn't slow much for the confetti onslaught, despite the poor visibility, until Jason loosed another arrow, which actually scored a mage and dropped him. Then they stopped and a couple of them started speaking spells of their own.

Calais was still scribbling furiously down the side of the brick with her red and black chalks. By now some of the aian men and women that were supposed to take the portal were joining the fight. Perhaps ten or so of various houses picked up the weapons of the fallen peacekeepers and mothguards and took positions in front of Eula.

"The fight to free our people is not only yours, my goddess," one of them, from House of Yol, said. "We stand with you and the Chosen One."

The mages in the alleyway finished casting their spell and some kind of wind ripple blasted out from their ranks. It surged toward everyone, a hurricane strength blast that not only blew the confetti back but forced the group to take a knee to prevent getting knocked down and bowled over.

Calais was now lying on her stomach. Her hands were outstretched drawing black and red lines toward the center of the clearing. The wind died, allowing her to stand and face mages who were significantly closing the gap in an all out run.

She reached into her satchel and threw some bright white powder onto the red and black chalk lines. The lines began to glow. Calais reached into the ground where the lines were and pulled out a fearsome black chain that throbbed with a wicked red light.

The mages were almost on top of them. Ruki could see various fire and ice spells springing to life in their hands.

Calais pulled the glowing chain and more of it emerged out of the ground, stretching taut as the chain ran up the side of the building Calais had been scribbling on. The chain stopped anchored around a circle of symbols that glowed black. She yanked the chain and, with a groan, the entire building came down into the alleyway on top of the mages.

A wave of dust and debris assaulted Ruki, forcing him to cover his nose and mouth with a sleeve. He could hear Jason next to him.

"Every time I see something like that I feel I rolled wrong."

"Save it," Mel said, nodding at the scant few civilians left to take the portal. "How about we bail?"

As if in agreement, the downed building started to tremble. No doubt the mages on the other side were blasting at it.

The sun was starting to rise, giving the city a fiery hue. Eula, her cuts and bruises noticeably smaller, turned to her new recruit from the House of Yol.

"Our people no longer dream here. I must rely on you and your knowledge of the city to guide us to them."

"Yes, my goddess," the aian replied with a deep nod.

He headed back through Second Chances, Eula and the rest of the aians close behind while the humans and Vincent brought up the rear. The ant aian burst through the front door and without pause took a right, first heading down the main thoroughfare before heading due east down an alley.

The sounds and smells of the city were changing. Over the constant clanging of alarm bells, distant screaming and the yells of men could be heard. Explosions. The stench of sulfur fires assaulted Ruki's nostrils.

As they ran, a door to the left burst into a shower of splinters. A pair of destruction mages emerged from the building. They immediately bent their robe sleeves, pummeling the four closest aian guards and keeping virtually everyone at bay.

Before they could get any more spells off, Vincent was on the attack. He closed the distance, sprinting under the bent sleeves like some sort of megrym lightning. Vincent took his hammer left then right into the knees of one mage, pulverizing the kneecaps. The mage yowled in agony only to be silenced a moment later by Vincent's hammer blow to the face.

Vincent wheeled to take on the other mage but by this time Mel was already on the robe. She deftly ducked and dodged the extended sleeves and chopped the mage in the windpipe with the edge of her hand. As he grasped his own throat for air, Mel grabbed handfuls of robe, fell backwards to the ground and kicked him toward Jason, whose arm club was waiting to faceplant the flying mage into an impromptu nap.

Jason looked down appreciatively at Vincent. "I see you learned your trigger."

Vincent scowled at the many wood splinters in his forearms. "Easy enough to tap into when jackasses are trying to turn you into a porcupine."

Some of the aians assisted the guardsmen that had gotten beaten about and disoriented by the black robes, and together they continued their flight down the alley. They turned northeast, down another narrow alleyway. Ruki looked up. Behind the roofs, the gray stone walls of Suusteren were growing closer. In places here and there along the walls, pockets of dense black smoke rose into the air. For the first time in his life, all his years of living here, the walls now seemed an ominous and looming presence.

They emerged out of the alley and onto the main street. The city walls were on their right. What was on their left made Ruki's breath catch in his throat.

He was never much good at remembering military units, but he was pretty sure fifty peacekeepers made one troop. And it looked to be as if a whole troop of peacekeepers were running towards them. They were led by six mages of various colors.

Vylar was all out of paper. Jason had about four arrows knocking loosely about in his quiver and Calais didn't have the time nor a building tall enough to bring down to fill a street this size.

What else could Ruki do as an army descended upon them? He cranked his diskbow and fired a shot.

Before he could tell who, if anyone, got hit by the disk, explosions in the middle of the peacekeeper's ranks set them flying about in the air. Ruki looked perplexed at his diskbow. Then he heard cheers from overhead.

Eagle aians from House Demir and moths from Eula's house were flying above them. Many carried satchels, no doubt filled with bombs. Three of them carried other aians, members of the House of Yol.

The ant-headed aian that accompanied Eula turned to her.

"Word of your daring raid has spread throughout the hive, my goddess, and from there to the siege captains outside the walls. They have joined your fight. They aim to take Suusteren this day for the Empire."

"This is exactly what I hoped to avoid," Eula said with a grimace as she looked towards the smoking, smoldering walls. "If the walls should break apart and fall, who do they fall upon?"

Chapter 14
Red Payment

If the purple green sky was a clue to Rich that he was experiencing a cost-dream, the waterfall made of spiders was the giveaway. Rich turned from the spiderfall and found a familiar face looking back at him. Far from malice, Richard Bates had an expectant look on his face, as if he had been patiently waiting for Rich to arrive.

"Welcome back, finally, to adult costs."

Rich hadn't seen his former face in so long he had kind of missed the little bastard.

"Been awhile," Rich said. "I see spiders are still all the rage."

"Blame yourself for that, mage," Richard Bates said. "If you had an irrational fear of puppies then you'd be swimming neck deep in a pool of adorable mutts. Like so."

Richard Bates snapped his fingers and Rich found himself in a giant vat of puppies. Puppies below, puppies all around, little dalmations and pugs and terriers and hounds and shepherds and setters, all of them with tiny bite-sized barks and wagging happy tails. Rich had never seen this many puppies and didn't know if it was real physics or some strange force which permeated the vat, but Rich had to swim to keep his head above the mass of adorable little dogs.

The voice of Richard Bates spoke over the whines and barks of the puppies. "But of course, costs aren't made to be pleasant."

Suddenly, the puppies turned vicious. Horns grew out of their heads. Their maws became distended, filled with jagged teeth, hot breath and forked tongues. They had snake eyes.

Rich let out a scream despite himself, jarred by the complete turn from the loveable fluffy puppy armada to demon dog horde. There was nowhere to swim where he could get away.

He heard a loud snap and instantly they were gone. Rich stood alone in absolute darkness. A moment later, a spotlight beamed down on him.

Another spotlight turned on, illuminating Richard Bates, who walked towards Rich.

Rich looked at the cost. The being more often than not wore his own face from his original Earthly body, as if it was a pair of floparound shoes, while he dispensed cruel and unusual punishments to the point that Rich despised and abhorred his own visage. And in looking at the cost, looking at himself, as it were, and listening to what the cost was saying, it occurred to Rich that he had failed to ask this being the most rudimentary of questions.

"Why aren't costs made to be pleasant?"

Richard Bates smirked. "I imagine you expect me to say something malicious and nonsensical, like 'because evil must feed mu ha ha ha' or some such," he said. "But no. It's a transaction, one you initiated. You took from the Onesource at your own pleasure. Hence, you have to give back at your displeasure. This, and only this," Richard Bates wagged a finger at Rich, "restores balance."

Rich shrugged. "I still don't get this premium you place on balance."

Richard Bates nodded grimly. "I imagine you wouldn't. Your world is a far different cry from the one you're on now despite their spiritual affinity. And your world's been out of balance your whole life. But the Onesource is there, permeating the planet as with all things. It cannot remain out of balance. Volcanoes erupt from pressure, storms clear the air and, even if it has to flood half a town, water always finds its level. Speaking of..."

Richard Bates snapped his fingers and the darkness around them evaporated, replaced with a morning sky. Rich looked down and noticed he was standing on air as if it were solid ground. Him and Richard Bates were suspended high above a seacoast town. The walls smoked in places. Fires raged in small pockets dotting the city. Halfway between Rich and the ground, moth and eagle aians flew in formation like jet fighter squadrons. They'd throw firebombs from sacks that would explode on impact. From the ground, intense beams that reminded Rich of railgun bolts in movies would shoot up and fry the aian flyers. Rich didn't know if those beams were magic, technology, or a wicked combination of the two.

Rich had only been here once and briefly, but still, he recognized the place.

"Suusteren?"

"Oh, Razzleblad, I had such high hopes for you," Richard Bates said. "I want you to note this isn't the future or the past you're witnessing, but the now. I tried to pull you to Suusteren because I so keenly wanted you to be part of this. It's nothing short of history in the making."

He pointed to the beach and as he pointed they moved in closer to the area, effectively zooming in on the action below. The battle was intense along the shore, with aian warriors from the squid house of Menanderus and the fish house of Baligoz fighting from the depths. Peacekeepers and mages trudged waist deep in the water to keep the aians from getting a foothold on the beach. Bodies, aian and human alike, floated along the coast, staining the water a foamy pale red.

The aians in the rear ranks, the furthest from the action on the beach, jolted unnaturally as if the water had become electrified. Their eyes rolled back into their heads until only the whites of their eyes showed. Then they disappeared beneath the waves as if they had been pulled under. Moments later, another back rank of aians were jolted and pulled under.

More spasmed and disappeared below the water. The ranks in the front noticed and turned. At the same time, something immense began to surface. Everyone, the aians in the water and the men on the beach, backed away as they stared in horror at the growing monster.

Rich didn't know if the thing was alive. How could it be? It was as if all the sea life in the bay had been thrust together into one large, writhing mass of fins and flippers, a patchwork giant. Twisted scales gave way to hard carapace shells that melted into the smooth skin of seals and dolphins and back again. The thing had a thousand eyes and a million teeth all over what constituted its body, a body that was devoid of discernible shape or dimension.

"What the hell is it?" Rich asked breathlessly.

"He calls it the Atrox," Richard Bates answered. "But I don't think the name much matters."

Rich's understanding stumbled on the first word. "He?"

"Now, that's a better question," Richard Bates said with a wicked grin. "Are your eyes ready to feast? I know mine are. Let's look!"

He pointed and their perspective zoomed in closer. They moved past the shore, where aians and human warriors alike had forgotten all about the battle to flee the monster together. Rich and his cost flew across large swaths of undulating scales and slimy skin until they came to rest hovering directly above creature. There, in the dead center of the beast, stood a man in a gray robe smiling gleefully.

Clemson Goodchild.

It almost looked as if the mage was a part of the Atrox. Barnacles crusted over the bottom of his robe, securing him to the creature. Dozens of fine tendrils similar to those of jellyfish extended out of both his sleeves and into the Atrox. Clemson grasped the tendrils in both hands as if they were reins.

The gray robe looked up at them as if he could see them there. It made Rich jump back in shock.

"Is this what you want?" he asked, the smile still plastered on his face. "Moloch pays you, Clemson Goodchild. Moloch will make these errant mages pay, and these aians pay, these worthless towns-people, too. They all pay! Everything pays!"

He finished with hoarse laughter. Clemson had addressed himself as Moloch, the equivalent of Rich calling himself Razzleblad. It was obvious to Rich the guy was past the point of reason, made mad by the cost. The gray robe pulled up on the tendril reins and the Atrox monster lurched high into the air until it towered three or four stories above the people running on the beach. It roared, a sound fueled by both rage and agony at its own tortured existence.

"I admit," Richard Bates said, "working with you would've been a lot less disgusting, Razzleblad. But it's not like I have to touch the thing. And, honestly, who can argue with this level of showman-ship?"

"How can such a thing... be?" Rich asked.

"Magelord magic is insanely powerful," Richard Bates said. "And when you couple insanely powerful with all out insane, you're bound to get things a rational mind just wouldn't consider. Case in point; check out the tentacles, man."

They zoomed out to take in the front of the monster. The beast had three giant tentacles formed from the fusion of countless squid and octopi. At the end of the tentacles clumps of giant jellyfish clustered like fists. From the fists, an obscene amount of jellyfish tendrils snaked haphazardly in the air.

But there were some tendrils that weren't waving in the air. Those tendrils were wrapped around and speared through the aians the Atrox had recently caught when it was below the water's surface. The aians dangled above the ground, suspended by the tendrils, now a part of the Atrox. Their eyes were milky white. Their skin was blue.

"It gets better," Richard Bates whispered in his ear.

The Atrox whipped its three tentacles around and the dangling aians flew about limply as if they were cadavers on a carnival ride. The Atrox lashed out at the people fleeing it on the beach.

As the tentacles extended, the limp aians suddenly came alive. They reached out with their arms and grabbed some of the fleeing human and aian warriors.

The captured warriors screamed, only for the sound to cut off in a sickly squelch as jellyfish tendrils wrapped around and pierced them.

They were now new additions to the Atrox. Their eyes went milky white and they too turned blue as they went limp alongside the ones who had grabbed them in the first place.

None of this was possible. Nothing halfway close to this existed in any spellbook Rich had read. Even the history of magic, the *Birleshik Arcana*, and the spellcraft theory books he had studied made no mention of being able to fuse living beings together, keep the new creature alive, and control it. Not even two houseflies, let alone something on this grand scale.

Richard Bates seemed to know what he was thinking.

"Even when you zoom way out, it's an impressive accomplishment. Observe."

The scene blurred. Rich and his cost were on the streets of Suusteren. Bombed out, crumbling buildings provided a clear view of the towering Atrox in the distance. The Atrox bellowed an agonized roar, lashed out its three tentacles and collected more people.

Rich became aware of someone sidling up next to him. It was Jason carrying his arm club in his bone hand. Jason looked at the monster with utter disbelief.

"What the hell is that?" he asked.

Rich faced Jason. "It's the gray robe from the Pendulum. He's gone mad."

Jason didn't respond. Suddenly Mel and Eula walked through Rich as if he wasn't there and the realization returned to Rich that he wasn't, not really.

"Never in all my immortal years have I seen such an abomination," Eula said as she stared at it.

As if in response to being called an abomination, the distant Atrox whipped its tentacles again, demolishing the closest buildings in a cloud of rubble and debris.

"I've got to go," Rich said. "I've got to stop this."

"Oh, you had your chance to stop this, Razzleblad, but you forsook that along with your gray robes. Don't get me wrong, I still have hopes for you, mage, not as high as they once were, but hopes nonetheless. Regardless, do you really think your power can compare to Moloch's now?"

"It doesn't matter," Rich retorted. "I can't just sit here and do nothing."

Richard Bates shook his head. "You forget what this is, Razzleblad. This isn't some simple bad dream you can awaken from when it perturbs you enough. This is the cost, muted as it may be now that you've taken the oath. And this cost requires you to sit idly by and watch, completely powerless as this abomination wreaks death and devastation upon the innocent and your friends alike. Now, as much as I'd love to see if your plucky courage and pure moxy can win against insane magelord magic, even I'm beholden to my one and only rule. Everyone, everything pays. Everything must."

Richard Bates sat on a pile of rubble. He leaned over to an adjacent pile of broken bricks and brushed some of the dirt off. "Have a seat, Razzleblad, and pay your cost."

The cost wasn't something that was going to drive him mad anymore, but it was still far from easy. If anything, it was a different kind of difficult. Rich was action-based, the kind of guy who needed to *do*. He was the same person that had stormed the Hierophane's dungeons as a brown robe when he had discovered Rew was held captive.

Stuck here watching was its own special hell.

"I'll stand," Rich told his cost. At least he had control over that.

"Uh, friends," a familiar voice called behind Rich. He turned. Ruki Provos? Apparently the merchant had hooked up with Mel, Jason, Vylar and Eula. Clemson's old gaming buddies Gina and Vincent were here as well, along with an entirely different team of aian warriors and a frizzy-haired black girl Rich had never met. Ruki pointed at the Atrox.

"What are we doing about that?" he asked. "I'm assuming it's portal time. At the very least we should be running the opposite way."

Mel shook her head.

"Can't you see what this thing is doing? It's growing, feeding on the people of Suusteren. We have to stop it."

Jason shook his head as the Atrox heaved its way steadily into the city, crashing its tentacles with a terrible shudder into any building in its path, grabbing any wretch unfortunate enough to not escape its ferocious reach.

"I dunno... I'm with Ruki on this one. This seems a bit over our current level, whatever that is."

The black girl took a step forward. "There's no running from this. The next time we see it, at the very least it'll be the size of a city. This city."

While everyone looked at the Atrox, Richard Bates leaned over to Rich. "That's Calais. I like her. When it comes to paying the cost, she's about getting the whole community involved. Socialism at its finest."

The Atrox was steadily moving inland. Aian flying squadrons dropped firebombs on it. Chunks of Atrox exploded.

It lashed its tentacles in the air but, for the most part, the flyers were faster. They expertly broke formation and flew around the tentacles and formed up again once they had cleared the threat.

The Atrox seemed to be learning from its encounters with opposition. Instead of lashing out at the last band of flyers, the Atrox retracted its tentacle into its side, to the point where only the giant clump of jellyfish showed, the aians and humans dangling from it inert and innocuous. Suddenly the tentacle shot out like a missile, quicker than what seemed possible. All the trapped blue warriors reached out and they plucked an entire formation of flyers into their ranks.

Standing next to Eula, an aian from House of Yol spoke. "Reports from the hive say there's a man on top of the creature. A gray robed mage."

Vylar grimaced. "I don't know what this thing is. I've never heard a beast sound like that, neither the roar nor the sound of it moving. The smell is dead, a stench that's everywhere yet nowhere specific. I can't get a mental picture of it. I'm blind to it."

Some of the rail gun devices in the city fired at the Atrox. Many of the beam blasts flashed harmlessly over it. A scant few scored near the top of the beast, blasting monster chunks to rain down on the city below. The Atrox howled in anguish.

The monster spread itself out, reducing itself in height while swelling at its base. Now Rich could barely see much of it, like a writhing horizon behind ruined buildings in the distance. All the rail gun blasts shot well over the thing. Apparently only the aian flyers would be able to score hits on it from a relatively safe distance.

But the flyers wouldn't engage. Instead they were flying to the city walls. In short order all the squads flew over the walls, away from the city entirely.

"Where are they going, Induryol?" Eula asked.

"Orders from the generals," the ant aian replied. Rich assumed he was Induryol. "All units have been recalled."

"Why?" Eula asked exasperated. "We need those flyers in the air against this thing."

Induryol shook his head. "This isn't our fight. Virtually everyone in the hive mind is unanimous in that respect. Let the mages kill each other. We hang back to claim the city in the wake."

"Tell them to press the attack!" Eula cried. "What if this thing *is* the wake? It's only getting stronger."

Induryol stood still and quiet for a long, tense moment. "I'm sorry, my goddess. The generals have spoken. They want me to inform you their power is vested in the war council of seven houses, the voice of Yol, of Inanna, of Menanderus, of Nadi, of..."

Eula waved her hand. She had heard enough.

"That's it, then," she said looking at the creature. "It rests upon us."

Richard Bates stood up and turned a sly grin on Rich.

"Man, right about now she is not a happy goddess. And it's not gonna get any better, you know? Any minute now, I think the full scope of what's in store will dawn on her."

"What do you mean?" Rich asked.

As if to answer his question, those oblivious to his presence explained. First was Vylar.

He shrugged and shook his head. "As much as you feel it's up to us, Lady of Tenth House, I'm in no shape to fight this thing, any more than you would be if someone blind folded you and turned you in circles. I'm leaving."

"We need you," Eula replied. "My people are still trapped within the walls. Surely you won't sit back and allow this thing feed on them?"

Jason pointed to it. "I know we can barely see the thing, but it's got speed now. And it's headed to the walls."

"Quick!" Eula cried. "We've got to evacuate them before it arrives!"

They all took off in a sprint, even Vylar.

Richard Bates raised two fingers in the air and flicked them towards the surging blob of Atrox in the distant foreground. The world blurred around Rich and the cost. When the blur ceased they were once again suspended over the city, close enough to the Atrox to get caught up in its ensnaring tentacles if it could touch them.

The Atrox, flattened out to the size of a one story building, was about as big as a city block. It had indeed picked up speed. The front of it, if Rich could call anything on it a 'front', moved by causing its flesh to lurch forward a pocket at a time in seemingly random places, like a hundred goliath fists trying to punch through a wall of dough over and over. It was demolishing any building in its way. All those pockets of flesh punching forward to drive the monster had serious power behind them. Beyond that, they were not just an amalgamation of fin and shell and skin, but also eyes, many of which had been gouged shut from impacts with the buildings.

And teeth. Teeth extended all over the creature in patchwork Frankenmouths that gnashed and snarled and frothed rabidly. Some of the civilians that thought they could bunker down to escape the war encountered those teeth as the creature punched through any structure in its way. They weren't snared by the creature but eaten. And in either measure, the creature grew.

The mages fought valiantly against the threat. A dozen black robes pelted its sides with fireballs, blasting chunks out of the beast. A handful of red robes levitated hefty slabs of building rubble, improvised missiles that they shot with crushing force through the creature. An orange robe had altered her own body into glistening steel. Blades protruded from her from all angles. She ran through the side of the creature to emerge a minute later gore soaked on the other side.

These attacks weren't enough. Any mage close enough to affect it with magic was also close enough to get grabbed by its enslaving tentacles. The mages were adept at maneuvering thanks to magical chains, bent sleeves and portals but despite their mobility some mages still fell to the Atrox's grasp.

There had to be over a hundred people dangling from the tentacles now, the blue, morbid fruit of the Atrox.

Portals opened up above the creature. Two blue and one purple robe fell from the portal to land atop the creature, near to where Clemson controlled the beast with its fistful of tendril reins. Rich was glad to know the mages had figured it out and were going to cut the head off the beast.

Clemson never bothered to look at them. He pulled one rein and tugged the other. The flesh of the creature parted with a sickening tear where the blue and purple robes stood. The mages unceremoniously fell into the Atrox, their screams silenced abruptly as the Atrox's rent flesh slammed shut once again.

"And to think, you wanted to run off and tangle with this thing," Richard Bates said. "You should be thanking me, Razzleblad."

"Thank you?" Rich asked incredulously. "You asshole, you caused this! You made Clemson Baines into this. Moloch's your creation just as sure as the Atrox is his. And for what?"

Richard Bates shook his head. "Don't ask questions you already know the answers to. A better question is what happens now?"

He pointed. They zoomed ahead of the Atrox. Now they were in the detention camp. The living conditions in the camp were deplorable. Shelter for the aians consisted of little more than broken hovels and crude shanties. Trash and refuse littered the ground everywhere. The sky was obscured like a prison yard, with the smaller yet still foreboding inner wall forming three sides of a square with the outer wall, which stood three times higher.

Jason and his team had arrived. Vylar had three portals open. The aian civilians were evacuating but portals are only so big and there were so many people. The evacuation was going too slow.

Rich didn't know if the cost was doing it, but the next moment everything seemed to slow down.

The short inner wall exploded in a cloud of dust. Out of the cloud huge chunks of rocks came crashing down onto civilians. Aians fled in panicked screams.

A huge chunk of rock fell towards Eula, threatening to crush her. Jason bounded to her.

"Onus!" he cried and raised his hands in the air.

The giant slab of wall came down and the two of them disappeared.

Where the inner wall had once stood, a cloud of dust dissipated to reveal the Atrox. It made its way into the detention camp.

The Atrox lashed out with its tentacles at the masses of people, all of them penned in with nowhere to run.

Rich couldn't count the number of people the Atrox claimed in those swipes. He looked for the people he knew. Ruki had already hit the deck before the tentacles lashed out. Calais pulled Gina down in time to avoid being scooped up and turned blue.

That left Vylar. The tentacle was fast approaching him. He couldn't see it coming.

Vincent dived at Vylar to bring him down before the tentacle claimed him.

Neither one made it. The tentacle passed the spot where Vylar had stood and Vincent had dived. After the tentacle passed the spot was empty. No Vylar. No Vincent. Both of them gone, now inextricably part of the monster.

Rich stared mutely, in shock, unable to process what he just saw. He turned to Richard Bates.

"You're fucking with me. That didn't really happen."

Richard Bates shook his head. "The truth is a lot more disturbing than anything I could invent. And sometimes when the end comes it is unceremonious, inglorious. It is what it is."

Rich was sure the Atrox wasn't going to stop lashing out with its tentacles until it claimed every last life in the detention center. Then he saw Mel. She was striding toward the Atrox, her feet sure, her jaw clenched.

The Atrox lashed out with its tentacles.

Mel, in an unbelievable display of both suicidal tendencies and acrobatics, leapt at the nearest lashing tentacle. She sliced the hands reaching for her with her sword, severing the appendages before they could grasp her. Mel grabbed at a blue arm and hoisted herself up, jumping and dodging the tendrils that sought to embed themselves in her.

She proceeded to run down the length of the tentacle with speed that didn't seem real. Once she was close enough to the bulk of the Atrox, Mel dived off the tentacle.

Mel landed in a roll on top of the creature and then sprang out of the roll into a run with that blinding cheetah speed.

Clemson was aware of the warrioress rushing toward him. The flesh of the Atrox opened in rifts under Mel.

But Mel was too fast, too agile. She'd jump deftly to and fro, dodging the openings as she continued to close the distance.

Clemson tried to open a giant chasm between himself and Mel. Mel hurdled the gap. She pointed her sword forward. She closed the remaining distance and drove the sword into Clemson's gut.

The mage gasped. The Atrox shuddered.

"It's time you die," Mel said with gritted teeth.

Clemson sputtered blood. He shook his head. "It's... time... you... pay!" he shouted.

The Atrox shook like it was the epicenter of an earthquake. Then the monster imploded. The bulk of the center sank down drastically, as if the fist of God had punched it down like dough. Both Clemson and Mel, still on top of the Atrox, sank out of sight. The tentacles curved up and folded themselves into the depression. Then it seemed as if the rest of the Atrox followed, with its mass feeding into the hole.

A gray wave boomed out of the creature, with light so intense Rich had to close his eyes. He could feel the whole city tremble.

When he opened his eyes, Suusteren was actively being destroyed. The booming explosion had created a sinkhole and half the city had fallen into it. Now the sea sat higher than the sunken half of Suusteren and water from the bay was pouring in.

Rich tried to find the part of the city Jason and the rest had been in. He needed to see who had survived that. It was impossible to get a clear view. Gray motes hung thick in the air. At first Rich thought it was dust from collapsed buildings but the gray motes began to clump together in the air. The motes spread more and more, forming a shell. Soon most of the collapsed and ruined city was covered by the shell, which glistened in the sun as it hardened.

There would be no seeing through that.

"You would do well to remember that I don't talk just because I like the sound of your teenage voice," Richard Bates said. "Instructions, warnings, advice, they're all there if you know how to listen."

Rich looked at the hard shelled chrysalis that obscured the depths of the sunken town and where his friends may have fallen. Richard Bates' words came unbidden to him, the thing the cost had said about balance.

"Even if it has to flood half a town, water always finds its level."

Chapter 15
Into the Blue

Rich stared at his reflection, his worry and desperation easy to see in the early morning light. Neither Mel nor Jason responded to his invocation of the mirror link. He called for Mel again. He only saw himself looking back, the modest campsite among short grass plains and Rew's slender hand caress his shoulder. She had been there to comfort him after awaking from the cost. He may not have woken up screaming his head off, but that didn't mean it was easy to stomach.

"I know I'm still an amateur at portals," Rich said, looking at her from the inert mirror, "but from what I've studied portaling over there is really stupid idea, right?"

Rew nodded. "From what you described with the battle and this Atrox monster, Suusteren's topography has changed too much to trust a portal. What was once open streets and empty rooms could now house mountains of rubble. A portal that opens into solid rock doesn't make the rock any less solid. No mage should portal there unless driven mad or desperate."

Didn't this count as desperation? A want bordering on need prodded at Rich to go to Suusteren and offer any aid he could, no matter how little. The only thing that kept him from acting on it was Rew's words. Jumping out of a portal into his own immediate demise would help no one.

He felt Rew's hand grip his shoulder tighter.

"Even though everything about your cost feels true and final," she said, "hold a measure of hope that you were shown some falsehoods, and all our friends are okay."

Rich nodded as he looked at Rew. She must understand the feeling all too well. In her many lifetimes lived, she probably could no longer count the times she had seen friends and allies die. Or worse, what if she could... each and every one she'd prematurely lost permanently etched into a memory that did not blunt with age. Did it ever get any easier?

He didn't ask that question. Instead, he asked, "into Lapis Deep, then?"

"Yes," Rew agreed. "Let's set upon our mission. The best way to honor our friends is to not fail them."

Reluctantly Rich put the mirror away. Together he and Rew cleaned up the campsite to finish the journey towards Lapis Deep. Rew had a healthy respect for the place and her closest portal was miles away from the cave system to prevent emerging into immediate danger when they took it. The distance turned into a small blessing when within a few moments after arriving the feeling of an upcoming cost payment cycle hit Rich and they decided to camp for the night. That said, Rich couldn't help feeling like a toddler who needed to pee two miles into a road trip.

But now the site was broken down and Rew had already done the work of creating, attuning and securing a wind channel while Rich had cost dreamt. It was a terrible shame because Rich had seen them in his studies, but the process was so convoluted and the warnings so dire he hadn't dared trying to build one. Seeing one built would've gone a long way to helping him master them.

Rew reached for Rich. Rich took her hand, felt a measure of reassurance in its warm grip and the next moment he saw the world blur around him. It was immediately familiar, like any of his favorite sci-fi movies where they turn on the hyperdrive. The world streamed past Rich.

"Whoa..." he breathed as they stopped and the scene unblurred. Lapis Deep was more canyon than cavern. Porous blue-gray rock stretched fifty feet into the air. It didn't seem like a cave because the roof was home to gaping giant holes. The remaining rock overhead formed slender archways bridging the cavern ceiling. Sunlight streamed in brightly. Vivid green moss grew down the sides of the arches, the cave walls and the floors of the cavern.

"It's like a blue Grand Canyon," Rich said as he looked around, looked up to take it all in. "Only greener and with holes... like it's made out of Swiss cheese."

Rew's eyes joined his looking up at the majestic vault of Lapis Deep. "In ancient times, a grand and powerful waterway had flowed topside, slowly eating away at the rock, leaving the archways and hollowing out the vast cavern we're standing in. No one knows how many millennia that feat took but no matter my years and accomplishments I feel small, inconsequential compared to the titanic forces that created this."

Lapis Deep smelled of old earth and new rain. It felt timeless, a place that seemed like it was always here and would always be, no matter what squabbles and troubles people got themselves into. It was beyond such things.

Rew turned to face Rich, compelling him to stop sight-seeing and return her gaze.

"Dangerous things dwell here, amongst the beauty. Are you ready?"

Rich nodded. He brushed his red robes off for good measure.

Rew led the way.

Together they set off further into Lapis Deep. The sound of their footsteps seemed loud to Rich, a jarring, unnatural commotion competing with birdsong and the crick of insects. The giant holes in the ceiling began to shrink, replaced by smaller, more numerous openings. Sunlight came down as if being directed through spotlights.

"All the world's a stage," Rich whispered.

The gray cavern walls started to change with deep blue mineral veins appearing in sharp streaks. That was the lapis lazuli.

They came to an abrupt halt. The cavern floor ended at a ledge, with a severe drop of fifty feet. A thousand spots of patchy sunlight illuminated a cave floor rich with green-blue moss.

"Not exactly wheelchair accessible is it?" Rich asked looking down. He looked over to Rew. "Magic our way down?"

"Normally, I'd say yes," Rew said. "But the Beautiful Ones, it's hard to know if they're drawn towards magic. While we can't be sure, the few mages that have braved this place all agree that the less magic they employed the safer they felt. Let's ascribe to that ascetic."

She led the way to the far cavern wall, which was covered with an intense lapis vein that practically glowed cobalt blue. The closer they got the more apparent the stairs were that had been carved out of the lapis. They looked like planks that floated, as if suspended by magic of their own.

"I didn't even see these things," Rich said.

"Lots of artists and artisans traveled here ages ago," Rew said. "Some of the first were architects."

They descended the stairs. Rich felt similar to how he felt when he first arrived in the Temple of Houses, like he was walking through a living, breathing rock giant. He entertained the notion of these stairs being ribs.

On this lower level of Lapis Deep the overhead sunlight seemed distant, as if someone had poked holes in a tall warehouse roof with a pencil. However, the light didn't just fall. Crystals and mirrors had been placed on knee-high platforms throughout the cavern, causing the light that filtered down to bounce, reflect, refract and dance. The cavern floor was home to lush ferns and mosses that thrived in dense patches in between large swaths of completely barren earth. The crystal and mirror platforms were largely overgrown with moss and ivy. Everything the light touched glittered. The contrasting darkness seemed oppressive, complete.

"So cool," Rich whispered.

"I like it too," Rew said. "This was done by the painters, like Iyla and Bazzel, who wanted to experiment with chiaroscuro—a treatment of light and darkness contrasting together on canvas. A few of their works grace the Hierophane. Remind me to show them to you if we ever restore things back to the way they were."

"It's not a matter of if," Rich replied, "but when."

Rew smiled. "I do love your optimism."

Together, they walked in this unique place. It felt like a park to Rich, one where light and shadow were more the focus than trees and grass. Because of the mirrors and crystals and the chiaroscuro effect, everything that could catch light sparkled, including Rew's eyes. Rich remembered there was a time when she looked at him in a way that was magic in its own right. The thought of it pained him.

"I talked myself out of us," Rich blurted out into a world of glittering lights and cascading darkness.

The words made Rew stop short. "Say again?"

"Us," he repeated, letting out an exasperated sigh. "You and me. After you found out what I had done to Druze, the stone spell, I told myself that you hated me. It was your eyes, you see. They looked so betrayed. I felt like the lowest grime on the planet, where I just wanted to slink away and hope you forgot all about me. Like there would be forgiveness in the forgetfulness, you know?"

Rich looked around, at a world twinkling back in sporadic bursts like a pocket universe, and rubbed the back of his neck.

"I'm terrible at explaining this," he said. He exhaled and looked back at Rew. Now she was staring at him intently.

"I'm sorry," he said. "Sorry for lying. For hurting you. I'm sorry things aren't different between us... I miss how we were."

The silence stretched long and taut between them. Finally Rew shook her head.

"You may be a special brand of foolish that borders insanity to worry about such matters in the most inopportune of places," Rew said. She reached out and stroked his jaw with delicate fingers.

"But you are ever sweet, Rich. I haven't forgotten."

She leaned closer, her lips slowly, softly pursed around his top lip. He returned the kiss, enjoying the delicate fullness of her bottom lip between his. She did it again, this time moving her mouth down ever so slightly to take his bottom lip into hers. It seemed so much more than a kiss, as if he was feeling a promise being made between the two of them.

She pulled away. They both smiled from the exchange. It was a perfect moment, one he saw ruining imminently with what he was about to say. Still, he felt he had to explain.

"About me and Mel..." he began.

"Is between you and her," Rew cut him off. "You don't belong to me, any more than you belong to her. I know because when that happens the whole world knows it, sees it and there's no room for anything else. Now, Rich, are you ready to continue?"

Rich grinned. "Lead the way."

The chiaroscuro park became darker and darker the further they went. Up ahead, a cobalt blue glow cut through the growing gloom, a welcoming beacon that undulated and wavered as if it was in motion. The light was fractured, broken into pieces by sharp angled silhouettes.

As they neared the silhouettes, the source of the blue light peaked out from the background, revealing itself to be netherfire. Unlike any netherfire Rich had seen before, like in the sconces throughout Fort Law or in the hands of Druze Wozencraft, this was not a ball of fire. This netherfire moved. It looked like liquid neon, blossoming upwards from a giant stone fountain to cascade down on all sides. The fire never stopped sprouting out of the fountain or flowing down.

Rich cast his gaze down to find the base of the fountain, to see where the fire ended. Instead, he found a four fingered hand reaching out to grab him from the darkness.

He jumped back in alarm. The hand stayed still, ever reaching. Rich's eyes followed the hand down the arm to a shoulder that disappeared into a block of stone. It was carved.

Rich looked around. The blocky silhouettes that had previously obscured the netherfire fountain were now clearly visible. All of them were unfinished sculptures. Men's muscular torsos and women's legs emerged from the stone pillars. Missing fingers, missing toes and other incomplete body parts dotted the stone. A few pillars displayed buildings, half of a carved Temple of Houses and other places Rich had never seen. A sea of faces, broken nosed and chipped mouth, stared at Rich with hollow, pupil less eyes.

"They call it the peculiar graveyard," Rew whispered. "This is where the sculptors honed their craft. They all chased perfection and the things you see here fell short of their pursuit."

The pillars, with their grasping arms and marred faces halfway steeped in darkness unsettled Rich. "Isn't this poor light to do this kind of thing?"

"There's many myths surrounding the peculiar graveyard," Rew said, her voice still a whisper. "Some say pure white light used to bloom here, powered by a combination of every kind of magical light, from red illusionary fire to the Black Calefaction you needed to summon to break brown. Now only the netherfire remains. Others say that it was always blue-dark this way on purpose, for the sculptor that could emerge from here perfecting their craft could chisel the most intricately detailed sculptures on demand anywhere in the world."

She leaned in closer to Rich, close until her mouth hovered right beside his ear. "One thing is sure," she whispered. "Many of the Beautiful Ones began what passes for their life here, born of the graveyard. It is not unreasonable to suspect they come back from time to time. For this reason, if you have something you need to say, do so in this fashion. Okay?"

She pulled away. Rich nodded.

Rew threaded her way through the assembly of half carved sculptures, Rich following closely behind. Absent of a fuel source like gas or wood, the netherfire flowing from the giant fountain droned like dull wind through the chamber. Over that eerie backdrop, their feet padded on hard packed earth like timid knocks on a stranger's door.

A scratching, scuffling sound arrested their trek through the peculiar graveyard. Slowly, they wove between the pillars, crept toward the sound. Suddenly, Rew held up her hand to stop Rich.

Looking over her shoulder, Rich saw an incomplete statue lying on the ground. Unlike the other statue of the graveyard, this one wasn't incomplete because part of it hadn't been carved but because it had been partially destroyed. One armed, it lied on the armless side, a side that had been blackened, heavily charred. The char extended down to its waist where the statue abruptly ended in jagged fragments. Its legs were nowhere to be found, but the inordinate amount of debris in the immediate area could very well have been the legs. Its other arm still existed, at least from the elbow down to the hand. This was the arm it reached for.

Rich thought it was some kind of modern art display until the arm reaching for the severed appendage moved on its own accord, scratching at the ground as if trying to pull its body closer to the arm. It scuffled itself and inch or so closer then reached out again in an effort to collect itself.

A Beautiful One. The thing seemed concerned with its task and hadn't noticed them yet. Rew retreated quietly and Rich followed suit, slinking back until the living statue was no longer visible. They could still hear the scritch-shuffle.

Rew approached Rich and spoke into his ear. "Netherfire hurled into it."

Rich nodded. *Druze*. He passed netherfire around like gym students passed basketballs. It looked like the two of them were picking up his trail.

They worked their way around the broken Beautiful One, continuing their trek through the peculiar graveyard. Rich realized as he swallowed down some of the butterflies fluttering that he had been hoping for an easier time, that Druze had picked elsewhere for his target. Rich had to admit there wouldn't be much of a mage duel if he and Druze got into it down here. He had only picked up a handful of red spells. Rich barely held his own back when he was gray. The thought of that made Rich realize something, a notion that should've been obvious to him the whole time. He leaned into Rew's ear.

"Druze is a gray robe, isn't he?"

Rew nodded. She cupped a hand around Rich's ear.

"One of the only two in the world, until you showed up."

Soon the liquid netherfire fountain was at their backs. The half carved pillars became less frequent. The darkness ahead seemed foreboding and ominous.

"Why didn't he wear the color?" Rich whispered. "Why didn't you?"

"I was Hierophant," she reminded him. "It has its own robe of station. And my father didn't care for the added attention."

Rich grimaced, not that anyone would see it in the dark. It seemed unfair, for these two gray robes to go around wearing everything but. Meanwhile, that gray robe had gotten Rich into all sorts of trouble.

Firelight, a traditional red glow, flickered ahead, filling in the shape of the cavern. The walls had converged to what was now a narrow pass. Rew sidled through first, followed by Rich. As Rich cleared the pass, the sight of what was in the new cavern made his breath catch in his throat.

The red firelight belonged to a mage wearing dark robes. The mage held the illusionary fire high overhead, making it hard to see if the mage was a man or woman. It could've been Druze for all Rich could tell. Under the mage's control the fire kept changing shape, morphing into a cat, a dog, a castle, a dove. The fire also gave ghastly definition to a sea of Beautiful Ones surrounding the mage.

These Beautiful Ones were so very far from their namesake. They were not mere living statues. They appeared to have been flesh and blood, the skin flayed off so the muscle could be seen in many places and in other places the muscle had been stripped off to reveal the bones.

It didn't just end with skin and muscle removal. The flesh and bone had been, for a lack of a better term, styled. On several, the skin had been flayed to curve like flower petals, with muscles sprouting out of the bloom. Bones had been added, where ribs extended like bat wings from the guts of some and skeletal arms burst out of the backs of others.

Despite all these badly mutilated and perversely shaped bodies, it was their faces that were the most disturbing. Devoid of eyelids their staring eyes seemed to bulge. A lack of skin gave their exposed teeth the semblance of smiling, a frozen rictus of a grin that made Rich shudder uncontrollably.

And all these staring eyes, those grinning smiles, were locked on the mage. The mage brought the illusionary fire down lower, revealing his face, the harsh scars and harsher blue hair.

Delv.

Chapter 16
They Hurt You Every Time

Rich gasped without thinking. A heady mix of both fear and rage surged through him at the sight of the mage that had gotten into his mind and tortured him within an inch of cost breaking him.

Even now, Delv's presence was posing a direct threat on Rich's life. Gasps make noise, especially in a cave. While the vast majority of the three dozen or so Beautiful Ones surrounding Delv and his impromptu magic show kept their attention on him, a handful of them turned their skinless heads towards Rich. Their heads turned in stuttery-jerk motions that were wholly unnatural, a testament that they were driven more by magic than by muscle. Their unblinking, bulging eyes fixed on Rich and Rew.

Rich dry swallowed. The Beautiful Ones didn't move. He risked a quick glance back to Delv, unsure of what kind of encounter this even was. He half expected the illusionary fire the blue robe conjured to become the real kind that gets hurled at the person dumb enough to take their eyes of the bastard.

That's when Delv cracked a wry grin.

"I would say welcome to the show," he said, "but with these things, who can tell if it's even a show."

Delv was right in that regard. The Beautiful Ones didn't look entertained, or delighted or angry or curious. They just looked. But whatever they thought, if they thought while looking at the fire, it kept them from ripping off Delv's nose to see how it worked.

Rich noticed a bead of sweat trickle down the blue robe's temple. Still, Delv kept that sick grin on his face and even shot Rich a wink as his illusionary fire morphed into a flaming bear.

"Better start working on your own performance," he said.

The five Beautiful Ones that were now focused on the newcomers moved in stuttery steps towards Rich and Rew. Every instinct in Rich told him that direct aggression against these creatures would lead him to that special place where poor choices were rewarded with agonizing pain. Instead, he followed Delv' lead and conjured illusionary fire into his hand and held it aloft.

The only problem was that he wasn't skilled enough in fire play to turn his simple fireball into anything noteworthy. The Beautiful Ones' gazes panned up to the fire for the briefest moment before panning back down to Rich's face, as if their exposed teeth and frozen muscle grins were laughing at his pitiful attempt.

"Don't copy," Rew whispered to Rich. "Draw from your nature."

Rich felt like arguing with her. These muscle-bone monsters were stutter-shambling closer and she was trying to turn this into a magic lesson. She was the gray in brown clothing; why the hell didn't she put on the magic show? Only there was no time to argue. They were almost within arm's reach.

Draw from your nature. Rich had seen that term more than a few times when going over his magic studies. Raw magic was uncaring—formless, waiting to be shaped into an instrument of the mage's will. And every person's will, including mages, was informed by their personalities. The influence of personality was the reason there were twelve distinct schools of magic, but it extended into differences even within the schools. Druze's nature pulled him toward fire within destruction while Brigitte's had naturally drawn her towards ice. But what was Rich's nature? He wasn't sure himself.

One of the Beautiful Ones reached a musculoskeletal hand towards Rich. Not to his fire, but to his nose. Images of the creature ripping it off came unbidden to Rich.

"*Kir bana gael*," Rich intoned without thinking. Dirt from the cave floor and walls gathered into his free hand, forming into a swirling ball of earth. The Beautiful One's hand froze in mid-reach and its head, along with the others in the troupe, panned toward the swirling ball of dirt.

Then the fire went out.

Shit! Hastily, Rich summoned more illusionary fire in his free hand and brought it closer to the ball of dirt that had possibly maybe hopefully caught the Beautiful Ones' attention.

"Keep them distracted," Rew whispered. She began to trace lines and glyphs into ground.

The difficulty of keeping two distinctly different spells going at the same time weighed on his focus, like being forced to recite the alphabet backwards while counting off prime numbers every other letter. The fire's light fluctuated from barely there to ultra fierce and back again. Fortunately, Rich found his ball of earth wasn't as hard to maintain as the fire and kept the dirt swirling smoothly.

Rich spared a glance at Delv. The flaming bear in his hand reared up on hind legs and opened its mouth in a silent roar.

A Beautiful One close to Delv reached through the illusionary fire bear, grabbed the mage's index finger and bent it to the left with a sickening snap that sounded like thunder in the hollow air of the cavern.

Delv grunted, the only sound that escaped through his clenched teeth. Either the mage's willpower or pain threshold was unbelievable. His flame did not go out. It barely wavered. Besides the finger that visibly swelled as it pointed backwards and leftwards unnaturally, his grimace of exquisite pain was the only sign that something was wrong.

"*Dude's a complete psychopath,*" Rich thought.

The bear in Delv' hand morphed into a phoenix. The bird spread its wings and blazed twice as high and grew three times its size. The phoenix launched from the hand with the broken finger and flapped majestically into the upper reaches of the cavern. Performing beautiful spins and spirals, the firebird captured the attention of every Beautiful One in the cavern, including those closest to Rich.

The phoenix dove sharply. It pulled out of the dive to hover directly above Rich. There it swelled and blazed its light brilliantly, forcing Rich to squint under the intensity.

Then it went out, disappearing altogether.

The cavern was left with Rich's lonely, fluctuating fireball for illumination. The shadows grew deeper, the bulging eyes and grinning rictus of the Beautiful Ones grew even more sinister. Rich looked for Delv.

The spot the mage had occupied was now only empty space.

Bastard. Delv had slipped between the Beautiful Ones while the phoenix performed its grand finale. Now Rich and Rew were the only things in the room to play with.

The Beautiful Ones further away began to stutter step towards the mages.

"What are we doing?" Rich whispered as he smiled awkwardly at the approaching Beautiful Ones. Hell, what was smiling going to do besides show them he had teeth they could yank out? Every instinct in Rich told him to run like he was on fire. But they couldn't go back the way they came safely... it was single file through the passage, meaning whoever was in the back would be exposed waiting for their turn to squeeze through. The way ahead was blocked by a sea of skinless bodies getting ever closer.

Rew continued to scrawl glyphs and patterns on the ground. "Keep at it. Trust," she replied without looking up.

The problem with "keeping at it" was that it was no longer working. Since the departure of the phoenix, not even the Beautiful Ones closest to Rich were concerned with his swirling ball of dust. A hand reached towards Rich's face.

"*Kir daha topliyor*," Rich said hastily, raising the swirling ball directly into the Beautiful One's line of sight. The spell he uttered pulled even more dirt and dust from the cave walls and floor, making the ball swell to twice its original size.

The Beautiful One continued to reach. Fortunately for Rich, his spell was more substantial than illusionary fire. The Beautiful One's musculoskeletal fingers came in contact with the swirling ball, causing a layer of rock chips to peel away. Rich buckled down his focus and kept the layer from flying off completely, forcing a ring of loose chips to orbit around the original ball. The thing began to look like a miniature brown Saturn.

More skinless hands reached for the swirling dirt. Rich focused and pulled the chips that flew off into separate, smaller orbs. He pulled them into orbit around dirty Saturn. If the Beautiful Ones kept this up, Rich was going to die exhausted around an entire solar system.

But there was no keeping this up, as another hand reached from under the spinning planetoid. The hand grabbed his wrist. The touch felt spongy, unnaturally cold with a grip like forged steel.

Rich's fire flickered and the moons and rings around his mini Saturn fell immediately. He didn't have the same focus as Delv; he could barely contain the urge to try to snatch his wrist out of the creature's strong grasp.

Another hand grabbed his flickering fire hand, this one warm and smooth. He looked down and saw Rew's hand in his. He looked up and saw a dozen more hands, all of them flayed skinless, reaching for him.

Then he saw nothing but a blur. A wind tunnel! Rich hadn't been able to see the intricate process it took for Rew to make it this time either, but this time he could give less than a damn about that. If he could kiss the hyperdrive blur he would. God, that call was too close.

Suddenly, the world unblurred. Rich found himself further into the cave system of Lapis Deep, led there by Rew, who kept her hand wrapped around his. The present cavern was nondescript, wonderfully devoid of Beautiful Ones. He turned around to get his bearings.

Taking up his entire view was a pair of bulging, lidless eyes staring at him.

"Augh!" he cried, jumping back with a jolt. The eyes and fleshless grin followed. Unlike back when he was surrounded by a horde of them, the jump scare caused by this Beautiful One made his fear intense and immediate. Rich heard himself speak flowing spellcraft he could scarcely understand. Instinctively, he opened his hand to let the spell manifest.

Nothing came forth.

He looked down at the empty hand, where he noticed the Beautiful One had a solid grip on his other wrist. It must've hitched a ride through the wind tunnel.

The Beautiful One released Rich's wrist. It simply stood there, staring.

This was... good? Maybe it lost interest? Rich took a step back.

With ungodly speed, the Beautiful One rushed Rich. A hand grabbed Rich's face in a vice-like claw grip.

The pain of the creature's squeeze was unbearable. Rich pulled with both hands to try to pry his face from the crushing grasp. The Beautiful One was unmovable. Rich swore he could hear his own skull cracking. Through the thing's splayed fingers, Rich stared back into unemotional, vacant eyes.

Rich saw a blur of brown and the Beautiful One's arm came away from its body. The blur revealed itself to be Rew Majora's sleeve, not bent as the usual for most mages but altered into a sword. She swiped with the sword-sleeve again and separated the Beautiful One from its ankle.

The thing fell on its face. Rew brought the sword down on its neck and it's bald, skinless head rolled away.

The sleeve transformed back into just a sleeve as Rich finally managed to pry the clawed fingers from around his face. He threw the arm down with a sigh of relief.

"We must hurry," Rew said.

Before he could ask why the need for haste, Rich got the answer. The dismembered Beautiful One's muscles swelled as if it was flexing, even the separated pieces. Its hands began to reach for its severed head.

If Rew ever had a problem with Rich talking at the wrong time, that wasn't the case here. He quickly grabbed Rew by her hand and ran in the opposite direction of the reconstituting Beautiful One.

Rich didn't stop running until he was well out of breath. The cavern they were in hosted stalactites and stalagmites. A soft blue glow illuminated resplendent pools of water between stalagmites.

Rich didn't care about any of the picturesque beauty.

"How the hell is that thing still alive?" he panted.

"Their biology is nothing like ours. They live on magic. What I did only fed it. It would be like someone giving you a jolt of fresh air or a nutritious meal and wondering why it didn't kill you."

"Nothing's ever easy here," Rich muttered. Why was this world so dangerous? Was it the multiple sentient races, the magic, the lack of convenient stores? No wonder the mages thought it worthwhile to import offworld help via the Rift Pendulum.

"At least we know we're on the right track," Rew said. "Druze is here. We simply have to find him."

Rew took steps further into the cavern, prompting Rich to shake off his reticence and hustle into step beside her. A small stream carved its way through the right side of the cavern and along the stream's bank bluish ferns grew lush and leafy. Rich didn't know how the cave got this glow, whether it was natural light or placed here by an early artisan. He couldn't identify the source and he wasn't about to ask Rew; at this point he just wanted to shut up and keep moving.

Somewhere up ahead, Rich heard a sound different than the babbling of the stream. Voices. He looked at Rew, who nodded. They made their way, slowly, carefully, using the stalagmites as cover. Rich and Rew leaned from behind the cover of a stalagmite and saw their target.

Delv sat down with his hand out while Druze knelt in front of him, tending to the injury. Behind Druze, two Ardenspar peacekeepers stood watch.

"There, the splint is in place," Druze said. "That should hold until we get you to a cleric."

"Thank you, liege."

"You should thank my daughter and her old boy for the distraction. I wrote you off as dead once we got separated."

"Yeah," was all Delv said in reply.

They kept silent for another moment, then nodded.

Druze helped Delv stand and together they turned towards something further down in the cavern. Rich could scarcely make it out with the mage and peacekeepers in the way, but it looked like a geyser with a rusted iron lid over it. Chains wrapped around the lid and anchored it to the cavern floor.

"They call it a wellspring," Druze said. "I was the one that actually led the mission to seal it, about, what? Four hundred years ago."

He looked at the peacekeepers. "Break it open."

The two peacekeepers took out their weapons and advanced on the wellspring. They severed the chains and lifted the rusted lid that groaned with protest. They tossed it with a jarring clang onto the ground.

As far as the wellspring itself, nothing of note happened. Rich had expected clouds of steam or blue sparks or something. But no, nothing really burst forth.

"Unimpressive," Delv said.

"If you were expecting a show, you left it back there with the Beautiful Ones," Druze told Delv. "This is an outflowing of the One-source, not lava. If you got closer, you'd see the shimmer of it. Now, if you please."

Delv opened a shimmery blue and white portal. Druze stepped in, followed by Delv and the peacekeepers.

Rich looked at Rew confused. Whatever Druze was doing in Lapis Deep, he had expected way more setup than removing a lid. He and Rew had had absolutely zero time to prepare an ambush. "That's it?" he asked her.

Rew rose from the cover of the stalagmite. "It would appear so," she said.

Looking at the shimmery portal illuminate the wellspring gave Rich an inspiring idea.

"I know, how about we put the lid back on, forcing Druze to come back to undo it again, only this time we booby trap the locks so it snares him?"

"He could always send someone else to investigate the cause," Rew said.

"He could," Rich agreed, "but it seems like removing this lid is too important for him to trust to anyone else. He's gonna come. Besides, I'm all out of plans."

Rew nodded. "I'm afraid I'm fresh out of them myself."

Rich nudged her. "It'll work. C'mon, help me put the lid back on."

Rich hurried over to the lid. Then blackness took him.

REW WATCHED HELPLESSLY as Rich spasmed on the ground. What was happening to him?! More importantly how could she stop it?!

A moment after Delv's portal closed behind her, another one opened right next to it. Druze, Delv and the two peacekeepers emerged from it. Druze smiled at his daughter.

"I swear, there's no better feeling than seeing a plan execute flawlessly."

Anger contorted her features.

"You knew this would happen?"

"I planned on it, my dear. I can stop it, before he dies."

She looked at Rich before looking back at her father. "And you want what?"

Druze, smiling, produced a small twelve sided stone from his library pocket. Rew immediately recognized it; she had devised the infernal contraption.

"I only want my daughter back."

She looked at Rich, writhing and helpless. Without much in the way of alternatives, Rew went over to her father, grabbed the witchlock that bore her name, and activated it.

Crushing weight pull her down to the ground. Druze smiled at her.

"I hate to sound overly fatherly, but this really is for your own good."

"Help..." she struggled through her words, "...him."

"Of course," Druze said. "All a part of the plan. Watch as it unfolds, with a bit of undocumented history."

Druze produced another witchlock. This one he tossed over the wellspring. The stone flared red as its tethers erupted out, encapsulating the spring before they disappeared. The witchlock hovered over the wellspring, glowing like an ember.

Rich stopped seizing. Druze nodded and the peacekeepers went to collect Rich off the ground.

"He wouldn't have known these wellsprings are impossible for pendulum heroes to approach. I did. It's the reason I had to come here myself to seal the damn thing four hundred years ago. You know, the good old days when I had my original skin."

"Why..." Rew began.

"Hush, daughter, no need to push yourself. I'll give you the answers."

Druze approached the wellspring, looking at it with an almost reverent gaze as he talked to Rew.

"Your question may have been as to why I sealed these things up so long ago. There were other schools of magic back then, older ones, more powerful and venerable, when I went to study under Kaftar Friese and his new way of thinking. When he founded the school, it was actually called the Magical Hierophane of the Free States. Lapis Deep was the Blue Grotto College of Enhanced Artistry. More to the point, every competing school of magic that existed reduced the Hierophane's power base. And that lack of power threatened the continued existence of the Free States. So we closed the other schools and any schools in the future by shutting off their taps."

He turned to face Rew. "This was all before your time, daughter. By the time you arrived and became the incredible student you were in the Hierophane's sacred halls, the tower was established as the only place in the world to learn true, legitimate magic. All the other schools had been deemed either myths or perversions."

He knelt before his captive daughter. "But perhaps that wasn't the 'why' you were going to ask. Maybe it was along the lines of 'why am I unsealing it after all this time?' yes? Again, I have you to thank. Observe."

Druze pulled a chain link from his pocket and let it dangle in front of Rew so she could see it. A shimmering metallic black, it was thin like a necklace with barb-like thorns connecting each link. Rew recognized it immediately.

A lifetether. Memories of when she was still a student, working her way through the colors came to her. She was naïve then, and always reaching, always striving to win her father's approval. She remembered when he came to her in confidence and told her his unnaturally long life was because of the undying, immortal monster he and Kaftar had discovered in the Eural Mountains. If the monster ever got free, Druze cautioned, it would raise an unstoppable army from the grave and bring death to the whole world. To keep it caged required Kaftar Friese's spell "Life Ending Chain" and the caster's life as the spell's cost.

That method was unacceptable to Rew. So she had studied and experimented until she perfected the Majora witchlock. The witchlock had saved some hapless mage from giving the ultimate sacrifice to trap the creature and her and Druze stowed it in the darkest confines of Fort Law.

"It's not enough," Druze had told her. "We need its lifeforce. The thing is immortal. What would happen if it outlives the witchlock's magic, outlives the only two people in existence that know of its infernal power and fear it enough to keep it trapped? We cannot trust this to future generations."

It hadn't taken much to convince Rew. Who didn't want to live forever? To accompany the witchlock, she had crafted the lifetether. One end adheres to the person who wanted more years and the other end binds to the lock, where it drains the life from whatever was caged under it. The two of them, father and daughter, had cast two lifetethers on the death creature's witchlock and then had proceeded to watch the rest of the world die around them.

Druze leaned closer to Rew. "I know what you're thinking. This time the lifetether doesn't get attached to either you or I. Hell, it would likely kill me... tapping directly into a wellspring isn't exactly a safe bet for the Pendulum Hero that I am now."

Rew wanted to laugh. The thought of Druze calling himself a hero, pendulum or otherwise, was its own special blasphemy.

"The other end of the tether goes to another wellspring," Druze said. He leaned over to his daughter's ear and whispered.

"You call it the Rift Pendulum."

Chapter 17
Tech Romancers

Mike popped up out of the cover of a broken marble pillar just long enough to fire off a shot from his diskbow. The disk twanged out, Mike popped down, and somewhere in the background a Clockwound Warder screamed.

He was gonna have words with Vylar the next time he saw him. Not only did all warders sport goggles, they literally wore moving clock gears and cogwheels on their chest pieces. Even a blind dude could see this wasn't Sons of Kaftar turf.

A fiery explosion to the left sent charred rubble flying along with three warders. Savashbahar emerged from the direction of the explosion and took position beside Mike behind the fallen column.

"Has Runt returned?" she asked, looking back once to observe her handiwork.

As if on queue, Runt burst onto the scene behind them. His massive hand held a Clockwound Warder by the face. The pitiful warder dangled uselessly, clawing at the half-weagr's bear grip with both hands. Runt drove the warder's head into a stone block and the defeated sprawlcrawler went limp, oozing out of Runt's grasp onto the ground.

Runt looked at the others and motioned with his head for them to follow. It was all the invitation they needed. They stayed on Runt's heels as he led them through the maze of ruins. Occasionally, Mike would turn and fire off a disk to keep the warders from full and open pursuit. Savvy pulled a hex, called it web and stuck it to a broken pillar as she passed.

Moments later, Mike heard yells. He turned to see four of the warders wrapped up together in netting like Spider-Man had swung through.

Close behind them, on both the left and right, the warders were closing the distance. Ruins everywhere provided decent cover to prevent clear diskbow shots but Runt was heading towards a clearing. Soon they would be open and exposed.

Twang! Twang! Twang! Twang!

Before they reached the clearing, a parade of diskbow shots went off. Clockwound Warders on both the left and right went down in a spray of red mist. The others hesitated, looked around, then broke into an impromptu retreat.

As they emerged into the clearing, it was easy for Mike to see why the warders had turned tail. An entirely different gang stood in the clearing, easily two dozen people of human, megrym, and aian persuasion. Just like Savvy, they wore slick black leather outfits, adorned in places with brass and silver fittings.

Mike recognized the human who stood at the head of the pack with his brown hair and black lensed goggles. Ego.

Ego tilted his head to the side, as if he was curiously assessing what had shown up at his doorstep. His smile was large and unreserved.

"I's roughs is back! Tread all the way from the start of dark Wozencraft to here to bring good news to I, no doubt."

"Ego!" Mike called. Both parties closed the distance and Mike met Ego with a hearty handshake. "You right on time! Thanks for giving them warders back there that work."

Ego waved his hand as if the warders were mosquitoes. "None of I's roughs is ever alone in the kingdom."

Mike smiled at that. A silent space entered the chill air of the Sprawl. Ego looked among Mike's party before returning to Mike.

"Where's I's friend Ruki of Provos, who tried to pass himself off as the friendly trader? You don his goggles, was I's goggles, was goggles from warder's dead leader. The good sight don't pass unless the friendship's warm or the body's cold. Tell, I, life no longer reside in the rough?"

Mike shrugged. "He should be good. He retired."

Ego laughed. "What nonsense you speak to I? Roughs only retire when they covered in dirt, know? I seen his kind plenty in the wastes and he a right rough. Not done yet, he."

He gave Mike a hearty clap on the shoulder before walking back towards his gang. Without looking back, he motioned for the others to follow with his baton.

"Clockwound will come again, like feral dogs once they grow the pack. Come. I and I's head to sanctuary."

Mike's party fell in step behind Ego. The Sons of Kaftar took up positions beside and behind them. All of them were the same kind of uniform ragtag, with smooth gray and black leather held together with brass buckles, bolts and fittings. They wouldn't look out of place as extras in a Mad Max movie.

Ego led the way to what appeared to be a decayed coliseum. Perhaps it was once a domed stadium before whatever cataclysm befell the Sprawl; what remained were circular walls that still stood between two to three stories high depending on the erosion. Thick vines of ivy descended down the sides.

Inside the stadium was a completely opposite world to the Sprawl outside the walls. Plant life blossomed in a way Mike could only describe as Eden-esque. Beautiful yellow and lavender flowers, corn, strawberry bushes, tomatoes, ferns, melon vines and a myriad of plants Mike couldn't begin to recognize flourished anywhere, everywhere. Deer, sheep and goats grazed among the plants, seemingly unconcerned with humans. And all of it was tended to by leather-clad Beyond Thunderdome warriors.

"I thought the Sprawl was lifeless," Mike said looking around. "I mean, that desert on the way in made it seem like you couldn't grow nail fungus out here."

"Thing about life, rough," Ego said. "Give her enough time and her, she always find a way to thrive."

Ego pushed through rows of corn and they emerged at the shore of a pond. Crystal blue water lapped the shore which was carefully fed into channels that branched throughout the stadium like spider webs. Across the far side, a couple of warriors tossed a net into the water. Ego turned to face his guests.

"Welcome to the Blood of the Sons."

Mike looked around before nodding appreciatively. "Nice. Completely wrecks the myth that you guys feast on the hearts of your enemies, though." Mike raised an eyebrow. "Speaking of hearts, I assumed you were going to take us there. That place is future-swank."

Ego shook his head and grimaced. "Things, them changed since you last saw I. Clockwound Warders with vile mage help, overran the Heart of the Sons. Not just. Warders seem near mindless, especially of late. Them attack all things that draw breath and some of the things that don't. Them running roughshod, no reason no rhyme, make it troublesome surviving in the fallen kingdom. So I and I's fell back here. Here I and I's plan, look, wait for opportunity. Maybe opportunity find I in the form of old friends, know?"

"Heh," Mike nodded. "Apparently, I got a destiny. Blood vision has me surrounded by Clockwound Warders, with them reaching up to me like I'm the sweetest snack stuck on the highest shelf. Figure that's a better direction than shoulder shrugging by myself, that's why I'm here."

"Who be I to question the kind of vision that see I's rough safely back from the start of dark Wozencraft?"

Mike smiled at the name. "Start of Dark Wozencraft" was what Ego called the town of Olukent, the place where Druze Wozencraft betrayed Ego's forefather Kaftar Friese for eternal life. The name reminded Mike of his first run in this world and the desperate bid to find his brother. Simpler, clear cut times.

A white woolly lamb came over to them, sniffing curiously. Ego knelt and began to pet the lamb behind the ears.

"Them say the young ones are the tastiest, but I, I got no appetite to see something so new meet its end. I's fine with never knowing. The problem is I's blood, it hunger for the oldest of prey."

Ego kept petting the lamb but turned his goggled gaze to Mike. "I hear he's back, Wozencraft. Or someone who claims it's he, calls himself the Second Hierophant Returned and is waging war with all the aian houses save Onus. Truth to this? Tell I."

Mike nodded. "'Fraid so."

Ego patted the lamb once more before sending it off to its mother. He stood up.

"Let I and I's roughs sup and plan. Our heads come together to take off the heads of all of I and I's enemies, a trail of bodies that start at the Warders and don't end until the treacherous Wozencraft pay his blood debt."

"I'm sorry," Savashbahar said. "For the time being, I cannot be among you."

Everyone looked at her with perplexed confusion on their face. "What are you talking, Savvy?" Mike asked.

"I have my own whispering blood, my own vision. I must go to it," she said to Mike. She looked up at Ego.

"The place among the ruins where a thick, dark fog grips the air and broods like an angry ghost, never leaving. You know it?"

Ego nodded. "Indeed."

Savashbahar returned his nod. "Show me."

Chapter 18
The Lost Tribe

Savashbahar moved through the waste of *yasak toprak* as a ghost, invisible to any onlookers save for a rippling outline. Directly in front of her another shimmering specter led. This was the aian called Danda, a Son of Kaftar that also belonged to the chameleon House of Sen.

The late afternoon sun was just beginning its descent below the horizon for rest. The clear, cloudless sky was bright, with just a touch of bright orange punching out to contrast the blue. Even in their near perfect camouflage, Savashbahar and Danda would have to stop on occasion. The Clockwound Warders moved in unpredictable patterns, with anywhere from two to a dozen in any pack. And there was something unsettling in their goggles, the way they would stare at the patch of the seemingly empty air Savashbahar or Danda occupied as if they could see them.

The two of them continued to slink their way through the ruins. They had to proceed carefully through a patchwork of downed marble columns, taller than Runt even now that they lay on their sides. There was no telling if there were any warders on the other side, or what may be around the corner.

Danda paused at the chipped, circular face of one such column. The rippling camouflage evaporated around his index finger, making it seem as if the digit hovered in the air. The gray finger floated to point around the column.

Savashbahar peeked around. There in the distance, the wasteland was shrouded in a thick, gray fog. It was a stark contrast to the clear air around her and the sight of it filled Savashbahar with unease. After all, there was a reason all the tribes, from the Maltep to the Jahnavar called this forbidden land.

She looked back at Danda. As she did so, his face appeared out of the camouflage that still draped his body. "Stay ready, my fellow rough." Then the camouflage returned to his face and his rippling body retreated, leaving her alone in the face of her quest.

She walked with slow care toward the ashen shroud of perpetual fog. Halfway there her invisibility hex died, leaving her open and exposed. Still, there was no need to seek cover; she knew just by the sight and feeling of this unnatural air the Clockwound Warders patrols stayed well away from this place.

The air felt slighter warmer, thicker, as she entered the fog. It carried a dirty metallic scent of rust. She brought the fold of her cloak up to cover her nose and mouth. The wasted city, the solitary pillars and broken structures that dotted the landscape, it all looked like a gaunt silhouette, a ghost that mourned its own fate.

Silence reigned here, making her footfalls sound like beating war drums as the detritus shifted under her feet. The ruins began to change. Now thick steel beams jutted from the ground, twisted and warped, covered in their entirety by red-brown rust. Savashbahar felt as if she walked among the scavenged bones of giants.

Up ahead, on a horizon made short for the fog, three small silhouettes moved. The shapes grew larger, obviously approaching her. Savashbahar looked down at her belt of hexes for reassurance but did not reach for one. Instead, she waited.

Soon enough the shapes came into focus as they cut through the fog. Two were obviously nasran by the way they walked with their front-hinged knees. All three had clothing far different than the black leather with metal fittings she wore. Instead of leather, they dressed in layers of fabric, first dark gray collared shirt and pants, then over the shirts were gray vests with many compartment flaps, then over that a thick black overcoat, then over that a black cloak that trailed listlessly behind their backs. Their boots came up to their knees, their hands gloved to forearms wrapped in gauntlets. Upon their heads sat frayed, tri-cornered hats. Like her, their noses and mouths were covered, leaving only their eyes exposed. Still by those eyes, Savashbahar could tell the third member appeared to be a human from the far eastern land of Oyoni. The fact that they were all so similarly garbed took any question away from her about who these people were. She knew she was face to face with members of Exhaust.

The nasran in the center spoke. "You're a curious one." The gravel in his voice identified him as male. "Who comes garbed as a Son of Kaftar yet bearing a belt laden with what they most despise?"

"I am Savashbahar, Hexenarii of Maltep."

"I am Balaban. Do you not heed the warnings of your people, Savashbahar of Maltep? This land is forbidden. Turn back, I say."

Savashbahar shook her head. "I seek what was lost, whether it lies in forbidden lands or not."

"What is it you seek in such a forlorn place, hexenarii?" Balaban asked.

"The Ah-irduman," she replied, speaking the true name of the Lost Tribe. "The ring of the Buyukata."

Balaban shifted his gaze to his two compatriots before returning his eyes to Savashbahar.

"Names I have not heard in quite some time. You come to these fume-choked wastes seeking power."

His words were not a question. There was no doubt why she would travel, why anyone would travel here. The only thing to ponder is how these strangely garbed men would react. Savashbahar remembered vividly how the Sons of Kaftar responded to the question of whether Ruki Provos was a friend or a trader the first time they had entered *yasak toprak*. The gangs of the Sprawl all had their peculiar ways about them. There was no reason to believe Exhaust was any different. She thought it best to be forthright and deal with any potential fallout.

"I seek enough power to end the destruction loosed upon my kind by human mages and their relentless thirst for magic, nothing more."

"You would raze a city to burn out mere maggots?"

There was weight to the question which hung as thick as the fog around them all. She thought for long, careful moments before answering.

"The maggots grow into flies and carry their filth on diseased wings to infect the world over. I would burn as much of the city as necessary to keep that from happening."

Balaban stared at her.

"Come with us," he said.

UNLIKE THE SONS OF Kaftar, who seemed to prefer the sanctuary provided by the Sprawl's underworld, the members of Exhaust dwelled above ground. They apparently lacked the aversion to magic the Sons of Kaftar carried and used spellcraft to bend and shape the ruins into functional edifices. Their builders had fused steel seamlessly to marble pieces and wove glass through stone as if it was thread. Homes and shops were made of entirely repurposed ruins, some round, some square, some two stories tall.

Here, for reasons Savashbahar couldn't fathom, the thick fog only came to ankle height. Yet surrounding the patchwork village the fog towered as a dense and impenetrable wall. She felt as if she was somehow on an island and the fog that listed at her ankles were shallow waves at the shore.

Balaban led her through the village. The other members of Exhaust while dressed in the same layered fabric and tri-cornered hats, did not sport the nose and mouth coverings. Men and women, mostly human or aian, milled about on their own affairs, children played and very few spared a glance in their direction.

Savashbahar took a small measure of comfort seeing the village and its inhabitants. According to the Sons of Kaftar, Exhaust lorded over a huge swath of the Sprawl, everywhere the fog touched. Any war parties sent into the fog by either the Sons or the Warders never came out again. Seeing civilization, patchwork as it may be, was a welcome sign that Exhaust was more than just bloodthirsty madmen.

Balaban escorted Savashbahar into a round building built of equal parts interwoven steel girders and red brick that culminated with an intact marble dome. Little occupied the interior save a grand circular table made of marble. Nine nasrans, two humans and a megrym sat around the table. Even the megrym wore the triangular hat, albeit child sized. The nasran woman in the center facing the entrance looked up as they approached.

"Inonu," Balaban greeted her, "I present to you Savashbahar, Hexenarii of Maltep."

Inonu raised an eyebrow. "You are welcome here, hex maiden, in the beating heart of your forbidden land."

"I am well met," Savashbahar replied, "if perplexed. You are nasran. Is this not your forbidden land as well? What tribe do you belong?"

"Do you not see Krager?" Inonu asked looking at the megrym, who bowed his head slightly. "Or Shima and Tegu?" The humans, one male and one female, both obviously from the land of Oyoni, curtly nodded. "We are beyond tribes here. We are Exhaust."

"My blood whispered to me that I would find the lost tribe here. It made sense when I saw the unending fog within the vision. I am hexenarii, trained to read and write the ancient words. Ah-irduman means heavy smoke. That is you," Savashbahar pointed at Inonu. "That is Exhaust."

Inonu leaned back in her chair, a catlike smirk on her lips. "The lost tribe found."

Savashbahar shook her head. "I do not understand what feels to be a great many things. Why are you here, in an exile that seems self-imposed? Why are there people among you that are not our kind? Why do you no longer proudly wear the mantle of Ah-irduman, the tribe that birthed our people's last Buyukata?"

"Your last question I've already answered. We are beyond tribes here, past your notion of what it means to be of Maltep or Antep or Jahnavar or Ah-irduman. Your twelve distinct tribes each with their own sacred mission and traditions mean more to us than you can know right now which is why these tribes mean nothing to us."

Savashbahar grimaced. "You play with what you know and what I don't as a cat with a mouse."

The smirk on Inonu's face didn't waver. "Forgive me, but we rarely see the uninitiated here and to talk to one whose eyes are yet to open is too tempting a thing not to embrace."

Inonu stood up and gave a nod to the megrym called Krager. While she walked around the table to meet Savashbahar, Krager called the seated members of Exhaust back to order and began to discuss the results of the salvage efforts of the northeast quadrant.

Inonu faced Savashbahar and looked her up and down. "You look to be about my height and build," Inonu said. "Perfect. Come."

Both Savashbahar and Balaban followed her out of the domed building as Inonu took to the fog licked streets of the village.

Inonu craned her neck to look behind her and spoke. "You are a bit of puzzle yourself, hex maiden. You are of Maltep but they don't teach hex magic to women, as with many tribes. Kahraman, Kastamonu or Balikesir, which tribe trained you?"

"Kahraman. Where are we going?"

"If you were strictly Maltep hexenarii I would say you leaned toward fire hexes but your learning came from those who have a reverence for blood. Your strong suit, is it blood or fire?"

Savashbahar wasn't particularly keen on this woman's line of question or the lack of response to her own question. She walked silently behind Inonu for a moment, looking at a couple of nasran men carry splintered wood and granite chunks to parts unknown. Finally she answered.

"My strong suit is knowing there are elements where I lack confidence which I may bolster through study and practice."

Inonu shook her head as she led the way. "If the tattoos on your skin didn't mark you as hexenarii your response certainly would. 'Too reveal your strength is to also reveal your weakness,' yes?"

The woman had quoted verbatim from the scrolls of sanctified knowledge, words and teachings seen only by hexenarii.

"Has your entire gang read from the sacred source? Shall the megrym recite the Seven Steps to me?"

Inonu stopped and faced Savashbahar. She rummaged through one of the small pockets of her overcoat, pulled out an object and tossed it casually in the air towards Savashbahar.

It landed in her palm. It was a rock, like much of the debris that littered the Sprawl, only covered in fine line carvings. Some of the shapes Savashbahar recognized—she carried them on her own hex belt. Others were completely foreign. Unlike her hexes, which only carried one shape per hex, this little rock held too many to count.

The stone seemed impossible. How had someone managed to carve the symbols so small, so precise? The stone itself was small, about the size of a hex, and it looked impossible for the rock to hold that many carvings without crumbling into powder.

Gloved hands gently removed the stone from Savashbahar's open palm. She looked up to see Inonu holding the stone eye level. Without a word, the stone glowed blue and crumbled. Inonu became as mist, almost as if the fog that dwelled at their feet had grown up her legs and swallowed her. The mist darted in short bursts, as quick as a buzzing fly. It did this four times and when it got about twenty feet from her the mist dispelled leaving only Inonu.

"How?" Savashbahar asked dumbfounded. It was hex magic not carved in wormwood, issued without a single word spoken.

"You are of Maltep," Inonu spoke to her, "even if you are not of their hex tradition. I'm sure you've used fire, which I prefer to the use of blood. Less cleanup."

Inonu fished another stone from her pocket. "Hurl your fire at me, Savashbahar."

Savashbahar plucked a hex from her belt, named it fire and threw it at Inonu. It became a flaming missile and careened with deadly speed at the woman.

Inonu simply reached with her free hand and grabbed the fireball. More than that, it appeared as if her hand was able to cram the fire back into the hex. An instant later, Inonu held the inert piece of wood that Savashbahar had pulled from her belt. In Inonu's other hand, the multi-runed stone glowed blue and crumbled into powder.

Savashbahar looked in awe of Inonu. No story of the hexenarii or word in the text could explain this. "Are you the Buyukata?" she asked.

Inonu closed the distance to Savashbahar, a slight smile on her lips. "No. There has not been one for a long time now. I am simply what you and every other hexenarii used to be, from a time quite lost."

"And what is that?" Savashbahar asked.

"Knowing," Inonu said. She placed a gloved hand onto Savashbahar's shoulder. "It is what you shall be soon. We are going to my home, where I'll outfit you with clothes such as mine. From there, you'll descend into the origin, where you'll learn what we all here have discovered. The Ring of the Buyukata is there as well, if you still wish to bear it."

Inonu took her hand away from Savashbahar's shoulder. Their eyes met.

"Are you ready to know, Savashbahar of Maltep?"

Savashbahar had never known such a heady combination of wonder and fear as she nodded.

Chapter 19
Broken Party

Jason awoke to a sword's sharp tip pointing at his face. He followed the blade up to see Eula holding it. Fury was etched in her features.

"This again?" he asked with a sloppy smile. "We really gotta work on your methodology for waking others up."

Eula pushed the sword at him further, forcing him to pull his head back to prevent unauthorized dental surgery. He held his hands up, which caused a splashing spray of water. While he didn't look down to confirm, he could feel he was sitting waist deep in water.

"You lying, filthy wretch!" she said, her anger unabated. "This whole time you've been in league with Onus."

"I saved your immortal life," Jason said. "Big falling pillar of stone crashing down on your head, remember?"

"That," she said between clenched teeth. "Is the only reason I haven't killed you yet. I just want to know why before I end you."

Jason took a moment to look beyond the sword in his face and Eula's angry countenance. Above them, the sky was obscured by a gray dome that appeared to be a translucent shell. It caused a strange kind of gloom to permeate the air. Not only was Jason sitting up to his waist in water, the entire area under the dome was half submerged. The tops of buildings jutted out of the water at haphazard angles. This likely meant he was sitting on a rooftop. Debris floated everywhere.

"Can I explain when we're in a safer place?" Jason asked. "I promise, I'll tell you everything you wanna know."

Eula looked at Jason with incredulity, as if he had asked her to grow another head out of her shoulders. "You want me to trust you, a thrall of the King of Maggots, after you've betrayed me once? No. This ends here. You end here. And if you don't tell me why you've joined with Onus then I'll find a way to make peace with never knowing. I will find comfort in your death. Explain slowly and measure your words carefully, for if I even hear a syllable of his name issue from your lips, I will ram this sword down your throat before you can finish calling on your dark lord."

Her angry visage coupled with her words became an unsettling realization for Jason. He knew without question she meant it. This wasn't a movie where the male and female leads have a quarrel about some plot related turn of events, they begrudgingly agree to continue to work together and finally patch things up near the end of the movie and then make out. Looking at Eula's fiercely oscillating eyes, Jason finally understood there was no bargaining, no bickering, no reluctant agreement. There was no later. She had no intention of doing anything other than kill him as soon as her curiosity was sated. Her immortal ass was done with him.

Jason had to dispel his own feelings of betrayal, a sense of hurt that came from her inability to see him as a good person after all they've been through together, despite her religion or belief in Onus or whatever you called this thing that had her at odds with him. He dispelled it because he realized this was his fault. Even after a death sentence at the Temple of Houses, even after a war was started largely because of his mere existence, Jason had refused to consider these people's religion seriously.

There was no true analog back home, but Jason tried to image what a devout Christian turned demon hunter would do if they learned someone they had met a short while ago was in league with the devil, one day away from becoming the conduit for the Prince of Darkness to reign on Earth. Probably not a whole lot of conversation to be had with that one.

"All right," Jason said slowly as he looked Eula up and down. She wore a battle dress, all steel and reinforced leather, arms exposed at the shoulder, gauntlets on her wrists. The dress ended two inches above the knee. Bare legs disappeared into murky saltwater. He knew she wore calf high boots. Because of the murk, he wasn't sure how her feet were placed and what potentially unstable material they rested on.

"I've got something to show you, which will explain most of this. It's on my neck, which is a bit difficult to get to because I've got your sword in my face and my o... my quiver pulling against my throat." Jason had to fight saying the word "own" for fear of if being confused with Onus. "I'll move slow."

With his bone hand, Jason pulled at the strap, allowing him to remove the quiver, his bow and severed arm that he placed beside him with a splash in the water. With his flesh arm he pulled out the heart pendant Onus had given him.

Only two maggots remained, waiting to writhe their way into the heart.

"After the High Fane sentenced me to death for no other crime than being markless, the Corrupter engineered my escape using Targhos and the other top-level flyers from the House of Demir, which was thoroughly infiltrated with Twelfth House by the way. The next time I met Targhos, he took me to see his boss. He gave me this. It was not a choice. My only choice would be whether I would use it or not. Since then my friends and I have been ruthlessly hunted by both mages and aians alike. This thing started off with eight maggots. And each time I've used it, it's been to save my friends from that danger. Like I saved you. I can't help how I look and what that means to your people or to the God of Power. All I'm trying to do is stay one step ahead of it all. Is that good enough for you?"

Eula blinked slowly, her eyes heavy lidded. "No," she said.

"I'm afraid it's going to have to be," Jason told her, "because for you, it's been a very weary day."

Jason allowed his skeletal hand to rise above the water line. Eula looked down dully to see the bone hand holding Jason's flesh arm club. Its four fingered hand had been touching her bare legs underwater and was now resting on her knee.

Eula's sword fell through limp fingers. Jason rushed off his feet to catch her before she collapsed.

"For the record, I have entertained the thought of you swooning for me," he said to her as she slumbered in his arms. "Also for the record, I never thought it would go down, least of all like this."

Gently, he propped Eula against the same wall he had been resting. He picked up his gear and surveyed the area as he replaced his quiver and bow on his back. His friends were somewhere out there in a half-drowned and ruined city. The first thing to do was find out where.

He rummaged through his pack and fished out his mirror link. His own reflection stared back at him. "Mel," he spoke to the mirror and the reflective surface seemed to shimmer into liquid, as if it would ripple if he touched the glass. He stared at the shimmering surface for long, tense moments trying in vain to not think the worst.

Finally Jason's reflection blinked and was replaced by Mel looking back. He could almost taste her relief as she exhaled.

"Jason! Oh god, I tried to call you earlier and you didn't pick up."

"Yeah, that was probably me sleeping off a giant rock or something. I guess mirrors don't have voicemail. How are you? Where are you?"

"Holding up," Mel replied with a grimace. "We're on a flat roof, one of the bigger ones, about a story higher than the surrounding water. We've got a fire going in the center. You see us?"

His eyes may not be as keen as they would be in stark daylight, but he was able to pick up the wan orange light of distant fire on the further buildings. He also saw that some of the things floating in the water used to have a pulse.

Until he could confirm the body with his own eyes, the whacked out gray robe was still out there, alive if not well. After all, one of the rules in this business was to always double tap.

"I should be able to make my way to you," Jason said. "Chosen One out." The mirror link died.

He got started. Fishing Eula's sword from the water, he returned it to its scabbard, picked her up, threw one of her arms across his shoulder and kept wading through the knee deep water until he ran out of solid ground and fell in with a splash. He swam one-handed, while the other held Eula, toward a building leaning toward one o'clock with two full stories sticking out of the water. If nothing else, it would provide a decent vantage point to scan for Mel's fire and possibly other survivors.

The swim was tiring and took what felt like forever. He was tempted to call on Onus just to speed the process up. Eventually, he reached a half-submerged window and climbed in, pulling Eula in after him.

It took awhile for Jason's crappy aian eyes to get used to the gloom. Half submerged as it was, the room looked to be an apartment. An overturned wardrobe stuck out of the water, most of its clothes spilled out. A mattress floated in the corner.

Being both inside and surrounded by a leaning building forced Jason to view the world through this slanted perspective. He carried Eula through a diagonal doorway into a hallway that likely had more of an open courtyard feel versus the inclined indoor pool aesthetic it had now.

He made for the stairs in this apartment complex somewhat awkwardly. There was no ideal way to carry a slumbering aian goddess. His bow, quiver and arm club all took up space, leaving zero shoulder room for him to use the fireman's carry. So he carried Eula in both arms, which was much weirder in practice than he would've thought. His bone arm felt no weight, so carrying two handfuls of goddess made it seem that his flesh hand had too much Eula. It messed with his balance and every other step Jason looked down to be sure of his footing and how he was holding the sleeping goddess.

She was beautiful now that she wasn't quivering with rage. Jason couldn't help but think it as he looked down and saw the peaceful expression on her face. Funny, as soon as she woke she was going to kill him.

Half a flight up, the environmental perspective began to make more sense in his head, most likely on account of them getting well above the water line.

"Ugh," Eula moaned.

Now Jason had to gently lay Eula down on the steps. He pulled out his arm club and placed the three fingers and thumb across her forehead like a priest blessing one of the congregation. In a few moments she stopped stirring.

The gods and their ridiculous tolerances, geez.

This would make for a slog with Eula treating the induced sleep like a snooze alarm. With little choice in the matter, he scooped her back up and continued up the stairs. He made the landing and as he turned to take the next flight of stairs he heard an unexpected noise.

Sobbing. Barely audible.

Jason proceeded up the stairs cautiously. When he reached the next landing, he saw a purple-haired aian girl sitting in the corner, hugging her knees, head bowed while she cried softly into them.

"Uh... you okay?" Jason asked.

The little girl jerked her head up in alarm. Her dancing, surprised eyes were wet with tears.

"Sethrin!" she exclaimed, speaking his name with a lisp. "You've come to resthcue me!"

The lisp, the purple hair. It brought back the vivid memory of when he spoke to Suusteren's aian population as the Chosen One. This was the little girl that told him she wanted his mark when she came of age.

"Rida?" he asked her name.

She nodded. "I lost my mom and dad," she said. "They told me to stay close and I tried hard but the water came and pulled me and now I don't know where to go!"

Jason smiled at her. "Lucky for you, side quests are my specialty. Let's go find your parents."

Rida smiled back, revealing small, tic-tac teeth. She wiped her eyes and stood up.

Jason continued up the stairs holding Eula while Rida followed close enough behind to grab his pants leg. After a few steps she broke the silent trek upstairs.

"Are you going to use your Chosen One power to find them?" Rida asked.

"If only," he replied. "I mean maybe, if my power happens to be luck and willingness to grind at odd hours, then definitely."

More silence followed. The passed another landing leading to an abandoned hallway. Nothing stirred down it and Jason assumed anyone would work to seek an open space like the stairway or the roof rather than staying in a room. Even a young child had that kind of sense. He continued up to the roof.

"Sethrin?" Rida asked.

"Yes?"

"What's a side quest?"

"It's when you help someone along the way of what you were planning to do, oftentimes just for the sake of doing it and maybe a little XP."

"Hmmm," she said in acceptance.

After another half flight they reached the roof. The door to the roof hung ajar. As soon as Jason emerged onto the rooftop, the sense of a slanted world returned as he looked at the bent and broken buildings from the vantage point of a leaning apartment tower.

"Ugh," Eula groaned and stirred restlessly.

"Yay!" Rida exclaimed with a clap. "Eula's getting up! Will you carry me next, Sethrin? Will she? She has wings!"

"Not yay I'm afraid," Jason said. It was unfortunate too because some winged reconnaissance would be useful right about now. He gingerly set her down on the rooftop, took out his severed arm and blessed her on her forehead again until she returned to resting.

"Eula's really cranky right now," Jason explained to Rida. "She needs her sleep to get better and only this arm can keep her asleep. Don't touch it or it'll make you go to sleep too."

Rida looked with awe at the arm in front of her and then back up to Jason.

"It's gross," she told him.

"So are your manners, kid."

"Are you going to carry me now?" she asked. As if he had already acquiesced, she raised both arms to the sky in front of him.

Jason shrugged a mini-'why not?' to himself and bent down to scoop her up. He carried her in the crook of his bone arm and what little bit she must have weighed completely disappeared. Apparently, quite a pro at being picked up and carried, Rida expertly nestled herself in Jason's chest and neck. Her purple hair brushed against his cheek and smelled faintly of almond.

He took her close to the edge of the building to survey the surroundings. The view was much better up here and Jason could see that the dome covered a huge swath of what was once Suusteren. Several buildings jutted out of the water, many at angles like the roof they were currently on, a few rare ones had managed to stay strictly vertical. Piles of wood, trash, debris, and other flotsam floated in groups throughout this waterlogged space. More than a few of the floating objects were clearly bodies. The light was beginning to fade under the dome, but Jason could discern shapes moving about on a flat rooftop in the distance and the flickering light of a small fire. Must be Mel.

Finding his comrades was a hopeful prospect, but Jason also became cognizant of the fact that Rida's parents could likely be among the floating dead.

"Sethrin?" Rida said his name as a question and looked up at him with curious, oscillating eyes.

"Hmmm?"

"What's eks pee?"

He smiled. "It's growth. After we're done, we'll both grow a little."

"We're going to get taller?"

"Yes, on the inside. The whole point of life is to get taller inside," he replied.

"I want a lot of eks pee!" she said.

"Awesome. You're well on your way to being a big girl."

While he cradled Rida with his bone arm, he used his other hand to clear a lock of purple hair from her face. "Speaking of being a big girl, I need you to do something really scary. Some of our people didn't get out of the water in time like you did and they died. I need you to be brave, really brave, and look at the people who are still in the water and see if any of them are your parents. Can you be brave for me, Rida?"

Jason didn't know if this was the right thing, but he didn't like the alternative. While he hoped her parents were safe on another rooftop, he was well aware that they may have drowned when the city flooded. Pretending otherwise wasn't going to change that and trying to shield Rida's eyes from the floating corpses may rob her of knowing what happened to her parents. Innocence is something everyone loses and if given the choice to lose it early for closure or keep it intact for awhile and always wonder if they somehow survived, he would chose the former.

Rida nodded. "I want to be brave."

She turned her head and looked out along the devastated city. While her eyes lingered on the bodies in the water, Jason steeled himself to focus on the task of getting off this particular rooftop. They were approximately two stories above the water line. There was no way he was built to the task of carrying both Eula and Rida and wasn't willing to bank on Rida's skill as a swimmer. If only she was of age and had the mark of Baligoz or Menanderus. They needed a boat of some sort. Nothing in the water looked shipworthy.

"I don't see them," Rida said shaking her head.

"Good," Jason said. "Thank you for being brave."

"How else am I going to get eks pee?" she stated.

"Right?!" he retorted appreciatively. He nodded back towards the rooftop doorway. "Let's go check on Eula."

While he was putting Eula back to sleep for the third time, he noticed the roof door. It was attached to the doorway on three hinges, a quality wood that appeared to be pine and despite all the damage to everything everywhere this particular door was still solid and whole.

For the first time ever, Jason was glad his mom had made him sit through the movie Titanic as if her tearful enjoyment of it was going to rub off on him.

He had to get the door off its hinges. "I've got to work, so I'm gonna set you down now," he told Rida.

"Can I help?" she asked.

Jason thought for a moment. He pulled his severed arm from behind his back and carefully covered the exposed shoulder socket meat with the sleeve fabric most of the arm sported. Soon only the hand and wrist was exposed. He held the arm out to Rida.

"I need you to be very careful and don't touch the hand. Only hold it at the base. Keep the hand touching Eula's face while I'm working. Can you do that for me?"

"Sethrin, you want me to do the grossest things for my eks pee," she said taking the arm. Holding it with both hands, she held it out in front of her as if it was a full diaper and carried it over to Eula. She brought the hand down over the bridge of Eula's nose and across her eyes with a soft splat.

Jason went over to the door. He wedged his skeletal index finger under the bolt in the hinge. He made a fist with his free hand and rammed it up forcefully into his skeletal elbow. The bolt popped up a half inch. He did this again and again, treating his hand like a hammer and his skeletal arm like a chisel. Soon the first bolt popped out with a clang onto the rooftop.

Jason worked quickly, sparing an occasional glance back to make sure Rida was still covering Eula. She was diligent for the most part, even though he had to spare some time telling her not to stick the fingers in Eula's mouth or up her nose. Especially the nose... he'd rather for Eula to keep whatever may lurk up there and not shatter his illusions of her femininity with what could potentially get stuck to his finger.

Soon the door was completely off the hinges. It fell onto the rooftop with a thud. He looked back at Rida.

"Ready?" he asked.

She nodded. She was stroking Eula's hair with the hand of his arm club.

He collected his arm club, braced Eula against him with an arm across her chest and dragged her while his bone arm dragged the door. He stepped backwards, pulling the goddess and the door to the edge of the building while Rida dutifully followed. When he got to the edge, he bent down.

"Hop on."

Rida put two arms around his neck. He stood up feeling the small but sure weight of Rida around his chest and Eula at his side. Never had he felt like such a pack mule.

He jumped into the water. The door floated easily. First thing he did was set Eula on the door. Then he helped Rida onto it. He knew there was a limit to buoyancy and wasn't going to test the limits trying to get himself on it. He stayed in the water, holding the door in both hands.

Jason smiled at Rida. "Keep your eyes open. We're about to get some more XP."

Rida smiled back with her tic-tac teeth. Eagerly she turned towards the front of their makeshift raft.

Jason kicked the raft into motion, heading towards that distant rooftop that held a fire and the promise of survivors.

Chapter 20
Reroll

Rich awoke staring at the one thing he didn't think he'd see for a long time, if ever again. He was back in the Hierophane looking directly at the Rift Pendulum.

The giant, golden bob of the pendulum moved in an unhurried sway over the stylized map that covered the whole of the floor. Inside the bob, entire universes blossomed and winked out of existence. He looked up to the ceiling, where liquid metal stars and gas nebulas changed colors. The air shimmered in the space between the pendulum's swinging arc as if it was tearing a hole in the air itself.

"Beautiful, isn't it?" a voice asked. Rich looked to see Druze gazing up at the starry ceiling.

Rich scrambled to his feet. A hot flood of panic surged through him. Seemingly unconcerned, Druze shifted his gaze to the shimmering golden bob that swung on its golden wire as he walked along the map.

"I hope you're not thinking of doing something stupid, like bending sleeves or some other amateur spellcraft," Druze said. "We both know how that duel ends, and if I wanted you dead what makes you think you would've woken up?"

Honestly, Rich had been three milliseconds away from bending a sleeve. It was kind of his go-to. He instead forced a breath in, getting himself into an uneasy calm.

"So what do you want, if not me dead?" Rich asked.

Druze kept strolling, his eyes dancing in the universes blooming and dying in the pendulum's bob.

"Megrym technology, nasran hexation, human spellcraft, it all went into this machine, all to turn the Onesource into what it was always meant to be... fuel. Now, no thanks to you I'll add, I've refined this fuel. It can power wishes and dreams into reality."

Druze stopped looking at the swinging pendulum to focus on Rich. "Turn around, Rich. I'd like for you to take stock of a unique situation."

Rich's breath caught once he saw. Seated in simple wooden chairs near the door were Delv and Rew. Delv's scarred face held a wry grin that reached mirthful eyes. Rew seemed as if they had poured her into the chair, like one nudge would send her spilling out onto the floor. Rich looked above her to see the silent red throb of a Majora witchlock.

Beside them both an aian man from the House of Yol stood. The man wore the black and red armor that distinguished him as Fane Armsguard. The aian didn't move, didn't blink. He just stared vacantly ahead.

"I don't understand all this," Rich said.

"A display of the Rift Pendulum's increased power," Druze said, "something that will become clear in a moment. If you will, Delv."

Delv closed his eyes. A moment later, the aian man blinked and looked around the room.

"Interesting," the man said.

"And the hive mind?" Druze asked. "Is it as you speculated?"

"Better," the aian man said with a twisted grin. "Their minds are like houses without doors lined along a straight, wide avenue. There are no protections or safeguards. I can go into any of these houses and take what I want or add as I need. I'll have no problem convincing them I've been here all along."

The growing realization became an unsettling truth in Rich's mind. "Delv's become a pendulum hero."

"Yes and no," Druze said. "Yes, in the same manner you and your friends used to be, occupying bodies, eager to be in my world doing incredible and impossible missions for the good of humanity. No, in a sense that the Rift Pendulum no longer needs to graft your people's otherworldly mindset onto the hero for it to work. Now it can create blank templates which can be occupied by one of our own provided they have worthwhile mastery of blue magic."

Rich took his eyes off of Delv back to Druze. He smoothed out the white and purple Hierophant robes.

"We no longer need your kind," he said.

Rich tried to think. Delv stood near the door, Rew sat helpless and he was the least accomplished mage in the room. Impossible to run and uneven odds unless he could crush the witchlock, but even then it took a long while to recover from the drain.

"It doesn't just create new blank pendulum heroes," Druze said. "It also alters existing ones. Observe."

He reached a hand out towards the swinging bob of the pendulum. The golden glow intensified and the swinging arc crept to a halt.

Druze's body began to change. He grew a foot taller, his dirty blonde hair changed to shiny black, his features became harsher, sterner, his eyes more East Asian. In moments Rich was looking upon a face he had last seen locked in stone.

The old Druze took a long, deep breath. "Home," he exhaled.

The pendulum had begun swinging again. Druze resumed his stroll through its arc, his boots landing with a hard knock against the floor map.

"You may think I want to torture or obliterate you, Rich, but I don't. It took you and your sloppy friends for me to realize the status quo was slowly failing, that it was unsustainable. Because you forced me into action I have become better than I've ever been, aware of the depth of my immortality in a body hewn from raw magic. And the Hierophane's stronger, the pendulum not only rejuvenated but reinforced. So no, I don't want to kill you. Besides, my daughter would never forgive me for that, and never's exhausting when it's forever."

Only now did Rich start to relax, shifting his mind away from some desperate and half baked escape plan. He looked back at Rew, her eyes pained, a grimace on her lips. A quick glance at Delv showed a blue mage who was curiously inspecting the ant armor of his new body's forearms with prodding fingers. Rich turned back to Druze.

"So what do you want from me?"

Druze smiled. "What all fathers want, to really get to know the person their daughter's so taken with, even if the daughter is wayward and thinks so little of her parent. She thinks you're intelligent and resourceful and even brave. Personally, I believe bravery is a cloak often worn by those who lack a path to be who they really are. So let's provide you a path."

Druze held his hand out to the pendulum. Once again, it stopped its swing and swelled with golden light. A portal opened, but not a blue and white swirl as in most portals. This one was black with white specks, like the pendulum had grabbed two handfuls of condensed cosmos and placed them in the room. A familiar scene opened in the middle of the portal; his house, his street.

Rich's eyes flitted from the scene inside the portal to Druze. "What is this?" he asked.

"You know exactly what this is," Druze replied. "A place free of mages and costs and battles and hardship. A place where you can be the carefree youth that you are, boy. I'm inviting you to go home now."

This had to be a trick. But how? His house was exact, down to the geraniums that mom kept in a state of perpetual struggle. The sight made him realize how much he missed his mom. She must be crazy with worry. He didn't see her that often with her working two jobs, but she was working so hard to keep that house, working herself to death for him. Recognition of all her sacrifice was made stark by his own hardships in this new world. The urge to see her and hug her was overwhelming.

His eyes welled up. "This is a trick!" he shouted at Druze. "What is it? As soon as I walk towards it, you close it and you and your goon laugh at me? It sends me to the Underthral? I'm not falling for it!"

Druze shook his head, his softened eyes and voice almost having a fatherly quality to them. "My daughter needs to see you not only gone, but safe. She needs to see the choices you make. If that choice is to go home, then by all means, go home. All you have to do is take the step."

Take the step. Home was so unbelievably close, Rich could be in the portal faster than a mage could bend a sleeve. And why shouldn't he take the portal? He had failed his part of the mission. Now he was stuck in a room with a psychopath and a sociopath, at their mercy. Who could fault him for leaving before they tire of playing with their newest toy and just kill him for expediency?

"What about my friends?" Rich asked.

Druze shrugged noncommittally. "What about them. You can either trust that I'll remain this magnanimous or trust they'll force my hand and arrive at their own way home but no matter which one you believe, it comes down to trust. You'll literally be a world away."

Rich stared at his home in the portal, silently, the moment stretching into an eternity. The scene seemed to pull at him like a black hole, a hungry maw that he yearned to be swallowed by. He may never get another chance to go home. Here it was—right here, right now. What if he never got to see his mother again? His friends would never fault him for taking the clearest, cleanest path home.

He clumsily batted the tears from his face. "Close it," he said. Before Druze could respond Rich shouted the words again. "Close it!"

The way home winked out of existence.

"Perhaps Rew is right about you," Druze said with an imperious nod. "Seems as if you've changed since you first came here. Back then you were all too ready to leave this world in worst shape than you found it after freeing the Death Null. Since you're not ready to leave, maybe you're ready to right the wrongs you've caused."

"Wrongs?" Rich asked numbly.

"Well, not so much you," Druze said with a wry grin, "after all, you were just a kid locked in a tremendously dangerous prison. I'm surprised you only carved out a piece of the High Fane instead of reducing the whole city to rubble. Let's blame this person instead."

Druze held his hand to the pendulum and as it glowed gray material began to coalesce on the floor and work its way up, like a magic-powered 3D printer. When it was done, Rich was looking at his original character, complete with gray robes and long, errant beard. The newly created Razzleblad stared at nothing with vacant eyes.

"I need you to deliver this miscreant to the Temple of Houses," Druze said. "Perhaps this will allow us to start peace talks and end this war before more innocent lives are lost."

Rich shook his head. "Are you crazy? This isn't going to work."

Druze looked at Rich then at the empty Razzleblad. He nodded assent. "You're right. There's no way you would've grown this much hair since blowing apart the Temple."

He reached out to the pendulum again and Razzleblad's beard shrank to mirror the stubble that was on Rich's face. Razzleblad's thick and unkempt mane transformed into a clean cut.

"Oh, now you want me to deliver an even more identical twin," Rich said.

"I've saved this part for last, this being where it all turns, mind you."

Apprehension grew in Rich as Druze reached out to the pendulum again. Rich felt himself changing, a weird sensation like being at the dentist, where you could see and feel the dentist doing stuff in your mouth but you couldn't feel it through your nervous system. He sensed himself growing, getting bulkier, saw the skin of his hands turning gray.

"*Havadan bir ayna yaratmam lazim*," Druze intoned. In the air next to Druze a mirror pane appeared. Cautiously, Rich stepped towards the mirror.

Rich was aian now. He had a head full of purple hair and a hard reptilian ridge across his brow. House of Sen, the chameleon aians.

Rich looked back at Druze, horror on his face.

"I didn't ask for this. I don't want this."

"You don't want this, you don't want to go home. I'm of the mind to think you don't truly know what it is you want."

"Not this," Rich said shaking his head vigorously.

"I know what you want. It's to serve a nobler purpose. I'm afraid you couldn't do that as Razzleblad. Why, he's wanted by the Holy Aian Empire. But what you can do as the newest member of the empire is end this war."

Rich didn't want to hear any of this, especially coming from Druze and his slick smiling lips.

"Why should I help you? I mean, why should I go along with any of this?"

Druze shrugged noncommittally. "The sooner you deliver the errant gray robe to Nasreddin, the sooner I can crumble the witchlock protecting Rew from her own sense of truth and justice. While she's storming about her offices in the Hierophane sulking, we begin peace talks. In the middle of those talks a group of mages conveniently kill a pendulum crafted clone of your friend Jason. The war ends. You and your friends go home with a clear conscious and my daughter finally starts talking to me in a decade after she's cooled her heels and realizes this plan was the best thing for the Free States. We all win, with me being the biggest winner of us all. That's my plan. What's your alternative?"

Apparently, his alternative was silence. He looked to Rew. Misery clouded her features.

"No..." she began.

"Hush, daughter," Druze said, batting a dismissive hand at her. "It'll take you until nightfall to hear your protest. You think the war's going to wait for witchlock speeches? Your boyfriend here has shown his bravery. Let's see his intelligence. Let him be the man you know him to be and let him reason his way to his own decision."

Rich chewed on his lip while he contemplated Druze's plan. He thought of possible pitfalls, possible alternatives. Everything in his gut said this was bad. Nothing in his head offered a reasonable alternative. Finally he thought of Rew.

He looked at Druze.

"So, how do I turn invisible?"

Chapter 21
Infiltrators

Rich bounced uncomfortably astride the destrier. He felt like he was seconds away from getting tossed from the horse. More than that, after thirty minutes of riding he felt like someone was rhythmically punching him in the ass. Not for the first time, he wished he could swap rides with the destruction mage at the front of their party. She smoothly glided across the plain on a hava-chaise. He spared a glance behind him, where the fabricated Razzleblad lay bound, gagged and tied across his destrier like a saddlebag, his eyes closed.

"You ride like shit," Delv said beside him. The mage-turned-aian rode his own destrier and looked much more competent on it than Rich felt. "We're not even at a gallop."

A gallop would've likely outpaced the two black robed mages who rode hava-chaises in front and behind the two fake aians. The mages were there simply for the appearance, to sell the lie of a prisoner swap and peace offering.

"You know you can go alone," Rich said.

"Apparently, you know psychology about as well as you know horseback riding," Delv replied. He looked dispassionately at the unending grass plains of the High Veldt. "Would you like to venture to guess why I'm not going alone?"

"Druze is an asshole?"

"Your thinking is feeble. It'll only make your trip in that saddle longer."

Rich absently rubbed fingers along his reptilian brow ridge as he bounced awkwardly on the horse. It had become a bit of a habit since becoming an aian. The brow made him feel like he was on the set of Star Trek playing an extra for random alien race X.

"Enlighten me," Rich said. May as well get a bit of insight into blue magic from a mage rather than the *Birleshik Arcana*. Anything to get his mind off the horse's assault on his rear end.

"We're convincing a whole society that you're Seratim, Commander of the fallen Crystal City. Furthermore, we're telling them that this garrison commander is an accomplished tactician versus the incompetent, unrememberable and unremarkable bungler that he really was. Convincing all of aiandom that the commander who lost one of their most impregnable strongholds is actually a legendary hero is highly improbable without help."

"So you want the hive mind involved."

"They are beautiful corroborators," Delv said smiling. "Across the hive I've inserted just the name Seratim into several minds. In a few others just a question, 'Who was it that led the stalwart defense at the Crystal City? Serati? Seram?' In others the sentiment that this nameless commander negotiated the safe return of civilians back to aian lands after the city fell. How he almost won despite overwhelming odds. The sheer number of cowardly mages he felled. And all of it just broken fragments in the back of their minds. So when I announced later that Seratim, Commander of Crystal City was getting released with the mage Razzleblad in custody, those distant, fragmentary notions I inserted got seized on and promulgated through the hive. Now, because of the hive, everyone's excited to see the return of their hero."

Delv talked with excitement about his success at group think manipulation. Rich remained unimpressed and not only because all that talking did little to take his mind off the ride.

"I still don't understand why you couldn't have announced yourself as the Commander of Crystal City."

"I don't exactly fit the description," Delv retorted.

"You can fit any description you want," Rich grumbled. Druze was able to throw out pendulum manufactured shells for Delv to wear like winter coats—a full body immersion at the cost of a simple scry.

Delv shook his head. "And who's left to guide the hive? They overly rely on it for their intelligence and it is the key to this infiltration. Rumors and lies can spread easily in this mindspace, repeated enough times by enough people and they will call them facts. But that doesn't make them true and doesn't allow them to stand up to scrutiny, which is why I can't be the lone hero. You are the one who has to stand on stage, waving and bowing to the cheering masses while I'm the one keeping the curious from looking behind the stage and seeing how the props work."

Delv looked at Rich. "In other words, learn to ride, hero."

Rich grimaced. "Easy for you to say."

"I can train you."

Before Rich could tell him to get bent more words echoed across his mind in Delv's voice.

Seriously, I can train you.

This was the same way it had felt when the two of them were locked in the same room in the Underthral. Delv Vereyn had tortured Rich relentlessly in his own head space while Rich, stuck under bind of a witchlock, had been powerless against the invasion.

There was no witchlock this time. Rich glared at Delv.

"Get the fu—,"

"Wait, wait," Delv held his hands up. "I know what you're going to say. Hear me out."

I can get you back into fighting shape to contend with Druze. Back to gray.

Delv's voice in Rich's head was unmistakable. Meanwhile, the blue-mage-turned-aian-grunt kept talking as if the voice projecting in Rich's mind wasn't his.

"Every aian Armsguard is accomplished on horseback, especially one with career long enough to become a commander, incompetent or otherwise. It will be much harder to sell your authenticity if you are falling off your destrier."

Druze doesn't want to sell your authenticity, the voice in Rich's head spoke. *He could care less if you come back from this.*

This time Rich responded to the Delv voice in his mind.

How are you in my head?

You never uninvited me from the last time we did this, Delv replied. *Our connection ended more with an abrupt severance than a declarative refusal, which means I'm still your guest.*

Not for long, Rich told him.

Understandable, but hear me out first. The alternative is to remain a rather helpless pawn in all this. That, friend, is a shallow pool you shouldn't rush to dive head first in.

"I'm not your friend," Rich snapped.

"No one inferred as much," Delv said in an even, calm tone. "But what does friendship have to do with instruction? Let's not get emotional about riding horses."

"Fool!" Delv's voice hissed in Rich's head. *"You think Druze isn't actively monitoring the most important covert mission of the war?"*

"Sorry," Rich thought, feeling more than a little strange that he was apologizing to Delv of all people. *"I'm not used to think-chatting."*

"What I meant to say," Rich said out loud. "Is that I don't understand why you would want to teach me anything."

"Because I'm good at teaching and the hive mind is boring." Not a second passed before Delv thought-spoke the real answer. *"I hold no illusions to what I am to Druze... simply a tool to employ until that tool breaks. How many lieutenants of Druze have you encountered already? The position has a life expectancy of about one weekend. I'd like to politely resign, and to do that I'm going to need someone on par with Druze to cause a bit of mayhem. That, friend, is you in gray robes."*

This had all the feelings of a setup. Between Brigitte and Samedi and the other barons, Druze had no problems fostering loyalty with depraved people, and Delv ranked up there as one of the sickest. *"Why would you betray him?"* Rich thought. *"Didn't he free you from the Underthral?"*

"I hold no loyalty to Druze or any other mage stupid enough to free me from the Underthral."

"Do we have a deal?" Delv asked "Because from my vantage point seated comfortably astride this horse, it's a veritable bargain."

"Yes," Rich both spoke and thought.

"Excellent. Straighten your back. Square your shoulders. Your legs should be turned inward. You want most of your weight resting on your seat bones."

Dutifully, Rich followed the spoken instructions as Delv gave tip after tip in terms of Rich's posture. After nearly a dozen different protocols, Delv thought to Rich.

"This won't hurt a bit."

Waves of memories that didn't belong to Rich hit him in an instant, a psychic jolt that made Rich's head reel back and almost made him lose his balance. For that instant it was as if he was living the lives of several people at once and all those people were vaguely him and all riding horses.

"See?" Delv said out loud. "You're riding better already."

Rich knew he was riding like an expert. He suddenly had the experience and muscle memory to go along with being an expert. Apparently, blue mages could Matrix someone into whole new skill sets.

"I don't know what this matrix is," Delv thought-spoke, *"but I'll take it as a compliment. And while we're out here, why not get you to the top of your tier in red magic?"*

Just as sudden as the memories of riding a horse, the memories of nebulous people casting insanely powerful spells assaulted Rich's forethoughts. Making a pond of water float, turning his own robe into solid gold, creating a wind channel, hundreds of spells cascaded into a blur of memory. And they all felt as if they were him despite Rich knowing full well he hadn't cast a fraction of those spells himself, not even in practice.

They rode in silence for a few moments with nothing to mark the passage of time but the clomp of the destriers and the engine whine of the hava-chaises speeding over the grasses of High Veldt.

"You know, you should thank me," Delv said. "Students are such ingrates."

"Erm, thanks." Rich was still in shock. All those spells he had barely read much less seen, he knew them now, just as intimately as he knew how to bend his sleeves. The feeling that Delv was setting him up came back strong.

"Why do you need me at all?" Rich thought-spoke. *"Why can't you or any other blue mage for that matter just download their way to gray robes?"*

"This is all short term memory," Delv replied. *"Transitory. Next week you'll remember how to ride a horse about as well as you'll remember what you ate for lunch today. Since you don't really know how to ride, all you'll really be left with is the practical experience you're getting right now. Granted, next time you ride you will be better because of this real experience coupled with the ghostly remnants of your implanted tutoring, but I wouldn't recommend galloping to anyone's res-*

cue. *That said, any spells a blue mage would attempt to learn without having used would surely evaporate in time."*

"So how is giving me temporary spell knowledge supposed to get me to gray?!" Rich thought. He didn't have to wonder if Delv could read Rich's emotions because the exasperation carried more emphasis than the words when Rich thought it.

"Idiot. You're a gray robe. I'm not dumping spells you've never used into your brain. I'm helping you recall the spells you already know, all the spells that took a lifetime to master to get you into those robes in the first place. Yours isn't the matter of fooling your short term memory, but unlocking the long term. Now is there any other trifling concern of yours or can we get down to the business of inciting revolution?"

"I could get used to this," Rich muttered. He recalled what Delv said about spies and turned to the blue mage. "The riding a horse, I mean."

"You know, I used to be a teacher at the Hierophane. The students always extolled that I was the best."

"Why'd you stop teaching?" Rich asked.

"The students," Delv answered with a wry grin.

Seriously, Delv thought to Rich, *what I'm teaching you will be of little help if we can't enterprise a way to return you to your Razzleblad form. This is the part of the plan I've yet to work through.*

After you popped into my head I was hoping this aian form was more cosmetic than anything else, Rich thought back. *You're casting as an aian, after all.*

You're reminding me of why I stopped teaching, Delv thought. *Right now you're looking at the House Yol aian riding beside you as if he is me, as if he is the one in your head right now. Must I remind you that I am in your head like I am in its body like I am in the hive mind while truly being in none of these places? Physically, I'm still at the Hierophane. You find yourself immersed and surrounded by thought magic without truly understanding it.*

Rich, for his part, had come to think of the ant aian riding next to him as Delv, differently skinned as Rich himself was now. *You unlocked red magic for me. Can you unlock blue magic now?* Rich asked. *It feels like the school I'm least familiar with.*

Delv's ant shell pointed toward the horizon. "I hope you're ready," he said aloud. "Because lessons are over."

The smudges in the far distance became clearer quickly thanks to Rich's new aian vision. Eleven Armsguardsmen sat astride their destriers in a line. Within a few more yards of riding to meet them, Rich could see there was an Armsguardsman from every house except Onus. Maybe even one or two from his house too, if Targhos had taught Rich anything.

"As much as I take a simple joy seeing you bungle through life, could you attempt to be a bit more visible?" Delv asked.

Rich looked down and noticed he had chameleon cloaked. He essentially looked to the outer world like a floating set of armor. The reins for his horse dangled in the air as if they'd been hit with the heaviest of starch. Apparently the cloaking state wasn't just a conscious decision but could be activated based on feelings, at least on the feelings of apprehension Rich was currently fostering. It made sense, because a large part of Rich felt like hiding right now.

Luckily Rich had practiced Sen cloaking a lot while waiting for the Hierophane and Temple of Houses to set up this exchange. He uncloaked with ease. An errant thought crossed his mind that being in the House of Sen was probably the worst for someone trying to overcome the fear of public speaking. *How are you gonna hide your stage fright when your body's blinking out of sight?*

Are you deficient? Delv thought to him.

It didn't take long for the black mage in the lead to arrive at the delegation of soldiers, all the while nervous energy building in Rich like electricity charging a battery. There were lethal consequences to him not pulling this off. The black mages ahead and behind Rich shut down their hava-chaises and let them settle on the plains in silence.

Rich recognized the Armsguardsman from House Marad. It was Mors. The snake-featured aian thankfully showed no sign of recognition. Mors looked at him with emotionless protocol, put his right hand over his heart as if he was pledging allegiance and bowed his head. All the other aians simply stared at Rich.

Ah... this was a courtesy Rich wasn't sure how to respond to. He cast a glance at Delv's aian shell, who was looking ahead at the soldiers. Then he realized it was very unlikely for commanding officers to look at foot soldiers for input in the middle of a maybe-salute thingy. Hastily, Rich returned the gesture, pledging with his hand over his heart and bowing back.

The aians across the field looked at each other quixotically.

Oops, Delv though to him casually. *Forgot to train you on military customs and courtesies. One moment.*

Imagery and information from a slew of aian battle scenes and military conversations rushed into his mind. He realized he had screwed up the custom called Assumption of the Guard, something done when someone of higher rank and authority enters into a unit he has right to lead. The one currently in charge relinquishes command with the gesture Mors performed. The person taking command puts their right hand over their heart just like the person who initiated the ceremony but then fully extends the arm straight out and makes a fist. Unlike Rich, the person taking command never bows their head.

"Uh... I'm afraid I can't, uh, take command," Rich said to Mors. "I don't consider myself, um, fit after my time in the Hierophane dungeons. This mission is too important to trust to a mind that has yet to have proper recuperation."

The leather in Mors' glove crooned with strain as his grip tightened on his spear. "Did they torture you, Commander?" he asked before casting his stare down to the black mage in front of him.

Better take charge of something, Delv chided.

"It doesn't matter," Rich said. "This mission is also too important to strike empty blows on account of my condition. Lead us back to the safety of Nasreddin, Captain Mors."

Mors raised an eyebrow. "You know my name, Commander?"

Oops again. "Even unarmed, a commander should always be armed with intelligence."

Mors nodded respectfully.

I'm impressed, Delv thought. *You work well under pressure. That line was so good, I broadcast it out to the hive mind. Both me and Restan there. Now everyone in the hive's talking about it.*

Great, Rich thought. *Just what I wanted to do... trend on aian Twitter.*

Speaking of twits, anytime you're ready, feel free to put your horse in motion so I can follow behind you and take our places with the aians. Unless you prefer to stay sandwiched in between two destruction mages and cause more military protocol breeches.

Rich nudged his horse to walk between the destriers of the Armsguard formation, turned and took a place behind Mors. Mors looked down at the destruction mages.

"You will hear from officials of the High Fane within a week. I needn't remind you to brook no hostilities until then."

The mages gave curt bows which Rich wasn't sure Mors had even seen as he immediately kicked his destrier into a gallop. The other Armsguardsmen followed suit in an instant, leaving Rich and Delv to respond late and last. It took a while for Rich to find his proper place in the formation, tapping into the temporary riding skills Delv had given him. He spared a glance backwards to see the two mages as receding black smudges lifting up on their hava-chaises and turning around.

The destriers sent clumps of grassy earth upwards as they tore a path to Nasreddin.

Congratulations in the short term, Delv thought to Rich.

Rich felt uneasy butterflies dancing in his gut. This was all too reminiscent of the first time Mors had escorted him, Jason and Mel to the Temple of Houses. That had started with open arms and culminated with the cleaving of the temple.

Somehow, these same open arms felt more ominous the second time around.

Chapter 22
Clockwound

M ike couldn't help but feel a sense of wonder as he gazed into the night sky. Stars were always scarce in the city where he grew up. Here they were a thick blanket, as if some mischievous god had spilled glitter in the bowl of heaven. The only other time he had seen so many stars was when he was in Afghanistan and in both places staring up made trouble feel as far away as the starlight, if only for a brief moment. This time, however, he entertained the brief thought that one of these stars may be home.

He brought himself back to the world, this foreign one where he was stuck and looked at the crude map he, Ego, Runt and three Sons lieutenants were all gathered around. Illuminated by the ruddy glow of copper lanterns, the map showed features of the Sprawl's undercity, with red marks to indicate Clockwound Warder strongholds and the captured Heart of the Sons.

The table came up to Mike's chest. He had to reach up and over to point a purple finger at one of the red marks.

"So you say this they headquarters?" he asked Ego. "Clockwound central?"

Ego shook his head and shrugged noncommittally. "I tell I's rough that is where their head was quartered back when them had a head. Ever since I bested Pramus, them have no head, at least none brave enough to emerge from its hole in the ground and announce themselves to I."

"Somebody's gotta be calling the shots," Mike said. "Can't have an organization without an organ. So there's some dude behind a counter handing lil clock-gear vests and goggles to the new recruits and they got somebody else suited up with their goggles and their vest maybe rocking a lil chef hat cooking up big vats of rat stew so everybody can get their protein for another day of marauding... there's somebody directing those efforts, know what I'm saying?"

"I think same," Ego said with a nod. "Reality not meshing with I's thinking though, rough. Them group in strange patterns, do odd patrols around regions none think matter, not even them back when Pramus ran things. Senseless."

"Maybe the new leadership is doing things to throw you off?" Mike suggested. "They stay at war with you and you already bodied their last leader, after all."

Ego set his jaw and shook his head. "Feels different to I. Them move in sync with each other, but out of sync with the rest of the world, know?"

"Let's look at the situation," Mike said. "Ok, so we want the warders to pull back from the Heart of the Sons and return to their not-so-happy but predictable selves rummaging through their own piece of the Sprawl, which will allow the Sons to deploy some of their forces to crack open the Hierophane without having to worry about if they've got a home to return to. But, Ego, you're saying in the months I've been gone no clear leadership has emerged and so there's no one we can wreck or negotiate with to get them going back to their old ways, right?"

Ego nodded. "Truth in gist."

Mike looked up from everyone at the table, his goggles shimmering in the lantern light.

"We need more intel. Instead of guessing at what the warders are about we need to know from the source."

He looked around at the party. "We need to nab some of them up."

Ego sucked his teeth. "Not an easy go about it. Warders, them fight hard, like cornered animals. Them run even harder. It's like that fear the purple mage put in them festered, made them all frantic in their own heads."

"Sheeet," Mike swore. "Easy? Last time I saw easy I was in a world of asphalt, street lights and breakfast cereal. I don't expect easy, but I do expect we can pull that off, get some questions answered and be in a position to make a more informed choice. Right now all we can do is bale buckets of water to keep the boat from filling up when we need to know how to plug the leak."

One of the Sons of Kaftar, a female aian from House of Yol, approached the group and faced Ego.

"News from the hive," she said. "This war with the mages may be ending soon. The Hierophane has returned the Commander of Crystal City to the Temple of Houses and handed over the gray robe who carved up the temple."

Mike stopped looking over the map lying on the table, his vision filtering out everything and everyone in the field camp except the aian from House of Yol.

"What do you mean they handed him over?"

The aian's eyes looked as if she was thinking something before focusing her oscillating eyes on Mike. "The Temple of Houses is celebrating the return of Commander Seratim and his deliverance of the rogue mage Razzleblad."

How the hell did that old kid go from checking out a cave to being locked down in the aian capital? Mike looked at Runt and Ego. "I've gotta make a call."

He went to the edge of the camp where he had stowed his pack. Bringing the mirror out, he invoked Mel's name. The mirror shimmered for a few moments until Mike's brother appeared, looking a bit cross.

"Not the best time to talk, especially if you're just gonna come at me about Rich."

"Man, do I look like a relationship counselor?" Mike asked. "Does this look like an intervention? I'm here to tell you if you wanna help your new boo, you'd best keep radio silent with him."

Confusion mixed with the irritation already present in Mel's features. "What the hell is this about?"

"Word from the hive mind. The aians nabbed up Rich, got him locked up in Nareddin."

Mel nodded slowly. "And this is to warn me not to go off and do something stupid to get him back?"

Mike stroked his chin, musing. "I forget, who teleported into the middle of the Hierophane and ran through it beating on mages like dusty rugs when their jump-off ran off to rescue their jump-off? Was that me or you?"

Mel glowered. "You're going to stop coming at me sideways, Mike, or we're gonna have more than words next time we see each other."

"I call it like I see it," Mike said. "If you wanna move some furniture later cause you in your feelings about that, we can get it, bruh. All I'm saying is if you wanna give him the best chances for getting out of there to smash again, you'd best keep your end of the mirror quiet."

Mel scoffed. "Ha! I'm in my feelings... seems like you're the one bent and twisted right now about how I spend my free time. Calling me in the middle of..." she paused and looked up and around at a scene Mike had no way of seeing, "...I don't even know what to call this, but you're hitting me up to tell me not to call a guy. And why the hell is it so important to keep 'radio quiet' anyway?"

Mike looked at his brother and spoke slowly, his expression deadpan. "He got captured, dude. If he's still got the mirror then he hid it, prolly somewhere in his pajamas. He'll likely wanna use it when no one's around interrogating him to coordinate rescue attempts from the inside. The last thing he needs in between is for it to go shimmering and shining because you're trying to set up a booty call."

Mel's eyes shot daggers. "What makes you such an asshole, you little fucker?"

"Maybe I don't like hearing about how my brother got his back blown out in the middle of a backyard barbecue."

"Go to hell, bitch," Mel said before ending the call.

Mike nodded at his own reflection in the now quiet mirror. Okay, so his brother thinks he can talk wild spicy and just hang up like that's the flavor? Bet. Yeah, they were definitely gonna move some furniture around next time they got up.

Mike stowed the mirror, turned and made his way back to the strategy table. Only when he arrived, no one was there, not even some of the anonymous Sons of Kaftar who were pretty much in the background minding their own business. It was as if Ego had put in the call to evacuate and left Mike alone to make the call.

"Did I pass anybody on the way back here," Mike asked himself. "Where the hell is everybody?"

Suddenly, the corn stalks behind Mike began to rustle. Moments later, Runt and four Sons of Kaftar emerged, led by Ego. The four Sons carried a gagged Clockwound Warder, each son holding a limb as the warder being carried thrashed about futilely. Runt carried another warder by himself, holding onto the warder's face like it was a suitcase and dragging the rest of him while the warder pawed at the half-weager's iron grip.

Ego looked at Mike. "Is the rough done with exploring his emotions in the looking glass?"

"Man, stop playing," Mike said. "How'd you get these dudes so fast?"

"Who better than I in the fallen kingdom?" Ego asked in return.

"Fair enough," Mike replied.

In short order the Sons of Kaftar had the warders bound to wooden pikes with rope from neck to foot. Despite this inextricable predicament, both warders continued to struggle against the binds like feral cats.

"All right," Mike said pacing back and forth between the two warders. "Cool it already."

They kept at their struggle, heedless to his words.

Mike drew back and cockpunched the warder on the right. His response was to grunt, lurch his head forward momentarily, then he went right back to the useless fight against the ropes.

"What the hell's going on with these dudes?" Mike asked to no one in particular.

"This is what I say, them wrong," Ego said. "In sync with each other, out of tune with the rest of all."

"Yo," Mike said. "This shit got sci-fi movie written all over it. Mind control, terminator robots, whatever it is, these dudes got some ill wiring. Runt, I need your height bruh... could you pull this man's goggles?"

Runt went over to the warder on the left. He grasped the goggles straps on either side of the warder's face and pulled them off. Immediately, the warder's head slumped forward. Unlike the other one who kept struggling against his bonds, this one stayed inert as if he was now lifeless. Runt put a palm on the warder's forehead and pushed his head up. Under the light of the lanterns, everyone could now see that the warder had no eyes, just hollow, cavernous spaces where eyes should be.

Mike flinched involuntarily. "What the fuck, man?!" He looked up at Runt. "And how the hell can you be all copasetic with touching eyeless tron dude?"

Runt shrugged. "Little fear in simple meat."

Meat. Mike turned the word over in his head, then spoke to Ego and Runt.

"I don't think it's human. We ain't been paying attention, not for real for real. These warders all look alike. Not just the uniforms and the goggles and the shaved heads. They mouths alike, they noses. Not exactly identical but close enough to warrant a feeling of sameness. My best guess is we dealing with a clone army that nutted up for some unknown reason."

"What be these clones?" Ego asked.

Mike answered. "They're like copies of each other. What I'm basically saying is the reason you've got so many warders running around everywhere is they keep making duplicates."

"You speak of things that make no sense to I," Ego said. "I fought Pramus. Pramus spoke to I during the duel and before. He was aian, flesh and blood, quick until I made him otherwise."

"Well, something's changed," Mike said.

For long moments no one spoke. The only sound was the gagged gurgling of the second warder struggling to get free.

Finally, Mike spoke.

"Pramus was aian and apparently able to have conversation, so they can't all be like this, just the ones we see roaming about, topside. But something happened after the purple mage Samedi came through terrormancing and terrorizing, something that made the clone warders nuttier than a Snickers bar."

Mike turned his gaze to Runt and Ego. "Looks like the only place to find real answers is in the undercity. And I don't like the prospect of going up against a clone army of who knows how many fighters in their home turf."

"Perhaps," Ego mused, "other potentialities present themselves to I." He took the pair of goggles from Runt and put them back on the face of the inert warder. Immediately the warder became alert and active again, struggling against its bonds as if nothing had ever happened. Ego took the goggles off and again the clone went lifeless. He looked inside the goggles, inspecting the frames and rim before removing his own goggles and donning the warder's. In that brief flash between eye protection, Mike noted Ego's irises were hazel.

Nothing happened to Ego. No secret chamber opened in the goggles and spat acid at his eyeballs. He turned to face Mike.

"Your goggles came from Pramus through Ruki through I, so fear nothing. Everyone else, clear from here."

Everyone retreated into the brush and corn to where they were no longer visible, except Runt, whose head extended beyond the height of the corn from the eyes up. Ego drew a diskbow blade and cut the remaining warder's bonds.

Hastily, the warder shed the ropes that still clung to him and removed the gag. Once it had, it merely walked past Mike and Ego. Ego motioned to Mike to get in line behind the warder. The warder continued to walk as if it was nothing out of the norm leading this procession. Mike raised a hand and beckoned Runt to come out of hiding towards him.

Runt emerged from the cornfield. Upon seeing Runt, the warder growled and charged full speed at him. Runt smashed down with a meaty fist on the top of the warder's head as he approached, a blow so hard it caused the warder's feet to go out from under him. The warder stumbled to the ground and remained there.

Ego went over to the prone warder and removed the googles. He twirled the goggles by their strap.

"Seems I and I's roughs found the recipe to cook this stew, know?"

Chapter 23
The Broken City

Mel stuffed the mirror into her pack a bit too forcefully only to pull it back out a moment later. She exhaled, calming herself, and leaned it gently against the pack, easily visible from most of the roof, just in case it shimmered.

From the edge of the roof, Mel looked out over the broken city. Under the translucent dome, the waterlogged, crumbling buildings, the floating bodies and debris, it all gave Mel the impression that she was trapped in a morbid snow globe. Somewhere out there was Jason, but from her vantage point on the roof she couldn't see him.

She turned her attention to the immediate roof space behind her. Ruki Provos was helping a peacekeeper hobble over to the other survivors, a ring of seven aians who sat surrounding a small fire that helped to warm and dry everyone. It was only when all seven aians glowered at the peacekeeper as he awkwardly angled himself to sit down on the rooftop that Mel realized the peacekeeper's presence probably wasn't overly welcome.

Ruki seemed aware of it as well. "War's over friends," he said. "At least for us. We'll likely need everyone to pitch in to get out of this situation, so let's try to not kill each other."

The peacekeeper took off his chrome helmet, revealing a blond man in his early twenties. He looked at the aians around the fire. "I did not relish the orders to separate the aian population, which I know came from mages," he said. "I'm a native Suusterene. My allegiance is to my city and the mages have destroyed my city. Their orders against your kind no longer hold."

The aians did not speak back, but Mel could tell that their ice had thawed as a couple heads nodded. Apparently no longer worried about people murdering each other while his back was turned, Ruki went over to the edge of the rooftop to Mel.

"Even though I was a bit busy, I couldn't help but overhear your call with Mike," Ruki said, pointing to an ear. "A keenly developed practice of eavesdropping that's contributed to its fair share of winning deals. Are you okay?"

Mel chewed her lip. "I don't think any of us are okay, at least not here. We should worry about what's in front of us and not what's trolling me from across the nether regions of the world."

She placed a hand on Ruki's shoulder. The act caused a slight smile to peek out on the corners of his mouth, bringing Mel's attention to the dark stubble of his square jaw. The smile reached his eyes, which twinkled in a way that seemed both mischievous and kind.

"C'mon," Mel said, returning the smile. "Let's check on Gina and Calais."

Together they went to the other side of the roof. Gina sat solemnly beside Calais, who was kneeling over the side arm outstretched, helping more survivors clamor onto the roof. Below her in the water two male aians of the fish house Baligoz were lifting a woman aian of the snake house Marad into Calais' waiting hands. Once the woman was safely on the roof, Calais helped her to stand and pointed behind Mel and Ruki.

"Find a place by the fire," Calais instructed her. The woman nodded, appreciably relieved and left. Calais turned her attention down to the fish men in the water.

"Traverys, Barum, how are you two holding up? Ready to make another foray into the unknown?"

They both nodded. "No rest until we've scoured every inch of this blasted place," one of them said. And with a return nod from Calais, the two of them dived into the murky depths.

"Our numbers are growing," Mel said to Calais.

Calais nodded. "I'm hoping what's left of Eula's moth guard will bring in some people too, but they seemed more focused on finding their queen, so who knows."

"Ladies," Ruki said, "any of you have experience escaping from giant magic dome shells? I'm afraid I'm slightly out of my depth here."

Gina shook her head solemnly. She held a distant, almost vacant stare in her eyes. Her friend Vincent had gotten taken by the monster right in front of her. There wasn't a whole lot Mel could say to help her deal.

Calais grimaced as she looked up at the dome. "It's a collection, a giant tapestry of seashells. I assume that gray robe was able to cast it from that stitched together abomination. The most incredible and perverse use of green magic I've ever seen."

She stood up and looked to the horizon. "In normal circumstances, it'd be easy enough for me cut through the shell using witchcraft once we got to the edge. We're far from normal though and I don't know how effective I can be."

"I don't understand," Ruki said. "Why would you be less effective now?"

"I'm a warm witch," Calais said. The subsequent look of confusion from Ruki made her roll her eyes disdainfully. "The witch community, small as it is, is divided between sympathetic witches or apathetic witches, warm or cold depending on how they use costshares, you know, the people who bear the cost. A warm witch farms the cost out to as many costshares as possible. Most of my costshare base was the aian population of Suusteren. Between all the destruction and the portal hopping, I don't have enough costshares within proximity to bear the weight of any heavy spells."

Mel pointed up to the dome. "I hate to sound callous, but you may have to seek your colder side today. We don't exactly have the luxury of sneaking costs past the unsuspecting."

Calais raised an eyebrow at her. "Mel, right? Well, look around, Mel. Anyone close enough for me to draw from has undoubtedly been through too much already without me inflicting them with more. These costs can break bones, shut down organs. If you're not willing to have both your legs snapped back like brittle twigs, don't go volunteering anyone else for the job."

Ruki, seemingly bristled by how Calais addressed Mel, took a step towards the witch. "You want to consign everyone here to new, permanent addresses under the dome because working within your medium all of a sudden agitates your moral fiber. A thief who can't bring herself to steal."

"I have lines I don't cross," Calais said with cold steel in her voice. "You're one to talk about thieves. You may think of yourself as a hero now that the city's collapsed, but it wasn't that long ago you were nothing more than a war profiteer, willing to let families starve to make some coin."

"A witch! Looking down her shrew nose at me?!" Ruki began. "You have about three sec—"

"Shut it!" Gina shouted. The sound came unexpected, forcing both Calais and Ruki to pause. They looked down at her while she continued to look over the ruined city.

"Put the cost on me," Gina said, her voice low and gravelly. "I'm tired of this place. Sick of this shit." She looked up at Calais. "One way or another, I just want out."

Calais' eyes were rimmed with sorrow. "Gina, honey, you don't know what you're saying. These spells can maim, even kill."

"I'm done playing," Gina said with a shrug. "I'm calling game over. And I'm leaving, one way or another."

Mel understood full well what Gina was driving at. It was something Mel had contemplated and discussed with her friends, something that she was sure all pendulum rejects sooner or later think about. What happens to them if they died here? This used to be a game and these bodies, simply game avatars. Back when it was just a game everyone playing had seen their fair share of deaths taking on insane challenges. Mel and her friends all kept some hope, even if it was just a sliver, that death here meant waking up in their original skins back in their own world. None of them were desperate enough to test it. It sounded like Gina, having hit a precipice of hopelessness, was all out of fucks to give.

"Hey!" a familiar voice shouted. "Before you game over, you mind helping me out?"

They all turned to see Jason in the water, steering a door towards them. Eula lay sprawled across the door. Beside her sat a little aian girl, who was rubbing the goddess' face with Jason's sleep inducing arm club. The sight was both strange and relieving.

"Jason!" Mel called. "You found us."

"A man with a scoundrel's crazy luck!" Ruki shouted. He wasted no time, hurrying back to the impromptu camp to retrieve a rope which he threw down to Jason. Jason tied the rope around himself and Eula and held the little girl while the four people on the rooftop hauled them up.

"I'm lucky I had the sound of your unnecessary, angst filled arguing to guide me," Jason said with a wry smile. "Otherwise I might've gotten lost and maybe run into a group of survivors who are actually trying to escape this place. And who needs that?"

"Great," Calais muttered. "Exactly what we all were clamoring for to get us out of here, comedy."

"Sethrin," the little girl said as she pulled on Jason's pants leg. "Can I have comedy instead of eks pee?"

"Rida, my dear," he replied. "You can have both!" He put a finger on her nose. "Boop!"

From the shadows, a questioning feminine voice emerged.

"Rida?"

Two of the aian survivors stepped out of the shadows, a man from House Ananna and a woman from House Otam. The woman saw the little girl and her horse ears twitched excitedly.

"Rida!"

"Ma!" Rida exclaimed. "Baba!"

She ran into her parents' outstretched arms. They hugged her fiercely. Mel smiled at the sight, the one ray of sunshine to be found under this dome.

"And that's why they call me the Chosen One," Jason said with a smug, self-satisfied grin as he looked at the family he helped reunite.

"Here I was hoping they called you that because you had an idea on how to get us out of here," Calais said dryly. "At least a better idea than your huckster friend here."

"*Huckster?!*" Ruki cried.

Jason held up a bone finger. "Before you two adopt each other as brother and sister, lemme make the observation that your two different points of view are not mutually exclusive. Guess how we resolve them."

Jason paused. Calais shot a questioning glance at Jason, then Ruki, then back at Jason. "Can't you... just tell us?"

"Simple," Jason began. "It's highly doubtful these are the only survivors and wooden doors in this huge swath of city. So let's make our way to the edge of the dome, collecting survivors and door rafts as we go. Every person adds to our resident witch's blood bank. By the time we've reached the end, there should be plenty of people to help spread the cost around."

Calais nodded sagely. "That could work."

"Of course it'll work," Jason said. "The people want us to find them and get them out of here. And it's not like there's some kinda time limit. We take it methodically, make sure we get everybody and get out of here."

Suddenly everything under the dome shook. A thunderous groan permeated the air. Their building and all the buildings around them started to tremor. It was an earthquake.

"Suusteren doesn't get earthquakes," Ruki said as he held onto Mel.

"This can't be good," Mel replied.

As if waiting for those words, chunks of seashells from the dome fell away, splashing down into the water below. Suddenly a huge spike, like a tooth made of coral, stabbed out of the water next to the building, so tall everyone had to crane their necks upward to see the cruel tip. This was definitely not natural, and no one had to say what this meant.

Clearly, the gray robe was still alive. And he was aiming to kill them all in this watery prison.

Chapter 24
The Other Front

Rich rode into Nasreddin to a hero's welcome. A huge crowd of aians packed the streets, forcing the horses to travel close together down the main avenue. Aian flyers hovered in the sky while more folks teamed out of second and third story windows to cheer raucously for the returned general hosting the captured gray robe.

Funny enough, this wasn't the first time he'd seen a hero's welcome. Jason got this same treatment the last time they were in Nasreddin, with aians of all stripes, spots and scales clamoring to get a glimpse of their Chosen One.

This time Rich rode through the city without Jason or Mel, and their absence caused a heavy-hearted sigh. Rich couldn't recall the last time he felt so alone.

"Alone?" Delv Vereyn asked in Rich's head. *"Perish the notion."*

Not alone, then. Somehow, that was even more troubling.

They made their way through the throng up the steep incline where the Temple of Houses sat, carved into the mountain.

Towers, parapets and spiraling staircases wove in and out of the rock over many tiers while a majestic waterfall spilled over the mountain and into the temple. The water collected in pools tier by tier, like watery steps, weaving its own course through the temple to eventually reach the city below.

In full day, Rich could easily see the jagged gash he had cut from the uppermost reaches of the temple months ago. He didn't know his spell had been that catastrophic. It was as if a giant had taken a bite out of the temple's once perfect symmetry. He would've thought it would've been fixed by now, or at least there'd be scaffolding or something.

"*The aians have sworn to not rebuild the temple until the culprits responsible have been brought to justice,*" Delv mind-spoke, reminding Rich that his thoughts weren't strictly his own for the time being. "*Nothing like having to look up every day at this eyesore of a sacred site to light the fire of resolve with the people.*"

Everyone dismounted at the gates of the temple, where stable hands came out to gather the destriers. Delv came over to assist Rich in getting off his horse and together they pulled the fake Razzleblad off the horse.

"Remember, you're a general," Delv cautioned.

Rich nodded.

Mors came to them with an assistant. "Seratim, let us take the mage to the council so they can more properly bind him."

"Indeed," Rich said authoritatively and in a move that was very unlike him, he stepped away from the bound and sleeping mage to let Mors' assistant and Delv carry the body. Apparently, high ranking officers of the High Fane didn't do actual manual labor but they still took the credit, so Rich and Mors were going to "take" the captured mage to the council by just walking there while their grunts did the hauling.

The Temple of Houses was just as stunning as Rich remembered. Polished marble columns and high ceilings were home to lush ivy tendrils. The brown stone floor was tinged a soft green in places where the waterfall pools had lapped and allowed moss to grow. The rock walls hosted vibrant red and yellow flowers among the moss and vines. The whole place felt alive.

It also bustled with traffic, dense with men and women of the Armsguard. Everyone cleared a path for them as Rich and Mors approached with their aides bearing Razzleblad. Rich felt extra shammy looking at their expressions of awe and deference.

They stopped at the huge double oaken doors Rich remembered from the last trip. The gods had interviewed them all in there, trying to assess whether or not Jason was indeed their Chosen One. Two armsguardsmen stood before the door. They came to brisk attention.

"Comport yourselves within the Accord of Communion!" they said in union.

Mors immediately dropped to one knee. Rich followed suit awkwardly, with no idea if he should be doing what Mors was doing or something else altogether in order to 'comport' himself. The act earned a suspiciously raised eyebrow as Mors side glanced at him.

Panic flashed hot in Rich. He may look the part, but he didn't know the first thing about aian military protocol. Now here he was in their templed out version of the Pentagon, faking like he had a storied career in the profession of arms spanning decades. Was it movies, Hollywood magic—what made him think he could get away with this charade? This was suicide in the making!

"Are you going to remember I'm here before or after you wet yourself?" Delv asked in his head. *"Listen to me instead of your rabbit heart thumping and you'll be fine."*

"What's the Accord of Communion?" Rich thought-asked Delv. *"Am I comporting myself?"*

"It's their military Armsguard way of saying 'prostate yourself because one of our stupid gods is inside,'" Delv answered. *"Consider yourself comported."*

Meanwhile behind a kneeling Rich and Mors stood their aides, both holding handfuls of incapacitated mage.

"Oh, don't mind us, we're like ghosts or pack mules," Delv said, *"Here but not here. They're about to tell you which gods are inside. Just keep saying yes and you'll get through it eventually."*

"Obeisance in the body, fealty in the breast, reverence in the breath for you soon bear witness to our gods. Beholden yourself to Ananna, the Grower, Weaver of Fates, Protector of Destined Lovers, the Keeper of the Third House within the Everlasting Temple of Houses, the House that bears her name. In her faith and covenant are you so bound?"

"Yes," Rich and Mors said together.

"Beholden yourself to Otam, the Measure, the Breadth of Competence, Defender of the Diligent, the Keeper of the Fourth House within the Everlasting Temple of Houses, the House that bears his name. In his faith and covenant are you so bound?"

"Yes."

"Beholden yourself to Baligoz, the Watcher, Delver of Thought, the Sustenance of the Hungry Soul, the Keeper of the Fifth House within the Everlasting Temple of Houses, the House that bears his name. In his faith and covenant are you so bound?"

"Yes."

"Beholden yourself to Nadi, the Hunter..."

They kept going but by this time, Rich had pretty well tuned it out. He just waited for them to stop talking so he could say yes at the end of it.

After Rich's fifth yes, the guard said "Stand and receive their blessings," while the other guard pulled open the doors. Rich and Mors got on their feet and proceeded into chamber.

The twelve thrones were in the room as Rich remembered. The first two thrones stood empty. Ananna the spider goddess, who Rich still suffered nightmares about, sat in the third throne. On her right sat Otam, a god Rich was seeing for the first time. His shoulder-length chestnut brown hair was mohawked, giving the appearance of the helmets Spartans wore and allowing full display of his long horse ears. He wore a metal breastplate the color of burnt umber.

Before he could continue going down the line, instructions from Delv piped into his head. He proceeded to the middle of the room, the same spot where he had previously interviewed before all the gods and their Elevated. Mors and the aides carrying the Razzleblad dummy fell in behind Rich where they were all single file. Rich bowed his head.

"We beseech you dear gods," Rich said. "Find favor in us."

"Look upon us and know our favor," Ananna said.

Rich looked up, silently glad she hadn't turned into a giant spider as some way to show her approval. Contrary to the customary words they were using, that wouldn't have done him any favors. Ananna pointed at Rich.

"Present the villain Razzleblad."

Rich stepped aside, allowing the aides to bear the dummy. Ananna looked the sleeping mage up and down while the eight thick dreadlocks curled tightly to frame her face. The disgust in her features was clear and unmistakable.

"The mages have surrendered him true," she said.

At her words, Otam rose from his throne. Now Rich could see that along with the burnt umber breastplate, Otam wore a blue and gray pattered skirt that stopped at his knees. Maybe it was a kilt but Rich wasn't really fashion expert enough to know the difference. A leather pounch hung at Otam's waist, held in place by an ornate silver chain. "True or not, sister, I don't trust gifts given by enemies," he said with a voice like a bass drum. He proceeded down the dais until he stood before Razzleblad. Reaching into his leather pouch, Otam produced what appeared to be a dull metallic twelve-sided die and what Rich knew to be anything but.

The sight made the cat god Nadi jump from his throne. He wore a breastplate and gauntlets of deep red over a green bodysuit with yellow tiger stripes. "A witchlock? You trust not the enemy but trust their tools? You would use their magic here, within the heart of the temple?"

"Yes and more yes, brother. I look at his binds now and wonder if they'll hold. Likewise, I question the suitability of our own dungeon to hold a gray robe. I don't have the same question with this," he said rotating the witchlock with two fingers. "I've seen mages of all ranks and colors crumple with this. Razzleblad here deserves nothing less."

The sight of the witchlock made Rich uneasy, and not just from his prior experience with it. Part of him wondered if employing it on the sleeping dummy would make it unravel. It was just a hollow shell fashioned from pure magic, after all. There was no telling what the witchlock would do to such a thing.

Without waiting to see if there'd be any more protest, Otam chucked the die at the sleeping Razzleblad. It flared to life with an angry red and indelible tendrils snaked out of it before they disappeared, leaving a glowing red cube to float above the mage.

Rich breathed a sigh of relief as the Razzleblad dummy continued to sleep through the lock.

Otam raised Razzleblad's head by grasping a handful of his hair. With his other gloved finger, Otam plucked Razzleblad smartly in the eye. Razzleblad's eyes stayed closed and the mage stayed slumbering.

"Venerated one," Rich said to Otam, "the mages informed me that the sleep they induced on... uh, Razzleblad is the strongest they know. It should hold for a few more days easily."

"I was hoping the witchlock would've killed the sleep," Otam replied with a grunt. "You can never be sure with human magic, my son. You've got to question anybody who's willing to treat the blessed Onesource as a damned spigot. Who knows how that kind of water splashes?"

"*Statements like these are exactly the reason I hate their imbecilic culture,*" Delv said in Rich's head. "*Imagine, finding a tall tree that provides shade and deciding to worship it. Or taking note that the sun makes crops grow and turning it into a sentient being worthy of praise and prayers. That's the whole host of their empire, a collection of sheared sheep licking sharp rocks."*

"Toss him in the corner," Otam said, pointing to a far pillar. The two walls that met the pillar had huge picture windows carved out to provide a spectacular view of the city below. "I want to be around when he wakes up; hard to do in a dungeon. Also, I wouldn't mind if he took the same trip down he sent my temple, but I suppose that's just wishful thinking."

"Indeed it is, brother," Ananna said from her throne. "We need him alive, at least until he confesses it was Rew Majora who helped him desecrate the temple and helped the false Chosen One escape. If we cannot expose the Hierophane we will come out of this war with our empire reduced."

Nadi the cat god looked at Ananna as he resumed his seat on the throne. "We can simply ask for the return of the Crystal City and any other territories during peace negotiations."

Otam still stood in front of Rich and Mors as their aides placed the sleeping fake Razzleblad into the corner. "Our sister is right, Nadi," Otam addressed the cat god without taking his eyes off Rich. "An armistice now keeps the territories as they stand to date. Druze Wozencraft is returned as Hierophant; he clearly remembers The War of Six Houses and the era when the Crystal City was a member of the Free States. He would not give that up now, especially as the nasran threat grows increasingly difficult to quell."

The whole time Otam spoke he had been looking Rich up and down. It was unnerving. Rich shot glances at some of the other gods, who affected to not notice at all, except Baligoz, the fish god of Fifth House, who sat on his throne while looking at Rich with a slight smirk on his lips that seemed both gleeful and knowing.

"*Am I supposed to be doing something?*" Rich thought to Delv.

"*You're doing it,*" Delv replied. "*This is Otam's fashion, thinking about two or three different tasks while discussing the first one. I think that's why they call him 'the Measure.' More preferable to 'the Unnerving,' yes? Just act like what he's doing is totally natural.*"

"I would consider it even exchange for the Crystal City if we held Suusteren, but the damnable mages blew most of it up before we could sack it," Otam said at Rich but not necessarily to Rich. "Now it's too dangerous to enter, what with that giant boil grown over it."

"Well, we have to call an armistice, brother" Nadi said. "We already agreed to this with the Hierophane on the condition they surrender Razzleblad. They've upheld their end."

Ananna leaned forward in her throne. "We can call the armistice and still come out ahead, dear family," she said. "I will call upon the Hierophant Wozencraft and agree to a temporary ceasefire. I'll express our concern that the captive Razzleblad may not recover from his unnatural slumber, which would destroy any chance we have for trying him for his crimes against the Empire."

"No one's ever died from mage slumber," Otam said, who was still looking at Rich like it was Rich who had spoken the idea. "But the Hierophane, they don't know that we know this. They think their magic and their processes so esoteric and mysterious so let's play to that. Meanwhile, the wait for Razzleblad to rise will give me an opportunity to face the nasrans without worrying about mages cooking our backs. And you're going to help me."

Silence grew uncomfortable as Rich stood there under Otam's assessing eye, waiting for Ananna or Nadi to respond.

"*He's talking to you,*" Delv thought to Rich.

"*For serious?!*" Rich asked. "*How was I supposed to know?*"

"*He was looking at you.*"

"*Don't be an asshole right now! What do I say?*"

"*Your will done,*" Delv answered

Rich repeated the line. Otam nodded. "Time in their dungeon has slowed your wit, perhaps. I will need you thinking with the speed of running feet if we are going to take them in battle. Follow me. Mors as well."

Without waiting for their acknowledgement, Otam took strides to the grand doors that Armsguardsmen swung open for him. Rich fell clumsily in step with Mors and they both followed Otam at his brisk pace.

"*Shit!*" Rich thought panicked. *"Is Otam taking me to battle?!"*

Delv's only answer was a maniacal laugh.

Chapter 25
The Vision

SAVASHBAHAR FELT THE doorway she stood in front of was more the maw of a monster than anything mortal hands had built. The edifice was simple enough, a rectangular entryway into a small half dome, made entirely of steel, somehow completely intact from ancient times. It was scarcely a building as it only hosted metal stairs that led down into the darkness. But the fog that licked the ground of the village and formed an oppressive wall around it seemed to emanate from this open doorway and the depths below.

"This is the origin, Savashbahar of Maltep," Inonu said beside her. "Do you still wish to know?"

The two nasran women were dressed identically with calf high black leather boots, heavy gray wool overcoats and black leather gauntlets that reached their forearms. Savashbahar even wore a tricornered hat the same as Inonu even though she didn't know if it served some other purpose outside of aesthetics. She answered Inonu's question by pulling her scarf up to her nose and mouth to where only her eyes were exposed.

Inonu nodded and placed a hand upon Savashbahar's shoulder. "The truth is deep as the seas. May you take to it as a fish being thrown back and not as a stone. I await your return."

Savashbahar steeled her nerves and approached the doorway. The fog didn't boil or bubble—it flowed more like a current, parting subtly as she got nearer. Now in the door frame, Savashbahar looked down to see only the first two steel steps visible while the fog flowed upwards over them. It felt like being in between two different realms.

She descended into the fog, holding a leather clad hand against the wall to feel her way each deliberate step down. The air got thicker and not for the first time Savashbahar wondered what this was she was breathing in.

After 24 steps she arrived at the bottom. The fog swirled all around her, making it impossible to see more than two feet in any direction. She fished a hex from her overcoat pocket.

"Illuminate," she named it. The hex glowed white and she held it aloft where it seemed to stab out at the fog like a beacon.

The underground structure seemed built of the same steel as the stairs. She couldn't see very far down but it seemed she was in a large hallway, with wide apertures on either side of her.

Savashbahar turned to the aperture on her left and held her light into the door to see what may lie within. Only the fog answered back. It swirled violently on her approach, as if the light agitated it. The fog began to take on depth, dimension, color. A scene formed which Savashbahar could see plainly. It showed her running, pursued by the blood drinkers, the wolf-masked warriors of the Jahnavar tribe. Her shadow self jumped into a ravine. The blood drinkers surrounded the cliff above the ravine, and parted for a man Savashbahar had grown to despise. Enverpasha.

This was where she had surrendered her tribal rings and with them the right to lead them into battle. The event had caused her to seek out the Ah-irduman, her last desperate attempt to unite the tribes under the banner of the Buyukata to march decisively on the Hierophane.

"The fog acts as the living dreams of the blood whisper," she said to the empty chamber.

She turned around and looked into the opposite aperture. Again, the fog in the empty chamber swirled into a scene. Dushenmek, only twelve years old, burst into their small, modest home on the outskirts of Maltep's sacred mound, holding a new bow up for his mother to see. He had been selected to join the warrior guard as an archer.

Savashbahar's breath caught in her throat as she watched the scene. The look on his face, the pride and unmitigated joy he showed had already been burned into her brain. This was one of her favorite memories. To see it play out before her as if she could step into it again made her heart anguish.

"Oh, my beautiful boy," she whispered.

The white light of the Illuminate hex held high, Savashbahar continued through the fog of the long hallway. It seemed thick enough to cut. She could no longer see the sides of the hallway without squinting, which made her wonder if they were even there at all any more. One more step and the fog was gone completely.

She found herself in a vast cavern. Unlike where she had previously passed, this was not forged out of steel but a natural cave. Nothing was in it and the light of her hex reached the furthest end to reveal dull brown walls. Savashbahar turned around and saw no fog in the metal hallway that had moments ago been a thick and impenetrable wall.

"*Is this a trap?*" Savashbahar wondered. "*Am I to come down here to succumb to these strange fumes? Inonu has already proven that my hexes would be quite ineffective against her magic. Surely there were easier ways for the Exhaust gang to dispose of unwanted guests than to send them into poison fog under the guise of friendship.*"

Then, before her eyes, the cavern started changing. Hexes started to scrawl themselves into existence on the floor in front of her. Neat, small, perfect symbols, only a fraction of which she recognized, began to appear at her feet and worked outwards until the whole floor was covered. Then they began to write themselves up the walls and up, up on the ceiling.

When the last of the ceiling's empty space was full of the magic symbols, the entire ceiling throbbed darkly. It became black like the night sky. Tiny pinpricks of white light like stars started to appear. The stars grew until they were the size of fists and their light began to flow like rivers between them.

In the middle of the cavern floor the hexes moved, forming what Savashbahar could clearly see was an eight point compass rose. Circles and bisecting lines appeared at precise points throughout the compass rose. It was a beautiful design, one that Savasbahar easily recognized. This same pattern appeared in the sacred hall of the Kastamonu tribe. It was revered, the chief reason they called themselves The Wayfinders.

The room was not done changing. Suspended high above the center of the compass rose, framed directly below the night time sky of the ceiling, the Emerald Sun blazed with green light. This was the most sacred object of her own tribe of Maltep, the divine fire she had temporarily extinguished so many months ago to help Ruki Provos steal hexes.

What is this place?

An ornate crescent shaped table appeared between the compass rose and the far wall, with twelve seats. It identically matched the council hall of the Antep tribe. Twelve nasrans in white robes sat in the seats, seemingly real but not, as they had no aura. Their faces were hidden behind masks, similar to the Jahnavar blood drinker warriors only instead of wolf bone, the masks were made of fine porcelain and held serene, peaceful countenances.

The twelve white robed nasran... elders?... got up from their seats and formed a ring around the compass rose. In unison, they began to chant words that no longer held meaning for nasrankind, but

Savashbahar immediately recognized them. It was the Aria of Erzinjan, from which the Erzinjan tribe derived their name.

As they chanted the aria, the twelve nasrans each pulled from their robes a large ring suspended on a long chain around their necks. They placed these rings on their thumbs. Savashbahar clearly saw they were the signet rings of the twelve tribes. She had been the custodian of four of them for a short time.

The rings flared green, matching the color of the Emerald Sun of Maltep. An image grew from a pinprick to an orb, suspended waist high in the center of the compass rose.

The image showed a backdrop of stars and in the forefront sat a marble. The marble was blue, with splotches of brown and green and thick swirls of white. The marble grew in size until Savashbahar could tell she was looking at clouds, land and water. It kept growing until the view went into the marble, past the clouds. And they were on the surface.

Humans lived here. The humans all wore various colors of shiny fabrics which seemed to be just a one piece garment. Their buildings gleamed with chrome and silver and lights that glowed fiercely in unnatural colors. But the land was sour, their crops failing. They wore strange contraptions over their noses and mouths which seemed to indicate the air was acrid.

Their world was dying and them with it. The twelve nasrans finished the Aria of Erzinjan and the image began to swirl into what anyone close to the factory mages would recognize as a portal. One by one, the humans with the strange breathing masks and one piece shiny suits stepped through. The humans took their masks off, smiling as they shook hands and hugged their nasran saviors.

Is this how we came to share this world with mankind?

The cavern changed again. Chrome and steel, glass and the fiercely glowing colored lights of the human's home world began to appear within the cavern itself, nestled cleanly, neatly beside the etched hexes of the nasrans. Now the cavern looked more like the long hallway Savasbahar had traveled to reach this place. It reminded her fiercely of the underground refuge the Sons of Kaftar had taken her in their first meeting, the one they called the Heart of the Sons. Strange devices peppered the cavern. In one corner misshapen men slept in giant tubes of viscous orange liquid. There were several tubes and it seemed that these men were growing in these tubes, giant sized until the last tube was a full fledged weagr.

As if to verify her suspicions, two weagrs with large goggles over their eyes and leashes around their necks were hauling huge metal devices on their backs under the directions of human and nasran handlers.

In another corner, humans and nasrans were studying lizards in a bin. The people had wires attached to the lizards as well as tubes with green and purple liquids. They chopped the tails and limbs off the lizards, watched and took notes as the lizards squirmed, measuring the efficacy in which the lizards grew back appendages. Next to the bin of lizards, glass display cases held what Savashbahar could only describe as lizards that had been developed or crossbred with human babies. They were scaly, fetal, crying for their needs with forked tongues. Next to those glass cages a holding pen held a half dozen megryms.

We, human and nasrankind, created both weagrs and megryms?

There seemed to be no other explanation for what the vision was showing her. She was so dumbfounded by all this that she still held her hand aloft for the Illuminate hex to work despite the fact that it had burned off some time ago and she was holding onto nothing. She became aware of the tiredness in her arm and lowered it as the twelve robed nasrans gathered again around the compass rose.

They chanted the Aria of Erzinjan once more and the cavern scene started shifting... ascending. It raised up through layers of rock and pipeworks and wiring and steel until it broke through to the surface. The desolate, burned out ruins of The Sprawl were completely restored, a vibrant city of towering glass and steel spires, resplendent white marble and shiny lights. Flying vehicles zipped along everywhere. The scene continued to rise and Savashbahar could see no end to this beautiful city, full of lush green parks and smiling people, that stretched from horizon to horizon.

Nasrans with their magic and humans with their technology, we built all this.

Despite the change in scene, Savashbahar could still hear the Aria of Erzinjan, an incantation droning in the background.

The scene kept rising away from the ground and the city became smaller, smaller, a dot on a lush green landscape, the landscape became masked by clouds, and further out until the land was its own green, blue, white marble. Then the marble blurred along with stars. The scene was rapidly moving through the heavens. Occasionally the blur would stop and there would be a different marble present, small marbles of desolate rock or giant marbles of colorful banded clouds. The scene would only settle on the marbles for a moment before the blur would resume.

It only took a few moments of watching the counter-clockwise blur motion before Savashbahar recognized the movement pattern, the way it seemed to radiate out as a spiral from a fixed central point. This was the migration pattern of the Kahraman tribe. It was identical to how the wandering villages moved across the steppes counterclockwise to the fixed center capital of Maras. "We wander as the stars wander," was a saying among the nomadic people.

The Aria of Erzinjan is the spell that powers this blur. The nasrans are searching for something. What?

Finally the blur came to rest on a marble that resembled the ones the humans came from. The scene descended into this marble, revealing lush forests and a landscape that was devoid of settlement.

Aians, devoid of house marks like Jason, huddled here in packs, fearful of gargantuan insects as big as buildings that roamed the wilds. Their clothing, if you could call it that, were jungle vines knotted together and tied around private areas. Their hair was matted, their faces dirt streaked, and they grunted at one another if they made any sounds at all.

The porcelain masked faces of the twelve nasrans appeared as specters over the huddled aians. If the aians could see them, they sounded no alarm.

"These things," one of the nasrans said. "I believe they'll suffice."

"No, Buyukata," another said. "They are in a primal state. Their planet is new. We don't know how intelligent they are, or if they can be trained in our ways. We should keep looking."

"This is exactly what we need, Kahraman," The Buyukata said. "They seem clever and intelligent. If they lack sentience, we can employ some of the modification sciences the humans brought with them. In other words, if they're not good enough we can make them good enough."

"Your plan is careless and hasty, Buyukata," another one chimed in, a feminine, smoky sound behind the mask. "None of our mage-scientists have worked in this realm of genetic manipulation. That means we would have to collaborate with the humans. We would prematurely tip our hand."

"What is the alternative, Urfa?" The Buyukata said. "Do we save another dying race from a dying planet? Isn't that how we find ourselves here right now?"

"Young Buyukata has a point," another elder said with a voice of gravel. "We need a species we can create in our own image."

"Thank you, Balikesir," The Buyukata replied.

The words 'young buyukata' caused realization to dawn on Savashbahar. This man in the center of the conversation wasn't *The Buyukata*, a title of unparalleled distinction and highest honor, his given name was Buyukata, of no more distinction or note at this time than her given name of Savashbahar.

Furthermore, the man whose name unites all nasrans addressed three of his peers as Kahraman, Urfa, Balikesir... all names of a tribe. She realized she was looking at the ancient ancestors from whom the twelve tribes were named. She looked at their rings and identified the other nasrans in the circle as Maltep, Antep, Kastamonu, Jahnavar, Sinop, Chorum, Erzinjan and Erzurum.

But if the one trying to convince the others was named Buyuka-ta, where did that leave the twelfth tribe, the one known as Ah-irdu-man?

"No, I agree with Urfa," Jahnavar chimed in.

"You would," Antep grumbled.

"My affections aside," Jahnavar said. "She's right. We don't have the knowledge to genetically modify beings without human aid. Human intervention would serve to make this species their tools like the weagrs and megryms."

"Or worse," Kahraman said, "the introduction of this species serves as the excuse they use to seize power from us by force. A coup."

"Please," Erzurum scoffed, his voice a deep bass voice. "Some of us on the council remain unconvinced that the humans seek to usurp us at all. It has been millenia since we rescued them, but they remember. They are beholden to us."

"Who remains unconvinced?" Kahrman asked. "You and your brother Erzinjan? Have you not read the histories they salvaged from their homeworld? There was one tribe that settled in the lands of another tribe. But they were idiots and nearly starved to death in the winter. The indigenous tribe brought them food, saved their lives and when the foreign tribe got strong enough not only did they kill the indigenous tribe, they celebrated it annually with a feast day. And that's their own kind... what do you think they would do with us, Erzurum?"

"Enough," Chorum said, her voice mature and matronly. "We've already discussed the rising human aggression and had quorum on our action to mitigate the threat they pose to society. The only thing left for the council to consider is whether this species before us is viable. Agreed?"

"Yes, Elder Chorum," the eleven other councilors intoned deferentially. She was clearly the chief among them.

"My point still stands," Urfa stated. "We cannot genetically manipulate these beings without human intervention. I say we continue looking."

"Perhaps they will not need genetic manipulation," Balikesir said.

"These things are seemingly incapable of basic speech," Kahraman said. "Yes, we do not need to save another dying race from a planet they destroyed as we have done with the humans, but we should find a species that has a least mastered communication, perhaps rudimentary agriculture. That is not these beasts hooting 'ay ay ay' at one another. I second the motion to continue the search."

"Third," Jahnavar stated.

"No," Buyukata said with authority. "Please, everyone. Let us not be short sighted. Have we forgotten what nasrankind is? We command power far beyond what the humans had even realized was possible. Their science did not save them from themselves. Why are we looking to it to save us now? Just as we delivered them with our magic, our salvation lies with that same force."

"There are no spells within any of our catalogs that pertain to making a creature sentient when before there was none," Sinop countered, his voice nasally and matter-of-factly.

"Dear Sinop, this is not a matter of turning antelope into philosophers," Buyukata said. "They are already thinking creatures, as evidenced by their desire to fashion clothing. This is a simple increase in intelligence, a little nudge to get them to where we need them to be quickly."

Sinop shook his head. "Any spell we could utter over them would be a temporary, nonpermanent solution. Such is the fleeting nature of magic. We cannot pretend casting enhancement spells over these things every two hours is a practical solution."

"Magic doesn't have to be fleeting. We're looking at these beings because of the Empyreal Engine, built by our magic, powered by our will. Just as this device is a standing, permanent part of our lives, I propose we make our change to these beings enduring. Irrevocable. We hex them."

Maltep, who had been silent this whole time, held up a hand in protest. "You may not be Hexenarii as I, Buyukata, but you know our most sacred rule, the one unbreakable," the man said with grave admonishment. "We do not mark living flesh."

"But we *can*!" Buyukata hissed. "We must."

"The hexenarii imbue our living essence in the inanimate, life where before there was nought," Maltep insisted. "to try to impose our living essence over another living being is a crime against nature."

"Do you think I care about nature?" Buyukata asked with a scoff. "Nature doesn't care if humans take over and drive us to the margins. It doesn't matter to nature one bit if humans make us slaves and exterminate us. That is what will ultimately happen, while we dally trying to find the perfect species in an infinite cosmos. I defy this outcome. And magic was made to defy nature."

After Buyukata's words, silence hung thick in the air around the twelve. They all looked at the markless aians scrounging berries and picking mites out of one another's hair. Buyukata held his hand out to them as if presenting them to the council.

"They are not perfect, but they can be made perfect. Infused with magic from the start, trained in our arcane arts, living weapons against the high science of the humans. Is there none among you who will second my choice?"

Balikesir raised a hand. "Second. We need an army, and more weeks and months searching for that army leaves us less prepared to mount a defense."

One by one the council raised their hands, all save Maltep, who shook his head when they all looked to him as the last dissenting voice.

"I cannot approve, but neither will I defy the council. My hexenarii and I shall mark them."

Savashbahar watched the scene disappear, replaced by one in which only Buyukata stood before the Empyrean Engine. A dull boom resounded in the chamber, repeating in measured intervals, causing dust to fall from the ceiling and make the whole room shake.

Buyukata's ring glowed green as he looked at the scene the engine presented. It showed the city above him, a city under siege. Fires and black, greasy smoke dotted the cityscape. The tallest building had been broken, the upper halves crashed into other buildings, the glass broken, the marble crumbled, the steel beams jutting and twisted. The wreckage of crashed flying vehicles punctuated the scene. Savashbahar could taste Buyukata's anguish.

Another boom from above. And another. The other councilors entered the room and faced Buyukata.

"The humans knock," Chorum said. "It is time, Buyukata. Time to make the engine cold. Time to surrender."

"My plan was beautiful," Buyukata said, his eyes wild behind the mask as he scanned the scene. "You'll see. Our aians will come to their senses."

"They cannot," Maltep said. "They did not evolve to accept magic as we have, it was forced into their being, written into their essence. They will all eventually go mad as the cost breaks them and their children and their children's children. We have failed."

"It is over, Buyukata," Chorum said. "And the engine cannot fall into human hands."

Chorum and the ten councilors took out their rings and began to chant. Savashbahar recognized it as the funeral hymn of the Erzurum. Above them all, the glowing green of the Emerald Sun began to darken and glow black.

"NO!" Buyukata cried. His ring flashed an angry red. The Emerald Sun blazed fiery red to match Buyukata's ring.

The other councilors stopped chanting. "You would defy the will of the council?" Chorum asked incredulously. "And you think your will is stronger than all ours?"

"Yes! Only I have the will to do what's necessary, what's final. The humans are vermin, maggots. I will not surrender my city to them. We will all burn first."

"You would raze the city to burn out mere maggots?" Chorum asked.

"I would crack this world open like an egg to deny them the yolk," Buyukata responded. "Such is my hatred. And they shall feel every vestige of it!"

At his words, the Emerald Sun flared violently. The waist high image of the besieged city seemed to shudder. In the sky above the smoldering city a light like a white sun bloomed and exploded. The people, the buildings, all of it was taken by the light, turned into vapor.

The wave of it not only shook the engine room and the councilors, it struck Savashbahar in the present, such was its force. The pain, the violent rage of millions of souls being ripped from existence, it made her eyes stream tears as her body rocked in the psychic stream of it.

Buyukata collapsed, his masked cracked, his eyes burned out. He was clearly dead.

The fog rolled in from the hall, permeating the chamber, swirling around the prone body of Buyukata.

"What have you done?" Chorum whispered.

The scene dissolved for a final time, leaving Savashbahar alone in the cold, dark chamber. No, not entirely alone. She wiped the tears from her eyes. On a small pedestal in the center of the chamber sat Buyukata's ring, glowing red like an entity onto itself.

Savashbahar stared at it for a long while considering all that she had learned.

INONU WAS WAITING FOR Savashbahar when she emerged from the chamber.

"The hexenarii of Maltep returns, illuminated," she said. "Tell me, Savashbahar, were you able to piece together the things that were not made plain by the sight? Do you know what happened after?"

"We could no longer dwell here," Savashbahar said, looking around. "The land was destroyed, made into a lifeless desert by Buyukata."

"Indeed."

"But the remaining council did not want to leave the Empyreal Engine. So each member took a piece with them, whether it was a physical piece such as the Emerald Sun of Maltep or a part of the process such as the invocation to start the engine now held sacred by the Erzinjan. And our people scattered."

Inonu nodded. "We were all one people, sister. Tribeless," she said. "The councilors formed the twelve new tribes to keep the engine from becoming whole again unless the situation became dire."

Savashbahar looked at Inonu. "And how did Ah-irduman come to be, sister?"

"His true name has been lost to time," Inonu replied, "I believe that's how the councilors intended things. Buyakata's young son, they renamed him Ah-irduman, the weighted, heavy smoke. What he carried away from yasak toprak was the knowledge of how the pieces of the engine fit, the shame of what his father had done, and the burden of the genocide."

"What shame, Inonu?" Savashbahar asked fighting back tears as the violent, psychic wave of Buyukata's cleaving washed through her anew. "His name is venerated. The monster has been deified."

Inonu approached her, placed a comforting hand upon her shoulder and squeezed with reassurance. "Tell me what this fog around us is, sister. The vision does not tell you but I know you know."

Savashbahar nodded. She did know the horrible truth of it. "It is the physical residue of millions ripped from the material realm by perverted sorcery." She cast her gaze down, ashamed of what their ancestor had done. "It is the source of the blood whisper."

"The people from the first nation," Inonu said. "Their blood now substanceless fog, their dying screams, mere whispers. It is why the tribe once called Ah-irduman is no longer a tribe of nasrans, but of all those that once dwelt in the Nameless Capital. It is the reason why the blood will whisper to all those who are inclined to hear it: megrym, nasran, human, even aian."

Inonu knelt down, reached a hand in the licking fog and picked up a small piece of white marble. "There is a reason why this city is nameless. Imagine the survivors, only handfuls from something once so vibrant, so many of their loved ones gone, their city destroyed, the land sour, their way of life irrevocably ended. I imagine talk of this place became too difficult to bear. It became forbidden land on the lips of all who uttered it. The people wanted to forget. For the nasrans in particular, a new history forged itself in that forgetfulness. Of the hero Buyukata, whose will was so strong it united all the tribes, whose ring is the key to which all other signets serve."

Another psychic wave racked Savashbahar's body, the anguish excruciating. "The ring," she gasped, "the cursed key."

Inonu's eyes tightened. "You bear it, do you not? Most flee the crushing burden the ring imposes. You have not. Why, sister?"

Savashbahar pulled the ring from the folds of her clothing to show Inonu. It dangled from a chain. It weighed little but it felt so heavy in the air.

"I wanted to when I touched it, to run from this oppressive weight, to think of another way to achieve my goals. But the mages, they have a device similar to the Empyrean Engine, a machine that pulls people from other worlds to do their bidding. I don't know if it can do what the engine from our lost age did, but I will not stand by and allow the possibility to exist. It must be destroyed."

Inonu nodded. "Then the army of Exhaust will help you destroy this engine." She smiled. "You are, after all, the Buyukata."

Chapter 26
Maharbal

Rich felt both relief that he wasn't directly on a battlefield facing down a charging nasran horde and dire apprehension as he looked at this alien table. The other commanders seemed as if they were in their living rooms sipping tea, so at home Rich wondered if they got paychecks to be here.

The thing wasn't a table as much as it was an oblong bowl the size of a table. There were no legs, just a solid marble base in which the bowl sat. The closest thing Rich could compare it to is taking a kitchen island and putting in a sink that left no room for countertop. In the sink basin, large brown bumps and little green smears sat around larger raised white and black pyramidal shapes. Red "X's" and blue "O's" congregated in their respective groups.

"I don't know what I'm looking at. I don't know what I'm looking at. I don't know what I'm looking at," Rich tried to think his thoughts directly into Delv's head, wherever he may be.

"I offered to teach you a bit of magic, not be your indispensable crutch every time you get confronted with a new mystery of life," Delv replied. *"You can't figure it out?"*

"What am I supposed to do, go over to the pack of gristled generals there and be like 'Seratim here, super experienced commander of Crystal City. So, what is this thing I should know all about, asking for a friend.' Yeah... a little help?"

"*A fine petition, quite persuasive,*" Delv said. He went quiet, and the silence seemed to stretch as Rich smiled awkwardly at aians who probably only use the facial expression themselves when they're feasting on the hearts of their enemies. One was of the ant house Yol, another of the mole house Zemishurus and the third of the eagle house of Demir.

"Have we all not met?" Otam the horse god said sidling up beside Rich. "My prickled ears, how long were you garrisoned at Crystal City?"

Otam was looking into the oblong bowl that dominated the room, his eyes dancing as he scanned the different shapes. But Rich was pretty sure the question was for him and the god expected an answer. Shouldn't Otam already know? Hell, shouldn't Rich already know?

"Uh... a long time, sir."

"Obviously," Otam said, still eyes deep in the bowl. "Your staff is Xerol of Brother Yol, Shamdon of Sister Zemishurus, Taruns of Brother Demir." Otam introduced them all without even a nod in their general direction. "Their roles should be fairly obvious," he finished.

All three officers bowed towards Rich. They kept their scowls on, probably part of the uniform.

"Yes... obvious indeed," Rich said. It wasn't.

"*It appears there's not a whole lot of information about the ISM in the hive,*" Delv said. "*No repositories that I can just stuff into that hampered mind of yours at any rate. That's what you're looking at, by the way, the Integrated Stratagem Machination, a collaborative effort between megrym technology and aian willingness to pay through the nose to end their dependency on human or nasran magic. It's fairly new.*"

"*How do I use it? Why do I use it? What do I do?!*"

"You're going to learn as I learn. And I have to learn, incidentally, because no one here at the Hierophane knew this thing existed. Now I have to relay my findings today. Thank you for the additional work."

Meanwhile, all the aians in the room looked at Rich expectantly, save Otam who was engrossed in the ISM.

"Ah... yes, the ISM," Rich said, moving forward and looking with manufactured concern at the stuff in the bowl. "So... what do we have here? What's the situation?"

"Maharbal has fallen to the nasrans," Xerol of House Yol said. "This is the offense to take it back."

"Marhabal," Rich grunted. "Understood."

"Now this is something in which I can enlighten you," Delv said. *"Marhabal is a small mountain town, quite scenic. In times of less conflict it's a tourist destination for aiankind. The best analog I can find within your mind is the town of Aspen, Colorado. What makes it of military value is the town sits on the bank of a large freshwater lake, Lake Baligoz. This lake feeds several key tributaries, one of them being the Heavensway. That, my dull knife, is the river you see pouring over the Temple of Houses and feeding the rest of Nasreddin."*

Delv had a remarkable talent for creeping Rich out. He was pulling towns like Aspen out of Rich's head as reference. What else was he doing in there?

Unfortunately, it was a question Rich didn't have the luxury of answering right now. The nasrans essentially had control of the capital's water supply and everyone was looking at him to get it back by using the ISM box.

"Update the map," Otam said while looking at no one, head down in the ISM.

"Shit, did he mean me?!" Rich thought.

Mors inadvertently answered the question by stepping up beside Rich, grabbing a crank on the side of the oblong table and turning it vigorously. Tiny squares of areas within the ISM began to change color and texture. It was almost like looking at pixels if pixels were much larger and could be raised or depressed. As Mors turned, the large blue of Lake Baligoz appeared on the northern end of the map. Below that, brown raised squares and rectangles appeared, clearly an aerial view of buildings, with sandy roads and pathways in between. Separating the town into two was a thick blue line which snaked its way down the southern end of the map before disappearing. Rich would've loved to ask questions about how the image updated and how it worked in general.

Ten red X's formed a semi-circle near the southwestern edge of the town. In the town and near the shore of the lake, five blue O's congregated.

"Do not be deceived by what appears to be our superior numbers," Otam said, still looking within the bowl. "The ISM wasn't built to handle these blended units composed of several tribes of nasrans. It's a fairly unprecedented affair, their unity. Apparently they have some new, shiny bright leader called Enver Pusher or something to that effect, does everything short of raise the dead and is one tribe short of being Puke Baba, King of Savages. That said, their blended units are either failing to register or only registering when enough of one tribe's warriors, like those annoying cat herders, move close enough together to be seen as a standard unit. You haven't asked how our forces are constituted."

"Ah... waiting for you to finish, sir."

Otam was silent as he gazed at the scene in the bowl. The moment stretched without a word from anyone.

"Uh... how are our forces constituted?"

Taruns of the eagle house Demir answered. "Commander, we have two aerial units, here" he said pointing at the two red X's that framed the semicircle. "Two subterranean units here," he said pointing at the X's directly next to the flying units. "Only one destrier cavalry, due to terrain, here," he said pointing out a center left X. "And the remaining five are ground forces, with this one," he said pointing, "built to be completely amphibious should the need arise to use the lake. All standard units, brightly lit."

"Your orders, Commander?" Taruns asked.

God, I'm so in over my head.

"Uh, a moment, please?" he asked the expectant aians.

"*Admittedly, it would be enjoyment of a special kind to watch you drown in all this,*" Delv said, "*but I'm curious to see if you can tread this choppy water if you're given just enough information to know how to swim. Let's unpack this from the bottom up. A standard unit is aian military talk to describe a force of one hundred-twenty warriors. Lit means the unit has members of the house of Yol integrated so communications can be relayed instantaneously through the hive mind, in this case integrated with extreme redundancy hence brightly lit. And I see that you have enough of an understanding of the different houses within aian society to know a subterranean unit is comprised of fighters from Yol and/or Zemishurus while an aerial unit consists of Demir and/or Eula. The only thing left is to discuss nasran warrior classes, like the vashokadama that Otam here blithely dismissed as annoying, but I'm afraid we're going to have to address that as you go. You have been in your own head space for some time, you see, and if you take a moment you'll notice they're all looking at you as if you're deficient.*"

Shit. So what were his orders?

"Um... okay. So how about we move the flyers out. The one North and the other one East." He drew his two index fingers out from a center point like an L. "The goal is to get better sight on what's in and around the town and relay it to our other forces."

Xerol nodded. "So keep enough distance to limit engagement, understood." he began to tap at something on his side of the table, Rich could only assume buttons but there was no way to be sure.

"*Be sure you investigate what's going on over there when you get an opportunity,*" Delv said. "*I have a report to produce and I like to pride myself on doing competent work, compulsory or otherwise.*"

"Anything for the sub-ground forces?" Shamdon, the woman of House Zemishurus asked. She produced a meaty digging talon, the mark of her house, and pointed to an X.

"Uh... yeah... um dig around to the back side of the village. Perhaps we can ready a surprise attack on their rear while our ground forces hammer at their fronts."

That sounded great. Commanderly. So why was Shamdon looking at him like he was let out of the circus to wander the street?

"Commander, this is the Heavensway," she said, pointing a claw at the path of blue snaking its way down to the southern edge of the map, effectively cutting the scene in half. "Trying to dig under it would effectively take us out of the fight."

"Did I say dig around? I meant dig under the town to, you know, the north back end, between the lake and the town but before you get to the river."

"And what of the entrenched defenses, Commander? Our standing count is sixty pieces of determent, not including what the nasrans may have added."

Delv chimed in. "*Entrenched defenses is the lady's way of saying there's all sorts of ghastly horrors dug under the ground and covered up. It's so easy for any of us to move earth, you see. Be it human mages with our magic, aians with their subterranean houses or nasrans with their hexes, none of us are simply shoveling dirt. So in any location worth protecting, we place things that make an invader cautious to say the least. You could call them land mines but I assure you, the stuff we have make those explosions you've seen in your movies quite tepid.*"

Shamdon was looking at Rich, expecting a reply.

"Move as safely as possible. Disarm what you can, navigate around the more elaborate ones."

"As you command," she bowed and began to punch more of those assumed buttons.

Xerol, the officer from the House of Yol nodded to no one in particular. "We have visual reports," he said. "The nasran force is beginning to push."

"*No reason you can't see what he's seeing courtesy of the hive mind,*" Delv said. "*Indulge your senses.*"

Rich's point of view shifted to that of a foot soldier from the House of Yol. He was surrounded by countless aians, all wearing the iconic red and black armor of the Fane Armsguard. In the distance, a small town of quaint wooden buildings sat nestled in the mountains. Behind it a giant body of water glistened serenely.

An army of nasrans approached from the town. Some wore leather armor, some wore cloaks and not much else, displaying a host of tattoos on their bodies. Others had their forearms wrapped in rope while others still had their faces hidden behind wolf skulls. As a tide, the nasrans began to rush towards the aian ranks.

"Your orders?" Xerol asked.

The silence in Rich's own head felt deafening. He wanted desperately to pawn this off on someone, anyone else.

"Uh, attack with our ground forces." It was all he could think to say through the pressure of seeing the swarm of nasrans grow ever closer.

"Done," Xerol replied as he pressed buttons. "And what of the cavalry?"

"Them too," Rich said. Mors started pressing buttons on his side of the ISM. Rich assumed this meant Mors was in charge of the cavalry.

Rich turned his gaze to the bowl of the ISM. The X's and O's were growing closer together, which was the only view of the battlefield for most of the aians in the room. Xerol and Rich, however, got the HD version because of the hive mind. The other generals couldn't see the nasrans growing so close Rich could see the rage in their eyes. Some of the nasrans led packs of cats the size of large dogs, their teeth bared into snarls as they bounded towards the aians on four legs.

Both sides loosed arrows. Now Delv switched the visual feed between different members of Yol. The blue robe was finding the most visceral angles, where arrows lodged into necks and faces, where the piercing mortal screams were the loudest, and pumping them into Rich's headspace.

Rich grit his teeth. The things he saw were so much more personal than a few dancing X's and O's. What other orders could he give to minimize the casualties?

The wolf masked warriors started moving southward in a serpentine, almost Z pattern, dancing and dodging in between the ranks of other nasrans who still proceeded in a straight line at the enemy. It would be extremely difficult for the archers to hit them. More arrows flew between both sides.

The *vashokadama* and their attack cats were the first to reach striking distance of the aians. The cats pounced upon warriors unprepared for their lunging speed, knocking the aians on their backs before ripping out their throats in lightning fast strikes. The *vashokadama* themselves were just as efficient, protecting their cats with long whips that had razors threaded at the tips. The *vashokadama* flicked these whips to wrap around the necks of their opponents. Then they pulled. The results were throats cut gruesomely, as if they had been clawed out.

It was so fast and brutal. God, the screams, the gurgling, the looks of terror and agony as these people died violently.

"We've gotta stop this," Rich said in horror.

"Stop what, Commander?" Xerol asked.

As if Rich had asked for more violence instead of total cessation, the rest of the nasran forces plunged into the aian ranks. On both sides swords and glaives and spears hacked, slashed and ran through armor and flesh. Fireballs, likely the work of hexes, arced in the sky to rain down on the back ranks of the aians.

Beyond the immediate fighting and explosion rocked the small town. A plume of magma shot up like a geyser at the edge of town, where none of the nasran force was.

"Reports of a lava trap unsuccessfully disarmed," Xerol said. "Approximate loss of sub-ground forces is at forty-eight."

"That's almost half the unit!" Shamdon swore. "And we haven't even made it to the town proper yet."

"Turn them back," Rich said.

"What?" Shamdon asked.

"Yeah, turn them around," Rich said "Have them surface directly behind the nasrans. Attack their rear."

"As you say," Shamdon said before going to the ISM console.

"The aerial units are at the northern and eastern periphery of Maharbal," Taruns said. "Any new orders?"

Rich had forgotten about the flyers.

"*I was just thinking,*" Delv said out of nowhere. "*You should learn purple magic. All of it. Now's a good time.*"

Rich's body rocked as his mind was instantly assaulted with the sum total of what the mage tower studied and classified as purple magic. He originally assumed it was a subset of blue magic. He could not have been more wrong. Purple consisted of accessing a plane of existence mortal men should never, ever be. Where fires raged and smog choked and vile creatures hunted not for meat but for psychic nourishment, feeding off the emotions and living energy of others. It was from this realm that the terrormancers summoned their binding chains, slathering demon dogs and a slew of other terrible weapons. Rich could only describe the horrible place as Hell.

His body shuddered as the thought of being stuck in that plane for eternity drove a spike of mortal terror through his gut.

"What ails you, Commander?" Taruns asked.

"It's nothing," Rich croaked, dry swallowing down the lingering stench of sulfur. "Shoulda ate breakfast."

"*Fucker,*" Rich said to Delv. "*You knew what that would do.*"

"*Yes, I knew it would make you a more competent mage should you ever get your robes back. You're welcome.*"

Otam shook his head, still looking at the battle in the ISM. "Our forces die while your mind is on your stomach. Does Taruns have to repeat himself or will you answer now?"

"Bring the fliers back," Rich said. "Ranged attack on their flanks."

The ISM showed the far flung X's coming back towards the pack of X's and O's. They seemed to take forever, especially since each and every passing second was a visual assault of death and carnage in his mind's eye. They seemed to arrive at exactly the same time, with aians pouring out of freshly opened holes in the ground as flying archers started loosing arrows down on the nasran flank.

It only took a minute of trying to adapt to the new threats before the whole host of the nasran warriors collectively turned their attention to east and fled, towards the Heavensway.

"Do we pursue, Commander?" Xerol asked.

"No!" Rich said quickly, his decision largely based around the desire to not have to see a battle up close ever again. "This could be a trap, you know, what do you call it? A feint. No, secure the town. That was our objective, so let's stick to it."

"Your tactics are strange to say the least," the god Otam said as he looked at the X's move toward the town while the O's slowly moved across the blue line of the Heavensway.

"I have commanded my fair share of battles in my undying," Otam said. "This one seemed like either a blundering accident or unabashed genius. Which one was it?"

"Um, I'm not sure I follow."

Mors placed a hand on the rim of the ISM. "What our lord means is you did things that made no sense. You sent the aerial and underground units away for seemingly arbitrary reasons, you had the cavalry hampered by surrounding ground units unable to ride, rush, flank, etcetera and you attacked an enemy who specializes in frontal assault head on. Why did you do any of that?"

"I uh, wanted to lull the nasrans into a false sense of security," Rich said.

"So why keep us in the dark about it?" Mors pressed.

"It would've, um, taken too much time explaining it rather than just doing it."

"What's your father's name?"

"Huh?"

"Your father. Who is he?"

"I don't see why that's important."

"Neither do I," Otam said. "Refrain yourself, Mors."

"*I do,*" Delv said. "*Mors is the one and only survivor of a cavalry rush of one thousand destriers. They were making their way to Suusteren to apprehend their chosen one and ran into Hierophane interfence at Dreft Esker. I know you remember that. You missed what happened after your unceremonious departure. It was at that point Druze body hopped into all of Mors' friends and subordinates and began to chop them all down. He intentionally spared Mors here so he could return to the Temple of Houses in defeat and tell them about the monster that was coming to kill them all for their transgression into the Free States. Imagine this man for a moment, the—your word is PTSD—he must have from seeing the Graverobber kill and kill and kill from beyond the grave. Why, you'd look at your own mother differently. Definitely someone the Hierophane just handed you.*"

"*He's on to me,*" Rich concluded.

"*For good reason,*" Delv said. "*He has experience seeing aian bodies being used as shells. And you're an imposter.*"

Otam smiled wryly. "All of these would seem to be gross incompetence but the nasrans, it seems they didn't realize how to take this abandonment of standard combat strategy so fell prey to your subsequent attack."

"*You seem to have a handle on the situation,*" Delv said. "*I'm withdrawing for a time. I feel my cost coming and I imagine it shall be very dark and wretched considering all the blue channels I've kept open. Oh, I can't wait to find out! Now, make sure you take a look at the other side of the ISM, for the control scheme, maybe ask a question. I'll sort through the details later. Goodbye for now, you unenviable bastard. Please don't get yourself killed.*"

Chapter 27
Exodus

Jason felt confident he could add "Fleet Commander" to his list of accomplishments. After all, here he was sitting on the lead boat of a flotilla. Thankfully, they had found an unmoored rowboat floating adrift early in the exodus and commandeered it. Ruki sat in the back manning the paddles, Gina and Calais sat in the middle, Jason and Mel sat at the helm while Eula lay curled up on the deck—uh, wait, are rowboat floors called decks?—anyway, she was curled up getting herself some beauty sleep whether she wanted it or not.

There had to be over thirty vessels behind the rowboat, any one of them holding two to a half dozen refugees. Over half of them were doors, strung together with ropes so they didn't drift too far apart, but being seaworthy had to count towards this being a flotilla.

They had gathered numbers rather quickly. Leave it to rising seismic activity to light a fire under the people stuck here. All their motley band had to do was shout as they made their way southward, where the glut of the buildings under the dome were. And people would shout back and wave at them from rooftops. Then they'd stop, look for something seaworthy or something that could be made seaworthy, ask the person to kindly volunteer for Calais' costshare program, and off they went.

"You know that's not practical," Mel said to Jason.

Jason sat beside Mel on the raft, placing the meaty hand of his arm-club on Eula's slumbering face. He simply shrugged and looked at Mel with dancing eyes.

"More practical than a stomach with an immortal's ultimate weapon running through it. Dude, swords are notoriously hard to digest."

Mel scowled. "Seriously man. She's goddess level powerful. We may need that if we run across the gray robe. Beyond that, we can't spare you just so you can be her glorified sleep aid."

He shrugged. "It's the only option at present. She'll want to kill me soon as her eyes snap open. Definitely not perfect girlfriend behavior, probably."

There were only three buildings left in this direction, a good thing since the earthquake rumblings had grown in duration and intensity. Jason felt as if they were in a giant snow globe in the hands of an energetic toddler. The world was being furiously shaken even now, and the people on the roofs of the three remaining buildings didn't bother waiting for a boarding party when the flotilla got close. Rather, they just dived into the water en masse and swam for the relative safety the makeshift boats offered, where waiting citizens hoisted them onto one craft or another.

"So much for signing up for the Witch Rewards Program," Jason said with a smirk.

Calais, stood up. Beside Mel they looked close enough in skin tone and hair texture to be sisters. The witch cut shrewd eyes at the newcomers.

"I hate to sound like the cost," she said, "but everyone pays."

She took out an orange chalk and began to draw the glyphs and symbols on her boat seat that in different times would earn her a hot brand through the heart. Jason was hung up on what she said though.

"Wait, how do you know what the cost says?"

"Reason through it," she answered. "I'm off."

And with that she took off across the rope tying their boat to the one directly behind it. She was so fast and nimble it was as if the ropes were made of paved highway. Maybe she had become so light the ropes didn't register her weight. Either way, she flew from makeshift boat to floating door to raft across the ropes. She signed each and every newcomer up for the costshare, which pretty much entailed reciting a pledge and kissing a doll she called her familiar. Meanwhile, for his share of the cost for whatever Calais had cast to navigate the ropes, Jason's feet felt numb in a "just realized I was sitting wrong and lost circulation" kind of way.

Jason, annoyed by the feeling more than pained, took her suggestion to pass the time and reasoned through it. He figured witches don't just sign up for a lifestyle of hiding and illegal spellcraft at the cost of a gristly and public execution upon discovery because it sounds cool. Maybe some do. Probably the bigger demographic tried legit spellcraft and didn't like the cost. Jason knew that cost was bad enough to have Rich flinching any time they needed magic cast. Hell, it almost drove the kid crazy. So what avenue's left for the individual who loves magic but absolutely dreads the cost? The only answer was the one that now had his feet feeling like bricks.

He could actually feel the tingling numbness lessen as Calais enlisted more and more of the newcomers into the costshare. By the time she had arrived back, it felt more like a heavy pressure than a numbness. Calais took out some black powder, sprinkled it over her orange scribbles and smeared the symbols with her boot. Instantly even the heavy pressure was gone.

"To think," Jason said, "anytime I caught a charlie horse or that itch in my back I couldn't quite reach, that was you all along."

"My nefarious plan, exposed," she returned.

A violent earthquake shook the boat, forcing Calais to fall clumsily into her seat while the rest held onto the boat as it tossed about the choppy water. Ruki tried to steer the rowboat between two of the buildings, heading towards the third directly ahead of them. Between the heavy flooding and the intense earthquakes, the buildings seemed as if they were built of cookie rather than brick; they all started crumbling.

The water turned even choppier as huge pieces of stone and masses of bricks fell from the buildings. The debris threatened to capsize the smaller vessels and floating doors or crush the people furthest out who were dangerously close to the buildings. Calais scrawled symbols with red chalk on the wall of the rowboat then clamored next to Ruki Provos, whose brow was furrowed in concentration as he tried to navigate. Calais grabbed the rope trailing from the rowboat. It glowed red in her hand and all the ropes tied to all the vessels in the flotilla joined the glow in unison. She pulled the rope gently and all the boats of the flotilla moved closer in a tight rectangle formation until there was scarcely any empty space between boats. Jason felt a lurch in his gut and he knew it wasn't entirely from seasickness.

"It's a bit difficult to steer while you're bewitching me," Ruki said with a grimace.

"This is nothing for you, Provos," Calais said. "A tiny distraction while driving a small caravan."

Ruki set his jaw and continued to row as both buildings on either side crumbled completely into the water. He was set to steer around the third building when out of nowhere it exploded into a shower of brick, stone, wood and mortar.

"The aian gods!" Ruki cried in conjunction with Mel's "Holy hell!" and a round of expletives from everyone else. A giant spike of blue whale sized coral had burst from the sea floor where the building had once stood. Huge pieces of debris were raining down on the flotilla. Shrieks of pain and panic filled the air as small vessels overturned. Citizens dived off one boat or another to avoid being crushed.

The world shook again and another giant coral spike, looking like a kaiju incisor, burst forth from the water to the immediate left of the flotilla. A voice boomed from everywhere, reverberating throughout the dome.

"It is time to die—pay!—pests, peons, perversions!"

Another giant coral spike burst out of the water, this one directly striking the back boats of the flotilla, sending five boats and over a dozen occupants flying through the air.

Jason felt like an ant, crawling uselessly between the splayed fingers of a watchful giant. They were sitting ducks out here, playthings for the mad gray robe.

Calais began to furiously scrawl her witchcraft on the rowboat interior with red and white chalk. She leaned over the back of the boat and thrust her hands into the water. "Steer!" she commanded Ruki as the boat leapt with newfound power. The water behind the boat churned with energy, as if Calais' hands were an outboard motor. Jason felt himself getting dizzy, nauseated and his palms started to itch.

Ruki seemed to feel the same way, clenching his teeth as he tried to angle the boat around the giant coral spike in front of them. The entire flotilla, tied to the lead boat, picked up the pace, narrowly missing another spike as it burst through the sea.

"Look!" Mel cried, pointing forward from the helm of the boat.

A giant island of coral loomed about a half mile away. It looked like a flat mesa formed from layers of green, pink and yellow coral stuck together. Strange shapes Jason couldn't quite make out populated the top of the mesa. Whatever those were, they weren't coral.

No one had to say the obvious. The mad mage was there.

The world exploded. A coral spike burst into the middle of the flotilla, launching Jason's boat and everyone in it into the air. Jason landed in a jarring splash of numbing cold water. He looked around frantically, then dived under the waves until he came up with a still slumbering Eula clutched in his arm. He looked back to see Mel, Ruki, Calais and Gina all treading water. Behind them, most of the flotilla had been destroyed or set adrift, with several refugees treading water as best they could.

"Swim!" Jason cried.

Jason followed his own order, swimming one-handed towards the coral island as he held onto Eula, doing his level best to keep her head above the dicey water. Mel swam over to him and helped carry Eula. Together, they both swam with one hand, Eula between them. Calais, Ruki and Gina overtook them and made landfall on the coral island first and waited patiently to pull Jason, Mel and Eula from the tumultuous water as they got close.

All of them helped to fish the remaining refugees from the water, who in turn helped others who flopped ashore, sputtering and spitting out dirty water. Jason went up and down the coral shore, helping where he could until he stopped dead in his tracks. Rida.

Rida's parents sat sobbing around the supine form of their daughter. Jason rushed to the girl's side. Did she hit her head? Her skin had taken on a pallid, bluish-gray hue. Were her lungs full of water?

"What's wrong with her?" he asked frantically. Both parents shook their heads as their tears flowed.

"Does anyone know CPR?!" he screamed to the onlookers. Reality reminded him he was in a completely foreign world where these people had never heard of the term CPR, had probably never developed the technique in a land where healing could be done through instant magic, and he, the Chosen One, was in all actuality a sixteen-year-old kid who had never bothered to learn it because death was such an abstract concept to suburban life.

He looked to Mel and Gina, who had rushed to the scene, the only other people who even knew what the term meant. Gina dived in immediately, checking for a pulse at Rida's neck. The carotid artery right? Fuck, Jason should've paid attention to this shit in health class! Gina shook her head and began doing chest compressions. Rida remained unresponsive. Gina stopped pumping on the little girl's chest, covered Rida's mouth with her own and blew in air. Still unresponsive. Gina went back to chest compressions. Still nothing. More air in Rida's lungs, more chest compressions. Still nothing.

Jason looked to Calais, the only one in the crowd who knew magic.

"I'm sorry," Calais whispered.

As if Calais' words had broken a spell, Gina stopped the CPR and sat back panting, exhausted from her fruitless effort.

Jason stood up. Fuck it. He knew someone who could help.

"Onus!" he cried. He felt one of the remaining two maggots squirm into the heart pendant lying against his chest, a sensation that surged with heat and adrenaline.

Onus appeared before him with a snap of thunder. The sight of the blood-robed adversary made everyone, including Rida's parents, scramble away in mortal terror. Jason didn't care. He looked Onus straight in his unnaturally still eyes.

"Fix this."

Onus panned his cold gaze down to consider the child before looking back at Jason.

"What you ask, Cephrin, is beyond me."

"No it's not," Jason said, shaking his head in disbelief. "You're the god of power. This takes power. So tap into the force you're the fucking god of and fix this."

"Redress your tone, cub," Onus stated. "You err in your grief to mistake me as some sort of wish-dragon, granting whatever boon strikes your fancy. I am of this world and power over it flows through me. Power over your friends, power over the fearful masses behind me, power over the husk before us. Would you like me to wiggle my fingers and command the meat of her to rise, to dance before us, a lifeless puppet show to massage away that feeling of powerlessness that I, like you, cannot abide? For this is all that is left of the girl in this world... useless meat."

Jason felt an overwhelming urge to beat Onus' face in. As his fists clenched, Jason felt something strike his neck and he was forced to close his eyes in a shower of shattered metal. He turned to see Eula, magnificent in her rage, glaring at him, her sword broken.

"Now, sister," Onus said. "The Chosen One did call upon me, which affords him the protection of my house."

She shot Onus a look that spoke daggers. "Do you think I will sit idle while you work to bring down all the houses and usher our people back into the Maddening Times?"

"Sit idle, stand alert, charge reckless, your action is immaterial," Onus replied. "The nature of what comes is out of your hands, the sole discrimination of The Chosen One." He closed his eyes and smiled as if savoring the smells of dinner. "Oh, oh sister! I can feel your powerlessness, it shrieks like a wounded lamb inside you."

Eula turned to Jason, her oscillating eyes failing to hide the rage and hurt. She spoke the same question she had asked him before he had slept her.

"Why?"

"Look around you, immortal, at a world that eats our short lives." He knelt down and moved an errant lock of hair from Rida's face. "The innocent and undeserving more than any."

He caressed her cheek. "Goodbye, Rida," he whispered.

Jason stood and faced Onus. "I'm going to need that maggot back. I have a bullshit mage I'm gonna go kill now."

Onus shook his head. "You issued a call for power and received that power and with it a lesson on its finite boundaries. It is a contract I will not revoke. That said, you have one more time to call upon a temporary surge of power before our merger, your ascension." He leaned closer to Jason, holding up one finger. "One more time to experience my might in your lowly, lonely form. Use it as you see fit."

He waved his hand and panned his steely gaze to his sister Eula. The broken sword she was holding reassembled itself, the metal shards flying towards it until the sword became shining, gleaming, whole.

"No hard feelings, sister. I know how much you treasure your Moonlight Blade. But know that your weapon will forever be useless against the Chosen One."

"Back to hell with you, worm," she spat.

Onus winked and smiled in reply. He turned to the crowd, huddled as far back on the coral they could get without being in the water. "Look at you," he said in disgust. "A bunch of defenseless, powerless half-animals. If any of you grow tired of huddling in fear and shame, if you ever weary of lacking the power to protect those you love," he said, eyeing Rida's parent's specifically, forcing them to avert their gaze. "You only need seek my house. You shall never know fear nor weakness again, such is my promise."

With that, Onus disappeared with the same crack of thunder in which he had appeared. The crowd huddled on the edge of the coral beach flinched in fright, reminding Jason of the munchkins when the wicked witch disappeared in a cloud of smoke in The Wizard of Oz.

Eula glared at Jason with nothing short of contempt. "Vile thrall of Onus, your deception, your thirst for power will doom us all to descend into madness."

Jason nodded, accepting her assessment. "I didn't ask for this path I'm on, goddess. All the same, we find ourselves here. If you're that worried about your precious empire, I'll turn myself over to you and the other gods for judgment. After I kill the mage that did this. Correction: After you help me kill the mage that did this. You and your people want my head on a spike, I want this mage ended. Deal?"

"Jason, no," Mel said, taking a step towards him. Jason raised a hand to stop his protests.

"Truth is, I don't know if I can stop the call to power, dude. It's a good feeling, a really good feeling. And me having god mode isn't exactly worth an entire race of people. Time for me to fess up and admit I'm selfish enough to push the button, that, not counting the gods, virtually all of aiankind was one large faceless mob to me. Except her." He looked down little Rida and felt his throat close. He had to look away so refocused on his best friend. "She had wanted my mark, whatever that could've been if such a thing could ever be. All I can do now is mark her gravestone, but first I'm gonna create his."

Eula nodded. "You have a deal Cephrin or Jason or whatever you are called. The mage is a threat to my people and the world at large. It must end."

Together they turned their attention to the upper tier of coral, where a demented mage was undoubtedly lying in wait.

Chapter 28
Less Than Ideal

Mike felt like he was in a zombie comedy movie where living survivors shambled about and moaned, pretending to be part of the undead horde around them. He moved alongside Runt and Ego, no shamble to be found in their purposeful strides through the Sprawl, while small packs of Clockwound Warders roamed in this direction or another with no discernible pattern to their patrols.

The goggles worked, which made Mike bug out a bit as all the clone dudes kept about their weird-whatever business completely oblivious to the folks who were clearly not gang affiliated stepping through their turf. Runt looked the most out of sorts. The man-sized goggles seemed small and tight, giving his face a pinched, beady-eyed appearance.

Despite the seemingly flawless immersion into Clockwound's hottest zone, none of them spoke, as if a word exchanged between them would break the spell, the final straw that would make the clone horde turn and realize there was something off about these three in their midst. Best not to test ancient technology none of them fully understood without reason.

Ego led the way, flanked on either side my Mike and Runt. He seemed to know his way through this region of the Sprawl, navigating through the crags, cracks and crannies of the rubble as if it was his ancestral homeland. It made Mike wonder how many rumbles the

Sons and Clockwound got into beefing over this specific piece of territory.

Ego stopped in a clearing at what Mike could only describe as Sewer Central. A giant chrome manhole cover, pitted and dirty brown from oxidation and forever's worth of neglect, dominated the clearing. Eight square holes, two foot square in size and spaced equidistantly in the concrete, surrounded the dilapidated manhole cover. The eight holes were a perpetual buzz of activity, with warders either climbing up or climbing down one hole or another.

Wu-Tang killer bees, we on the swarm. The thought came unbidden to Mike as he looked at the hive-like activity.

"What I and I's want be down there, seen?" Ego said finally breaking their shared silence. "Puppets not stray too far from the hand holding the strings."

If that was the case, they had a problem. Ego could fit down those square holes and there was no question with Mike, but Runt was small weagr sized. Trying to stuff him down one of these holes would look like all the Christmas movies of Santa getting stuck in the chimney.

"Not digging the logistics," Mike said. "I ain't trying to be one short in the heart of darkness down there."

Runt seemed just as motivated to not be left two short topside. He made powerful strides to the giant rusty manhole cover in the center, pushing aside some warders milling about aimlessly in the process. He put his fingers into two of small holes on one end and began to heave.

The thing looked unmovable, stuck in place for eons. Mike could see the veins popping out in Runt's forehead. Wordlessly, Ego and Mike went over to help.

The manhole cover barely even groaned, let alone move. There was no way the three of them were going to lift it. Still, Runt kept at it, which meant fuck it, Mike and Ego kept at it.

And then the warders came. All the warders that had been milling about or climbing up and down the access ladders formed a circle around the manhole with Runt, Ego and Mike. They all grabbed a piece of manhole cover and began to pull.

Now the thing began to move with a heavy groan and rust started breaking at the cover seams in chips. Slowly the cover lifted up and Mike could see there were also warders underneath the cover pushing it. Soon Runt was able to get his hands underneath the lid and with a mighty heave, he pushed the cover away, forcing some of the warders on the opposite side to scurry out of the way lest they get crushed. Once the job was completed, the warders went back to milling about as if nothing had changed.

Ego looked at their handiwork with a crooked grin. "Seems them still come together for purpose. I in wonderment about the particulars."

Mike shrugged. "Maybe they just need to see something worth doing. Y'all ready?"

Runt and Ego nodded. They proceeded down the ladder of the large manhole, their major highway to the underworld. The bottom was bone dry concrete. If there was ever any liquid sewage it had dried up a long time ago and now only a stuffy odor of stale sweat clung to the place. A large circle of light came down from the recently uncovered manhole, like a noonday sun, along with smaller beams of light from the holes the warders had already been using. They found themselves in the center of a "+" intersection. Immediately outside the light drenched crossroads, the four passages were swallowed in darkness.

Mike immediately thought of Jason and his dumbass "go left" theory. Only there ain't no lefts when you start in the middle of some crossroads. Mike halfway wished the kid was here so he could call him an asshole but figured Jason would just say something else that was equally dumbass.

Ego took out his baton and pointed it down one of the darkened corridors.

"I not one to stand rooted before a bounty of quality selections. Let I and I's feast on choices, starting with this dark offering. I think this one will leave I and I's little left to hunger. It smell of warder. It taste of warder. What follow now is the sight, know?"

Mike nodded and led the way down the passage. His megrym vision came alive in the darkness, where he easily navigated past dislodged stones and various detritus. Soon the tunnel began to slope downwards. Instead of looking assembled from bricks, the tunnel walls began to appear as if they were cast in stone, one smooth uniform piece machined to be there. The tunnel continued to travel down as well as expand on both sides and ceiling.

Light appeared, a soft white glow emanating further down, which displayed the end of the tunnel. They emerged in a cavernous chamber with ceilings so high Mike couldn't believe they had traveled this far down. The white light came from orbs the size of portholes that dotted the walls all over, like glowing eyes staring into the vast square room. There were a glut of warders here, some of them milling about, most of them standing still like vacant stares.

The opposite side of the room housed five giant tubes filled with viscous green liquid. The tube on the far right contained a whole warder minus eyeballs. The tubes left of that one housed various stages of meat and Mike had seen enough sci-fi movies to know exactly what this was.

"They growing them here," he whispered.

"This be the reason for the warder's unthinkable numbers," Ego said. He nodded. "Also the reason for their lack of martial prowess says I. But a blunt horde still be a horde, know?"

Thick lines ran from the tank to a huge device that dominated the center of the room. A large chrome metal base that gave way to a dense bundle of shiny wiring, glowing lights and spikes midway up, followed by more chrome metal pipeworks and fittings that went all the way up to the ceiling. The dense bundle of wiring was reminiscent of brain matter or intestines and the pulsing lights and brass spikes around it made it no question this was the main feature of the device. The only thing that came close to what Mike was seeing was when he had played *Metroid* as a kid and first encountered Mother Brain.

Ego tapped Mike's shoulder and pointed to a far, neglected corner of the room. A large iron cage sat there, full of warders if their tattered clock bearing uniforms were any indication. These warders, all human, had eyes, every one of them cheerless and despondent.

"Why they locking up their own?" Mike asked. "Drunk tank? Small crimes... they stealing each other concrete down here?"

Ego shrugged. "Maybe as far as the ones without pupils can see, them view the sighted ones as a threat. Maybe them in the cage not grown warders like their sightless brethren but indoctrinated as Pramus was or any of the Sons of Kaftar that find their way to I."

Mike had to admit, the latter explanation made sense. At least the not vat-grown part. Still, there had to be some leader to the organization and all the clone type ones Mike had met didn't look like they could lead a fly to garbage. So who was in charge and locking the more capable variety of warder in the holding tank?

"If they're like how Pramus was, then that means they can talk," Mike said, reasoning out loud. "Then they might talk to us, the enemy of our enemy and all that."

As if they were intentionally trying to add more mystery to this confused situation, eight of the free warders went over to the cage and opened it. The ones inside scurried over top of one another to cower in the furthest corner from the entrance. Unperturbed by the instant huddle, the free warders went into the cage and pulled one of the captive warders out. The captive struggled at the hands holding his arms, legs, neck and body, his screams hoarse and futile as his captors took him before the machine.

They held his head down before the machine, on a curved dais just big enough to hold his chin. All he could do was squeal between clenched teeth as the many hands held his head in place. The man attempted to squeeze his eyes shut, but that only resulted in more fingers groping his face, pulling his eyes open.

Like a scorpion strike, two brass needles shot out of the machine. The needles came within a hair's breadth of puncturing the man's eyes. The needles glowed white and a fine beam of light erupted from their tips, shooting directly into the man's pupils. He let out an anguished scream.

The machine's lights throbbed. The goggles on all the warders in the room shimmered in the light. Ego and Runt's goggles shimmered as well but their reactions were remarkably different. Ego just cocked his head to the side, seemingly bemused by whatever was playing out in his goggles. Runt took three staggered steps back, his features contorted in pain and took lumbering swipes at ghosts no one else could see. Mike's goggles remained unchanged so he didn't have the first idea what was happening.

"Runt! You good, man?"

Runt kept backing up, swiping at invisibles, until he tripped on his own feet and landed on his butt. He was panting in hard labored breaths. Mike and Ego rushed over to him, putting a hand on either side of him.

"Runt!" Mike called.

Runt's only answer was to shake his head.

Mike looked up at Ego. "What just happened?"

"Just an oddity to I," he replied. "Symbols I never seen fly up the glass of them goggles, come with a feeling of warmth. Not much else."

Runt snatched the goggles off his face. He looked at Mike.

"Symbols are purpose," he said. "Tasks to do. Places to be. The feeling is compulsion. Nothing matters but the purpose."

"Why'd it affect you two differently?" Mike asked "And me not at all?"

"Matters not, Mike Ballztowallz. I only know I cannot wear them. They seek to write over my own will."

Fuck. "Between the ones topside and the ones in the room, we're in a goddamn warder sandwich," Mike said, "and those goggles are the only thing that keeps them from peeling up the bread to look at the meat."

"I will face them," Runt replied. "And it will be my choice."

Ego sucked his teeth. "Cannot blame I's rough, any more than I would barter with a mage to save I's own skin, know?"

Mike looked at Runt. "Aight. Post up here. Stay in the shadows and don't let the goggles see you. Come in bruising at the first sign of scrapping, cool?"

Runt nodded and picked himself up off the ground. Ego and Mike shared a glance. Time to head into the mixer.

As they were walking down into the room the captive warder was already being tossed back into the cell, where he collapsed in the waiting arms of his fellow captives. Mike and Ego, their hands fingering the weapons on their hips, warily made their way through the uncaring crowd of warders on either standing or milling about.

By the time Mike and Ego arrived at the cage, the captive warders had formed a circle in the center of the cell around their prone cellmate. Ego leaned towards the bars.

"What go on here?"

As if his words were plates shattering, everyone in the circle flinched and snapped their necks at the sound, fear etched on their features. Then they saw who it was and noticeably relaxed. A good dozen crept quietly to the bars while a couple stayed to look after their injured cellmate. One of the captives, a man with knotted red hair, pockmarked face and green eyes leaned the closest and whispered with a strained voice.

"We've had our rivalry, blood spilled on both sides. But will you free us, Son Leader? Is it too late for us to be proven friends?"

"Illuminate I, gear man," Ego said. "Why stand caged amongst your own kind?"

Knotty Red spared a conspiratorial glance at the free warders, who seemed unconcerned with the conversation before turning his attention back to Ego. "A while back, feels like forever ago, a purple mage descended here. Your worst enemy, yes? No friend of ours either. He cast his fearsome magics on us. Our lessthans went crazy. Everyone here in this cage started seeing demons, monsters in our goggles, so we cast them off. Once we did that the lessthans killed several of us, then captured the rest."

"Lessthans?" Mike asked.

"The ones that surround us," Knotty Red said, looking around the large room for emphasis. "Our former workforce. Less than men."

"What them want with you?" Ego asked.

Knotty Red hesitated. "We may not have enough time to explain before they come for us again. Please, Son Leader, free us!"

Ego sucked his teeth. "One moment after seeking I's friendship and already you not proving to be a friend to I. You try to impose your sense of urgency on I when it is not I's urgency. I remain unrushed and newly skeptical. You bear this life for months but now you cannot spare the time for a few sentences for I's understanding. You hide secrets from I."

Knotty Red's countenance flashed in anger. With speed that belied his emaciated body, he snatched Ego's goggles off his head. More hands reached for Mike's face. Mike instinctively jumped away from the bars. Ego lunged for Knotty Red but he retreated to the relative safety in the center of the cage. Knotty Red hurriedly donned the goggles.

"The Masters!" he cried euphorically.

As if an alarm was blaring in their heads, all the lessthan warders turned to face the naked hazel eyes of Ego.

"Wait!" Knotty Red said. He looked up and around as if trying to see something in the goggle lenses. "These aren't." He turned to Ego and Mike. He pointed his finger at Mike. "He's got the Masters!"

The lessthans were moving with purpose towards Ego. He took out his baton. Mike pulled his diskbow.

Knotty Red rushed to the cage door, his fellow prisoners following behind him with renewed zeal. He reached a hand through the bars to fumble at the latch and the lessthan guards did nothing to stop him.

The first couple of lessthan warders reached Ego. He met them with a rapid succession of strikes with his baton so fast it could've matched a boxer working two speed bags at once. Both warders fell silently. Ego rushed to pry a pair of goggles off a prone warder and don them.

The lessthans still came for Ego regardless of the new goggles.

"Maybe them got better eyes than I gave credit," Ego said with a smirk.

Whether these lessthan warders in the room were special, or whether there was some kind of awareness the lessthans had where taking goggles in plain sight didn't work, it didn't matter. An army of lessthans were still mobbing towards Ego.

Meanwhile Knotty Red had gotten the cage open. The two guards made no move against him but were actively coming for his fellow cellmates. Knotty Red tackled one guard while his cellies rushed the other.

Some of the lessthans broke from their path to Ego to face the new threat of the freed prisoners.

A loud roar on the other side of the room let everyone know Runt wanted to play. He had his Z blade disassembled into twin axes and was moseying down the main ramp as if he was a Hollywood star walking the red carpet to his premiere.

Mike fired a disk through a lessthan who ran at Ego, while Ego cracked the skull of another one. Swarming lessthans were starting to fill the gap between Ego and Mike and separate them. The lessthans ran past Mike to challenge Ego. There were too many bodies moving erratically for Mike to trust the chain lighting of his gloves to not leap to Ego, so he took out his club. He didn't know how many he'd sleep before they decided to notice he was a threat, and now was a good ass time to find out.

The violent shoving and commotion around the cage let Mike know the prisoners were headed his way. Shouldn't they be moving toward Runt and the only visible exit to this place? Mike spared a glance back at Runt who was swinging on a flock of lessthans while shaking two of them off his back. Wouldn't now, with all the commotion happening, be the best time for these convicts to pop smoke?

Knotty Red broke through a line of lessthans intent on overrunning Ego. One of his cellmates ran through the gap and lunged for Mike. Mike ducked and sidestepped. The cellmate swiped desperately at Mike's face. Another two cellmates ran through the gap Knotty Red was forcing open to attack Mike.

Mike jabbed his club with flash speed at the hand reaching for his face. The club hit the fingers and kept going, bending them back with a sickening crunch. The other two cellmates were almost on top of Mike, forcing him to jump back, turn and slide between the legs of an approaching lessthan. The lessthan paid Mike no attention as he grabbed one of the cellmates.

More cellmates swarmed around the lessthan. There was no question Mike was their target. They wanted his goggles, Pramus' old goggles, the ones they called the Masters and they wanted it more than escape or the consequences of dealing with a horde of lessthans determined to stop them.

Mike couldn't collapse back to Ego, who had his back to the cage and was busy defending himself from at least a dozen lessthans. And retreating back to Runt was even less ideal, as the swarm from topside had made it to home base and the half-weagr was practically wading through a sea of lessthans with at least three riding him like an amusement park attraction at any given time. That left Mike to deal with a contingent of free thinking ex-prisoners who seemed rabid to have his eyewear.

"Three fingers can't carry this load, know?!" Ego shouted as he hit one warder with his baton, face pushed another and headbutted a third.

Indeed. This battle of attrition only ended one way. They did not have the numbers.

A cellmate jumped at Mike. His muscle memory from his high school football days kicked in, and Mike juked the tackle. A plan hit him, in the height of his desperation. He started running, not sideways towards Ego or back towards Runt, but forward, towards the approaching cellmate warders.

He treated his goggles like the football. He faked left, spun right, ducked around lessthans he treated as defensive linemen. Hands from all over reached out and tried to stop and grab Mike. He was aware of the hostile convict presence like a sixth sense, stutter-stepping and dashing and weaving around and through like a highlight reel.

Finally, he broke through a pack of lessthans, to an area where no one occupied, where the machine dominated the room.

Behind him he could hear the howling and scraping of the cellmates to get to him. The heightened urgency in their voices let him know they were beyond desperate.

"God, this is fucking stupid!" he yelled to himself as he ran to the machine. Without ceremony he laid himself down before it, placing his chin in the same position the cellmate was forced to take before he got his eyes probed by the machine's scorpion needle. Only Mike wore goggles and with that extra space he wasn't so sure the scorpion strike of the machine wouldn't break through the goggle lenses.

Mike dry swallowed as the machine lashed out with its brass needles.

The needles landed with a dull tap on the goggle lenses. Light erupted from the needles, causing the lenses to glow searing white. Symbols flowed across the lenses.

The energy changed in an instant. The lessthans stopped fighting Ego and Runt and all of them converged on the convicts. Without the added distraction of Ego and Runt, it was child's play for the lessthan to capture the convicts.

The spikes retreated back into the machine. Mike fell back from the dais to lie on the floor, breathing heavy.

Touchdown.

Mike heard the clink of boots on the metal floor as Ego approached. The man looked down at Mike, his head tilted slightly, a crooked smile on his face.

"How I's rough know what the recipe call for?" he asked bemused.

"Fuck me, I didn't," Mike answered panting. "Between the convict warders chasing me for eyewear, seeing this machine work on eyes and being fresh the fuck out of options, I just took a goddamn guess."

"Highest compliments to the chef, same," Ego said. He turned to face the convicts, who were each held in place by a good dozen hands each. He strolled over to Knotty Red.

"This was what you tried keeping from I, go snatching I's quality eye sight over?" Ego pulled the goggles from Knotty Red's face, to reveal the man's glowering green eyes.

"I saw a way to restore order to Clockwound. Maybe end the Son's leader as he ended ours in the process. I took it."

Ego nodded. "I not begrudge you. Would do the same if I's feet were in your boots. Now, if your feet were in I's boots at this moment, what would you do to I?"

Knotty Red shook his head. "You know as I know. No love to the other side in the Fallen Kingdom."

Mike picked himself up off the ground. Runt joined him at his side, his Z-blade safely attached to his back, looking stoic as if he had just had a leisurely stroll instead of a life and death fight with twenty at a time.

"Times change," Ego said to Knotty Red, "even in a realm frozen in time it seems. Factory mage invaded, hit I but first hit you, led to conditions that put you in a cage, a prisoner of your own people. I intend to hit back. Even if you knew with no doubts this room is the last one you'll ever see, would you not want to see I prosecute this intention? Would you not seek to arm I with the knowledge that tells all from the outside world, dread them fearsome techromancers? Come, tell I the secrets of this machine."

Knotty Red looked around at his captive brethren's forlorn faces and nodded grimly.

"It is too late to best you, Ego, but I can get these men a taste of vengeance from the grave through you. We call it the Instruct Engine, or I.E. The vats in the back take six weeks to grow a lessthan from nothing but liquid. Once the lessthan pops out, we put goggles on him, which are keyed and tuned to the Master goggles. The I.E. is how Pramus interfaced with the lessthans, to change their instructions if needed. After you killed Pramus and took the Masters, we couldn't change the instructions, which were set to general commands such as 'patrol the area, attack any and all non-warders.' We managed this way for months, with no way to set new instructions without a full on invasion of the Heart of the Sons. That was doomed to fail because we couldn't instruct the lessthans to join the invasion. So we attempted to find another pair of Masters. Then the mage came, his magic scrambled the lessthans and their instructions with no way to reset them. This is how you found us."

Knotty Red looked at the goggles resting on Mike's face. "They are tuned to the megrym now. He can issue general instructions that will stand even if the goggles are removed or he focuses his will and gives specific commands to one or more lessthans in an area. He will have to figure out the nuances of the control for himself. After all, none of us here have donned them save Pramus."

He looked back at Ego, "I ask your end for us to be swift. We have all spent enough time languishing in pain."

Ego tilted his head and a crooked smile formed on his lips, "What savage do you take I to be, to go killing proven friends?"

Chapter 29
Dire Blue

"*Ör*," Rew uttered. Her raven hair braided itself just a little more.

She said it again, and the braid lengthened. And again. And again.

She could feel the witchlock she was under tremble. The simple spell was slowly chipping away at its wards and defenses. Rew was able to stand now under her own power, without the lock being so oppressive it pulled her to the floor. "*Ör*," she uttered again as she stumbled with shaky legs in her bedroom turned prison. She gripped her dresser and looked into her mirror, where she could see fatigue in her eyes and nearly all her tresses neatly braided.

The mirror was spelled with a communication link. But whom could she call? Her allies were either in the Sprawl or Suusteren, and if Rich's cost vision was anywhere close to accurate, the team in Suusteren needed all the help they could get against the demented gray robe. And then there was Rich. Had his mirror been confiscated? Was it even safe to try to contact him if it hadn't?

Rew looked beyond her bed, out the window to the leaning Aphelion Tower shining dully in the daylight. Rich and Rew were beyond each other's help. Still, she needed to know. She let the weight of the witchlock pull her back to the floor.

Just the ability to stand let Rew know she had poked sizable holes in the witchlock. She opened her mind up to scry and spoke Rich's signature. Doubt poured into the silent stretch of space while waiting for him to answer. She had seen Druze turn his body aian. Could Rich even scry anymore? Sure, aians couldn't cast their own magic but they could have spells cast on them so the scry should technically work. What worried her more was what Rich had gone through. Between choosing to remain here when the easy portal home was thrust in his face and the jarring transition into another race perhaps the traumas had changed his scry signature. Her scry requests could be going into a void. And then there was the other void, the cold and final one where Rich could be for attempting this mad gambit to infiltrate the High Fane.

She was still trying to reassure herself against the worst case when Rich appeared in the scry. Only the familiar feeling of Rich was all that was left for her, as the gray body and the ridged chameleon brow gave her sight no comfort. Not even his eyes were the same, as now they kept dancing as he looked at her with visible relief on his face.

"Rew! Are you okay?" he asked.

"I have fared better," she said with a strained smile. "But I am safe for now. I worry that you are not."

The scene behind Rich was very much the Temple of Houses. It seemed he had been afforded private quarters. Moss encrusted stone walls framed the room much like the one she had paid him a visit in back when they had sat side by side on his bed and he had read to her from the Song of Ardor Swain, back before there was a war between temple and tower.

"I think I'm doing alright," Rich said. "I miss my old self... it kinda sucks that I've got no magic in a pinch, but they haven't found me out yet, so I guess that's a win."

"Oh, Rich," she sighed. "I wish you hadn't agreed to go along with my father's plan. That man always has motives and schemes hiding within his motives and schemes. There's no telling how this will end."

"I honestly wanted to tell him to go to hell on general principle, but I had no real reason to refuse." Rich shrugged. "Seems like he wanted the war over, too and the last thing I wanted to do was to say no to that just because I don't trust him."

"As well you shouldn't trust him." She shook her head. "His plan has put you in the heart of their lands, with no easy way for you to extricate yourself from that city or that body. It would appear he has no use for you any longer, which means he won't care either way if you survive this or not."

"Well, they're agreeing to an armistice, so that's good news. I figure I can wait for a quiet day, use it as an excuse to take a relaxing destrier ride on the High Veldt, then keep on riding til I get to the Free States. I still got my phone mirror, so I'll call the guys and hopefully work on a plan for getting you free and getting me back to my former self. Man, I didn't think I'd miss being Razzleblad this much."

"I understand being suddenly bereft of magic," Rew said, her gaze panning up as if the witchlock had followed her into the scry. "The feeling of helplessness, vulnerability." She looked back at Rich purposefully. "Implement your plan. I shall implement my own. Next time we talk, it shall be under more pleasant circumstances, yes?"

Rich smiled, the sweet boyish one, the only thing that still seemed unchanged from his transition. "You bet."

Rew killed the scry. Back in her room, the air seemed thicker.

"Ah! my immortal enchantress wakes," said a man's voice, one dripping with smugness.

An icy chill ran down Rew's spine. She turned her gaze to see sitting in her chair a mage that before his rightful confinement had been called the Dire Blue.

"Ver... eyn," she said flatly.

"Please," he said with a vicious smile that made his facial scars bunch up, "call me Delv. I imagine it would be a bit easier for you under the witchlock. Just as I imagine it must be hard to sleep under the lock. You didn't seem overly comfortable, despite how beautiful you looked. And you are beautiful, especially when your face isn't contorting into disdainful glares."

Vereyn leaned back in her chair and shook his head as if he had just realized something important. "But what am I saying? I bet you get compliments like this all the time from the men whose hearts you've captured, or bodies you've captured and locked in the Underthral. Perhaps both?"

Rew didn't answer. The man was bent and twisted. There was no answer to give a person such as Vereyn, no right answer that would make him go away or at least make him see reason. So she stayed stoic and silent, her only weapon against a foe that fed on her reaction.

He leaned closer, his icy blue eyes growing earnest. "Was it a cost? Have you been at war with this cruel bond in your sleep? Do you dream cast?"

Vereyn held up a finger. "Don't answer. Allow me. *Sorgulama*," he intoned.

Powerless under the witchlock to refute Vereyn, Rew let out an involuntary gasp as she felt his vile intrusion. His presence probed and prodded her mind like crude, eager fingers.

Vereyn smiled. "Now this is the kind of reaction I expect. Unlike your latest beau, you have studied blue magic. You know exactly what this is, even if it isn't inherently painful."

He emphasized the word "painful" by shooting jarring, seizing spasms down her spine. She yelped as her back locked up in an arch.

"But let's not rule anything out, shall we," he crooned. "And I mean anything."

Just as suddenly, the spastic pain subsided, replaced by a tingling warmth, like a lover's touch, that spread down from her neck and radiated through her entire body. The uncontrollable feeling of pleasure, dispensed by Delv Vereyn, sickened her more than the pain had.

"Allow me to tell you about my most recent cost," Vereyn said casually, leaning back in her chair. "Pretty steep one, I surmise from animating empty shells and entertaining new friends, getting back into teaching—how I've missed my students! All these things add up, and well, I know you understand how it feels when things start to mount."

He looked at her knowingly as the waves of tingling warmth rippled through her body, bouncing, creating echoes, intensifying. Her breath quickened as her mind raced for escape. Waves of utter disgust washed hollow, the natural feeling muted against the manufactured. She bit her lip to bring back the pain she now longed for.

"So the cost brings me back to the day I chose a color, and this time I chose orange. I went on to do amazing, praiseworthy things in orange. I was the mage that discovered for the world how to turn one's body into living netherfire. Imagine! Not only that, I developed a way to slow time itself by turning one's own system into something I had dubbed a gravity well. I lived an entire lifetime in that cost, praised by all, even you, Hierophant, in my other life. Along the way I met a beautiful woman named Asono. We had a romance even you'd be envious of despite all the lifetimes you've already had to find a love such as that. She bore me a daughter, my sweet Miri. Miri had my eyes and her mother's flaxen hair. She was a daddy's girl, followed me into the tower. I was there for her every degree of brown. She finally mastered the Black Calefaction a week before her sixteenth birthday and when she went to pick a color she said 'Blue'. That's when her eyes liquified and the flesh of her face melted. Then I awoke, having paid my cost. I spent a good hour mourning the loss of a wife and daughter that felt so real I can still smell my daughter's hair and feel my wife's warm fingers and I know without doubt, in that way you fully understand the cost is showing you truth, that they would've existed if I had only chose a brighter color."

He leaned forward, and the waves of pleasure he had been causing in Rew ceased abruptly in the motion. An involuntary gasp escaped her lips while she continued to glare at him.

"In the midst of my grieving, I realized Miri was quite like that one student of mine who actually did melt her own face after a bit of my suggestive nudgings took hold. I really should be under that witchlock, not you. Didn't you tell your father about me? Terrible parent, that one. I would've listened to my dear Miri."

Vereyn shrugged. "But there's no Miri in this world. And I helped melt the only girl here that could've been the closest thing to her. What's to be done? I chose this color. And in blue there's none better."

He smiled and winked.

"The cost, in trying to show me this better life I could've lived, actually showed me I was always destined to be this person, a mage pushing the boundaries of his color. Orange is harmless, manipulating skin and blood and bone. All the harm lives here," he said pointing to his temple. "Pain, sadness, madness, fear, greed, deviancy, all shades of blue, my house, my color palette. Naturally I couldn't stay away from a gift such as this." He extended his arms to her. "What lies in a mind centuries old?"

Rew's only answer was to glare. She felt his presence in her mind, over hers, like a heavy burden pressing his weight down.

"The loss of my wife/never-wife Asono and my daughter/never-daughter Miri inspired me, Rew. Surely, you have a legion of lost loves in that head of yours. Druze can have children in his immortality, why not you? Are you barren? Do you miscarry? Or have you had them, some dark secret never shown the light of day? These are important questions I'm sure you'll answer in time. And then there are the experiments to be had in love and hate. For instance, how would you come to view my visage once I overwrite each and every one of the special romances you've ever had and replace the man with me?

All those intimate moments we'll share! First I'll be your sweet Rich and then, hmmm..."

She could feel his dark, grubby fingers rifling through her memories.

"Maris Runember," he said with a smile. "Eventually they'll all look like me. The question is, will the hate you have for me now be muted by all the beautiful memories? Or sharpened by the thought of this very one-directional conversation?"

"Grave... mis... take," Rew spat.

Vereyn's eyes widened gleefully. "I certainly hope so, Rew. Mistakes are where we learn the most, where our best growth occurs. Life happens in the mistakes. *Dushunjeye zinjeerle bahla,*" he intoned.

Rew knew the spell. It allowed her mind to be chained to his, so he could show her things as he saw and experienced. As much as Rew didn't want her mind attached to his, the blue spell itself had nothing to do with the torture he had just proposed.

Vereyn knew what she was thinking. He wagged a finger at her.

"Before you and I have fun, though, we really should check on our aian friends in the Temple of Houses."

Chapter 30
Godsend

Rich was alerted to the returning presence of Delv by the sudden infusion of the entire school of creation magic into his brain. He saw white robes create a lake oasis in desert sands, erect a marble fortress in the heart of lush jungles, pull gleaming weapons and armor out of thin air. Unlike bending materials out of shape and form or altering them to similar things, the act of creating stuff out of nothing required an extreme amount of focus. But Rich saw some white robes creating materials that didn't exist in the known world, gases that glowed in the dark, strange winged and legged vehicles and smooth polymer-like materials that Rich could only liken to plastics.

"Miss me?" Delv asked in Rich's head.

"Why is your nose bleeding?" Mors asked, pointing at Rich.

He would notice. Of all the notable bodies in the High Fane's command center, Rich's body was the only one Mors took special interest in. While the aides and attendants and generals were ever-watching Ananna, Otam, Baligoz or Nadi while the gods themselves sat in their thrones pouring over charts and maps littering a table before them as they discussed a counteroffensive against the nasran forces. Well, Baligoz was the one exception. The fish god called the Watcher seemingly found it far more interesting to alternate his attention between Rich and the Razzleblad dummy sleeping in the corner under the red glow of a witchlock.

Unlike the god, Mors' eyes did not alternate but rather stayed glued to Rich, probably waiting for the moment Rich would go full Grave Robber so he could point and yell "imposter!"

Rich touched a finger and felt the thick warm of his nostrils oozing the byproduct of a fresh Matrix-like download.

"I really should see this thing you call a 'movie,'" Delv thought-said. *"They sound highly entertaining. Meanwhile, you should send for your attendant to, you know, attend you."*

"I'm fine," he said both to Delv in his mind and Mors out loud.

"Are you?" Delv asked.

Before he could answer, Rich was assaulted with the full barrage of destruction magic. Black robes throwing ice, fire, earth, metal and air, the whole purpose to destroy whatever the spell was aimed at. Hundreds, no thousands of spells invaded his brain, the full catalog of mankind's ongoing experiment in ways to end life. It didn't feel like a coherent school like the others, but more of a catchall for any and every spell that had no other purpose but to maim or mar beauty. Perhaps destruction needed no other purpose. Then at the end, Rich got the final teachings of black, the importance of a name, and the dark secret of how to unmake a thing as if it never was, even a person.

Rich felt himself shiver uncontrollably, and it was all he could do to fight the nauseating disorientation that came with a back-to-back blast of a full school download. Mors took a step forward, his hand on the hilt of his sword.

"I require my attendant," Delv said slowly.

Rich repeated the words to Mors verbatim.

"Good student," Delv said. *"You learn quickly."*

Mors nodded, keeping his hand on his hilt while he looked at the guardsmen at the door. "Fetch the commander's aide."

REW'S DREAD SPIKED to new heights as she watched Rich willingly obey Vereyn. There was no way she could warn Rich to reject the psychic link without exposing the fact that she had worn down the witchlock. She didn't know how long Vereyn had lurked in Rich's mindspace and his continued presence only increased the danger.

The physical Vereyn was sitting unblinking and glassy-eyed in Rew's chair in her bedroom, a presence Rew had to concentrate her attention on just to see, much like trying to look at objects in one's peripheral vision. Veryn had control of her focus, which he shifted to see from the eyes of the pendulum shell his mind manipulated, an Armsguardsman from the House of Yol. The guards outside of the war room called for Vereyn's shell, to which he casually strolled into the place as if he owned it. Someone pointed to Rich and his bloody nose.

"Seems as if he could've just called for a handkerchief instead of an aide," Vereyn said.

The remark caused the entire room to stop. It would. Aians held protocol, decorum and station in prime regard, especially within the Temple of Houses. This room had probably never been witness to this level of insubordination.

Rew felt the initiation of something dreadful in the making. She fought to regain her sense of self, to see the bedroom where she was that had been relegated to her distant vision. Once she felt her own body and her own presence, she whispered a solitary word under her breath, praying that Vereyn would not hear.

"*Ör.*" And again. And again. "*Ör. Ör. Ör.*" The braid lengthened.

Meanwhile, back in her primary focus, A wide-eyed Mors fixed Vereyn with an incredulous look. "Are you mad?!"

Vereyn smiled. "Perhaps. Though I like to think of myself as the lone sane person in a sea of crazed and rampant idiocy. Notice how I can plainly see he needs a handkerchief and all of you can likewise plainly see he needs a handkerchief, yet instead of just giving him one, it made more sense to you that I'm brought in here to give him one and it makes even less sense in your primitive minds that I call out the particulars of what we all can plainly see before us. Yet I'm mad?"

"*Ör. Ör. Ör.*" Rew went as quickly as she dared.

Mors reached for his sword but with lightning speed Vereyn closed the distance between the two and grabbed his wrist, keeping Mors from pulling the blade out.

"So violent, this one," Vereyn said with wide eyes and an even wider smile.

"*And you,*" Vereyn thought in Rich's head. "*You have too much random heroics in you, which is more of a wild card then I'd prefer at the moment. Please, friend, take a much deserved respite. Uyun.*"

Rich complied with the sleep spell, closing his eyes and falling back into his seat.

Mors struggled to free his hand from Vereyn's iron grip. Vereyn kept his smile and spoke as if they were comrades having tea. "I don't see why we should go decorating this room with our blood just because you find observational truth unsavory. I imagine this place has a tapestry master or some other artisan who wouldn't care much for your scarlet vision after already working so diligently on the decor."

"Splendid!" from across the room, the bass voice of Otam filled the space. "I haven't seen a mortal with balls this big for some three hundred years! Now, this is refreshing! Who is this aide who never learned it's the station of an aide to remain ever afraid?"

Vereyn held his free hand up to stop Otam from rising from his throne.

"*Ör. Ör. Ör.*" Rew's spell had been continual, the braids growing with her fear of both being discovered and what was unfolding before her eyes in the throne room.

"What do you remember of fear, dear god?" Vereyn asked, smiling. "From your lofty throne, in your ageless body, have you lost it entirely? And can one such as I remind you of it? I aspire to try."

Vereyn exhaled serenely in his shell. Rew felt another presence that made her stutter her braid spell and lose focus of herself and her room altogether. Tainted like a poisoned well, putrid like a decomposing body, a slimy warmth spread into the body and mind of the shell. A voice that sounded like writhing maggots or feasting pigs chittered to the shell.

"Be reborn in the Twelfth."

A dark aura blossomed out of the shell. In the space of a moment the shell swelled to stand over nine feet tall, its muscles and armored forearms becoming hulking and meaty. Two more grossly hulking arms burst forth from its ribs right below the first set of arms. The ant aian's antennae extended and its eyes elongated and became all black like onyx. Mandibles protruded from its mouth.

"Onus!" Mors cried. He was still under the grip of Vereyn now turned hideously monstrous under the power of the Corruptor. All the gods save Baligoz bolted up from their thrones. The generals and other mortals shrank from the presence of the giant ant monster in the center of the room.

Vereyn tossed Mors at Otam with power akin to tossing a sack of potatoes. A screaming Mors hurtled with arrow speed at Otam. The god, with hands faster than humanly possible, caught the flying aian deftly. Otam set Mors down, never taking his eyes off Vereyn.

"You are a fool to unmask yourself here and desecrate the temple. The god of your foul house cannot protect you from my wrath."

Vereyn tilted his glossy black eyes at Otam. "Protection?" he asked, his voice now deep and unearthly. "To use the vernacular I learned from another world, it's best you not run up... you do not want these hands."

The monstrous Vereyn took a stride forward. Unconcerned with the gods near their thrones, he walked towards the slumbering Razzleblad held under the witchlock.

Oh no.

"*Ör. Ör. Ör. Ör. Ör.*" Rew could not whisper the spell fast enough.

Meanwhile Otam had drawn his sword and rushed to meet Vereyn. Otam's strike was a blur. Vereyn met the blur with a quick raise of his arm. The blade met the armored forearm with a jarring clang and a shower of sparks.

Otam followed the first strike with more blurring swipes. Strike after strike met one arm, another arm, a third arm, all of them sparking on contact. Vereyn's fourth arm smashed Otam in the face. The god took several steps back, his face contorted in rage and pain.

"Has that familiar feeling of fear come back to you yet?" Vereyn crooned in his demon voice. He took another two steps towards Razzleblad.

Otam rushed again, his sword blurring. Again Vereyn's many arms moved slower but countered the strikes with ease. Nadi bounded over with supreme agility to help Otam. The cat god struck fast with angry claws.

Vereyn couldn't block every blow from both gods. Otam's sword found a home in the shell's gut while Nadi's claws gripped the shell's throat. Nadi pulled with his clawed grip with enough force to rip out a larynx but came away with nothing. Otam's blade emerged from the shell's back completely clean.

The abominable thing Vereyn powered was a pendulum hero. It would not bleed. Nor would it easily dispel. For all Rew knew about the improved capacity of the pendulum she wasn't sure it could be dispelled at all.

While both gods looked on in shock and horror. Vereyn used one hand to grab Otam's sword hand by the wrist. With two other giant fists he punched the god in his face and gut. The fourth hand Vereyn grabbed Nadi's face, which seemed so small in the giant ant's claw grip. Vereyn threw the cat god across the room, forcing Inanna to duck to avoid getting hit with her brother. Nadi landed into a couple of generals who had retreated to the other end of the throne room.

Vereyn kneed Otam, forcing him to bow over. He let go of Otam's sword arm and kicked him across the room. Otam flew through the air and crash landed into the large center table, breaking it in two. Rich was in one of the chairs that surrounded the now broken table, still slumbering despite the incredible din.

Nadi, exemplifying the catlike grace of his house, sprang on his feet and into a sprinting dash the second after he landed. Unconcerned, Vereyn took more steps toward Razzleblad. He was almost in arm's reach.

Rew forced herself with all her will to bring herself back into her conscious self, desperately trying to see her room, herself prone under the witchlock. She pushed the imagery of Nadi and Vereyn's combat. *Ör. Ör. Ör.* She knew with absolute certainty Vereyn could not reach that Razzleblad. *Ör. Ör. Ör.*

Rew was aware of Inanna joining the fray as a giant spider. Vereyn's giant body ignored the two gods' blows while his massive hands landed their own. They would not last against this.

The witchlock Rew was captive under had not fallen apart yet. But all Vereyn needed was a single step and an outstretched hand to reach Razzleblad.

Rew was one of the few mages that knew what was in a witchlock. Desperate, she began a new spell, not the braid, but one invoking the components of the witchlock. She spoke of truesilver and the salt of dried tears, of charred coral and heavenglow, the warmth of stars.

As Vereyn pushed away the gods' assault, made his final step and grabbed the witchlock binding Razzleblad with a meaty hand, Rew's own witchlock was disassembling, taking itself apart into a hundred small components, all of them radiating with the heavenglow that had been infused throughout.

Vereyn crushed the witchlock with his unholy strength. The entire Temple of Houses shook with the untimely release of the witchlock's energy.

The energy of Rew's witchlock hadn't been destroyed but redirected. She felt her own power rush into her. The small stars of the witchlock's hundred components glowed all around her face, robes and braided hair as she stood.

Now Vereyn became aware of what was happening back where his actual body sat before the now freely standing Rew Majora. His real eyes blinked as focus came back to them.

"Beautiful..." he whispered, almost to himself as he took in the mage dressed in starlight and unquenchable rage.

Wordlessly, Rew pushed. The starry components of the witchlock shot forth into Vereyn and continued on to explode her bedroom wall in a shower of dust and flying brick.

DRUZE OPENED HIS EYES, the bulk of his consciousness now in the body of Razzleblad's crafted shell. He picked himself off the floor to see the destruction he could only listen to before the witchlock got snapped. Beside him lay the prone body of Vereyn. Not a part of the plan. No matter. He looked across the room where Nadi, Inanna and Otam readied themselves for combat while Baligoz keenly watched with oscillating eyes on his throne. If these gods had such a time with Vereyn's shell, they were scarcely a match for Druze in this form.

He extended a robed arm, uttered his spell, and hurricane winds erupted from his sleeve. Inanna spread her arms and a shield of spiderweave appeared to protect her. Nadi crouched incredibly low to the ground, his claws digging into the floor to secure his grip. Three of the aian generals were flung to the back wall, where the wind kept them stuck and continued to flay their skin off.

Only Otam, who had his arms criss-crossing his face, pushed against the deadly wind. Slow step after agonizing step, he made his way towards Druze. "To what end?" Druze mused. This god was the most stubborn among them.

"I am Otam, mortal! The Measure! I cannot, will never yield!"

"Yours shall be the first house I raze," Druze said. It should be easy enough. He had crafted this Razzleblad shell with all of his own tattoo augmentation.

While Otam made his slow gains against the wind coming from Druze's raised sleeve, the mage turned his attention to the opposite wall. In his free hand he summoned raging blue netherfire. He pushed the destructive flame and it hurtled into the wall of the temple, blasting out the ancient stone. Azure sky appeared outside the smoking ruin of the hole.

Otam, his forearms heavily nicked and bleeding finally got within arms reach of Druze. The god closed the gap by lunging past Druze's hurricane sleeve. Otam grabbed Druze by the throat, likely an attempt to stop more spells. As the god squeezed the mage's throat, Druze grabbed Otam by the breastplate. Idiot god didn't understand Druze didn't need to speak to summon netherfire into existence. Druze pointed the sleeve still blasting out hurricane winds down to the floor right behind Otam. In that same hand, Druze summoned netherfire and let the hurricane winds push the fireball with sickening force. It blasted the floor and the resulting explosion pushed both Otam and Druze out of the hole he had just created in the wall of the temple. Still locked in their deadly embrace, they both hurtled to the ground a mile below.

REW STOOD IN THE THICK swirls of dust, anger contorting her features.

"*Defol*!" she shouted the spell that pushed Vereyn's presence out of her mind completely. Somehow, the man was still alive.

"Vereyn!" she shouted as she emerged from the hole she had created with the witchlock's release. She scanned her library, the room adjacent to her bedroom, for the telltale glimmer of blue illusion magic.

"You do not get to defile me and live," Rew said. "Show yourself, Vereyn!"

She saw a flash of blue by the window. She pulled fire from a candle into her palm, grew the fireball and hurled it at the flash. The wall exploded into fiery chunks, exposing a large view of the courtyard gardens and distant towers. She saw another flash of blue hop through the newly created hole down to the gardens below.

She jumped down after it, altering her robes as lighter than air to float her to the ground. She surveyed the gardens for glimmer and movement.

"Vereyn!"

She saw a lizard scurry. "*Toprak eskeri*," she pointed and the ground below the scurrying lizard erupted upward into a cruel spike.

In some nearby rose bushes, Vereyn's face appeared. It was covered in blood. Seemingly oblivious to his wounds from the witchlock, his smile was large.

"You know quite well a duel with a blue robe isn't exactly dangerous as it is tedious. While you play out your revenge fantasy you should at least try to know what your father's doing in Nasreddin."

"Die!" she replied, sending up another dirt spike that obliterated the rose bush.

The marble figure of a boy pouring water from a jar into a fountain glimmered and started speaking.

"He goes to break the spell wards from the Nasreddin mage delegation tower," the fountain boy said. "Once those are broken, every mage under his command will portal in."

Rew transformed her sleeves into sharp blades. She lengthened the blades and swung them together to meet at the statue, cleaving the fountain boy into three pieces of marble that fell in a heap into the fountain.

Next to the fountain, a tree branch rustled. "Those mages are going to raze the city and kill all the aian inhabitants. All the aians, to include one that has only recently fit this description. He will die in his sleep if you don't stop your father. Tell me, Rew, are you willing to pay for your revenge with this much blood?"

Rew's only answer was to scream as she sent the pieces of marble she had just cleaved flying towards the rustling branch.

DRUZE TOOK REPEATED blows to the face from Otam as they both plummeted to the ground below. He was fine with this. A moment before the ground came rushing up to meet them, Druze turned and pushed out with his arms, holding Otam below him. The ground smacked into Otam's back and the continued momentum forced Druze into Otam's front. Unfazed, unhurt, Druze rose on one knee and summoned netherfire in which to cook the god.

The god did not dwell on the pain of a fall that would've been fatal to mortals. He grabbed a fistful of Druze's gray robe and tossed the mage sideways. Druze tossed the fireball errantly, where it sped past Otam to hit a small, one story building and collapsed it.

Druze landed in a dusty street. Civilians scattered like roaches. The god sprinted towards Druze. Druze rose to his feet and dusted himself off, looking around for the Mage Delegation Tower.

Otam hit him with a left, a right. He picked Druze up, turned him in the air and brought the man's spine down across his knee. Otam then turned Druze upside down and drove his head into the dirt. Then he kicked the mage's head and sent him flying across the street.

After a brief roll, Druze rose from the ground. The Mage Delegation Tower was a few blocks from here. He had made this shell extremely hardy, but nothing was infinite, not even the health of this shell. He would not make it to the tower with Otam beating on the shell like this.

But then again, nothing was infinite, including the lives of gods.

He spoke in the old tongue, one of the few spells he respected from the book of Kaftar Friese. This one was loosely translated as "life fueled kindling." It converted with each utterance of the priming word a body's life force into physical energy. He converted this shell's overwhelming banks of life force into this physical energy. He could see the energy rising off the body like heat waves.

An enraged Otam charged. Druze kept pumping more fuel from life.

Otam grabbed the mage by his gray robes. Druze clamped onto Otam's arms with his own. Otam grappled for control.

"I know you cannot best me!" he cried.

"Know?" Druze asked. "Know the grave! *Patlama*!"

The energy ripped into an explosion that made all things bright white. Druze found himself lying on the ground on the outer fringe of a crater. Nothing existed in the crater, not even rubble. Around the crater, every building was blasted, charred and leaning. On the other end of the crater Otam lay unmoving.

Druze got up in a stumble. He could feel how weak the shell had become, as if a stiff breeze could unmake it. He was only a block away from the Mage Delegation Tower now. Druze spared a glance back at Otam, where Ananna and Nadi both knelt by his side, unable to rouse him. Nadi looked up at Druze with what could only be wonder, horror and fear.

Nadi was known as the Curious, the Grace of Motion, the Brace of Risk-Takers but Druze knew with that eye contact the cat god would not be taking any risks to pursue. Druze had given Nadi a gift today, the knowledge that death can come for him as surely as it does for everyone. And the god was facing death too soon after millenia of it being absent to face it bravely. The mage turned and stumbled towards the tower.

Druze hobbled his way up the stairs of the tower. He arrived at the door and reached a hand towards the wards to crush them.

As his fingers touched the ward, he felt a jarring pull. He screamed against it but to no avail. His consciousness rushed back into his own body at the Hierophane.

He saw his daughter tower over him, her eyes furious. Directly above his head, the glow of a witchlock throbbed red.

Chapter 31
Game Over

JASON EXPERIENCED A feeling that superseded calm as he navigated the thick, tree-sized spines of coral on the island. This was in spite of knowing somewhere in this twisted forest was a boss level enemy with insane levels of magic and equally insane brain space. This feeling wasn't produced simply because he was surrounded by compatriots whom he trusted: Mel, Ruki Provos, Gina, Calais, and Eula—well, definitely not Eula, she'd run him through with that Moonlight Blade of hers if she could and would probably haunt his dreams his next nap on general principle. No, this emotion was a calm actually powered by having something he had to do, not obligatory tasks he should do like homework or something he thought might be fun or cool to do but having something he absolutely needed to do, a thing he could easily walk away from but everything in him drove him decidedly forward.

Holy hell, was this *purpose*? He had had wants, needs, desires, wishes, tasks, missions and goals, but never purpose. Even without the necklace of Onus radiating warmth on his chest, he would've felt invincible.

Rustling ahead in the coral forest slowed their movements. Jason and his crew peaked around some cone shaped coral to find a clearing. Five hulking monsters congregated in the open space. A shark body and face walked about on giant, skittering crab legs. Instead of fins a writing mass of squid tentacles protruded out both sides of the body. The thing was completely armored in a thick crab-like shell, with only its shark face exposed to reveal rows upon rows of dagger teeth and cold, black eyes.

Calais raised an eyebrow. "Those don't look easy to take down," she surmised.

Eula nodded. "That armor would be daunting to pierce with our blades. I imagine the sole purpose of the horde of tentacles is to grab you and bring you into the shark's firece, fatal maw."

Mel looked at Gina. "Was this dude Clem into anime?"

Gina nodded.

Mel shook her head. "Geez, what is it with these anime dudes and tentacles? Ugh!"

Out of nowhere, Ruki Provos stepped away from the cones and into the clearing.

"Excuse me, roving shark monsters, could you kindly direct me to your stark raving creator?"

The shark-squid-crabs all jerked up in attention at Ruki's words. They all skittered towards him, tentacles lashing forward, dagger mouths open.

Ruki clapped his gloved hands together. Lightning arced between his hands as they separated. He shoved his hands forward and deadly bolts flayed out, catching all five of the shark monsters in spastic seizures as the electricity fried them.

Jason was glad to see some game rules were universal. Sea monsters are always weak to bolt.

Ruki smiled as he surveyed his handiwork of freshly blackened sea abomination, still smoking in their heavy shells. "Well, let's hope we don't run into more," he said, holding up his gloved hands. "These things take obscenely long to build a charge."

Epic cooldown on awesome weapons, another universal rule. As much as his friends swore this wasn't a game any more, it certainly behaved that way in certain respects.

They continued past the clearing, back into the coral forest. The coral here were more twisted than the conical spines before, turning into themselves to form arches or resembling gnarled fingers that seemed to point accusingly at the transgressors. Jason made his way through and around the curved coral, every step making him feel as if he was walking across the giant palm of an arthritic hand that would bunch into a fist and crush them all.

The next threat loomed quite visible well before they got to the clearing where it dwelled. They treaded carefully, trying to remain as silent and invisible as they could, using the twisting coral as cover. It looked like a giant frog, easily ten feet tall, standing on its hind legs quite human like. Instead of a right arm, the appendage was some kind of small whale or walrus with an extremely wicked horn, easily ten feet long and incredibly pointed, protruding from its forehead. The monster's head was a fish face with pointed teeth so large it couldn't close its mouth. A light dangled above its fish face, hanging there from a long spine and glowing bright white.

"Another chimera," Mel whispered. "This time it looks like a giant bullfrog, a narwhal and a viperfish."

"So..." Gina began, "bumrush it?"

Jason held up a bone hand. Why was there only one of these viperfrog-narwhalfish standing there, just waiting, still as furniture? It was setting off heavy mid-boss vibes for him.

"Hear me out," Jason said. "I know Clemson Goodchild's playing the mad necromancer and all, but if there's any sanity to his machinations, then he would've made more of these things unless they were incredibly resource-intensive to frankenstein together. And heavily resourced baddies tend to come with a whole menu of nasty tricks. Running out there full speed seems like a terrible way to find out."

Calais nodded. "Let's see," she said. She produced a blue chalk and started scratching symbols into the hard coral ground. Her glyphs and arrows were jagged and muddled as the coral chipped and chewed at her chalk.

"Only thing worse than this surface is mud," she muttered, grimacing every time a piece of her chalk broke off. She gave a cursory nod to all her handiwork, then opened a pouch of blue powder, dipped her fingers in and sprinkled the dust above her head. She began to shimmer while Jason began to experience a dull headache.

"Damnable witchcraft," Ruki Provos muttered, massaging his temples.

Calais didn't respond despite her knack for smart ass clapbacks. Instead she stepped out of herself as if the magic had created a clone. One stood stark still while the other one, a Calais that shimmered as if she had gotten dusted with glitter, kept walking. This one walked around and under the coral fingers, arrived in the clearing and then began to move cautiously toward the hulking frog monster.

The light dangling above the monster's fish face throbbed bright white. Then it moved impossibly fast. The narwhal arm lashed out like machine gun fire, that ten foot long horn striking the shimmer-Calais so fast Jason couldn't count the reps. It struck like a jackhammer and each blow caused a spray of concrete-like coral ground to shrapnel in all directions. While the narwhal arm was obliterating the space the shimmer-Calais occupied, the fish face extended from the frog body, as if it was more eel than neck. The eel-neck fish face struck at the shimmer-Calais, trying to chew the sparkle off with its icepick length teeth.

The shimmer-Calais disappeared. Safely behind the cover of the twisted coral, the real Calais shuddered and wobbled in place. Gina grabbed her by the elbow. Calais nodded a silent thank you.

"I don't think any one of us is fast enough to avoid this dude's patented Narwhal Strike," Jason quipped. "He might not be able to get us all, but one or more of us is going to die if we try to mob him."

Calais shook her head. "You all didn't see what I saw," she said brushing an errant lock of frizzy hair from her concern-rimmed eyes. When that light above its head flares and you're close to it, the whole world disappears, like you're in the bottommost depths of the blackest waters. All you can see in this darkness is that white light swimming toward you... and then that face appears, those teeth!" She shuddered as she recalled the sight.

Ruki shrugged. "We can always wait half a day for these gloves to replenish," he offered.

Eula shook her head. "I am loath to let this mage have that time to indulge his imagination."

Mel grimaced. "Goodchild's recovering from that near fatal wound I gave him. Now's the only time to finish him. If we can't take this thing down we'll never be able to stop a demented gray robe at the height of his power." Mel looked at Jason. "Kinda like how you wanted us to prove we could handle the Death Null by stopping Sentry Triptoe, remember?" he asked with a wink.

Jason smiled. "Can't forget, dude. You were mad A.F. Kept telling me to stop treating this like a video game..." he trailed off. His eyes got big.

"Dude!" he told Mel. "You gave me the key! I just figured how to beat it."

Jason smiled smugly as he surveyed his companions, waiting for them to guess what he had arrived at. None of them even ventured to guess as they looked at him expectantly. Come on... nobody? It was easy! Their countenances changed to ones of annoyance. Seriously, nobody?

"Speak, motherfucker!" Gina swore.

"Okay, geez," Jason said. "So, this island and everything in it has been triggering me since we started walking on it. Now I realize why. This thing was built by a gamer. A mad gamer, sure, but one whose deep, deep psyche is familiar with level design. That's why those initial mobs were all grouped up in the clearing instead of roaming around independent of each other, also why they collectively had that instant aggro moment in perfect synchronicity. That's also why this one is just standing there, not moving, just waiting... because it's not alive as much as designed. Game designed. This is Mid-Boss. After this, expect a short walk followed by End Boss, i.e. Clemson Goodchild."

"How's knowing all this help beat Mid-Boss, though?" Gina asked.

"Well, if my theory's correct," Jason said putting his bone hand up next to his mouth as if he was whispering a conspiracy, "and I'm always correct, then Mid-Boss has been built with a weak spot. If he was made of pixels, it'd be glowing red. But since this is a real world this mad gamer's playing in, it's glowing white." He finished by pointing a skeletal finger at the white light hanging above the creature's fish face.

Mel raised her eyebrow. "You're saying if we destroy the light, we drop the creature?"

Jason grinned. "Yep."

"This seems implausible," Eula said.

Jason nodded. To a nongamer it would seem totally nuts. "If nothing else, we nullify the attack Calais warned us about. Maybe disorient it enough to make it an even fight. If someone else has a better plan, well I'm stuck in the middle of the coral level and dying to hear some elite strategy."

"We'll have to shoot it off," Gina said. "And only one of us has a range weapon," she finished by looking meaningfully at Ruki Provos.

Jason could hear Ruki's hard swallow as he looked down at his diskbow and back up at the giant monster. "Um, I'm a terrible shot at this range. I haven't played these games you're all so fond of, but it seems to me that missing isn't exactly an option here."

"Oh no," Jason, Mel and Gina all said instinctively. Mel clarified. "If you start the mid-boss fight, it's going to aggro. We only get one shot at this."

Ruki offered the weapon to Jason. "Here, sharpshooter."

Jason waved it away with his bone hand. "Yeah, sharpshooter with a bow. I'm only good with other weapons if I call upon a certain dark lor—"

"No," Eula said pointedly.

"Magic to the rescue again," Calais said. She looked at Jason. "Take the wrappings off your severed arm and set it on the ground." Next, she turned to Eula. "I need a strand of your hair, goddess, if you please."

A question formed on Eula's face, but she complied, pulling a long, blonde strand and giving it to Calais. Carefully, the witch lay the hair across the arm. She dabbled into three separate pouches, sprinkling red, green and orange dust on the arm until you could scarcely see the hair. Jason entertained the thought of her seasoning the arm for roasting. Calais got on one knee and started drawing in orange and white chalk. She stood up, checked her handiwork then sprinkled some white dust over everything.

Everyone grabbed one of their own arms as they locked up in a severe cramp, all except Calais the cost skipping witch and Eula, who had absolutely refused to tie herself to a witch's dominion. Meanwhile, the arm at the elbow, almost resembling the Arm and Hammer logo but with fingers outstretched while narrow bone began to protrude out from the shoulder meat and the elbow thinned. Jason shut his eyes and grit his teeth to try to focus on not making noise as his arm's cramp started screaming at him.

Then the cramp was gone. Jason opened his eyes and found himself looking down in awe. Calais' magic had turned the arm into a bow, with Eula's hair running taut from the extended thumb to the bone tip peeking out from the shoulder meat. The elbow had been slimmed down and shaped into a grip and arrow rest while the bi and tricep had been elongated slightly to provide perfect symmetry with the forearm. Four fingers crowned the top of the bow like a rooster's comb. It was a bit macabre, a lot of weird, extra cool, supremely unique... all things that seemed to speak directly to Jason's soul.

"My ultimate weapon," he whispered to no one in particular. He grabbed it and held it up in the air as if the sun was going to find a way through the shell dome above them and shine its blessed rays upon it. Just marvelous.

"Uh..." Gina began. "You gonna keep holding that thing up like Simba or are you gonna, I dunno, shoot the monster?"

Jason had literally forgotten the whole point for a moment. Reaching behind his back, he found three arrows knocking about in his quiver. He took a few steps forward, pulled up to a coral, nocked an arrow, pulled back and breathed out calm, Cephrin focus filling his being as he aimed at the towering monster's light.

He loosed with a razor sharp twang of the bow. The bulb exploded. The monster grabbed its face with a thunderous roar. With its narwhal club arm it took angry, blind swipes at the air, swinging madly. Despite the hand covering its face and its blind swipes, it took fast, sure steps toward the source of its pain.

So much for an insta-kill.

Mel brandished his sword to meet the monster. Eula placed a hand on his shoulder to stop him.

"No need," she said. "The hard work has already been done. Allow me."

Her wings unfurled and Eula took to the sky. Jason could hear her Moonlight Blade whistle, cutting through air as she unsheathed it. She fluttered high above the rampaging monster. When it got directly below her, Eula turned the blade downward and fell from the sky. She landed on a crouch on top of the monster, her blade driving through its face all the way up to the hilt. The thing stopped its forward motion after that, stumbling back two steps. It almost seemed as if Eula was driving the monster with her sword hilt, moving it backwards and then commanding it to fall straight back. She pulled her blade out and walked away as the body hit the ground with a jarring thud.

"Perfect girlfriend," Jason said to no one. The whole world had disappeared while he watched her.

Eula wiped the Moonlight Blade on the monster, her expression unreadable, dancing eyes regarding Jason. She looked to the others.

"Please, you all scout ahead. I need to have a word with the Chosen One."

Mel, his sword still out, looked around at the rest of the crew and gave them a nod before leading the way.

"I better not turn around to see them making out while we're getting into boss fights," Gina muttered as she followed Mel into the coral.

Eula came within touching distance of Jason. She looked in his eyes with purpose.

"I need you to turn back."

He shook his head. "I can't."

"Yes, you can. We've gotten this far in no small part thanks to you. Let us handle the rest."

"I'm sorry, I can't. I'm sure you'll be fine without me, but there's no way I'm going to turn around and leave my best friend and everyone else up there to go head-to-head with a crazy gray robe. I absolutely can not go back and look Rida's parents in the face and tell them I tried a little but gave up at the end. That little girl deserved to live, but having failed her in that she deserves justice. And everything in me compels me to see that happen. Seriously, Eula, I can't go back."

Eula took a moment to look at Jason. "Your purpose is noble. Perhaps your soul is as well, Jason, despite the touch of the Corruptor. Will you swear on that soul an oath before me?"

"As much as I'm dreading getting some moth shaped jewelry from you when I say yes, I kinda gotta say yes."

"Promise me you will not invoke Onus."

"But what if—"

"There is no what if!" she spat. "No scenario of need dire enough for you to invoke the name. Onus has waited millenia to fully arrive in the flesh, he will not suffer to abide another fleshless moment while you freely channel his power. As soon as you speak it, the darkness will spread from that necklace through your body and it will no longer be yours. This is why you must not continue. You only have two arrows and what are those to a demented gray mage?"

"Sounds like twice as much stopping power than I had for the last dude I came across," Jason answered with a wry grin.

Eula shook her head. "The prophecies say the Chosen One restores the Twelfth House. Depending on how one interprets it, this could be a completely new house or Onus' old house made whole. You have no idea what the return of Onus would mean for aiankind."

"Does anyone?" Jason asked in all seriousness. Ever since Onus had forced the necklace on him, he had tried to figure out what his return meant. Did it simply mean a real physical body for the god? Did it mean all his followers could no longer masquerade under the guise of other houses, and would that transition kill them? Or was it even more sinister, a breaking of the long held covenant between aiankind and the Onesource, something that was desperately required to prevent all aians from eventually becoming mad like this gray robe lying in wait?

Eula didn't have an answer in her concern-rimmed eyes. "I haven't felt fear like this, Jason, mortal fear, since the Maddening Times. The fate of our kind rests on you. On your true soul, I need you to swear to me."

Jason raised his hand. "I swear on my true immortal soul, on pain of death, not to invoke the Corruptor's name," he said in all seriousness.

Eula nodded. "Since I cannot dissuade you, the only road left is to continue."

Together, they walked through the coral to catch up to the others. It was only a short distance, five or so rows of the twisted coral before they emerged in another clearing where the others waited. Jason did not have to guess this was the final clearing. Before them, aians, humans, even nasran and megrymkind lay prostrate as in supplication prayer. Facing the same direction towards a rising mound of coral, they all had blue skin. These were the people the mage's giant monster had grabbed up. A vast field of dozens, perhaps over a hundred of the blue skinned people, all evenly spaced among the coral wasteland, were face down in silent prayer towards the mound.

Now that Jason and Eula had arrived, Mel continued to lead the way up the hill. Everyone followed down the aisle created by the blue skinned worshippers. They crested the hill and Jason's jaw dropped.

It was hard to take it all in. It was a giant fish, whale sized, but gelatinous with a droopy, human like face. All black eyes, big bulb nose, and a perpetual frown sat on a face that seemed to be stuck in mid-melt.

"Blobfish," Mel whispered as if he knew Jason's question of what the hell was this thing.

The blobfish's face reminded Jason of an old comic strip character named Ziggy. The whale-sized blobfish had two large human arms. Both these arms reached out from the fish towards a hole in the coral ground directly in front of the fish. The hands seemed to be pulling the hole open wider, big enough for a weagr to dive in. From the top of the blobfish, a thick crystal stalk dangled, hanging in the air in front of the blobfish. The crystal stalk terminated directly over the hole the fish's hands pulled open. Coming out of the crystal like a butterfly halfway emerging from a cocoon was the face and half the body of Clemson Goodchild, his face euphoric and mouth wide open as it dangled over the hole. White shimmery light seemed to flow up from the hole and into Clemson's waiting mouth.

"So you have come at last." The voice came from the blobfish's frowny mouth.

"God, Clem," Gina said, her hand covering her mouth in horror. "What have you done to yourself?"

"Clemson Goodchild had to die," the blobfish said. "My cost to evolve. Only Moloch remains, the new lord of this realm, the righteous deliverer of its unpaid cost. Bow before me and know my benevolence."

Jason fully encouraged and endorsed villaintalk. Them telling the hero directly what they were planning and potentially revealing any weak points was always good in his book. It was rather weird addressing the giant Ziggy-faced blobfish, though.

"Uh, what's your old self doing over hanging over that pit?"

"It is the finger in which I touch creation," Moloch stated. "A god's control over this world."

Mel sidled up to Jason. "Something tells me this was the ley point that used to be underwater off the coast of Suusteren."

"You have passed my challenges," Moloch said. "So I have received you in my court. Now bow and be rewarded as harbingers of my new age or stand defiant and be consumed. I care not which you choose."

Jason decided to answer for everyone. In a blink he drew an arrow, nocked, and loosed. The arrow flew straight into one of the blobfish's giant black eyes.

The blobfish made no cry of pain despite half the arrow shaft being buried in its eye. It simply slurped the rest of the arrow into its face and a new black eye formed over the hole.

"Your weapons are made to manipulate flesh, which I am more than," Moloch said. "And my will is forged from the exacting fires of the cost. It is stronger than you can know. Witness my power over this world."

The air seemed to shimmer all around Ruki, Calais and Eula. Then the air became substantive, like a thick glass that surrounded the three of them in separate clear cages.

"The hell!" Jason cried.

Eula tried to strike the glass surrounding her with her Moonlight Blade. Mel rushed over to Ruki's glass cell and struck it with his bastard sword. None of their strikes marred or cracked the glass. Ruki took out his diskbow but Mel shook his head emphatically. The disk could break the cage or more likely it could ricochet and in a space that small the latter would be fatal. Calais fell to her knees and got to tracing patterns with her chalks.

"They will pay their cost, as this whole world pays its cost," Moloch decreed. "You remaining three come from a realm out of balance, one that has overpaid. I cannot render payment from you but neither can you stop me."

Jason looked at Eula, anger on her face as she continued to strike at her cage. This magic was beyond even gray robes. He looked back at the blobfish and the dangling spire that held the last human remnant of Clemson Goodchild.

"We gotta stop him from eating," Jason said. "Sever the hands, close the ley hole."

Mel and Gina charged at the massive hands pulling at the ley hole, blades out. When they got near the ley hole the two of them stumbled, fell and began to convulse.

"Mel! Gina!" Jason cried.

"They are unevolved, unworthy," Moloch said. "They aspire to touch the source and the source will break them down to their raw essence for their insolence. And I shall remain, to consume them."

Jason grit his teeth. "I'm not losing to a Ziggy fishface," he said. Nocking his final arrow, he loosed it at the head of Clemson Goodchild dangling over the gaping ley point.

Before the arrow could reach its mark, it dissolved into nothingness.

"I will not be denied my purpose," Moloch stated.

A feeling of panicked hopelessness, uselessness blossomed in Jason's gut as he watched his friends convulse on the ground or futilely beat against their cages. They were all going to die while he sat around watching.

He only had one option left to him.

Jason looked at Eula. She seemed to know what he was thinking. She shook her head, her lips mouthing "No."

He had no doubt the goddess was right about Onus having an instant new meat party as soon as Jason said the name. He needed to access Onus's power without the god being able to take over his body through contact with the pendant. He couldn't throw the pendant away and invoke the name because it always found its way back to his body.

If the pendant needed contact with Jason's flesh, that's what he'd give it.

"God of Loopholes, find favor in this," Jason said, taking the pendant off his neck. He placed the chain of the necklace over the thumb of his bow and placed the maggot heart pendant into the bow's palm. Then he curled the four fingers of the bow around the pendant.

He set the bow on the coral ground. "I just got this thing," he swore, shaking his head.

Jason didn't dwell, but took off at a sprint. Halfway towards the ley point he brought both his hands up to the sides of his mouth.

"Onus!" he cried.

He felt the power surge through his being. Jason arrived at Mel and Gina seizing on the ground. He grabbed them by a single leg in each of his hands and slid them backwards with unholy strength. They rolled and tumbled across the unforgiving landscape. Damn, they were going to probably curse him out for the scrapes and cuts, but at least they were out of harm's way of the ley point.

Jason picked up Mel's sword and with a single mighty swipe, came down on one of the blobfish's hands stretching the ley point. The severed hand was pulled into the hole and the size of the chasm immediately shrank from weagr-sized to Runt Half-Weagr sized. Progress.

"How?" Moloch asked, almost dispassionately, as if the hand that got lopped off was a fast food receipt that fell from a pocket.

"You're not the only one with power over this world," Jason told him. He looked back at his arm bow. It had blackened, and was throbbing an angry blood red. From the shoulder he could see a large mass writhing out. No, not a large mass, a sea of small masses. Maggots.

Better work fast. Jason turned his attention back to Moloch, bringing Mel's sword down hard on the remaining hand. This one also got pulled into the hole, which in turn shrank down to man sized.

Dammit, wasn't it supposed to close?

"You cannot stop the dawning age," Moloch stated.

"Cephrin!" An angry bellow called behind him. Jason turned to see the writhing maggots had formed into the shape of a man. Onus didn't run as much as the maggots at his feet wriggled towards Jason with alarming speed.

"You will not deny me my flesh!"

Jason fought the urge to run. Those maggots would chase him all over the world to get at him. And he wasn't about to allow Moloch to Mu Ha Ha his way into world domination and leave his friends and the goddess who hated his Onus-indebted guts to suffocate in indestructible glass prisons.

Nothing left but the last and greatest measure.

Jason jumped, feeling a slight pull from the open ley point below him as he grabbed onto the half exposed body of the original Clemson Goodchild. They both hung suspended over the ley point by Moloch's crystalline stalk.

Jason began to pull at Clemson.

"It is mine!" the cry came behind Jason. He looked down to see the maggots were writhing their way up his legs. They felt hot. Heavy.

Moloch's blobfish face looked alarmed for the first time since this encounter. "You must not! The cost demands everyone, everything pays. Everything must!"

Jason could feel Clemson tearing away from the stalk, his own muscles groaning in protest as he pulled with all his borrowed strength at the only thing left on the monster that was human. Skin separated from the crystalline stalk, exposing intestines.

The maggots had wriggled their way up to his chest. A spike of maggots came up and shot into his mouth. Jason could feel them writhing down his throat, into his gut.

Jason felt his vision tunneling. He was blacking out. He looked down at the sea of maggots crawling up his body to enter him as he dangled over a hole that led to an infinite abyss.

"*Maybe,*" he thought, "*this is a warp zone to the final level. Maybe it's where all heroes go, in the end.*"

He used his last reserves of summoned power to rip Clemson Goodchild free of Moloch. Together, with Onus, they fell into the void.

Epilogue

Mike looked at his brother through the mirror. Melvin looked like he had been through a shitstorm without an umbrella. His eyes looked tired and pained.

"You good, bruh? No immediate danger, right?"

Melvin shook his head. "The dome disappeared, no more coral spikes shooting out of the ocean or anything. The rest of the demented mage literally melted after, after Jason..." Melvin didn't finish the sentence, but instead looked up and away from the mirror to some spot Mike couldn't see.

"I'm sorry," Mike said. He knew too well what it was like to lose people close to you on the battlefield. There weren't any words he could really give him that would make a dent in that feeling.

"Well you tried to tell me we were in a war," Melvin said. "Didn't matter if I wanted to be in one or not."

"For real, bruh, the only thing that matters is what you do next. I say we ride for your homie, blaze a path straight to those mage towers and blast out this bitch."

Melvin looked back at Mike, his eyes carrying a serious weight and a hard edge. "Agreed."

"Word. Big brother got you," Mike said. He killed the mirror feed and placed the mirror back in his back.

"Is I's rough ready?"

Mike turned to look up at Ego. Beside him stood Runt. He turned the other way to regard Savvy and her latest partner in crime Inonu. He was prolly gonna call her Noni-girl or something.

In front of them all stretched a vast, seemingly endless desert of fine sand and green glass. Behind them, the ruins of the Sprawl ran as an unbroken line from one corner of the horizon to the other, a magnificent ruin even from this distance.

In between them and the start of the Sprawl stood a legion of fighters. Warriors from the Sons of Kaftar, Exhaust and Clockwound Warders stood deep as hell out in the middle of this nowhere. It looked like Burning Man out here.

Mike had his army. He nodded to his crew and turned back to face the desert.

Time to see some mages about his ticket out this bitch.

About the Author

James Beamon is a science fiction and fantasy author whose short stories have appeared in places such as Fantasy & Science Fiction Magazine, Apex, Lightspeed and Orson Scott Card's Intergalactic Medicine Show. He spent twelve years in the Air Force, deployed to Iraq and Afghanistan, and is in possession of the perfect buffalo wings recipe that he learned from carnies. He currently lives in Virginia with his wife, son and attack cat. He's serious about the attack cat... do not point at it.

Read more at fictigristle.wordpress.com.

www.ingramcontent.com/pod-product-compliance
Lightning Source LLC
Chambersburg PA
CBHW070627260626
47161CB00007B/2620